THE SOUND OF NOTHING

NICOLE AISLING

Phoenix Flight Press

ISBN-13: 978-1-964430-04-1 (Paperback)
ISBN-13: 978-1-964430-05-8 (Hardcover)

Cover illustration by JV Arts
Maps by Cassie McDonald
Chapter/scene break images by Lexi Scherkenbach

First Edition, 2025 Published by Phoenix Flight Press

For my parents, the strongest warriors I know.
In this family, nobody fights alone.

*"Sometimes life throws things at us that we're not ready for.
It's how we handle it that matters."*

Emirdom
Western Plains
Forests of Payan

The Far North
Konota Valley
Pajair Desert
N
E
S
W

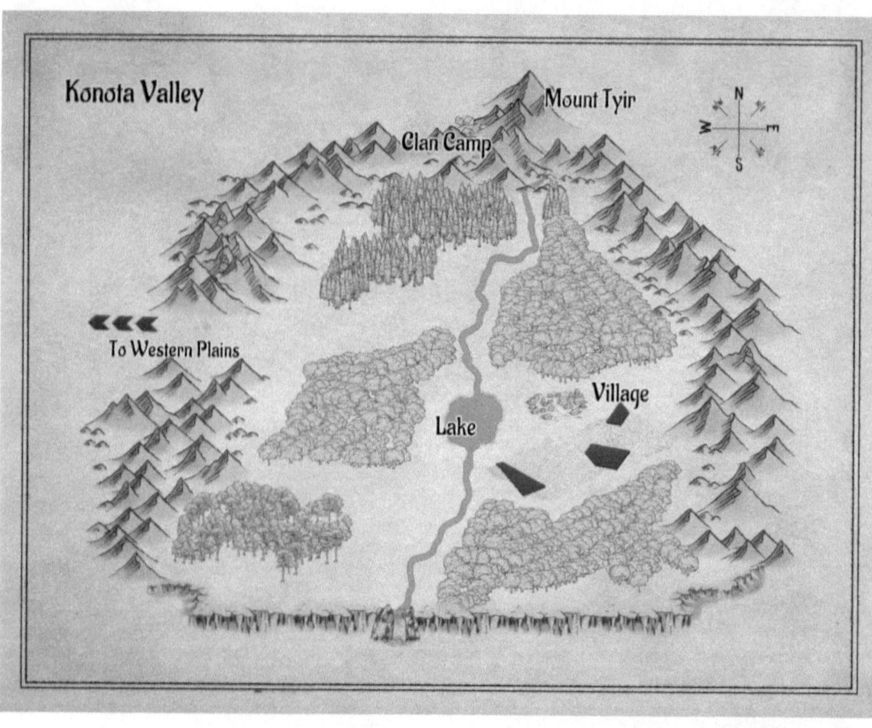

Konota Valley
Mount Tyir
Clan Camp
To Western Plains
Lake
Village
N
S
E
W

CONTENT WARNINGS

Intended for audiences 13+. Fantasy violence and death, including animal death. Brief bullying.

PROLOGUE

Kota

THE BLAST EXPLODED CLOSE enough that it stirred the walls of my tent. My eyes snapped open. Outside, Ryn already stood alert, tension rippling through her body. I scrambled onto my hands and knees, reaching for the leather armor I'd stashed in the corner the night before.

Shouts rose throughout the camp, followed by the low drone of a horn. A call to battle. Another boom rolled through the air like thunder, then another. What *was* that? I had never heard anything like it before.

Still lacing the left side of my armor, I shoved past the tent flap into the crisp morning air. A rush of wind accompanied a drakon shooting by overhead. I squinted against the glint of the rising sun but couldn't catch the rider's colors.

Took you long enough, Ryn growled inside my head. The drakon lashed her tail, the bone spikes dangerously close to slashing a hole in my tent. Ignoring her impatience, I threw the leather saddle over her back, but she kept shifting while I tried to cinch it tight.

"Hold still," I snapped at my keeper. I knew she was itching for battle. We both were.

When I finally secured the saddle, I swung onto Ryn's back and grasped the loop at the front of the saddle. My other hand drew my sword from its sheath, the weight of the weapon comfortable and familiar. My father's sword. Even before I became a warrior, I had known the feel of this sword's hilt against my palm.

Ryn leaped forward without hesitation, her wings unfurling. In moments, we were airborne, the camp shrinking beneath us as she climbed higher. By then, the battle raged at its height. Drakons swarmed the sky, some riders wearing Valere colors and some matching my blue and red painted leather armor.

Below, ruined tents burned throughout the camp, their pale animal hide shredded into tatters. Smoldering strips littered the ground, some pieces still drifting through the air.

"They finally came for us," I murmured.

We had known this moment would come. They had hit four other clans already, including the third drakon clan. *Join or die*, their chief had declared.

Another blast decimated a tent in the center of the camp. Ryn beat her wings, hovering in place while I watched burning scraps flutter toward the ground. They must have been searching for Chief Rajik's tent. Though his tent looked like all the others, they knew it would be in the middle somewhere.

"The stories are true. It's magic!" someone shouted nearby. "The gods have brought their wrath down on us!"

It's not magic, I thought. And it certainly wasn't the gods, either. Whatever caused the explosion, it sure as Atu's furry backside wasn't some mystical force.

"Kota, at your peak!"

I looked up on instinct in time to see something small plummeting toward my head. My stomach flipped as Ryn rolled to avoid it. The object whistled past—a sack of some kind? Fire erupted when it collided with the ground, the heatwave knocking Ryn off balance. For one horrible second, I thought she might lose control. My grip tightened on the saddle strap to keep myself seated until she leveled out into a glide.

The clang of clashing swords overhead wrenched my attention upward. Varrin's brown drakon fled from an unfamiliar black-scaled beast whose rider wore white and purple. Her pale hair streamed out behind her, the braid peppered with colorful beads.

The two drakons engaged in a deadly dance, swooping above and around each other while their riders traded blows. Varrin's cry cut through the chaos as the enemy's blade plunged through his shoulder. His own sword slipped from his grip and went spinning toward the ground.

Varrin tried to bank away, but the black drakon sank its claws into his keeper. The drakon swooped and released them, sending Varrin and his drakon hurtling toward the earth.

I didn't see them crash. Two drakons shot by, close enough that their flight stream disrupted Ryn's glide. A gray drakon with purple feathers and white streaks painted along its sides pursued another I recognized as Nikat's keeper. The gray drakon's rider clutched a bow instead of a sword, remaining seated with his legs alone. It was a feat both impressive and reckless.

Nikat's drakon dodged and twisted, throwing every evasive maneuver they had into shaking the Valere warrior off their tail. But their pursuer was relentless. All he needed was one clear shot.

I leaned low against Ryn's neck and directed her after them. With a few powerful strokes of her red-feathered wings, she gathered speed. When we were within range, Ryn swooped upward before folding her wings into a dive.

She timed it perfectly.

The enemy never saw us coming. I clung to the saddle as we slammed into them and lashed out with my sword. Screams of pain ripped through the air, from both drakon and rider.

Dive, I commanded. Ryn rolled to the side, her wings still tucked, and we dropped like one of those exploding sacks. The wind whipped my braid in my face and stung my eyes. Tears rolled down my cheeks, but I resisted the urge to squeeze my eyes shut.

Seconds away from crashing, Ryn snapped out her wings. We skimmed over the ground, close enough that her claws brushed the tall grass.

I twisted in the saddle, searching for the enemy rider. What I saw startled me so badly I almost dropped my sword—the other drakon was a tail-length behind us, the tip of the Valere warrior's arrow pointed straight at me.

Spin! I ordered.

Ryn's reluctance pulsed through our bond. *Are you sure?*

Yes! Now.

She relented nearly too late. We tilted to the side as Ryn tucked one wing to spin us in a circle. The arrow's fletching brushed my ear as it zipped by my head instead of through it.

The maneuver also slowed us down, bringing the enemy in range of Ryn's whipping tail. With my vision spinning, I couldn't see what happened, but Ryn's tail hit *something*. Bone spikes sank into flesh, then were wrenched free as we spiraled away.

We had practiced the move for countless hours but had never employed it before. It had been a favorite of my father's, one that most warriors rarely tried—and almost never saw coming. Watching it always reminded me of falling maple seeds, their blades sending them in a spiral to slow their descent. Of course, it didn't feel slowed when you were the one getting spun around. I desperately clutched the saddle as the world twisted around me.

Unfortunately, we didn't have enough altitude for such maneuvers. Ryn couldn't recover fast enough, so we spiraled straight into the ground.

My keeper took the worst of the impact, but the crash launched me from the saddle. I tumbled across the ground before skidding to a stop several paces away. Pain flared through my body, but a quick assessment told me none of my injuries were life-threatening.

"Ryn?" I called.

I'm okay. Her response came weakly, her breathing labored. Returning to the battle was out of the question.

"Kota," someone gasped. Varrin. He was sprawled on the grass nearby, chest heaving. He had survived the fall. His drakon, on the other hand...

Pity stabbed at me like a sword through my heart. Varrin probably wished he had died alongside his keeper. Pain lanced through my ankle when I got to my feet, causing me to stumble back to my knees. Unable to walk, I crawled the rest of the way over.

As soon as I reached Varrin, he shoved a knife into my hand.

"Please," he whispered. "For Atu's sake, please."

I stared at the blade I held, feeling numb aside from the throbbing in my ankle. I knew I should do it, and soon, because soulstealers flocked to battlefields. He didn't have much time.

My brief hesitation was too long. I saw the moment his soul left his body, the moment his eyes went dark. Not literally, but whatever gave someone's eyes their light, their *life*... It was gone.

Varrin—or the thing that had once been Varrin—threw himself at me with a feral snarl. He grabbed at the knife he had given me while I desperately tried to keep it out of his reach.

"Varrin!" I shouted, as if that would stop him. Varrin was gone. A demon had his soul because I had failed in my duty to free him from his body once his keeper was dead. He wouldn't make it to the next life. He was just... gone.

A wave of nausea washed over me, so strong I almost vomited all over the soulless man on top of me. My arms trembled as I parried his attacks, struggling to angle the blade for a strike.

Panic clawed at me when his fingers closed around my wrist. He started to pry the knife away with inhuman strength, but then a flash of white streaked toward his head. Bone spikes sank into his skull. I flinched as hot blood splattered my face.

Ryn wrenched her tail spikes out of his head, and his crushing weight left me as his body toppled over.

I stared at the body in shock. Nausea rolled through me again, lodging itself in my throat. It wasn't like I hadn't seen death before. I had killed. I had watched my fellow clan members die. But I had never killed one of my own before.

A series of sharp notes from a horn snapped me back to the battlefield. It wasn't the low, full note of my clan's battle horns, but something higher pitched, almost a whistle. I tilted my chin to look at the sky and was surprised to find the enemy drakons retreating.

"Why would they retreat?" I murmured. They had been winning.

They don't want us dead.

I blinked at Ryn, who watched me steadily with her deep bronze eyes. As the Valere warriors disappeared into the distance, I realized she was right. They wanted us to join them. They would kill us if we refused, but they would much rather our warriors join their army instead. This had been a show of strength, nothing more.

Bracing myself against Ryn's sturdy body, I hauled myself to my feet and clambered onto her back. I would have been ashamed of the awkward scramble if anyone were paying attention.

All around us, drakons landed among the remnants of our camp. Medics rushed from the cover of the trees to tend to the wounded. One approached me, but I waved him off and directed Ryn to carry me back to my tent. I prepared myself for the worst, expecting to find it blasted to scraps. By some stroke of luck, it remained standing. The tents on either side of it... not so much.

Three quick notes from a deep horn signaled a warrior meeting. As I made my way through the ruined camp, others bustled around me. They tended to the aftermath the way the medics tended to the wounded. Their keepers helped in any way they could, carrying debris away or pouring water on any flames that still burned.

Rajik stood beside the wreckage of his tent, his face taut, rage simmering beneath a mask of restraint. I had learned to keep my distance from that look. His drakon was sniffing through the remnants of the chief's tent. He had a long scratch down his side, but the wound had stopped bleeding already, dried blood crusted on his black scales. The other warriors and drakons bore the marks of battle. One man cradled what looked like a broken arm. A drakon's tail spike had snapped off, leaving behind a jagged stump. Another keeper had a deep gash over its eye.

I was suddenly thankful for my measly throbbing ankle. Aside from some scrapes and bruises, Ryn was unharmed.

Since attending the meeting mounted while Rajik stood grounded would be disrespectful, I slid from Ryn's back. My ankle twinged when my toes touched the ground, so I shifted my weight to my other foot.

"Our enemy made a bold move today," Rajik said once all who were coming had arrived. We were missing four warriors, because they were dead or too injured to walk. I thought of Varrin's body, a spike-hole in his head, his keeper dead nearby. The way he had attacked me like a rabid animal. My stomach churned at the memory of his soulless eyes.

"The Valere chief is greedy," Rajik went on. "Arrogant."

"He's powerful," Tam said. He leaned against his drakon, the one with the broken tail spike. "He has magic on his side. How are we supposed to fight that?"

"The gods themselves have sided with him," said the warrior with the broken arm. "We should stop fighting their will."

"The gods don't take sides," Nikat scoffed. As a warrior with even more experience than Rajik, her braid was decorated with nearly a dozen tokens. Mostly red, yellow, and purple beads, but other colors as well. "All must face Zera's fury. The chief might have a mage fighting for him, but he's still just a man."

"Whatever the reason, we can't beat him," Tam said. "Today proved that."

Nikat nodded. "This I must agree with. We have two choices, sir: we leave or we die." She didn't even offer surrendering as an option.

Rajik looked skyward, as if expecting to see more drakons dive out of the clouds. "Then we leave," he said softly. "If the North can no longer be our home, we will find a new one to claim."

"Leave?" I said before I could think better of it. Eyes turned to me. I was the youngest warrior among them and had no right to speak here. I forged on anyway. "We are warriors. We don't run with our tails down like Zera-forsaken cowards." Eilzar would never have allowed it.

But Eilzar wasn't chief anymore.

Rajik's eyes narrowed. "I understand your objection, but you are young. Inexperienced. Sometimes a warrior must recognize when they are beaten. There is no sense in dying in an unwinnable battle."

There is honor in not giving up, I thought, seething inside. I didn't care if we were hopelessly outmatched. Running away made us cowards.

But this time I held my tongue. My opinion held no weight here, not yet. They must have all thought I had gone dizzy, speaking out like that.

When I didn't speak again, Rajik moved on, issuing orders for our departure. As far as I knew, no clan had ever left the Home Range. Who knew how far we would have to travel to find a new home?

He's going to destroy us, I told Ryn. The red feathers on her ears quivered. She could sense my agitation, though I doubted she fully understood what had me so furious.

The meeting drew to a close, but before we could disperse, Nikat stepped forward. "We have one more matter to address," she announced.

Rajik looked annoyed, but even he couldn't dismiss the elder warrior without drawing dishonor on himself. He had already done enough, in my opinion, to lose one of his tokens today.

Nikat gestured me toward her. My injured ankle made it difficult to walk with dignity, but I used Ryn's support as little as possible as I approached.

"Kota fought well today," Nikat said. "She risked her life to save my own. I would not be standing here before you if it were not for her bravery."

Something stirred inside me, a flicker of hope I tried to smother in case I was wrong. But then Nikat reached into a pouch attached to her keeper's saddle and pulled out a red bead.

"Kota Ryn, today I reward you with a token of courage," she continued. "May the gods bear witness and recognize your strength as a warrior."

I accepted the offered token with trembling fingers. The other warriors stared, probably as shocked as when I had spoken out of place.

I didn't thank her, and she didn't expect me to. Tokens were earned, not gifted.

The meeting broke up after that. I turned toward my tent, though not before I caught the disdainful look Rajik gave me. Apparently, I had inherited his hatred for my dead father. I didn't care. Rajik was my chief, which meant he had my loyalty, but he didn't deserve my respect. With his decision to leave the North, he would never earn it back, no matter how many tokens adorned his hair.

The next day, we said goodbye to the Northern mountains and the only life I had ever known.

Part I: Crossing

Jurian

¤ ⌒♀〇

Prot Kyn

Sgielan

夫 冂

CHAPTER 1

Shaya

THE FALCON'S TRIUMPHANT CRY pierced the silence that had settled over the valley in the still hours of the morning. Whispers stirred around me, but my eyes never left the bird as it circled the village and glided back toward the tree line. I held my breath, praying the falcon signaled what we all hoped.

A human stepped out of the trees at the top of the hill. Once fully illuminated by the sunlight, he raised his spear. When the falcon landed on his other arm, a cheer rose like a wave among the crowd and crashed back down around us. I remained silent, but I shared their joy.

Makai had returned, alive and well, with a falcon as the new guardian of his soul.

The bird took flight again as Makai began his descent to the village. Family and friends rushed forward to congratulate him, with his mother and father in the lead. I stayed with my own family at the front of the crowd, watching from a respectful distance. It wasn't my place to greet him yet. We weren't friends, despite how much I wished we were.

Makai's grin stretched wider than I thought possible as his father clapped him on the back. His mother wrapped him in a hug until he protested that he couldn't breathe.

When she stepped back, I got my first clear look at him. Dirt smudged his face and clothes, but it didn't diminish his appearance. His chin-length black hair was brushed behind his ears, revealing dark eyes shining with pure exhilaration. His tan skin glowed in the sun, even after weeks without a proper bath. A few scrapes littered his arms, and one cut drew a sharp line down his cheek, but nothing serious.

Beneath his joy, I could see the weariness. His shoulders rested a little lower than normal, his steps the slightest bit unsteady. The inevitable toll of a solitary two-week journey.

Once the crowd finished welcoming him, Makai came to stand before my father. Our chief smiled warmly as the two clasped forearms, a greeting reserved for full members of the Konota people. Makai was a man now, a complete person.

"Welcome home," my father said in his deep, gravelly voice.

"Thank you, Chief Tahck." Makai managed to contain his excitement enough to keep his tone respectful. "Nahdi?"

My father shook his head. "Not yet. Don't worry, I'm sure she'll return soon."

Makai and his twin sister had left the village together but would have gone their separate ways somewhere along the journey. Everyone had to make the Crossing alone.

Makai's face fell, a brief flicker before his grin returned. He dipped his head to the chief and stepped past him.

For a fleeting moment, his eyes met mine. I usually existed outside Makai's notice, overlooked and unimportant. This was my chance to say something, to congratulate him on his return, but the words got stuck somewhere between my mind and my tongue.

The moment of opportunity slipped away. Makai stepped past and waded through the crowd behind me, clasping arms and exchanging hugs with others.

Everyone but me. Because I had been too hesitant, too slow. My shoulders slumped, and I silently berated myself for not saying anything. How could I get him to notice me if I froze whenever he looked in my direction?

"Don't worry, sis. That'll be you soon."

Ayla's voice broke through my thoughts. She smiled knowingly at me, but I wondered if she understood the real reason behind my despondent expression. Yes, I envied him. I wanted to be the one wading through a crowd of admirers.

But the knot in my stomach wasn't from jealousy.

A hand fell on my shoulder as Papa stepped up beside me. "Ayla is right, Shaya. You'll return with your keeper soon enough. Maybe Tyir will even bless you with a wolf." He winked, and I couldn't help but smile. I certainly wouldn't complain about a wolf—the same keeper as my father, an animal that signified intelligence and independence. Tyir allowed only the best of us to receive his own animal as their keeper.

"Maybe, Papa," I said.

"Or a fox," Ayla chimed in.

"Or a fox," our father agreed, casting an amused glance toward Mama, who had joined us. Nearby, two foxes lounged in the grass beside Honovi, my father's keeper. The huge black wolf watched us like an obsidian statue, his expression shrewd.

"Come, you three," Mama said. "Tonight is for Makai, not pining for the future." Her fox slunk after her as she turned her back on Mount Tyir. The crowd had already begun to disperse, people returning to their work. We followed her, the other two keepers trailing close behind.

That evening, a few hours before sunset, we feasted in Makai's honor.

Everyone gathered in the commons, a sprawling area by the lake, its tables this full only once every few months. I sat beside Ayla at one of two tables closest to the head table. Rows and rows spread out behind us, enough for the entire village—no less than four hundred people.

Delicious smells mingled with the fresh air: newly baked bread and cooked meat from that day's hunt, though the portions of venison seemed smaller than usual.

Makai sat between his parents and mine at the head table, facing the crowd. Only for occasions like this did anyone occupy those seats. His falcon perched on the back of his chair, looking noble and haughty as it surveyed the crowd, while the other keepers rested in front of the table.

"A falcon, huh?" Adann said from Ayla's other side. His cougar lay in the open space beneath our table, along with Ayla's fox. "I should have known Makai would end up with a bird."

Ayla smacked his arm. "Jealous?"

He leaned over to plant a kiss on her cheek, then another on her lips. I averted my eyes, focusing on my meal.

"Never," he said. "Illari is the best." The cougar looked up at the mention of her name, but she only flicked her ear before resting her head back on her paws.

I chewed thoughtfully on a piece of meat, watching Makai as he chatted with my father. He still radiated delight, his grin a seemingly permanent fixture on his face.

"I wonder what he'll name him," I murmured.

The falcon turned his head toward me, as if he'd heard my words. Makai followed suit, and our gazes locked for a split second before I looked down.

Adann leaned forward, peeking past Ayla at me. "You've hardly touched your potatoes. Are you going to...?"

I gave a small smile and slid my plate toward him. Typical of a nineteen-year-old, Adann could eat more than his fair share. He grinned as he claimed the rest of my food.

Ayla rolled her eyes. "Be careful," she teased. "You might have to watch what you eat eventually."

Adann set down his spoon and pulled up the bottom of his shirt, revealing the toned muscles of his abdomen. "Perhaps, love, but that day is not today."

Ayla wrinkled her nose in feigned disgust. She stole a glob of mashed potatoes with her fingers, earning a shout of protest from Adann. She smirked, at least until he retaliated by smearing more potatoes across her mouth. Her gasp of mock outrage trailed into laughter as she licked the potatoes off her lips.

"Just eat your food like a good boy." Ayla reached up to ruffle his short black hair, but he swatted her hand away.

"Shaya's food," he corrected.

"Right, eat Shaya's food."

When most of the attendees had finished eating, Papa rose from his seat and lifted his arms. The crowd fell silent.

"Tonight, we welcome a new member to our people," Papa announced. "He has returned from his Crossing with his soul complete."

He gestured for Makai to stand. The legs of Makai's chair scraped against the wooden platform, the sound startlingly loud in the expectant silence.

"Thank you, everyone," he said. "I am honored to stand before you and present my keeper, Farin."

Papa dipped his head. "Makai Farin, your focus, determination, and clear sight will protect our people. I, Tahck Honovi, chief of the Konota, am honored to welcome you, brother."

Makai straightened at the virtues that characterized any avian keeper. Every piece of him radiated pride, from his smile to his puffed chest. He met my father's eyes, then turned to address the crowd. "I am Konota now."

Behind him, Farin spread his wings, and the falcon's call cut through the air. Cheers erupted in the crowd.

In one month, I would make the journey to find the other half of my soul, and I would be sitting up there with my family. One month.

Chapter 2

The village waited four days for Nahdi to return. That was the cut-off. The journey shouldn't take more than three weeks. Anyone who didn't return by then would be declared dead. It didn't happen very often, but it did happen. I'd witnessed the heartbreak shared by our people when someone failed to return, but I hadn't been old enough to understand it until now.

I hadn't known Nahdi well, but she was adored by everyone, same as her twin brother. The two were inseparable, notorious for their mischief. Troublemakers, but in a way that made adults smile and shake their heads and say, "Great Tyir, those kids."

When night fell, torches were lit throughout the commons. Only her parents had to be present at the ceremony to confirm Nahdi's death, but nearly the entire village showed up. Makai should have attended as well. No one could find him, though, so they began without him.

Five words in, I slipped away.

I didn't bother checking the places others surely already had. Instead, I took the well-trampled dirt path down the hill to the lake, the place *I* would go if searching for somewhere to quiet my raging mind.

Makai sat on the rocky shore with his legs crossed beneath him, a knife and a chunk of wood in his hands. Shavings littered his pants, though I couldn't tell if he was carving something or meticulously reducing the wood to dust. Farin watched motionless from a tree nearby.

As with Makai's happiness four days ago, the hurt radiated off him. That was how deeply Makai felt. He ached so badly it permeated the air.

I didn't know where my sudden bravery came from, what had prompted me to leave the ceremony and now to sit beside him, mirroring his position.

His hands stilled as he glanced over, surprise and confusion clouding his expression. "Shaya?" My name sounded awkward on his tongue, as though he'd never spoken it before. "What are you doing? Why aren't you at... why are you here?"

I took in the tired, resigned look on his face and knew I'd made the right decision. "Because you're here," I answered. "And I don't think you should be alone right now."

"Maybe I want to be alone."

"No," I said softly. "I don't think you do."

He held my gaze, his eyes drawing me in, but the spell shattered when his shoulders sagged. He let out a shuddering breath. "I can't believe she's really never coming back. Everyone wants me to *talk* about it, but I can't..."

I tried to imagine what he was going through, how I'd feel if Ayla hadn't returned from her Crossing. Panic welled in my chest. Even though I shoved the thought out of my mind, the ache lingered.

I didn't respond, not to be rude but because I didn't have anything to say. I couldn't offer any comfort, any words of reassurance. His sister was gone, and the only thing left to do was grieve. If he didn't want to talk, I wouldn't force him—no one understood the need for silence better than I did.

I stared out over the dark water, acutely aware of how his eyes darted toward me now and then, and the way he opened his mouth like he wanted to speak but didn't know what to say.

Eventually, he managed to put words together. "Do you think there's still a chance she'll come back?"

I wished I could tell him yes, but giving false hope seemed cruel. "No one ever has."

This wasn't the answer he'd hoped for, but it didn't surprise him either. The sorrow left him in a burst, hitting me like a wave that forced the air from my lungs. I turned away, focusing on the line where the water brushed the shore. When I looked back, Makai was staring at me. His brown eyes looked almost black in the moonlight.

"What?" I asked, uncomfortable.

"I'm just... surprised you're here. You don't talk much. Definitely not to me."

I shrugged, not sure if that was an insult or an observation. Though my tendency to stay quiet had never bothered me before, it made me self-conscious now. "Not that it's a bad thing," he added hurriedly. "My mother always says you should listen closest to those who say the least."

I smiled faintly. "I doubt most people believe that." But it sounded nice. I'd worked with his mother a few times, in the Crafters Guild. Makai got his warm eyes and broad smile from her.

Yet, when I thought about it, I realized my family did fall silent and listen attentively whenever I spoke. Did they think I had something important to say or were they simply surprised to hear my voice?

He shrugged, marking the end of that conversation, which I thanked Tyir for. I wasn't here to talk about myself.

"I should be there, shouldn't I?" he murmured. "Am I dishonoring her by avoiding it?"

"Probably."

He let out a slow, ragged breath. Another truth he didn't want to hear but already knew.

I lifted my chin, watching as he stood and brushed grass from his pants. When his eyes met mine again, the sadness in them was softened by gratitude.

"Thank you," he said.

"For what?"

"For not making me talk."

He offered a hand to me. After a brief hesitation, I took it, far too aware of how his skin felt warm and rough against mine. I had never touched him before, and simply holding his hand sent tingles down my spine.

Makai helped me to my feet and together we climbed the hill, walking side by side to the ceremony that confirmed Nahdi would never return.

That night, I went to sleep with my chest aching, as if Makai had somehow infected me with his pain, his grief passing to me with the touch of his eyes and the brush of his hand.

The village spent the next day celebrating Nahdi's life—feasts and music and dancing—then the night in silence to mourn her death. After that, life returned to its normal rhythm, the village moving on from the tragedy.

Makai and I didn't speak again, but he no longer ignored me. At least once a day, we crossed paths in the village or at communal meals. He would meet my eyes and give me a smile that told me he hadn't forgotten our conversation. Always the same smile, grateful but tinged with sadness.

The village had moved on. Makai hadn't.

His guild choosing should have been the fifth day after his Crossing, but they had delayed it for Nahdi's funeral. On the sixth day, he had announced his choice. For him, at least, it had been an easy one. Everyone in the village had already known what he'd choose, and the Hunters Guild had welcomed him with open arms. His falcon's sharp eyes would be invaluable in the forest, finding prey to feed the village.

I watched as he passed my hut that evening, surrounded by other hunters celebrating a successful day. Some familiar light and excitement had returned to his eyes, chasing away the emptiness I had seen there recently. I hoped it meant Makai was healing from the loss of his sister... and I hoped it didn't mean he'd start ignoring me again.

"Shaya." My mother's voice broke through my thoughts, and I snapped my gaze away from Makai. From her amused smile, I knew I had been caught staring. Heat rose to my cheeks.

"Sorry, Mama," I said, and I meant it. I was supposed to be helping her mend torn clothing, not admiring a handsome boy.

"If we finish this, you can help your father with dinner." She nodded to the remaining pile of clothes in need of patching.

I didn't know what the Builders Guild had been up to lately, but half the torn clothing belonged to them. Most of the clothing the Crafters Guild had to fix came from builders or hunters, understandably, but it felt like more than usual.

Brightening at her encouragement, I set back to work with twice the diligence. Yet, even as I threaded my bone needle through the fabric, I couldn't keep my mind from straying back to Makai. Since the lake, his eyes had lingered on me instead of sliding past, but how long would that last? Were lingering glances all I'd get to share with him?

When we finished mending the clothing, we folded it and stacked it neatly in baskets to be returned to the owners tomorrow. The evening had deepened as the sun sank toward the ridge surrounding our valley.

My eyes traced the top of the ridge until they fell on Mount Tyir to the north. The great mountain always gave me a sense of excitement and anticipation deep in my stomach. It called to me, tugging at my heart and soul, beckoning me with promises of a new life. A better life.

I wondered if all children felt that call, if it was normal or maybe even something real, not something in my mind.

I climbed to my feet, using one of the wooden poles of my home's frame to steady myself. Tala, my mother's fox, rested with Honovi in the shade beneath the lincloth awning that slanted down from the roof, providing shelter for the keepers. Honovi lifted his head when we stood, but he promptly went back to sleep.

Inside, light from the fire illuminated the hut. Shadows flickered across the walls, cast by our limited furniture—a round table, three beds, and wooden chests at the foot of each bed for personal belongings. As the chief's hut, it was bigger than most, though not by much.

I set my basket in the corner beside my mother's, then we joined Papa by the fire. Smoke wafted through the clay chimney, up and out to keep the air inside safe for breathing.

Papa stirred the large pot in front of him with a wooden spoon. He looked strange sitting by the pot. Broad-shouldered, with bulky muscles that indicated his time in the Builders Guild before becoming chief. He didn't look like the sort of man who should be cooking, but he was the best in our family, aside from Ayla perhaps.

"Ayla's not back yet?" Mama asked as she took a seat beside him. Papa sat on a chair, but she preferred to rest cross-legged on the floor when given the opportunity.

I grabbed the wooden tray of spice pouches from the table and copied her, mimicking the quirk I had always found amusing and endearing. I didn't think I had one of my own, so I borrowed hers instead.

"I'm sure she'll be here soon," Papa replied. "There was an accident with the builders earlier today. She's probably still treating them."

"That's terrible," Mama said, her eyes widening. "Was anyone injured badly?"

"Nothing permanent," said a new voice. We all turned to see Ayla by the doorway, letting the flap of animal skin fall back into place. "Misni broke her arm, but we set it and Grandpa thinks it will heal fine." She grabbed a chair from the table and joined us by the fire.

The red-tinged light of dusk spilled through the doorway again as another person pushed back the flap. Grandpa Enzi poked his head inside. "I hope you don't mind if I join?"

"You know you're always welcome here, Papa," my mother said with a touch of exasperation. "Hurry along, Tahck is hungry."

Papa's deep laugh filled the hut. "Yes, I might drop dead from hunger if you don't join us immediately." The look he gave her made my stomach flutter. Someday, I wanted someone to look at me like that.

Ayla and Mama's laughter lifted my spirits, chasing away the storm cloud that had hovered over my mood for days. The mix of apprehension about my Crossing and worry that my moment with Makai had been nothing but that—a moment—faded away. For now, I focused on my family and the happiness that warmed me from the inside like the fire warmed my skin.

I sorted through the spice pouches, sniffing each one and trying to decide which would go best with the rabbit stew Papa had started. A savory aroma already filled the hut, as familiar as my family's laughter.

"Tahck mentioned an incident with the builders," Mama said. "What happened?"

While Grandpa and Ayla told the story, I sat in silence with my spice pouches, listening as the conversation flowed into the other events of the day. Everything they did sounded interesting. Then there was me, spending my time on menial tasks for the various guilds: stitching clothes with Mama, carrying supplies for builders, fetching water or herbs for the Healers Guild. It was supposed to help me decide which guild I wanted to join after my Crossing, but with less than a month left, I didn't have a clue.

I could be a healer like my sister. I liked spending time with Grandpa Enzi, and healing sounded like a good purpose. Yet the sight of blood and Ayla's description of setting Misni's broken bone made my stomach turn. I didn't have the strength of a builder, nor the patience and creativity to be a crafter.

The Hunters Guild was tempting, if only because Adann once told me I showed promise in tracking. And maybe joining would bring me closer to Makai. That thought eased some of my worry, but the perpetual pit of emptiness lurked underneath, reminding me I still didn't know where I belonged.

One way or another, I would have to choose when I returned. My decision would define my path for the rest of my life. Only a stray lacked purpose, and strays had no place here.

Once I settled on a couple spices, I held the pouches up to Papa, who took them without question. He added some of each to the stew and breathed in the fragrant steam with a contented smile.

When dinner was ready, I spent the meal listening, speaking only when spoken to. This was the way it had always been, but I realized it wouldn't last forever. When Ayla and Adann made their partnership official, they would share a new hut and start their own family. Eventually, I would have my own partner, my own home.

I decided to savor this as long as it lasted. My family. Grandpa, who had always encouraged my curiosity and fed my hunger for stories. Ayla, a little overbearing and controlling but kind at heart. Mama, patient and warm, who loved her daughters with a fierceness I wouldn't have thought possible. And finally Papa, who carried the weight of the entire village and somehow made time for his own family. He could gaze across the table and smile at me like he knew my thoughts.

I didn't know how life could get any better than this, yet some part of my soul still longed for *more*. I just didn't know what *more* might be.

Grandpa stayed for hours after we finished eating, sharing stories and trading jokes until the conversation wound down.

"I should get to bed," he said as he stood. "These old bones need their rest."

Mama rose to give her father a hug and a kiss on the cheek. I stood as well, less gracefully than my mother, and crossed the room to my bed. I was already looking forward to the comfort of heavy woven blankets and the feather-stuffed pillow.

"I brought you something."

Grandpa's voice at my shoulder startled me. My family always said *I* moved quietly. I must have inherited it from him.

He held out a folded piece of parchment with the outline of a bird—a hawk, maybe—drawn on the front. Curious, I unfolded it to reveal some kind of map.

As Grandpa raised a candle so I could see it more clearly, the flickering light shifted over his face, illuminating his skin paled from spending too much time inside. Tending to the injured and preparing medicines took up most of his day. He smiled at me, his face settling into the ridges of wrinkles he'd developed over the years.

The map was painstakingly drawn with such detail that it took my breath away. It wasn't merely cartography but a work of art, every valley and mountain shaded with care, every tree sketched so I could differentiate pine forests from oaks and aspens.

Along with being the lead healer, Grandpa was a knowledge keeper of sorts. As a young man, he had traveled far beyond our valley, returning with stories and legends, as well as the occasional treasure—like this map.

The rest of the Konota might not think much about the lands beyond our home, but I loved the stories about far away places and courageous heroes. I still remembered the first story he'd told me. I'd been ten, sitting around a firepit with several other children, including Ayla.

Now, years later, I had every word of it memorized.

NokaMia had been born in the Pajair desert, in the city of Darajin. When her queen was poisoned, she ignored all the warnings and embarked on a perilous journey to find a mythical plant to save the queen's life. Ayla said it was just a story, a foolish tale meant to entertain, but I believed there was at least some truth to it. I knew deep in my soul that NokaMia had lived. Even if she hadn't, I could still admire her bravery and refusal to give into hopelessness.

"I thought you might like this," Grandpa Enzi said. "Keep it as long as you like."

"Thank you." I carefully refolded the map. "I'll take good care of it."

"I know you will." He smiled and pressed a kiss to my forehead before leaving the hut.

After he had gone, I realized only Papa remained. He sat at our table with a wooden box in front of him. It was like the one hidden under my bed, only half finished. A single candle illuminated the project, though it was poor light to work by.

"Where did Mama and Ayla go?" I asked as I took a seat across from him. I set the map down and folded my arms on the table, then rested my chin on my wrist to watch him tinker with his box.

He didn't look up from his work, his deft fingers sliding a narrow peg through one side of the box. It looked too small for such a big man to be working with, his muscles and large hands more suited to constructing huts than crafting delicate boxes.

"They went to fetch some water. I believe they'll be gone for another twenty minutes or so." He finally glanced up and gave a knowing smile. The trip to the river only took ten minutes to get there and back. They would likely spend much longer talking at the water's edge.

A few minutes passed in comfortable silence before he nodded toward the parchment sitting by my elbow. "A new gift from Enzi? What's this one?"

"A map." I brushed my fingers against it, pondering what I would find when I studied it more closely. In my brief glimpse, I had seen our valley in the center of the page, but the rest remained a mystery. Grandpa had told stories of the desert and the Far North, even tales that spoke of a place where land met infinite water. Some people took boats out on that water, crafts larger and sturdier than any we used to fish in the Konota Valley.

Papa set aside his tools and the partially finished box. "You know whatever you choose, I'll be proud of you," he said, guessing my earlier inner turmoil.

"I know."

And I did. Some parents wanted their children to join specific guilds, usually their own. Mine had never cared. They wanted us to pursue our passion, wherever we felt most at home. I loved them for that, but sometimes I wished I had been pushed toward a guild from a young age. Maybe it would make the decision easier.

Papa watched me quietly in the flickering candlelight. I started to wonder if this anticipation was how people usually felt while waiting for me to collect my own thoughts.

Finally, he asked, "Are you worried about your Crossing?"

He waited patiently for me to respond, the same way I had waited for him. In the end, I only shrugged.

"Don't rush," he said. "You'll have plenty of time. This is truly about the journey, not the destination. Follow your instincts and let your soul wander."

I nodded. It wasn't the first time I had heard similar advice. Nearly my whole life had been spent preparing for the Crossing. It would mark the moment I passed into adulthood—the moment I found the animal that would keep my soul safe.

When I was eight years old, I had asked my father why I needed to wait so long for my keeper. I'd been terrified that the soulstealers would find me before then. He had assured me that the demons weren't interested in children—our souls weren't mature yet, so why bother stealing them?

Laughter outside announced Mama and Ayla's return. While Papa turned away from me to greet them, I unfolded the parchment again to sneak another look at the map in the candlelight.

My soul had been wandering for years, sometimes aimlessly, sometimes drawing me toward Mount Tyir and whatever awaited me there.

Hopefully, it wouldn't wander too far.

CHAPTER 3

AFTER SIXTEEN YEARS OF waiting, it was finally time.

"Shaya," my father said, his powerful voice loud enough to carry over the silent crowd.

Everyone, adults and children alike, had gathered outside the village. Horses, cougars, wolves, and other keepers were mixed in with the people, all here to send me off.

"The time has come for your Crossing." Papa sounded formal, but there was pride in his eyes. "You have three weeks to make your journey to Mount Tyir. May you find your other half along the way and return complete. Good luck."

And that was that. My family gave me encouraging smiles. When my eyes sought out Makai in the crowd, he offered a smile as well, but his was laced with sadness and... was that fear? Was he afraid I wouldn't return, like Nahdi?

I tried not to dwell on that. I would survive this and return complete. The emptiness and longing inside me would finally go away.

I turned my back on my village and jogged toward the forest. My pack bounced against my back, its contents a comforting weight. Dried food, two waterskins, flint, and some healing supplies. I also carried an unstrung bow, a quiver of arrows and a sheathed knife on my belt.

With every step, I found it more difficult to breathe. I paused at the edge of the forest, fighting the urge to glance back one more time. The tall pines and ancient oaks waited before me, daring me to enter, and I finally identified the feeling I had mistaken for excitement or anticipation.

It was fear.

My grip tightened on the bow. Only a fool would be unafraid. I would face many dangers and wouldn't return unscathed.

Steeling myself, I plunged into the forest.

My footsteps on the soft earth were the only sound as I wove between the trunks. The silence wrapped around me, not oppressive but comforting, peaceful enough to settle my nerves.

After an hour, I paused in the shade of a maple tree. The morning was pleasantly cool so far, but my brisk pace had caused a light sweat to break out on my forehead. I slipped off my pack and dug out one of my waterskins.

I allowed myself a long drink, well aware that my water supply wouldn't last the entire trip. Rivers or streams would provide a place to refill the waterskins along the way.

I traveled for most of the day, pausing at noon to hunt, eat, and rest before pressing on. A few hours after lunch, I started actively searching for a stream. Children were taught survival skills from the age of six, but the first time someone ventured into these woods was for this journey.

I had no map, no knowledge of the landscape. I was on my own in a strange land.

When the sky began to darken, worry settled in. I hadn't found a stream, and my second waterskin held only a few precious swallows. Nightfall meant I would need to stop and find shelter, but training and instinct told me I had to find water first.

Though weary from the long day, I turned toward the river that ran down the valley. Maybe I should have followed it for the first day, but I couldn't rely on it the whole way up the mountain. It was against the rules. As my father had said, I needed to let my soul wander, which it couldn't do if I stayed by the river.

When the hunger gnawing at my belly became too insistent, I pulled jerky and hard crackers from my pack—a meager dinner but better than nothing since I didn't have time to stop and hunt.

Soon, the forest darkened enough that I had trouble seeing. The shadows thickened, hiding unearthed roots and patches of brush that tugged at my boots. As much as I wanted to reach the river, I couldn't go stumbling around in the dark. Resigned, I shifted my focus from water and searched for a place to settle down for the night.

After scouting the area for a suitable tree, I detached the rolled-up cloth of my hammock from the bottom of my pack. With the ropes slung over my shoulder, I climbed the trunk and found two thick branches that could easily hold my weight. I tied two of the ropes around the first branch, then leaped like a squirrel to the second so I could secure the other anchor points.

By the time I scrambled down to retrieve my pack, the sun had fully set and the darkness pressed in around me. I thought I heard something rustle in the distance but told myself it was probably only the wind. I would be safe in my hammock high in the tree. After climbing back up, I lowered myself into the hammock and pushed the pack down by my feet.

I soon found that sleep would be more difficult than I'd thought.

The sounds of the forest—rustling and crickets and strange animal calls—made my heart beat faster. I turned restlessly in the hammock as the night went on, my thoughts churning. I was almost out of water after my first day. I had no idea what dangers awaited me over the next few weeks, and I worried I would have many more sleepless nights ahead of me.

I woke with my mouth parched and throat raw. My body felt stiff, my mind groggy, and my stomach cramped from hunger, since I hadn't eaten much the night before. Dawn had passed and light flooded the forest. The sunlight on my face must have been what woke me.

My stiff muscles didn't respond right as I climbed out of the hammock. Unbalanced, my foot slipped, and I clung to the branch to steady myself. From this height, a fall wouldn't necessarily be fatal, but it could leave me injured and unable to continue.

Once safely on the ground, I wrapped the ropes around the hammock to keep it rolled and tied it to the loops on my pack. I drained the last mouthful of water from my waterskin, which did little to quench my thirst. After fishing out a few strips of jerky, I continued northwest toward the river.

When the land began to slope downward, I picked up my pace, hope unfurling in my chest. Soon, I could hear the tell-tale sounds of flowing water. I tripped in my eagerness and slid halfway down the slope, but I didn't care. I sprang right back to my feet and ran the rest of the way to the wide river.

Relief rushed through me as I staggered to the bank. I fell to my knees and splashed the cool, clean liquid over my face. Cupping more in my hands, I took a long drink, the water easing the pain in my aching throat.

After filling my waterskins, I decided I had time for a much-needed bath. I stripped off my clothing, most of it made from sturdy leather that would hold up for the journey, and plunged into the water.

The cold river came as a shock at first, but washing away yesterday's dirt and sweat felt amazing. I scrubbed every inch of my body with my hands and rinsed out my hair in the running water.

Reluctantly, I waded back to the bank and stood there for a moment while the water ran off my body. A sunny patch of grass on the shore provided a place to stretch out like a cougar and enjoy the warmth while I dried.

Once most of the moisture had evaporated from my skin, I made my way to my clothes. As I bent down, I heard something nearby. The crunch of leaves, the snap of a twig. This wasn't vague rustling of leaves in the wind. Something was out there—something large. I held my breath as my eyes scanned the forest, ears straining for any sound. They found only silence.

I snatched my knife from the pile of clothing. Still naked, I felt exposed and vulnerable, despite the knife in my hand.

"Get out of here!" I called, trying to sound as menacing as possible. I waited, scarcely breathing, counting off the seconds in my head. One, two, three, four...

When I reached five, a loud crash broke the silence as something plowed through the undergrowth. I jumped back, my body tensing, but the sounds moved away from me. The creature had retreated.

I let out an unsteady breath. My body shook as I picked up my clothing. It could have been anything out there, concealed in the shadows. A wolf, a cougar, even a rare bear. Or maybe just a deer or some other non-predator. The uncertainty frightened me most.

As I dressed, a question nagged at me. I was supposed to find my keeper out here, but how would I know it from a creature that wanted to eat me?

You'll feel it, I told myself. When the moment came, surely I would know.

As I followed the river up the mountainside, refilling my waterskins whenever they ran low, the morning progressed into a sweltering day. Soon sweat rolled down my face and soaked my clothing. No one was around, so I stripped off my shirt and carried it as I walked, keeping to the shade as much as possible.

I had to force myself to take a break beneath the shelter of an ancient oak. My eagerness to reach the mountain's peak urged me to press on, but it was only the second day of my journey and exhaustion had already started to set in. I needed to pace myself.

Don't rush, my father had said. *This is truly about the journey, not the destination.*

When my breathing returned to normal, I pulled on my shirt to protect my shoulders from the sun. By then, hunger pawed at my stomach. I decided to reap what I could from the forest, conserving my supply of crackers and jerky for emergencies. A bush of familiar wild berries staved off the hunger until I was able to shoot a rabbit a few hours later.

I gathered dry sticks and grass, setting up a fire pit in a shaded area. Adann once showed me a trick for getting a good fire going and practiced with me again and again until I got good at it. I smiled at the fond memories of his patience and encouragement.

As soon as the meat was done, I tossed dirt on the flames to put it out. I ate my fill of rabbit meat and berries, squirreling away most of the edible leaves and roots I'd found into my pack for later. Sitting in the shade, my stomach full, I wondered if this would be one of my few good meals. I doubted my luck would hold for the rest of the journey.

I had started to drift off when I heard it again: the crackle in the forest. I stiffened and reached for my knife, my nerves on edge. I *knew* something was out there, the same creature from the river. Something was following me. When a twig snapped behind me, I spun toward the sound, every muscle tense and ready for an attack.

Large eyes of molten gold with slitted pupils peered out at me from between two shrubs. The eyes blinked once and vanished, then footsteps retreated into the forest again.

I stood there, gripping my knife in a sweaty hand and taking deep breaths. What *was* that thing? I had never seen eyes like that before. I shuddered, as if trying to shake off my fear, and gathered my things.

After seeing the mysterious beast staring back at me, I was too on edge to stay in one spot any longer. I marched on, hours sliding from one to the next, until there was only my footsteps on fallen leaves, the sun beating down, and the rapid pulse of my heartbeat.

Every now and then, I'd hear the snap of a twig or the crunch of leaves. The creature stalked me through the forest, a hidden watcher that made the back of my neck prickle with unease.

Chapter 4

Each day grew more grueling than the last. I accumulated various scrapes and bruises, and my cheeks felt raw from a mild sunburn. The heat hadn't let up, either. Despite bathing and rinsing my clothes in the water, I smelled like sweat and dirt.

After three days of following the river, I refilled my waterskins for the last time and forced myself to leave it behind.

All the while, I sensed the thing following me. The occasional rustling and snatches of movement out of the corner of my eye. By the fifth day, the prickling on the back of my neck had become so constant that I felt strange during the rare moments it went away—and relieved when it returned. Whatever stalked me didn't seem interested in killing me, and I somehow found knowing I had a companion, even a mysterious and invisible one, comforting.

On the sixth day, my food ran out. I pulled out the last two strips of jerky, my stomach sinking. I should have gathered more food from the woods instead of relying on my supplies when I was too weary to search. Night had already fallen, though, and I couldn't scavenge for food until morning. I choked down my meal, despite apprehension souring my appetite.

Sleep remained elusive. Every time I started to drift off, some noise in the forest startled me awake. I didn't know if it was the wind or a bird or a deer. Maybe my watcher was out there somewhere. Watching.

The next day it *poured*. I would have welcomed a light shower, a break from the heat, but this was a river falling from the sky. The clouds turned the day to night, and I staggered around in the darkness before giving up on making progress.

My boots slipped on the wet bark as I scaled a tall basswood tree with my hammock. I hoped the thick foliage would provide some shelter from the rain, but little could be done about this onslaught. After getting the hammock set up, I set my waterskins on the forest floor to catch the rainwater. The narrow openings wouldn't collect water quickly, so I plucked a few leaves from the tree to use as funnels.

I shivered in my hammock that night, sleep coming with even more difficulty than before. After hours of cursing the weather and wallowing in my misery, I realized I pitied the children born in the winter. I had to deal with rain. They faced freezing nights and snow and ice.

That knowledge restored my resolve the next morning. After foraging a small meal, I spent the rest of the morning covering as much ground as I could, keeping a look out for a stream now that I had left the river behind. My collected rainwater wouldn't last long.

I ignored the grumbling in my stomach until well into the afternoon. A few hours before sunset, I hunted. I set up simple snares in the area, which I planned to check in the morning. My first attempt to shoot a quail failed, the bird disappearing into the treetops before I could loose the arrow.

My stomach rumbled angrily, and I silently berated myself. I could do better than this. The second time I found prey, the creature didn't escape. I had pheasant for dinner after building myself a fire pit.

In the morning, I found a rabbit in one of my snares. A second snare had been tripped during the night but sat broken and empty. Rabbits and squirrels rarely had the strength to break free, which meant some larger creature had gotten snared... or something had taken it. Had my watcher stolen the prey? That thought made me smile—because it had taken one catch but left the rabbit for me.

Once I'd finished eating, I left my campsite and forged on. I wished I knew how much farther I had to go, but even when the branches didn't block my view of the peak, I couldn't tell how far it was. The mountain loomed above me, even more intimidating now that I stood on it instead of at its base. The slope of my journey gradually increased, making each step more and more difficult.

A shriek tore through the forest.

I froze like an elk catching wind of a predator, my ears straining. The forest went silent for a few seconds, the quiet followed by snarling and a distressed cry unlike anything I'd ever heard. I couldn't imagine what kind of creature would make that sound, but something deep in my soul told me my watcher was screaming for help.

I raced toward the source of that shriek, not really following the sound but something intangible that called me onward. When the snarling grew loud enough that I knew I was close, I ducked to peer beneath a tree trunk that had fallen against a steep hill, leaving half a pace between it and the ground. I didn't have a clear view through the clump of bushes on the other side, but I could see movement in the clearing beyond. The gray fur of wolves and... something else.

I dropped my pack near the base of the broken tree trunk. As quietly as I could, I scaled the next tree and climbed out onto a branch to get my first good look at the creature that had been following me.

It looked like nothing I'd ever seen or could possibly have imagined. It stood at about my height on four muscular legs. Feathered wings of deep purple and bright gold were tucked against its back. Leathery black skin covered most of its body. At the tip of its long, lizard-like tail were forearm-length feathers of that same deep purple, and as the creature swung its tail toward one of the wolves, I saw a flash of ivory. Bone spikes? More purple feathers ran down its long neck and along its spine. Right then, the feathers stood up like hackles.

The creature lashed its tail at another wolf, driving it back, but they circled closer. Its motions became more frantic, and though it still snarled at the wolves, it looked more frightened than menacing.

Shouting as loudly as I could, I launched myself from the branch. I didn't think about how reckless it was. I just did it. The three wolves jumped back, startled, when I landed between them and the creature. I whirled around, swinging my unstrung bow like a staff, and caught one wolf on the nose. It yelped and backed away as I aimed another swing at a second wolf that side-stepped to avoid it. The third wolf snapped at me, but the creature batted the wolf away with its long tail before teeth could close on my arm.

The wolves paused, cautious now that they faced two enemies instead of one. I stilled, holding my bow in front of me. The wolves growled, their teeth bared. I was well aware of the strange creature still standing behind me. For some reason, a part of me felt safer for it, my watcher guarding my back.

"Get out of here!" I shouted at the wolves. I swung my bow again, not aiming to hit anything but simply to frighten them. The wolves gave one last snarl before disappearing into the forest.

Slowly, I lowered my bow and turned to face the creature. It stared back with those huge golden eyes set on either side of a narrow snout. They had to be the size of my fist, and I could have sworn the color shifted like molten metal. The fear from the wolf attack lingered, but the creature mostly looked weary now. We locked gazes for a few heartbeats. Then it turned and vanished as well.

I went the rest of the day without feeling my watcher's eyes on my back. Before, its persistent gaze had made me uneasy, but now the absence left me feeling vulnerable and alone. Had I frightened it off?

I had never heard of a creature like it—a mixture of bird and lizard, something beautiful and frightening at the same time. For a heartbeat, I had thought the creature was the reason I was out in this forest, that my soul had found its other half. Perhaps it had been following me because we were meant to be together. Now that it was gone, though... maybe I had been wrong.

A few hours past midday, I happened upon a narrow stream, a blessed place to pause for a much-needed drink and to refill my waterskins. They were both almost empty. After a short rest, I crossed the stream and continued north.

I came to a stop at the base of a cliff. I had to crane my neck to look up at it, the sheer surface intimidating and almost taunting. *You can't climb me,* it said. The mountain was daring me.

Or maybe it was my exhaustion speaking.

I turned my head to one side and then the other, finding only more of the steep climb either way. I could pick a direction and try to find an easier path, but I had a feeling that would merely waste time, maybe a full day of wandering with no guarantee. I was getting closer to the mountain's peak. My journey would only grow more difficult from here.

I set my jaw and adjusted my pack. Scaling such a sheer surface would be difficult, but maybe I could find a way to make it easier. High above me, a tree grew off the edge of an outcropping near the top of the cliff. The trunk tilted precariously toward the world below, several of its roots dangling into thin air like petrified tentacles. A plan started to form.

I glanced around, assessing my surroundings. A patch of grass nearby grew nearly to my hip. That would do the trick. I left my pack at the base of the cliff and got to work, picking the longest strands of grass I could find. The wider blades I sliced in half with my knife, then started twisting one blade until it grew tight enough that it looped in the middle. With the loop pinched in one hand, I used my other to continue twisting one end of the blade. When it grew tight, I twisted the two sides together so I could work with the other half. Once I neared the end of the blade, I spliced in another piece, folding it and laying it over the ends of the forming cord so it seamlessly became part of the rope.

On and on it went. I twisted so much my fingers began to cramp. Adann could have made a cord five paces long in ten minutes, but it took me much longer, especially since I had to keep going back for more blades of grass. The longer I worked, the more I questioned whether this was the best idea. But something told me I *had* to do this, so I kept going.

I needed to twist multiple cords together to make a rope thick enough to hold my weight, but eventually I had a rope I was confident would be long enough and strong enough for my climb. I tied one end of it to an arrow and shot it up so it looped several times around the trunk of the tree growing off the side of the cliff. A few hard tugs confirmed the rope was secure. The other end I tied around my waist. I used an extra bit of cord to attach my bow to my pack, so I wouldn't have to figure out how to carry it—or worse, leave it behind.

One grueling motion after another, I made my climb. Left hand. Right foot. Right hand. Left foot. I focused on the rhythmic movement, my eyes searching for my next handhold. When I couldn't find one, I used the rope to pull myself upward. As I climbed higher, I looped the rope around my body each time there was enough slack to do so.

I pushed past the protests of my muscles and the sharp pain in my fingers from gripping the rough surface of the cliff. Sweat collected along my collar and above my cheek bones. It rolled down my forehead and stung my eyes. When I licked my lips, salt coated my tongue. My heart pattered an uneven rhythm in my burning chest. Before long, each heavy exhale left a metallic taste in my mouth.

My heart faltered when my foot slipped. I tried to cling to the face of the cliff, but the small lurch was enough to tear my fingertips free. I dropped a full pace before the rope went taut and halted my fall. I jarred my shoulder against the cliff when I swung inward, but I was alive, rather than broken on the ground below.

I took several deep breaths. My heart raced. My shoulder throbbed. I thanked Tyir for my decision to take the time to weave the rope. When I no longer felt dizzy, I started up again, reclaiming the distance I had lost. Then onward.

I didn't dare look up more than an arm-length the whole climb. I was suspended in a brutal eternity, uncertain how far I had come or how much farther I had left. The only thing I knew was the press of rough stone under my fingers and the way my whole body ached.

Then, finally, my fingers curled around the edge of the cliff.

I hauled myself up and over, sprawling on my stomach like a corpse. Eyes closed, I panted, trying to fill my lungs and slow my heart. I didn't think I could have stood, could have moved one muscle, even if I'd wanted to.

I failed to hold back a whimper. The soft sound of my own exhausted pain shattered the thin wall that held back my emotions. Tears started to roll down my cheeks, mixing with sweat and dirt.

How did every man and woman in our village get through this? How could they expect their children to do it? Prepared from an early age or not, this was more than a journey to find your soul. It was a test, one of mind and body and sheer willpower.

As I lay there, I thought of Makai and Ayla and my parents. They had all done this. They had succeeded and returned. If they could, I could.

I forced my heavy eyes open and lifted my chin.

My muscles screamed as I dragged one knee under my body, then the other, and pushed myself up onto my hands. My head spun as I hauled myself to my feet. I had to lean against the rock wall beside me... and that was when I realized my climb wasn't over.

I stood on the wide outcropping of rock, the tree that had kept me from falling to my death beside me. My safety rope no longer had much use. From the ground, I had thought the outcropping was close to the top, maybe even close enough for me to reach up and pull myself over. Now that I stood there, I realized I had underestimated the distance. I still had at least twice my height to climb, with no place to reanchor the rope.

I rested my head against the cliff and fought back another rush of tears. After blinking several times to clear my blurry vision, I noticed the narrow path that led along the side of the cliff.

"Path" wasn't the right word. The ledge, barely a few hands wide, jutted out from the cliff face. The outer edge slanted downward, but it was horizontal enough to walk on. The path sloped upward, gradually climbing the cliff... all the way up to the top.

I let out a sharp breath and let my tears fall again, this time from relief. I could walk the rest of the way, provided I could get to the ledge. It started a couple paces away from where I stood, the space between entirely vertical and smooth as a river stone. No hand holds—I would have to jump. While I thought I could make the distance, I didn't have complete confidence that I wouldn't lose my balance.

I tilted my head back and squinted at the top of the cliff directly above me. Another four paces up the vertical face or take the risk of attempting the jump.

My muscles would probably give out before I managed to drag myself even another single pace up the cliff, which made the decision easy. I kept the rope tied around my waist and gave myself a little slack for the jump. A fall would send me swinging back toward the tree, but it would be better than plunging to my certain death. I took a few steps back to the far side of my little outcropping, which allowed me a short running start before I flung myself across the gap.

I made the distance easily. In fact, I overshot it, so I stumbled when my feet hit the ground. The top half of my body pitched forward as I went down, and I crashed onto my hands and knees.

I was too relieved to feel any pain.

My palms rested on the edge of the narrow ledge, my fingers stretching out into empty air. I let out a shuddering breath and rocked back to sit on my heels. *You're okay,* I reassured myself. Flooded with adrenaline and a little scraped up, but still breathing.

With one hand on the cliff to steady myself, I stood. I untied the rope, figuring I wouldn't need it anymore, and started along the path. After my vertical climb, the steady slope was nothing. Before long, I was only a few steps away from being able to throw my arms over the top and haul myself up.

In my eagerness, I picked up my pace, and that was my downfall. I stepped a little too close to the edge and the world lurched as my foot slid sideways off the path. My stomach dropped. Terror rushed through me, and a panicked scream ripped free of my throat.

Then the straps of my pack tightened around my shoulders, jerking me to a stop. I dangled in the air, the straps supporting my weight. My foot bumped against the cliff face as I swayed in the wind. Something pulled me up and dumped me on the ground at the top of the cliff.

I rolled over and scrambled away on my hands and knees. When I raised my gaze, golden eyes stared back at me. My watcher crouched in front of me, its body between me and the drop off that had almost killed me. Its spiked tail swayed a hand-width off the ground, moving languidly like a mesmerized snake.

I swallowed the rest of my panic and let the tension slump out of my body. I expected the creature to run off again—half-expected it to dive over the edge of the cliff and spread those feathered wings—but it didn't move.

"What are you?" I asked, still breathless. It was the first time I had heard my own voice in days.

The creature made a quiet sound, musical and bird-like, and tilted its head to one side. I didn't know why—logic told me I could lose a finger if not more—but I reached a shaking hand toward the creature's muzzle. I held my breath, waiting for it to flee or attack, but it did neither. The distance, no more than a hand-width, stretched on forever until my fingers finally brushed my watcher's rough skin.

Fire flooded through my veins and ignited my blood.

Lightning darted across my skin, sending fine hairs on end, a tingling burn that felt good and agonizing all at the same time. A rushing like wind over the meadow filled my ears. Dark dots spread over my vision until everything went black.

I didn't know how long the sensation lasted, but it ended as abruptly as it had started. I blinked, and my vision cleared again. Huge gold eyes, less than an arm-length away, gazed back at me. I don't know how to explain it, but I felt different. Like something I never knew was missing had suddenly clicked into place. It felt like waking up from a dream. A haze had lifted from my mind and all my senses honed the world to a new sharp precision.

I felt complete.

Chapter 5

WHEN I TRIED TO stand, I found all my strength had left my body. I stumbled against the creature—*my* creature—and caught myself on his shoulder. His. I knew with instinctive certainty the creature was male, even if I still didn't know what he was. He made a soft sound in his throat, a gentle clicking, and a question blossomed in my mind. Not in words but in feelings—concern mixed with a sense of confusion and wonder. He felt what I did, that new feeling of completion, but he didn't understand it.

"It's okay," I said. "Don't be afraid." Even though I knew he wouldn't understand the words, he would understand the meaning. Did that make any sense? Nothing made sense anymore. I felt heady from excitement and the rush of new sensations.

Up close, I could see that small scales made up the black surface of his skin. They felt smooth and leathery, the scales hot under my fingertips, his skin hot. I lifted my hand and ran it down the gold and purple feathers on his wing. I'd never felt anything so soft, the fine threads of the feathers gliding against my skin like silk.

"What are you?" I whispered in wonder.

The same question echoed back from his mind.

The full weight of what had happened finally hit me. I stepped away, grinning, and spun in a circle. Luckily, the strength had returned to my muscles, so I didn't topple right over the cliff he'd saved me from. He watched me curiously, his feathered ears erect and his long tail curled around his feet. The spikes at the tip were indeed made of some bone-like material, sharp and gleaming white in the sunlight.

"Navi," I said. He blinked at me, his head tilting to the side. "Navi, that's your name." My parents had once told me that's what they planned to call me if I'd been a boy. It felt right now.

He gave a soft rumble of pleasure that emanated from deep in his chest. *Navi.* The name formed hesitantly in my mind, originating in his.

"That's right," I said. "And I'm Shaya."

The rumble intensified, not like a growl, but akin to the soothing sound of Illari's purr. Navi's happiness flowed through me. I had to lean against him again, faint with the emotions rushing through my head.

Then I remembered finding my keeper wasn't my only task to complete on my Crossing. I had to reach Mount Tyir's peak. Without asking, because I already knew it would be fine with him, I reached over Navi's broad back and pulled myself up, careful not to tug on any feathers. I settled myself near his neck, my legs resting on top of his folded wings.

"Let's go," I said, a bit breathless with excitement. He bounded forward like a playful wolf cub, and I had to wrap my arms around his neck to keep from flying off his back. I laughed at his enthusiasm, which mingled with my emotions until I couldn't separate his from my own.

He sensed where to go from my mind, and together we worked our way up the mountain. We passed the tree line a few minutes in. I finally noticed the air growing thinner, as if we'd stepped out of a bubble, not to mention the cold. The thin, frigid air bit at my arms and face, tiny needles of ice that pierced beneath my skin and wouldn't dislodge. Navi seemed better suited for it, despite his lack of fur, his thick skin resistant to the wind. I leaned closer to him as he lifted his wings slightly to shield me from the worst of it.

Navi had to climb steep, rocky hills a few times, his claws scrabbling against stone and a light dusting of snow. I wondered briefly why we couldn't fly the rest of the way, but the answer echoed back to me immediately.

Navi didn't know how to fly.

He was a young... whatever he was, and he hadn't known any of his family. Whether this was normal for his kind or not, we had no way of knowing. The rush of his knowledge—what little he had—left me light-headed again.

Despite his lack of flight, Navi could move far faster than I could on foot, and we made good time to the peak. I had started to doze off, partly from tiredness and partly from the lack of air, when Navi stopped suddenly. I peered over his head and was met with a sight that left me even more breathless.

The world fell away before us, vast and unknowable and achingly beautiful. The lands beyond our sheltered valley: the plains to the west and the snowcapped mountains of the Far North. The map Enzi gave me came to life, pale parchment replaced by the blue-purple mountains and forests ranging from deep pine to vibrant green. A river wound its way down from the mountains and along the eastern edge of the plains.

It terrified me and called to me all at once, whispering terrible and alluring promises. I didn't know much about what waited out there, only what I had learned from stories. As far as I knew, out of any living Konota, only Grandpa Enzi had ventured past the safety of the valley.

I tore my eyes away from the spectacle that spoke of freedom and danger, my sense of purpose returning. After sliding from Navi's back, I knelt on the rocky ground. From my pack I drew my flint, my iron knife, and a bundle of kindling I had gathered days before. It took me several tries to get a spark to catch. The cold wind extinguished any flame that flickered to life, leaving behind only a wisp of smoke that was swiftly carried away.

Navi curled his body around me, his wings extended to guard me from the wind. Finally, fire licked at the kindling and spread quickly, the edges of the grass and twigs curling as the flames blackened them.

We didn't have much time before either the kindling ran out or the wind stole the flames away. I plucked a feather from Navi's wing, offering a silent apology at his sharp chirp of protest, then pulled a strand of hair from my own head. I twined my brown hair around the vibrant purple feather, then held the pair to the flame.

It caught quickly, the fire spreading across the hair and feather and leaving only ashes behind. I dropped the end of the feather a moment before the flames reached my fingertips. It fell into the fire and vanished a few seconds before the small blaze burned out.

"We are one," I said. "Soul and keeper. Guard this piece of me until we both draw our last breath."

The wind swept the words away even as I spoke them. It carried them to the north, toward the majestic mountains that made Mount Tyir look like a mound of sand. Had Navi come from somewhere out there? The plains or the northern mountains or even the deserts to the east.

When I looked over at Navi, my keeper, I felt a flicker of fear. He blinked and turned his head to me, his confusion stirring in my mind. "What if they don't accept you?" I whispered.

I doubted he would understand the concept, but I said it anyway. I had dreamed of this day in part for the acceptance—the inclusion—returning from my Crossing would bring. But now I was bonded to a creature I'd never heard of, not even in legend, and I didn't have a clue what our reception would be.

Don't be afraid. The words, not my own, resonated in my head. I blinked at Navi. He had repeated my words from earlier.

How can I not be? I thought back to him.

I couldn't avoid the inevitable. We had to return home and face what awaited us there, whatever that may be. After one last glance over the endless unknown, I climbed onto Navi's back, and together we made the long journey down the mountain.

CHAPTER 6

I WOKE TO A gentle rumble that vibrated through my body and made my skin tingle, its source deep in Navi's chest. I opened my eyes to early morning light filtering between the leaves overhead. Glancing around, I realized this area was familiar. We were close to home, and somehow Navi knew that too. It was why he had woken me. The trip that had taken me a week on my own had lasted only a few days moving at Navi's pace.

"Home," I murmured. A warm feeling echoed back to me from Navi, along with a faint sense of confusion. "Haven't you ever had a home?"

He didn't seem to recognize the concept, though he liked the feelings it elicited from me. I wondered what his life was like before he started following me in the woods. How long had he been alone?

Home. He repeated the word with a tentative wonder, testing it in his mind.

That's right. We're almost home. My home, and yours too now.

He chirped happily in response.

Navi slowed as I slid from his back, opting to walk the last stretch by myself. I felt stronger after letting him carry me through the forest, and most of the bruises from my adventure had faded or turned an ugly brownish green. Navi matched my pace perfectly and without protest.

Time seemed to slow the closer we drew to the village. The possibilities of what awaited us there yawned in my mind. I didn't know how my people would react to Navi, a foreign creature I had no name for. I managed to summon some of my mother's optimism and assured myself everything would be fine.

Soon, we reached the edge of the forest.

The grassy hill sloped away from us, our little village nestled at the bottom. In my mind, I saw Makai standing at the top of this hill, his arms raised victoriously, but I didn't have his flair for the dramatic. I picked my way down the slope, my hand resting on Navi's folded wing. I focused on the feel of his soft feathers under my fingertips and blocked out unwanted worries.

With nothing to announce my return, the way Farin had for Makai, the village wasn't gathered awaiting my appearance. The sun, barely above horizon, washed the village in a warm glow. Few people were awake, aside from the first group of hunters who would hopefully bring fresh meat back later that day. Early-rising farmers dotted the fields as well, but aside from that the village was quiet.

I'd made it halfway down the hill when one of the hunters spotted me. Shouts rose as the hunters roused the rest of the village. I slowed my step to savor the moment, watching as my family gathered. Not only my mother and father and sister. Right then, the entire village felt like my family. None of them knew me well, few had ever held a conversation with me, but they were family all the same. They amassed at the edge of the village to welcome me home with open arms.

Then, like a flash of lightning splitting the sky, the mood changed. The cheers died down, replaced by an uneasy hum as murmurs passed between people. Panic washed over me. I went rigid, my fingers curling around Navi's feathers.

They'd seen him. They had seen Navi and didn't know what to think. Even though I couldn't see any faces clearly, I imagined looks of fear, confusion, and disgust sweeping over the crowd. My eyes darted from one indistinct face to another until finally settling on the broad-shouldered, towering man at the front.

My father, waiting to greet his youngest daughter as an adult. He stood tall, shoulders back. Unafraid. I never took my eyes off him as I crossed the last few dozen paces to the village.

I no longer needed to imagine the fear and distrust. The people before me didn't feel like one great family anymore. My father, however, offered me the same loving smile he'd been gifting me since before I could remember.

"Welcome home, Shaya." His voice was formal, but his gaze retained its warmth... and yet beneath it I could see an undercurrent of confusion. *It's okay,* I reminded myself. *You would be confused. Confusion is better than fear.*

I took his offered forearm in my hand. "Thank you, Chief Tahck," I said, matching his formal tone. My voice sounded far more strained. I glanced past him to my mother, who stood nearby with Ayla. They both gave uncertain smiles that made my chest tighten.

"But what is it?" a voice cried from the crowd.

"I've never seen such a creature!" Misni of the Builders Guild called. A dozen other voices echoed her, and I stopped trying to identify them. This was the moment I'd dreaded, the moment when my village refused to accept Navi—and therefore *me*.

"Enough!" Papa bellowed. Except... he never actually raised his voice. The deep timbre carried over the crowd anyway, and everyone abruptly fell silent. The absence of sound left a void in my ears that was somehow worse than the grating clamor of a hundred voices.

My father broke the spell. "Shaya has returned with her keeper, making her a full member of the Konota. It does not matter what her creature is—" he paused for a heartbeat, which made it sound like maybe it *did* matter— "she is one of us and now an adult. We will celebrate her Crossing tonight."

No one argued, but the crowd still bristled. The air quivered with tension that no one could possibly miss. I met Papa's eyes and tried to draw strength from his steady gaze, but it wasn't enough.

Then someone repeated, "But what *is* it?" and I cracked.

I pushed through the crowd, ignoring my father shouting my name. People parted for me, or rather for Navi, who followed in my wake. As I fled from the fear on their faces, I stumbled and fell into another person. Strong hands steadied me, and I looked up into Makai's face. I wished I hadn't. His expression mirrored that of everyone else, confusion and fear, and I *couldn't* take that from him. Not him.

Fighting back tears, I pulled out of his grasp and kept running.

When I reached the hut, I threw myself onto my bed and buried my face in my pillow. Though the bed was far too small for both of us, Navi jumped up beside me. The bed frame—sturdy and well-made from wood poles like the frame of our hut—protested under his weight. I worried it might break, but the creaking ceased when he curled his warm body around mine and went still. I focused on the feel of him at my side. Navi was part of me, a piece of my soul. Whatever anyone else thought, at least I still had him. I would *always* have him.

I had never really cared about what other people thought in the past, so why did I care now? A soft rumble sounded in Navi's chest in response to my thoughts.

"You're right." The words came out breathless and bitter. I did care. Whatever I told myself, I had always cared.

I closed my eyes and didn't open them even when I heard the rustle of the pelt that covered the entrance to the hut. I knew they all stood there without having to look. My family, the people who cared about me more than anyone, but I couldn't look at them. I pressed my face tighter against the pillow until I couldn't breathe.

"Shaya." Papa's deep voice was not that of the chief. It was gentle and warm, the voice of a man who loved both his daughters unconditionally.

I rolled my head to the side, freeing my face from the smothering pillow. I took a deep breath and wished the pain eating at my soul could be soothed as easily as my burning lungs.

"I'm sorry," I whispered, though I don't know what I was apologizing for. For bringing home an impossible creature, for being *other?* If Navi was something dangerous and mysterious, then I was too. We were one in the same. What did it mean that my soul had chosen him?

"Oh, Shaya. There's nothing to be sorry for." My mother crossed the room. I waited for her to rest a hand on my shoulder, but she didn't. She stopped a pace away, not looking at me but at the creature behind me. My keeper lay still as an ancient oak, though I could feel his agitation—a mirror of my own—thrumming beneath the surface of his rigid body.

The hesitation contradicted her words. It said so much more than empty reassurances could.

"Please go away." I pressed tighter against Navi. If I could have melted into him and escaped the weight of my family's eyes, I would have. "I don't want to talk."

"Shaya," Papa said. "Whatever it—"

"He," I said.

We stared at each other. His expression wasn't angry, but rather dumbfounded. I didn't think I'd interrupted another person in my life, especially not my father. "Whatever *he* is," he corrected himself, "it changes nothing."

It changes everything, I thought, but I didn't say the words. It didn't matter. Nothing I could say *mattered.* I didn't know how to make them understand the turmoil that chewed at me.

"Please talk to us," Mama said. She sounded so desperate, with an undercurrent of guilt, that I felt compelled to obey. Or try at least.

I struggled to find words. There was too much spinning around to voice, a hundred snippets of thoughts and fears and other feelings all tangled up so I couldn't quite single one out. When I finally separated one thread from the mass, it hit the core of my worries well enough.

"You saw the way they looked at me." My voice, quiet as ever, sounded too loud in the room. I could feel the tension that pervaded the air when I breathed in.

"They're surprised," Mama said. "Give them time. It's not every day that..." She trailed off, lacking the words to describe exactly what had happened today. I had returned from my Crossing with a strange creature, but somehow that simple statement didn't sum up the entire truth.

"They don't like him here. They don't like *me* here. We're different." And different was always, *always* bad. People feared what they didn't know and couldn't explain. I didn't realize my voice had risen until my next words came out small and fragile. "What if I don't belong here anymore?"

"This is your home," Papa said. "You will *always* belong here." The way he spoke... with such certainty that it almost made me believe.

"You're still one of us, sweetheart." Mama finally stepped forward the rest of the way so she could brush a lock of hair away from my forehead. The gesture was familiar and should have been comforting, but I felt only hollowness inside.

I glanced at Ayla, who had remained silent. She hadn't looked at me once, her eyes trained on her hands folded in front of her.

"Ayla?" Mama prompted gently.

"I think she should do what feels right," Ayla said. "Maybe there are others out there... like her." She kept her eyes down, which I was grateful for. I think eye contact would have made the betrayal a hundred times worse.

Had Ayla told me she thought I should leave?

I pushed my mother's hand away and stood. Navi bounded off the bed beside me, causing my family to instinctively shift away. I pushed my way between Papa and Ayla and reached for the door flap.

"Shaya, wait," Papa said. I paused, but when I glanced back, it was at Ayla. I waited for her to speak, to take it back, to even *look* at me. She didn't.

I turned my back on my family and fled, but I couldn't flee the misery and fear and the thoughts that circled in my head like vultures waiting to pluck out the last vestiges of happiness.

The village bustled with its normal activity, but hands went still and conversations fell silent as I passed. People stared and crowds parted. My steps grew more rapid, to match my heartbeat, until I was flat-out running. I didn't know where. Just away, away, away...

As my feet followed the well-beaten path down the hillside, I realized where they were taking me.

The lake shore was empty, everyone working elsewhere. I stopped at the edge of the water, the wavering line a few finger-widths away from my toes. My reflection stared back up at me. My tired face and brown hair that I hadn't bothered to brush since my return. And beside me Navi—the creature who held a piece of my soul and whose very existence no one here could comprehend.

Ayla's words echoed in my head as I collapsed on the shore and pulled my knees to my chest. This wasn't how it was supposed to be. I found myself starting to wish I could do it over again. Maybe things could be different... but I knew I would never trade Navi for anything else. He was a part of me, the way it was always meant to be. It couldn't happen any other way. I had felt complete on that mountain.

Now I had no idea who I was.

When my tears had run dry, I dragged myself off the ground and wiped my cheeks with my sleeve. I still wore the clothes from my Crossing, and the tanned hide left a smear of dirt on my face. I didn't care. The dark smudge on my skin was nothing compared to the hollow look in my eyes, reflected back at me in the surface of the lake. I had once thought the lighter shade of brown hair I shared with my mother and grandfather was pretty, but now it only made me feel more different than the rest of the Konota.

I had *always* been different. Now the differences were more obvious.

I turned my back on the lake and marched with renewed purpose toward Grandpa Enzi's hut. Navi's ears quivered as he followed me, an uncertain question touching my mind through our bond. Lira, Enzi's fallow deer, grazed on the patch of grass alongside the hut as we approached. She eyed Navi as we passed, her slender body tense.

Grandpa looked up from whatever he was grinding with a mortar and pestle when I entered. "I wondered when you would show up." He spoke in an even, powerful voice that made him sound younger than his years. I had no idea how old he truly was; he had an ageless quality, but old enough to have grand-daughters.

Grandpa Enzi could be my salvation. In all his travels, surely he had heard something about Navi's kind.

"You know what he is, don't you?" I asked.

His hands went still, his expression thoughtful. "I know legends," he said. "From the North. They speak of an ancient, powerful beast with great feathered wings, four legs, and a bone-spiked tail."

Navi chirped from the doorway, his huge ears erect and twitching. The opening was a bit narrow for him to squeeze through, so he remained outside with his long neck poking in.

"A name," I said. "Did these legends give a name?" I didn't know why it mattered, only that it did. Maybe if his species had a name, a story, he would seem less *other* to my village.

Grandpa nodded. The seconds stretched out. My breath was trapped in my chest, awaiting his answer. "Drakon," he said. The word rang through my mind and echoed back to me from Navi's. I mouthed it silently, feeling the shape of the name on my lips and tongue. It felt foreign. It felt like a warning, and unease prickled at my spine.

"Mysterious creatures, the drakons," he went on. "They're said to dwell in the treacherous mountains of the Far North where few men get to glimpse them. Some people fear them as demons. Others worship them as sacred animals, keepers of the gods. Their virtues are strength, protectiveness, and ferocity. The fearless guardians of the North."

That sent more than a prickle down my spine. I shuddered, and Navi stretched his neck so he could press his nose against my arm. I rested my palm against his forehead, my fingertips tracing over the scales. Demons. Keepers of the gods. Both of those sounded terrifying. I wanted neither to be true.

"If they live in the northern mountains, what is he doing *here*?" The Far North was at least a two-month journey from our village.

"That is the baffling question," Grandpa agreed. "Along with why he's alone. Drakons are supposedly social creatures, living in large colonies in mountain caves."

"Drakon," I murmured. Fourth time hearing it. First time saying it. "Are there legends about people bonding with them?"

"One story speaks of a great hero. They say he fought the gods themselves on the back of his mighty drakon."

"Fought the *gods*?"

He shrugged. "It's a legend. Perhaps one part truth, but certainly three parts fiction."

"The gods," I repeated. I leaned heavily on Navi's neck and silently begged the world to stop spinning. "What was his name?"

"Tavlin Lamere."

I had never heard the name before, but the way he said it—the sharp T and fluid pronunciation of "La-meer"—gave me another chill. Tavlin Lamere, hero of legends. A man on the back of a mighty beast.

"Thank you," I said softly. I took a step toward the door but stopped and looked back at the old legend keeper. "Grandpa... how does the story end? What happened to Tavlin Lamere?"

He didn't answer right away. The longer the seconds dragged on, the more sure I was that I didn't want to know the answer. I shouldn't have asked. Before I could take it back, Grandpa said, "He died, killed by someone he trusted. Some say he grew too ambitious and forced her hand, while others say she stabbed him in the back. Either way, he died before his time, taking many of his friends and allies with him."

On that morbid note, I pushed aside the door covering and slipped outside. Navi trailed me through the village, his movements tense. I didn't know if it was due to his agitation or mine. Maybe there wasn't enough of a difference to matter.

Chapter 7

Like my return to the village, my ceremony fell pathetically short of my expectations. People gathered in the same manner as the dozens of ceremonies I had seen in the past, but a blanket of unease had settled over the crowd, muffling the few conversations that took place. My imagination ran wild with what those people whispered to each other.

My parents sat on either side of me at the head table. Papa surveyed the crowd, while Mama stared ahead at nothing at all, a hand resting lightly on my arm. I think it was meant to be comforting. It wasn't.

I wanted to run and hide. Hundreds of eyes stared up at me, humans and their keepers, the pressure of each gaze pushing against my skin until I thought I would crumple in on myself. I didn't want to be here, but running from my ceremony would upset everyone even more. So I stayed.

Both my parents attempted to start conversation, but I either gave short answers or simply didn't reply at all. Eventually they gave up. When most people had finished eating, Papa stood, as he had during Makai's ceremony. The difference was Makai had sat up here with triumph, while I wanted to slink under the table and curl up with Navi.

When the chief spoke, his voice was strong, no sign of the doubt that plagued the rest of the village. "Tonight we welcome a new member into our people. She has returned from her Crossing with her soul complete. She brings with her a keeper none of us have seen, a drakon from the northern mountains that somehow found its way to our valley. Shaya, if you would introduce your keeper."

Grandpa Enzi must have told him about the drakons. Papa's words danced toward reassuring, like he was trying to put everyone at ease, but they never quite reached their goal. They only served to remind me how different we were.

Wrong. It was all wrong. This was supposed to be the happiest moment of my life. I should be standing before my people with pride, not trepidation.

I couldn't breathe. I opened my mouth to suck in air, but I may as well have been inhaling water. My fingers curled around the edge of the table, so hard I thought they might snap under the force. My head spun. My heart raced. Droplets of sweat rolled down my forehead and along my collarbone.

I thought I would pass out, but a gentle weight pressed against my leg. Navi's tail, the only part of him that fit under the table. The contact jolted me back to myself. Air filled my lungs, my heart stopped trying to outrun itself, and the cool breeze kissed away the sweat on my burning skin.

My father's worried face came into focus. He and everyone else watched expectantly, and the weight of their attention almost sent me into a panic again. I honed my focus on Navi's presence and rose from my chair.

I spoke the words expected of me, but my voice sounded flat and far away to my own ears. "I am honored to stand before you and present my keeper, Navi." My gaze swept over the crowd, at the people I could easily name but few I'd ever spoken to. They stared back with expressions ranging from uncertain to outright disdainful.

"Shaya Navi, your strength, fierceness, and vigilance will serve our people well. I, Tahck Honovi, chief of the Konota, am honored to welcome you, sister."

Strength, fierceness, and vigilance. None of those words sounded like me, but Grandpa must have told my father the virtues so he could use them in the ceremony. Would I live up to what my keeper was supposed to embody? Maybe bonding with Navi had been a mistake.

Even as the thought slithered into my mind, I knew it wasn't true. The gods guided us toward our keepers, the ones we were destined to walk beside for the rest of our lives. Tyir had brought us together, which meant there was a reason.

The last four words were the hardest to force out, because they didn't feel true. Not one bit. "I am Konota now."

When Makai had spoken those words, the village had erupted in cheers. My declaration dropped into the tension-strung crowd and was met with only silence.

I stared across the lake, watching the way the wind blew ripples through the crescent moon. As soon as I had announced myself as Konota, I had left the ceremony to circle the lake shore and return to my favorite spot, the one where Makai and I had first spoken. Light conversation and laughter had drifted from the commons for an hour or so until the sun set, people enjoying themselves after the uncomfortable part was out of the way.

Now only the sound of the water lapping against the shore and the occasional hoot of an owl reached me.

I heard him before I saw him, soft footsteps on the grass, and I didn't need to turn my head to know who sat beside me. The rustle of wings announced Farin as he landed on a branch nearby.

I never took my eyes from the unsteady glow of the moon's reflection. "Did you come to tell me 'you'll always be one of us' too?"

"Is that what they said?" Makai asked.

"Everyone but Ayla." I didn't bother to hide the bitterness.

"Oh."

That was it. Makai fell silent, a would-be stone carving as he followed my gaze out over the water. Normally, I would have been content to sit wordlessly, listening to the crickets and the soft brush of water against the land and the sound of his breathing. But at that moment I wanted—needed—some form of reassurance from him. Maybe it hadn't meant anything from anyone else, but maybe from him... Which was a stupid thought. What could he say that had more impact than my family?

Was this how he felt the day Nahdi had been pronounced dead? Not wanting people to make you talk but having so, so much to say. The silence stretched out until it became too unbearable.

"Ayla thinks I don't belong here." I felt an almost physical sense of relief when my words filled the silence. They left me in a burst, like they'd been taking up room in my chest and now I could breathe again. It was as if the world had paused and suddenly started again, the motion the only thing that made me realize how wrong the stillness had been.

Makai shifted to face me. "She said that?"

"She said enough."

"I'm sure she didn't mean it like that," he said. "People say strange things when they're caught off guard."

"Then maybe they shouldn't say anything at all," I snapped, then instantly regretted it. He was only trying to help.

Makai didn't seem distressed by my sudden anger. "Give them time to adjust. They'll come around."

Another hush fell over us, but it took me less time to break it. "Do *you* think I don't belong?"

He didn't respond right away, which made me fear his answer. What if he said yes?

"I think you belong wherever you're happy," he said finally. "And I really hope that's here."

It sounded so close to what Ayla had said, yet somehow different. Had I overreacted to her words, read into meanings that didn't exist?

Or maybe I'd been waiting for someone to tell me I didn't belong. Someone to confirm how I felt. I glanced at Navi and again wondered how he had ended up in the valley. Everyone else must be wondering the same, along with "Can we trust it?"

"Thank you," I whispered. I didn't specify what for, and I didn't think I needed to.

Ayla would have said something along the lines of "returning the favor." Mama would have told me she would always help and she loved me very much. Papa would have said, "Anything for you."

Makai only nodded.

CHAPTER 8

I HAD FIVE DAYS following my Crossing to choose a guild. Most people made their decision long before the official cut-off, because most people knew what they wanted before they reached sixteen years. Ayla had known. Makai had known. Everyone but me.

Officially, the five days were meant to give someone one day with each of the five guilds, to help them finalize their choice. Some people would use a few of the days to narrow down their decision if they were uncertain, but I still had *no* idea.

The first day, I joined the Farmers Guild in the fields south of the village. It was the guild I least wanted to join, so I could have skipped it, but I wanted to drag out my five days as long as possible. Whenever I thought about announcing a decision, my chest tightened and my heart lurched.

I spent most of the day in the flax field, tending to the blue flowers. The plants would be harvested soon, lincloth made from its stalks and oil from its seeds. More fields of potatoes, corn, and other crops stretched as far as I could see. I worked diligently, ignoring the farmers around me. Few people were outright rude to me, but the same unease I'd sensed before lingered wherever I went. They avoided looking at me, spoke to me as little as possible, and at the end of the day everyone—especially the Guildmaster—looked relieved when I didn't choose their guild.

Next I picked the Builders Guild, my second to last choice. By the time I was released from my duties, I regretted not skipping it. I wasn't weak, but my muscles didn't compare to the strong arms of the builders. After a day spent carrying supplies and chopping logs with a hatchet, my arms felt like liquid.

I planned to head straight to my hut and collapse into bed, but a commotion at the edge of the village drew my attention. I peered between two huts to see what had caused the stir. At first, I saw nothing, but then a horse-drawn cart rolled into view across the bridge that spanned the river north of the lake. Traders.

Wait here, I said to Navi.

Why? He knew exactly why or he wouldn't have felt so wounded.

I gave his shoulder a reassuring pat. *I just don't want to startle anyone.*

With Navi no longer at my side, I was able to slip between other people unnoticed, the way I used to. No one paid me any attention as I wormed my way through the crowd to the front to see the cart rattle its way into the village.

One trader walked beside the horse that pulled the canvas-covered cart. A second man jumped off the back once it came to a stop. He waved at the gathered villagers, a grin on his face.

The two were an odd pair. The first trader's dark skin told me he probably came from the Pajair Desert, but his companion looked like he hailed from Emirdom on the west coast. His long black hair was pulled up in a bun, his tanned skin shiny with sweat from the midday sun.

"Greetings, valley folk!" he said grandly. He spoke the Konota language with hardly any hint of an accent. "We come to you bearing the many wonders the world has to offer. Spices and clothing from Pajair. Metalwork from Emirdom! Silk from the southern forests. What treasures do you seek today?"

The children fidgeted with excitement, and I found myself among them. I may have been an adult with my own keeper, but traders brought a piece of the outside world to us. When the other trader threw back the canvas that covered the cart, revealing their wares, the children pressed forward. I had to order my feet to remain rooted, against their instinct to run forward and join in.

The adults hung back while the traders showed toys, exotic foods, and colorful clothing to the gathered children. A few of the younger ones ran off to find their parents, probably to beg for something to offer in return for a plush from Emirdom or hard candy from the desert cities.

The other trader spoke with a much thicker accent than his partner. I could hear it even over the clamor of other voices, children asking to see this or that from the cart. His words rolled off his tongue, smooth and rhythmic in a way that made the familiar words sound musical. Like the other trader, he wore brightly dyed clothing, probably cotton or lincloth like my own. A wide-brimmed straw hat kept the sun off his face.

Once the children had finished with their fun, it was time for the serious trades. Metal tools and weapons for the builders and hunters. Foreign fabrics for the crafters to work with. I saw my father buying candles, both those with enticing scents and ones meant only for light. My people offered food and a variety of other goods in exchange. Sturdy leather, bottles of linseed oil, sheets of lincloth, carved figurines, and woven rugs.

"See anything you want?" Makai said at my shoulder. With the flurry of activity, it wasn't surprising I hadn't heard him approach. Farin perched on his shoulder, the falcon's talons digging into the leather shoulder guard he wore.

"Not really," I replied. Mostly I wanted a chance to talk to the traders. They often came with stories, both recent events and legends of old. When I saw an opportunity to step forward, I took it.

The trader with the hair bun gave me a smile, though his eyes flickered around me as if in search of my keeper. "Greetings. I am Roubin, the humble trader. Can I interest you in a whistle stick or plush toy?"

My face flushed. He assumed I was one of the children, late to the gathering, and I didn't bother correcting him. "No, thank you. I was hoping you might share a story instead."

"Ah, but of course." Roubin tilted his head, a mischievous twinkle in his eyes. "I knew you were the curious sort when I first saw you." He glanced toward his partner, who was busy haggling with a hunter over a bundle of metal spearheads. "I think he has it handled."

I followed the trader around to the other side of the cart, away from the frenzy. Makai trailed behind us with Farin still on his shoulder. "No, I don't think he has any fresh voles for you," he muttered. I suspected I wasn't meant to hear.

"So, what sort of story were you hoping for?" Roubin asked.

I didn't have a good answer to that, so instead I asked, "Are you from Emirdom?"

"Avarttha," he said. "The last remaining independent city in the west."

Avarttha. I mouthed the word to myself. I had heard the name before but not much else. "Tell me about Avarttha, then. Please."

"A brilliant choice. Not that I'm biased." He winked at me. Meanwhile, Makai tried to fend off Farin, who kept pecking at the side of his head. I fought back a smile and tried to remain focused on the trader.

"Once, long ago, the western lands were made up of individual villages that governed themselves," Roubin began. I already knew this part, but I listened attentively anyway. "They fought each other often, disagreements over what lands belonged to which people. Then came King Emir, now known in the west as the Great Uniter. He saw the people who died every day over petty squabbles, so he decided to unite his homelands under one rule."

"Conquer them, you mean," Makai said. I elbowed him in the side for interrupting, but the trader grinned.

"Aye, that's what the people thought then, too," Roubin said. "They didn't want to be united under his rule, but none could stand against his army. None but Avarttha. They saw his armies sweeping over the land and decided to prepare their defenses. They built a great wall around their village, taking example from cities like Darajin in the desert. When the king's army arrived, they were ready."

"So they were able to beat the king because of some wall?" Makai asked skeptically.

"That was part of it. But not all. Avarttha stands thanks to something no other village possessed—a very powerful mage."

"Magic protected it?" Makai sounded even more skeptical about magic than about the wall. "Magic doesn't exist."

Roubin shook his head sadly. "You Konota have myths and legends, but for the people of Avarttha, magic is still real. It's what ties our souls to our keepers, protecting us from the demons. It's what allows souls to be reborn into the next life... where they must find each other again and keep each other safe. It's what allows the human body to repair itself from grievous ailments."

Makai snorted. "That's not magic."

"Is it not miraculous?" Roubin asked. "There are those who can harness this energy. To control that which binds the world together... and tears it apart. Avarttha's guild of mages remains the most powerful in the six lands, aside from perhaps the legendary White Hall. When the army came, the town's magical defenses were too much for it. Fire rained down from the wall. The earth split beneath soldiers' feet. The weather itself turned against them—brutal sun turned to blizzards and back again, all in one day. A mere two days after arriving, the king's generals sounded the retreat."

Makai's expression shifted from cynical to eager during the story, but that didn't mean he believed in magic now. To him, it was just a story, but I wanted to believe the truth in it.

"Since that day, the rulers of Emirdom have left Avarttha alone, aside from one or two foolish monarchs who tried to breach the walls," Roubin continued. "The small town has transformed into a great city over the years, but one thing will always remain the same: It is protected by the strongest magic this world has seen."

I tried to picture the great city and the massive wall wrapped around it. My village would seem like a drop of water in the lake compared to a place like Avarttha.

Makai pulled a lock of his hair away from Farin's beak. The young man might have gotten enthralled in the story, but the falcon certainly hadn't. "Well, that's enough magic for me," Makai said. "I'm going to see if there are any sweets left." He gave me a quick smile before disappearing around the side of the wagon. I remained behind, itching with more questions but unsure where to start.

With Makai gone—or more importantly, Farin—a small creature made its appearance, poking its head out from beneath Roubin's shirt collar. It looked a bit like a mouse, with a long nose and round ears. It had a band of darker fur over its eyes, almost like a raccoon. When it crawled the rest of the way out of Roubin's shirt and onto his shoulder, I realized how long its body was.

When the trader noticed me staring, he reached up to scratch the small critter on the head. "This is Nilos. He's a ferret."

"He's your keeper?" I asked. No wonder Farin had been so demanding. He must have known the small animal was hiding in Roubin's clothing. I had never seen such a small keeper. We had wolves and cougars and horses. Sometimes a fallow deer like Enzi's. Falcons and foxes were the smallest creatures I knew of anyone in the valley bonding with. My people would laugh if someone came home with such a small creature—no use for helping with hunting or pulling farm plows or carrying building supplies.

"I suppose you would see ferrets as small prey, like a rabbit," Roubin said. "In my city, we have all sorts of keeper animals you would never guess." He gave me a dry smile. "Even rabbits."

"I don't mean to be rude. I'm just surprised."

"It's alright, young Konota." Roubin gave me a look so analyzing that it made me want to run after Makai. "You have a traveler in your soul, don't you?" the trader said. "A restless spirit."

"Of course not," I replied with little conviction.

"It's a big world out there," he said. "The Plains of Eleir to the west, Emirdom beyond it. The southern forests of Payan. We get to visit them all." He folded his hands in front of him and tilted his head. "You could come with us."

The offer startled me so badly that I couldn't find the words to respond right away. *No. My home is here.* But they wouldn't come out. "Why would you take me?" I asked eventually. "Do you make a habit of picking up random people on your travels?"

He laughed. "No. Never, actually. But I sense something in you—a desire to be free. I know that feeling. It's what drove me to leave home in the first place. Then I met Ditu and... well, the rest is history."

Again, I tried to refuse. I couldn't leave my family. But the words remained stubborn, unwilling to leave my lips. Navi sensed my distress all the way from the hut—he wanted to come to me, but I ordered him to stay put.

When I said nothing, Roubin rested a hand on my shoulder. "Think about it. We'll be here until tomorrow morning." He stepped around me and went to help his companion, leaving me standing alone behind the wagon. I felt numb. I had tried so hard to convince myself I still belonged here, but when offered the opportunity to leave, I found it all too tempting. *I could see the world,* I thought.

Do you want to? Navi asked.

I don't know.

That was what it came down to. The problem I'd had since before my Crossing, and it hadn't gone away. I didn't know what I wanted.

CHAPTER 9

THE TRADERS LEFT AT dawn. I watched their wagon rumble away from the village from behind a hut, as if I were spying on something I shouldn't see. With every heartbeat, I went back and forth on whether to run after them. On Navi's back, I could catch up easily. What would they think of the drakon, though? Maybe Roubin would change his mind, or Ditu would refuse me. I had left Navi behind yesterday for a reason.

Go. Stay. Go. Stay. Indecision kept me rooted to the spot until the wagon disappeared into the forest.

I turned my back on what could have been a different future. It was the third day after my Crossing, so I should have sought out the master of the next guild, but choosing between the final three proved as difficult as deciding whether to leave with the traders.

My feet led me to the north side of the village. The group of hunters preparing to leave eyed me as I passed. They probably thought I was looking for Guildmaster Caldin so I could request to join the hunt, but I continued walking without meeting anyone's gaze.

"Shaya Navi," a voice said.

I didn't need to look at his face. I could hear the sneer in his voice. Eldin had rarely spoken to me, but I didn't need to interact with him directly to know that Guildmaster Caldin's brother was a prickly creature. Like Adann, his keeper was a cougar, but he took the self-assurance associated with the animal to new levels. I had seen him in action, though. He was a good leader and a better hunter. I still wished he had decided to ignore me like the rest of the village.

"You should pick a guild and be done with it," Eldin said. "Why draw it all out? If you're looking for one to want you, it's not going to happen."

My eyes snapped up, unfamiliar anger flashing through me. When a low growl sounded in Navi's throat, I realized the fury had come from him, not me. I put a hand on his shoulder and pushed the anger away. Yelling at Eldin would do me no good, nor would Navi threatening him.

I drew strength from the fierceness boiling in my keeper as I met Eldin's eyes. My voice didn't waver as I said, "I will make my choice in time."

He blinked, surprised that I hadn't risen to the taunt. I stared at him and waited for his next words. Eventually, he turned his back, but not before I caught the flash of irritation. He'd wanted me to start a fight.

I jumped onto Navi's back and let him carry me up the slope that had begun my journey to Mount Tyir. Last time, I had ascended this path in search of myself, but now I was running away.

People like Eldin were the reason I had been so tempted to accept Roubin's offer. The reason my stomach twisted whenever I thought about my future in the village. People like Eldin would never accept Navi—accept me.

The drakon's strong legs bounded us through the forest. We wove between trees with a speed I hadn't thought possible. We had taken it slow on the way down the mountain, but this... this was freedom. I could only imagine how flying felt, how breathtaking that would be.

Navi, I said silently, so as not to disturb the quiet morning. *I want to fly.*

The response was so clear, he may as well have shouted it. *No.* The single thought was accompanied by anxiety and, beneath it, shame.

But you have wings.

Navi's wings shifted, spreading slightly before tucking tightly against his sides again. *I can't. Scared.*

So am I. But we can learn together. I pointed up at the trees overhead, where songbirds flitted between the branches, calling to each other with their repetitive melodies. *See how they do it?*

Navi followed my gaze upward, his ears twitching. His head turned as he tracked a robin's motion before it disappeared into the foliage. A vague thought came from him, which after a pause I translated into words. *How do they get up there?*

I don't know. They jump, I guess. From their nests in the trees.

Navi's golden eyes widened and the firm *no* resounded in my head again.

Are you afraid of heights? I asked.

Not heights. Falling. Navi made a soft sound that was a re-markably good imitation of something splattering against stone.

I ducked my head to avoid a low branch and let out a sigh. "Fine," I said aloud. "But you're going to have to learn someday."

Navi didn't respond to that. He kept walking, his eyes trained ahead and his ears so erect I thought they might pop off his head. I wanted to fly so badly, to go up and up until we left the ground and the judgmental stares far behind us. Maybe fly to the

North, to look for answers. But Navi's fear tempered my need for freedom, so we remained grounded.

We passed the section of river where I first met Navi's eyes. From there we crossed the water and veered north, away from areas familiar from my journey. Navi bounded and leaped, agile as a cat and tireless as a wolf. We climbed higher, pressing through new territory. Navi sprang easily from boulder to boulder, carrying us up a steep hill to a spot where I could see part of the valley between a gap in the trees.

I slid from Navi's back, my fingers running over sleek feathers and then rough skin. My boots hit the forest floor with a soft thud, fallen pine needles crunching beneath the soles. I leaned against my keeper, eyes closed, breathing in his already familiar scent.

When I opened my eyes again, my gaze settled on the village nestled by the lake. The sun was well into the sky at that point, the valley awash with a bright morning glow. I could see tiny dots moving between huts and among the rows of crops, people going about their tasks for their respective guilds. Builders would repair huts or work on constructing new ones. Crafters would make clothing and tools for the other guilds. The hunters were already out in the forest somewhere, finding food for everyone. Enzi, Ayla, and the other healers would be looking after the sick or gathering supplies from the forest.

I should have been down there with one of them, helping with the tasks that kept our village running.

Navi settled down a safe distance from where the land dipped sharply. It was a far cry from the cliff where I had almost fallen to my death, but a tumble down the hill would still leave me bruised and scraped up. The memory of that split second of falling, the terror and utter certainty that death awaited me, drove me a few steps away from the steep slope.

I understood why Navi was afraid to fly. But if he learned to use his wings, we'd never have to worry about falling. We would never be trapped on the ground again.

I tucked myself comfortably against Navi's side, his body like a fire behind my back. We should have returned to the village, but I didn't want to. I wanted to stay in this forest forever.

Hiding, Navi said. I dropped my head against his shoulder and squeezed my eyes shut. Yes, hiding. Was that so wrong?

The longer I spent away from the village, the more I wondered if I should have left with the traders. At "home" I had felt suffocated and terrified, waiting for the people I cared about to stop pretending they wanted me there. Out in the forest, I felt alive. I felt free, with only Navi at my side. Maybe that was the way it was supposed to be.

"Maybe we could go," I murmured. The words were lost under a rush of wind, but Navi didn't need to hear them. "Whatever is out there... we could see it. Explore the world, just like the stories." The traders were long gone from the valley by now, but I could track them. And if they didn't want me, Navi and I would find somewhere else. Somewhere to start over.

I wanted to pretend I hadn't noticed the sound of boots scuffing the dirt, but I knew ignoring the person wouldn't make them go away. Sometimes that worked, but I knew this time I had to face whoever had hunted me down.

When I turned my head, I expected to see Makai standing there, but it wasn't Makai.

"Some people thought you had left the valley for good," Adann said. Illari stood at his side, watching me with her intent feline eyes.

"Not you?" I asked.

Adann's expression was as still as his keeper's. "No."

"How did you find me?"

"I tracked you." He sat down in front of me, while Illari settled a pace away. "Makai wanted to come. I convinced him to let me talk to you. Alone."

I raised my eyebrows, the silent question clear. When Adann didn't answer it, I said it out loud. "Why?"

"Because he can't possibly understand what you're going through."

"And you do? Don't pretend with me. I know you always wanted to be a hunter."

"I didn't, actually." He smiled at my surprised expression. "Just because I'm the best hunter in Konota history doesn't mean I always knew."

I rolled my eyes at the statement—part joke and part arrogance, I think. Even if there was a fair amount of truth to it.

"Really, though." His smile faded into seriousness. "I spent my entire Crossing trying to decide. Everyone always assumed I would join the hunters, so I was afraid to do anything else, but part of me wanted to be a builder. Or a healer, like Ayla. I was tempted to join the guild if only for the reason to spend time with her."

He smiled again, wryly this time, and I couldn't help but smile back. They had only started officially courting a year ago, two years after Adann's Crossing. Had he been seeking her attention that long? Maybe even as long as I had yearned for Makai.

Underneath his amusement, though, I caught something... sad. Regret. I had never seen it before when he spoke of Ayla. "What happened?" I asked.

He let out a breathy laugh, devoid of any humor, and looked away. His eyes ran over the landscape below us before he finally replied. "I should have known you'd see it. You were always too observant for your own good."

"Adann."

"We fought," he said. "About you. Right after you returned, but again today. Worse today."

I looked down at my hands, folded together in my lap. My fingers tightened around each other as guilt swept through me. I couldn't be the cause of a rift in their relationship. They were perfect together. They always had been, right from the start. "You shouldn't defend me," I whispered.

"Someone needs to," he said.

"Let Makai."

"*I* need to," he amended. "I can't stand by while you struggle through this alone." He kept his eyes trained on me. Steady. Certain. "You're right. I can't understand what you're going through, not completely. No one can. But I'm here for you. I'll *always* be here for you. Even when no one else is."

I blinked at him, this young man who had no reason to stand by me but did anyway, even when my own sister wouldn't. "Thank you," I said softly. There was nothing more to say.

He rested a hand on my shoulder. "No need for thanks. It's the right thing to do."

"Still, I'm sorry about Ayla. I'm sure she'll come around. She loves you."

"She loves you, too."

I didn't respond to that. Adann fell silent, perhaps for the longest time I'd seen him breathe without speaking. Adann existed to be heard, to be noticed, and that was okay for someone like him. He deserved to be noticed. Now, sadness had driven him to silence. My silence was comfortable and easy; his was pained.

His hand fell away and he leaned back, bracing his palms on the grass behind him. "She'll come around," he echoed.

I grimaced, regretful that I couldn't do something to help him. It wasn't as if Ayla would listen to me if I spoke in his defense. I would probably only make it worse. They would have to work it out themselves, and I had to believe they would. I wanted them to be happy, *together,* the way it was supposed to be before I ruined everything.

"We'll be fine. Really," he said. "Just as long as you come back. You *are* coming back, right?"

"I don't know."

"Shaya." He managed to sound simultaneously reprimanding and pleading. "You still belong with us. Whatever anyone else says, you are Konota."

"Am I?" I lifted my chin, a mix of panic and frustration flooding through me. "I still don't know what guild to join. No one wants me."

"*I* want you," Adann said. "And so does Makai. Join the Hunters Guild, or at least join tomorrow's hunt. We'll stand with you. And you're *good* at it. I always thought you belonged with us."

I stared at him. He tilted his head in question and stared back. Never in my life, that I could recall, had anyone told me I was good at something. Enzi had applauded my determination and ability to memorize stories, but not even my parents had ever acknowledged any exceptional skills I possessed. Was it because I didn't have any? Adann seemed to think I did.

When I was sure I could speak without choking on the words, I asked, "You think so?"

"Of course." He took my hand and gave it a squeeze, then stood. "Come on, little mouse. Let's go home. You can hunt with us tomorrow morning. Everything will work itself out."

I took his hand when he offered it and let him help me to my feet. I looked up at him, the tall hunter and the little mouse, then stepped forward and threw my arms around him. He gave a surprised laugh and folded me into a hug, letting me cling to him as long as I wanted without protest. His body was solid and warm, something to hold onto when everything else was crumbling around me. Whatever else happened, I knew I could count on him. He could be the rock I so sorely needed.

CHAPTER 10

I RETURNED TO THE village with Adann at my side, several hours past midday. I'd eaten my lunch on the way, berries we'd found in the forest along with some jerky Adann had brought me, while Navi caught himself a couple rabbits.

It was too late to join the afternoon hunt, so I busied myself helping the Crafting Guild for the rest of the day. Mama kept asking where I had disappeared to that morning, but I returned only vague answers.

The next morning, I met Adann outside my hut and we joined the hunters milling around the edge of the village. When their eyes turned to me—including Eldin—I wanted to slink back home, but Adann rested a hand on my shoulder and strolled right up to Caldin. The Guildmaster's black hair was held back from her face with a leather cord tied high on the back of her head, and she held a spear in her hand.

"Adann." She greeted him by clasping forearms, then did the same with me. The gesture surprised me, even though I was an adult now. Somehow, because I hadn't yet chosen a guild, I felt like I hung in some halfway limbo until I declared my purpose to the village.

"Shaya is going to join the morning hunt," Adann said.

I fidgeted with the hem of my shirt, my eyes darting around at the other hunters who all either pointedly ignored me or shot me sidelong looks. When I looked back at Caldin, I expected to see the same dislike the other Guildmasters had worn, but her face was blank. Dark, unreadable eyes, a set jaw. She didn't know what to think of me, but she wasn't glaring at me with disgust the way Eldin did at her shoulder. Even once my focus returned to Caldin, I could feel his disdain, as if it had burrowed under my skin. That feeling would linger with me long after his gaze withdrew.

"I look forward to serving your guild and hope to find my place here," I said. My voice was weaker than I wanted, frightened and threadbare, but I didn't react to Eldin's snort.

"You can join my party," Caldin said, ignoring her brother as well. "We'll head east while the other party goes north. The afternoon hunt yesterday was unsuccessful. Perhaps we'll have more luck today."

I bobbed my head. To my disappointment, Caldin directed Adann to the second group. He gave my shoulder a squeeze before he left to join the others.

"I'm so glad you're joining us today!" Makai said. I jumped at his voice, and my boots tore grass beneath my soles as I spun to face him. He gave a sheepish smile and shifted away. "Sorry."

"It's okay," I said, though I was still breathless from surprise. "You're in Caldin's party?" Relief surged through me when he nodded. I wouldn't be alone. Navi cooed happily, and Makai smiled at the drakon. Warmth swelled in my chest. At least not everyone was afraid of Navi.

"Attention, hunters!" Caldin called. Individual conversations fell silent as the hunters from both parties turned to listen to their Guildmaster. "A herd was spotted down the valley yesterday. We're hoping they followed the river toward Mount Tyir."

"Prey has been scarce lately," Makai murmured to me. "We don't know why."

I frowned at Caldin, then looked at the other two in our party, Nell and Emry. All seemed extremely agitated, and I could understand why. Prey could be harder to find in the winter, but it was still early autumn.

Caldin turned away, our only signal to set off into the forest. The four of us fell into step behind her. Nell was the strongest tracker in the group, so once we spotted the trail, Caldin dropped back to let the other hunter and her wolf take the lead.

Midday had come and gone by the time we found the herd grazing in a clearing. Our group fanned out silently around the clearing, hunters and keepers working as one. Caldin let out a low whistle from her place at the edge of the clearing. *Archer, take aim.* The elk didn't know we were there yet, so it meant we might have a chance to take one down before they spooked. Emry had the steadiest aim, so it was the young hunter who nocked an arrow and selected her target.

I could barely make out the flicker of motion as she drew the string back. A moment before she loosed the arrow, the wind changed and the elk raised their heads in unison. By the time the arrow cut through the air, the elk were already in motion. It struck the target in the hip instead of through the heart, deep enough to make it bark in surprise and pain.

Enough to slow it down, too. As the herd charged out of the clearing, the injured one lagged behind. The hunters followed in its wake, spears at the ready. Unfortunately, the animal still moved faster than we did. We could track it, eventually run it down, but it would take hours rather than the easy take-down we had hoped for.

"It's getting away!" Nell shouted. If Adann were there, his cougar might have been able to help, but Nell's wolf couldn't do it alone, and the three birds that soared overhead were useless.

That didn't stop the wolf from trying, though. He launched himself at the elk's flank and sank his teeth into its hip. I watched in horror as the elk bucked, shaking the wolf loose and sending him flying into a nearby tree with a sickening thud. I thought I heard bones crack.

Navi! It wasn't so much his name that flew from my mind as an overwhelming call to action. My keeper came out of nowhere, launching himself from the cover of the trees and crashing into the elk's back with enough force that its legs buckled. The hunting party stopped running, everyone—me included—staring as Navi wrestled with the elk.

The elk flailed, trying to gouge Navi with massive horns, but Navi dodged nimbly away. The elk tried to haul itself up, but even if it hadn't been too injured in the fall, it never got the chance. Purple and white flashed as he swung his tail. The spikes struck the elk in the face, one of them sinking right into an eye. The animal went still.

The other hunters gaped as elk blood ran over the grass and soaked into the soil. Navi pulled his tail free and turned to me, his ears perked and his head held high. I didn't need our bond to know he was proud of himself. I was proud of him, too, but the other hunters looked a little frightened. Silence fell over the forest until a strangled sob shattered it.

I whirled toward where Nell cradled her wolf's limp form. Dread sank into my stomach. Caldin approached cautiously, but Nell's head snapped up, her eyes wild and wet with tears.

"Stay away," Nell snapped.

Caldin froze, her body tense. "We might be able to help—"

"You can't." Nell's fingers curled into the wolf's fur. "He's gone."

Beside me, Makai drew in a sharp breath. Emry whispered a fervent prayer to Tyir. I only stared, horrified, the reality sinking in like the elk's blood seeping into the ground. Nell's keeper was dead, which meant her soul was no longer protected from the soulstealers.

Caldin drew her knife and took another step forward. "Let me help," she said gently.

"No," Nell snarled, so vehemently that it made me jump. She scooped the wolf's body into her arms and took off into the forest before Caldin could stop her.

"Tyir help us," Caldin breathed, barely loud enough for me to hear. "Makai and Emry, get the elk back to the village. Shaya, you're coming with me."

"Where?" I asked, even though I already knew. I knew what had to be done, with the same level of certainty as I knew I didn't want to be a part of it.

Caldin sheathed her knife, though she kept her hand on the hilt, her face grim. "We're going after her."

I probably should have said something, or at least nodded. Instead, I stared at the spot where Nell had been only seconds ago, holding the husk that once contained the other half of her soul. Navi pressed against my arm and let out a concerned trill.

Makai took my hand to give it a squeeze, but then he had to join Emry to help carry the elk. It would be a strained task for the two of them, neither very tall or muscular. They were strong but better suited to long hikes through the forest rather than lifting heavy objects.

"Shaya," Caldin said. "Are you ready for this?"

I wasn't, but I nodded anyway. She led us in the direction Nell had gone, employing the same tracking techniques we had used to follow the elk herd, but we no longer tracked prey.

It was still a hunt, though.

We remained silent as we followed the trail as quickly and quietly as we could. Nell should know someone would come after her, but in her state, she might not have the capacity to care. We traveled deeper and deeper into the forest, toward Mount Tyir. The longer we walked, the more I worried we wouldn't find her in time. If we found her at all.

I had to sidestep Caldin when she stopped suddenly, her eyes trained upward. "What is that?" she murmured.

I followed her gaze to a patch of sky visible through the foliage. A cloud of brownish gray obscured the otherwise clear sky. Smoke, but it didn't look like a forest fire. The cloud would have been larger, probably darker, unless the fire had only just begun.

Caldin's keeper swooped down between the branches. The eagle had probably seen the smoke first and alerted Caldin. She started forward again, her keeper gliding over her head, but she had changed direction away from Nell's trail and toward the source of the smoke.

"What about Nell?" I asked.

She shook her head. "Nell can wait. We need to know what caused that smoke."

Nell can wait? That surprised me. We didn't know how long Nell had left. It could be weeks. It could be within an hour. We needed to find her before a soulstealer did.

But the smoke was a mystery that potentially posed a danger to the entire valley. Caldin was right.

The closer we got, the more the smoke looked like a campfire, though the column was larger than I had first assumed.

A bonfire? Who would be building a fire all the way out here, though?

The fire definitely looked controlled, which told me there were people. That thought was followed by a sting of fear from Navi. He jerked to a halt, his head swiveling from side to side.

What is it? I asked.

Smell, he answered.

I frowned in confusion. *What smell?*

Familiar. But not. That second part came as a vague after-thought that only left me more bewildered.

"Navi smells something," I said, keeping my voice down.

"What?" Caldin asked.

I shook my head. "I don't know." Which was what worried me. Whatever he smelled had put him on edge. "Something is wrong."

Navi didn't want to continue, but I ordered him to keep going. Though my keeper obeyed, each reluctant footstep heightened the tension bleeding through the bond. His anxiety infected me. I almost caved and let him turn away, but I didn't want to show weakness in front of the Guildmaster.

When the source of the smoke was just on the other side of a grassy hill, Caldin held up her hand, signaling for us to approach with caution. I already had an abundance of caution, thanks to Navi's nervous twitching. We crept up the hill, staying low to avoid being spotted.

Surprise swirled with fear when we reached the top and I laid eyes on what waited over the crest of the hill.

A large camp had been erected in the forest clearing. It had been there for a long time, the grass between the pyramid-shaped tents trampled into dirt. Two men walked around the edge of the camp. What prowled beside them jolt-ed my heart so badly I couldn't breathe. Two drakons, one brown-skinned with blue feathers and the other dark gray and purple. They were larger than Navi, probably because my keeper wasn't full grown.

The urge to flee radiated from Navi, but I wrangled his fear under control and kept him from running.

The sharp crack of wood striking wood drew my attention. In the space between tents, two women sparred with thick staffs. They moved with a speed and grace I had never before witnessed, not even from our best hunters. As I watched, one hit the other on the shoulder with the tip of her staff. Not the restrained tap of friendly sparring, but a brutal strike that drew a cry of pain.

Caldin waved her hand and hurried back down the hill. She didn't speak until we were well away from the camp. "Go back to the village," she ordered. "Tell the chief what we saw."

"What about you?" I asked.

"I'm going to find Nell."

I couldn't help the rush of relief. Someone had to release Nell's soul to the next life, but I wouldn't have to be involved. Instead, I had an equally important task: warning my people about the strangers in the forest. I didn't know for a fact they were dangerous, even though what I had seen scared me enough that I felt nauseous. These people must have been in our valley for months and hadn't disturbed us, though it did explain why the hunters had struggled to find prey.

I pulled myself onto Navi's back. "Be careful," I said softly to Caldin before Navi bounded forward.

We reached the village well after nightfall. Makai and Emry had clearly shared what had happened on our hunt, because a veil of anticipation hung over the village when Navi and I arrived. Everyone should have been in their huts sleeping, but torches had been lit along the main paths and people milled about.

My return without Caldin caused a stir. I ignored the expectant stares and went straight for my family's hut. Inside, a candle burned on top of our table—not the simple kind for light alone, but the sort that came from Emirdom and smelled like vanilla or wildflowers. The kind of candle families burned when they were praying for a loved one to return safely. When I was six, my father had told me a person's favorite scent would help guide them home.

The whole hut smelled like honey and lavender.

Though keepers usually remained outside, especially ones too big to fit inside the huts, Honovi was curled up at my father's feet, while Tala sat with her head in Mama's lap. My parents jumped to their feet when I entered, though Ayla was absent. With Adann, probably.

"Shaya!" Mama said as she rushed forward to pull me into her embrace. She had more strength in her slender arms than I thought possible. "I was so worried when I heard what happened."

I buried my face against her shirt and breathed in the lavender that had settled into the lincloth. How long had they been burning that candle? "I'm okay, Mama." I attempted to pull away twice before she finally released me. I slid my hand into hers and gave it a reassuring squeeze before turning to Papa. "I have to tell you something."

His concern for me shifted into something sharper, a father's worry for his youngest daughter turning into a chief's worry for his village. "About Nell? Or Caldin?"

I shook my head. I didn't know their fates yet. All I could do was pray Caldin had found Nell and freed her soul, and that the Guildmaster would return to us safely. "It's something else. Before we could find Nell, we came across a camp in the forest. Strangers. From the North, I think."

"A camp?" Mama said. She sounded more confused than worried, but Papa narrowed his eyes.

"How do you know they're from the North?" he asked.

I looked down, struggling to form the words, which died somewhere before they could leave my lips. *He'll know what to do*, I tried to convince myself. *Everything will be fine.*

"Shaya," he said gently. "What did you see?"

Navi's encouraging coo from outside loosened my tongue. "They have drakons with them," I answered. "I only saw two, but Navi could smell them. I think there are more."

"And the camp? How big was it?" my father asked.

"Big." I didn't have a better answer. I had been too startled by the drakons to assess the size of the camp. There had to be enough of those white tents to house at least fifty people, maybe even a hundred. "And it looked like they had been there for a while."

"That's why the hunters have struggled to find prey," Papa murmured. "Shaya, I need you to keep this news to yourself for now. The Guildmasters and I will discuss what to do, but I don't want to cause a panic in the meantime. Understand?"

I nodded. Keeping the secret wouldn't be difficult. The longer the rest of the village didn't know, the better for me. The regular unease around Navi was bad enough without whatever reaction would come of them learning more of his kind were in the valley.

Part II: Invaders

Vitanas

Indigers

Agriskutār

Chapter 11

Caldin didn't return that night, nor the next morning. Normal activities resumed, though a tension remained throughout the village, tight as a bowstring ready to fire. I should have been more concerned about her and Nell, but the strangers in the forest pervaded my every thought. I still worried about their intentions and how the Konota would react to the drakons.

My father had called the Guildmasters for what could have been a routine meeting, though I knew their topic of discussion was anything but routine. Caldin should have been present, but this problem couldn't wait for her to return. If she returned at all.

I still hadn't officially announced a guild, even though I had settled on the Hunters in my head. Interrupting an important meeting so I could tell everyone seemed foolish, so I decided to leave it for later. I gathered with the rest of the hunters that morning, ignoring the sidelong looks some of them gave me.

Without Caldin around to direct the morning hunts, Eldin stepped in. He put together two parties, neither of which contained the hunters from the day before. Our success yesterday meant we could stay closer to home today.

Even after he'd finished assigning everyone to their duties, he had never called my name. He didn't acknowledge my presence. I couldn't decide which was worse: that or blatant hostility.

I jumped when Adann brushed his fingers against my elbow. "Come on, little mouse," he murmured. "You can stick with me today."

Relieved, I followed him toward the farming fields to check the traps for any small prey that had gotten snared overnight. Illari and Navi wandered into the forest to do their own hunting while we worked. By the time my keeper returned with a belly full of rabbit and pride, Adann and I had a load of rodents and a single pheasant to prepare for cooking. Some would be distributed with lunch. The rest we would make into jerky.

The remainder of the day I was left to my own devices, which gave me too much time alone with my thoughts. I spent the early afternoon in the shade of the hut with Grandpa Enzi's map spread out on my lap.

I wanted to know where the strangers had come from. Their camp had been erected on the north-western face of Mount Tyir, no more than a day's journey away from the village, but far enough around the mountain that we couldn't see their smoke. Their light skin and hair, plus their drakon keepers, made me think they came from the Far North.

I traced my finger over the mountain range that made up the North on the map. That was where Navi came from. Somehow, he had made it down to the valley. Made it to me.

I reached out to rest a hand on the soft feathers that ran along Navi's spine. He had curled up beside me and promptly fallen asleep, but his ears twitched when I touched him.

Everything good? he asked.

Everything is fine. Both of us knew that was a lie. I could hear voices inside the hut, though the words were too muffled to make out. Had our village leaders come to a decision? Did they think the strangers posed a threat?

I folded the map and got up. As much as I had been enjoying sitting in the shade, the warm autumn breeze caressing my face, I was growing restless. I couldn't go inside, not with the ongoing meeting that had claimed my hut, so I started toward the commons for a change of scenery if nothing else.

I paused when the view between two huts showed the hill that began the journey up Mount Tyir. Would Caldin come from that direction? Or would she have to follow Nell all the way across the valley, even south to the Falls?

"Are you okay?"

I tore my eyes away from Mount Tyir, startled by Makai's voice. He stood only a pace away, having approached without my noticing him in that way he had. And Adann said *I* was like a mouse.

"I'm worried about Caldin," I said. "She should be back by now." With or without Nell. Almost a full day had passed, but Caldin wasn't the type to leave a job unfinished. She would track Nell beyond the valley if she had to. Caldin would return with a body or not at all.

"You could use a distraction," Makai declared. "Maybe you'd like to spend the rest of the day with us."

"Us?"

"Oh. Me and my friends. We're going to the lake."

I eyed him, frozen like a deer mouse trying to decide whether to hide or bolt. Despite everything else going on—maybe *because* of everything else—I did want to spend time with Makai. But meeting his friends? I didn't mingle in groups for a reason.

Makai noticed my hesitation and his excitement turned to pleading. He was a wolf pup with large, staring eyes, precious enough that my resistance melted away.

"Okay," I conceded. "Let's go."

The others were already gathered around the lake when we arrived. The boy had on nothing but a loincloth, while one girl wore cloth wraps around her chest and bottom. The other girl, Iliya, wore nothing at all, comfortably stretched out in the sun like a content cougar. I averted my eyes. Modesty wasn't exactly a standard in our village—and some, like Iliya, lacked any at all—but I wasn't secure enough for that.

Unsurprisingly, Makai was like Iliya. While I stripped down to my undergarments, awkward about doing even that, Makai simply removed his clothing and dropped it in a pile on the ground.

Iliya rolled her head languidly to the side, raising an eyebrow at him. She didn't even glance at me. "You're late," she said.

"Relax. I was getting a newcomer." He gestured me toward him. What I *wanted* was to snatch up my clothing and retreat, but I pursed my lips and moved slowly to Makai's side. He put an arm around my shoulders, unabashed under the stares of his friends. I tried not to think about my limited clothing and his lack of any at all. "Shaya, this is Iliya, Deira, and Trev."

I knew their names already, of course. It must have been a courtesy that he felt the need to introduce me, though I wished he hadn't. None of them looked particularly welcoming. I glanced at Makai and tried to work up the nerve to tell him I wanted to leave, but no words came out.

"Whatever," Iliya said. She rose from her lounging position and looked from one boy to the other. "Race you there?" she asked with a grin.

Makai's arm slipped from my shoulder as he stepped away. The closeness of his body had offered some form of protection, and with him gone I suddenly felt twice as exposed. At least no one's attention was on me anymore.

"Only if you want to lose," Makai said, then took off around the lake.

Iliya laughed and sprinted right on his heels. Trev, still on the ground, scrambled hastily to his feet. "Hey, wait!" he called, dashing after them, but the other two were already ten paces ahead. Trev's horse trotted behind him, while Iliya's fox keeper struggled to keep up.

Deira rolled her eyes and started along the shore at a leisurely walk, her wolf at her side. That left me to trail behind with Navi, my arms wrapped around my torso as if my skinny limbs could shield my body.

Makai remained two paces ahead of Iliya the entire way, with Trev gradually falling even farther behind. I watched as Makai sprinted up a steep hill to where a narrow bit of land jutted out over the lake. A tree stood at the top of the hill, its branches reaching out even past the overhang. A roped crafted from grass, like the one I had made on my Crossing, dangled from one of the thicker branches. Without slowing his step, Makai grabbed the rope and launched himself over the lake.

He gave a loud whoop as he swung out and let go of the rope. He flew another pace through the air before pulling his knees to his chest and dropping like a boulder into the water.

Iliya had to wait for the rope to swing back so she could follow him in. Her entry was more graceful, her body pitching forward so she could dive headfirst into the lake, her arms outstretched. She hardly made a splash as she plunged into the water.

The rope swayed back and forth, waiting for Trev to catch up. The boy paused with the rope in his hand, as if gathering his nerve before jumping after them. He let go of the rope with poor timing, a moment too late, so he fell straight down rather than his momentum carrying him out like the other two. Makai and Iliya laughed as Trev flailed wildly in the air. I winced at the sharp slap of his back hitting the water.

Trev sputtered when he emerged from the center of the ripples. "Every time, huh, Trev?" Makai called. The other boy scowled and swept his arm through the water, creating a wave that fizzled out before it reached Makai.

"Hurry up, Deira!" Iliya shouted, waving her arm at the straggler. And then there was me, a step behind her but practically invisible. Even Makai's attention was on Deira rather than the girl he had invited to spend time with his friends. Now I realized I never should have agreed.

"Calm down, I'm coming," Deira called back. When she reached the rope, she swung out over the lake like the others. Not as dramatic as Makai or as elegant as Iliya, but less clumsy than Trev, at least.

The keepers waited at the bottom of the hill, watching their humans play in the water. I stopped at the tree, reluctant to follow. Navi chirped in encouragement, but it didn't do much to ease the sick feeling in my stomach.

A flutter of wings drew my attention as Farin landed on a branch above me, and Makai finally realized I had lagged behind. "Your turn, Shay!" he said. "It's easy. Just don't be an idiot like Trev and you'll be fine." Trev splashed at Makai again, and this time he had paddled close enough that the water hit Makai in the face. Makai shook his head, dispelling water from his eyes. Grinning, he slapped the water, which sent a spray back at the other boy. Just like that, his focus was back on his friends.

My reluctance had nothing to do with fear of the jump. I didn't want to join them in the water only to be ignored. I didn't mind being alone. This was worse somehow, being surrounded by people and still feeling isolated, overlooked even by Makai. One-on-one with him, the center of his attention, I felt wanted and secure. With his friends around, he hardly looked at me for more than a heartbeat.

I took the rope in my hand, running my fingers over the rough surface. Unlike my rope, the blades of grass had been dried before weaving them together. It had been tied to that branch for a long time. Years. Ayla and I used to play out here when we were younger, before her Crossing. Now I felt like I hardly knew her, but we had started growing apart long before I'd brought Navi home. She had found other people to play with.

The sound of splashing and laughter finally ceased, long enough for Makai to remember I still stood on the land. "Come on, just go for it!" he called.

Before I could take the leap, Navi launched himself off the overhang, creating a splash big enough that water sprayed my legs. The drakon let out a loud, playful squawk, calling for me to join him.

My hands tightened on the thick rope. I could do this. If I waited up here, the others would only assume I was frightened, and I would never earn their approval.

"She's not going to," someone muttered from down in the lake.

That was the prompting I needed. Holding onto the rope with a death grip, I sprinted forward and hurled myself into the air. The rope went taut, swinging me upward. When I felt it start to slacken, I let go. My momentum carried me in an arc through the air, but my release had been awkward. I flailed a bit, managing to get my feet under me so I didn't smack into the lake back-first like Trev had.

Navi was at my side when I resurfaced, and I put a hand on his shoulder to steady myself. When he was certain I wouldn't panic and drown, he pushed his strong legs through the water and paddled away from me. The others watched him warily, all except Makai, whose eyes were bright with amusement when Navi rolled onto his back and slapped the water with his tail. It sent a spray of water at my face. A high chirping accompanied the amusement that passed through our bond.

I scowled at him, but when he flicked water from his feathered ears, my annoyance melted into a smile.

"Hey, maybe Navi can fly us over the lake for a higher dive!" Makai said. The others looked dubious at the idea of riding the drakon. "Oh, please. Not you all too."

"I'm not getting on that thing." Iliya side-eyed Navi with her nose wrinkled. Picking up the meaning of the conversation through me, Navi flipped over and laid his ears back.

"He won't hurt you, Il," Makai insisted. He looked at Trev, then at Deira. Both only shrugged, so Makai rolled his eyes and swam back toward the shore. "Well, *I'm* going to try it out. You all can be boring and watch."

"Makai," I said, but he didn't seem to hear it, so I tried again. "Makai, wait." When he finally paused and looked back at me, I said, "Navi doesn't... fly yet. He hasn't learned."

Behind me, Trev snickered quietly. "Oh, so he's a defective monster." The two girls laughed in response, but Makai gave them a disapproving frown.

"That's okay," he said. "I'm still going again."

I stayed in the water while Makai climbed the hill to swing out over the lake again. The others followed him shortly, all of them shouting and laughing. Eventually, I pulled myself onto Navi's back and let him paddle us to shore, near the tree where Makai and I had sat together in the past. I watched the others play while Navi stretched out in the sun to let his feathers dry.

As soon as my undergarments were dry enough, I retrieved my clothes and redressed before settling back down against Navi's side. I didn't know why I didn't go home. Watching them only reminded me that I existed outside the center of Makai's world and always would.

After the others left, Makai came to sit beside me. "What's going on in that head of yours?"

I only shrugged in response, unable to articulate my insecurities and fears. Or maybe I didn't want to.

"Do you not like my friends?"

I shrugged again. I wasn't fond of Iliya, but the others seemed friendly enough, aside from their dislike of Navi that the entire village shared. More than anything, I was afraid they wouldn't like me.

"It's okay if you don't," he said gently. "I mean, I want you fit in with us, but I don't care if you don't. I don't want you to feel like you *have* to."

I swore Makai was a different person, sitting here with me rather than playing around with his friends. Come to think of it, he was different when with the other hunters, too. Makai was one of the chameleons that lived in the southern forests, changing his colors to fit in wherever he went. In that moment, it was a skill I envied.

We stared at each other. I think he was still waiting for me to say something, but I remained silent. When he shifted toward me, like he might kiss me, I turned my head and stared out over the water. I had daydreamed about kissing Makai since I was old enough to no longer think kissing was gross, but the thought of letting him do it—of letting him in—made my stomach twist in painful knots.

Makai let out a slow breath and we lapsed back into silence. I spent the time debating whether I was a coward for not kissing him. I *wanted* to, or thought I wanted to. So why did it terrify me so much?

Makai leaned forward and waited until he caught my eye. "Can I ask you something?"

"Can I stop you?"

He took that as permission. "Do you not... you know, like me?"

My face grew warm again. "Of course I like you."

"I mean *like* me," he said. Great Tyir, was he blushing too? Embarrassment tinged his cheeks brownish-red, and I wanted to crawl into the water to cool my own burning skin.

"I—" My response got stuck. I had *liked* him for over a year, but even I didn't understand my own panic. "I do. But I... I can't." I gritted my teeth, frustrated at my inability to string a full sentence together.

"Shaya... please, talk to me." It was the first time he had said something like that to me, pleading for me to open up instead of waiting for it. He had spent a lot of time waiting, I realized.

I buried my face in my arms, my skin hot and clammy against my forearm. "I'm sorry."

"For what?" He sounded genuinely bewildered.

"I don't... let people inside. I don't like saying what I'm thinking, or what I want." I lifted my face and rested my chin on my knees. I had a hard enough time understanding my own thoughts. How was I supposed to tell other people?

"You don't have to apologize. I don't care." He scooted closer so his shoulder touched mine. "I don't care if it takes me a year to get to know you, or ten years, or the rest of my life. Because you're worth knowing."

"Thank you," I whispered. When I leaned against him, he put his arm around me. I still didn't know what I would do if he changed his mind about me, but it was nice to pretend, for a little while, that someone cared enough to deal with the more frustrating parts of who I was.

We stayed like that until shouts rose in the village. They sounded excited, not frightened. Hope shot through me like a bolt of lightning, hot and sharp and maybe a little dangerous. *Caldin.*

I jerked away from Makai and scrambled to my feet. Makai's footsteps pounded behind me as we raced back to the village. Caldin approached from the east, carrying a limp body over her shoulder. Though I couldn't see her face, there was something determined and grim in her strides.

We reached the crowd at the same moment a man stepped forward to meet her. Tears streaked his face, and he accepted the body from Caldin. Nell's partner of ten years dropped to his knees, cradling her lifeless form. Caldin bowed her head and rested a hand on his shoulder.

"Til the next life," Makai murmured beside me. I leaned against him, and he put an arm around my shoulders without hesitation. When I couldn't watch any longer, I turned my back on the heartbreaking scene and let Makai draw me into a full hug, my cheek pressed against his shoulder.

There had been too much loss lately. Something cold whispered inside me, insisting that Nahdi and Nell were only the beginning. It felt like a warning from Tyir himself.

CHAPTER 12

THE MEETINGS BETWEEN MY father and the Guildmasters went on for a full two days, long enough that the village realized something more than routine was going on. We should have been celebrating Nell's life with feasts in her honor and games for the children. Instead, rumors flew around the village, people theorizing about the reason for the long meetings.

Before the current meeting started, the chief had announced that they would reveal everything soon, so of course nearly the entire village had gathered to wait for the big announcement. Hundreds of people packed the area around the chief's hut, sitting in the shade or leaning against nearby structures. A small group of children played on the ground nearby. I should have been working on weapons maintenance with Emry, but all tasks had ceased for the moment.

I hadn't moved since I'd sat down with Ayla outside. Ten minutes, twenty, I didn't know. Navi lay on the ground beside me, his spiked tail curled against his side. His chin rested on my knee. Staring at the hide hanging over the doorway, I was a statue next to Ayla's fidgeting. I could see the movement out of the corner of my eye, and it was making me crazy. She was one of the few who already knew what discussion was taking place inside the hut. Our parents had told her the night before.

"What do you think they'll do?" she asked.

"I don't know."

"Do you think these people are dangerous?"

"I don't know, Ayla."

She didn't expect me to have the answers, but the questions grated on my nerves. She had asked a dozen already and was now recycling earlier ones. It was the most we had spoken since I'd returned from my Crossing.

I turned my gaze away from the hut to find Makai in the crowd. He stood with his mother and father, staring at the doorway with a faraway expression. I tried to catch his eye, but Makai never once glanced in my direction. I pushed down the disappointment that stirred inside me.

I counted off the minutes in my head—five of them—until the Guildmasters and Papa emerged. My father's face was grave. Mama's was as serene as ever, but Belvir and Pashir both looked afraid. From Caldin's furious expression, I knew an argument had taken place inside. The Hunters Guildmaster had her arm in a sling, a stark reminder of what had happened with Nell.

Any conversation abruptly fell silent, nearly four hundred people waiting with bated breath for the chief to speak.

"It recently came to our attention that there are visitors in the forest," Papa said, his voice ringing over the crowd. The voice of Chief Tahck—the kind that demanded attention. "We don't know who they are, where they came from, or what their intentions are."

A murmur swept through the crowd, the voices too muddled for me to make out individual words.

"Adann," Tahck said, turning to the hunter. "You will lead the mission to speak with them and find the answers to these questions. You are one of our most accomplished trackers and perhaps one of our strongest fighters. We have a general idea of where these people are—or at least, where they were—but you may have to track them down. Pick three others to accompany you."

I stared at him in confusion. Why would the hunters need to track them down when I could lead the group straight to the camp? Caldin obviously couldn't lead the party, not with her injured arm, but why wouldn't my father volunteer my help? He didn't even look at me.

Adann dipped his head to Papa. His eyes swept over the hunters, his expression thoughtful as he scrutinized each of them. He knew their strengths and weaknesses and needed to decide who would be best suited to the mission. "Eldin and Rena," he said finally. "And..."

The moment I stood and stepped forward, I regretted it. My vision tunneled on Adann, ignoring everyone's focus turning to me.

Papa was protecting me. He didn't want me in the party, in potential danger. He wasn't acting as the Konota chief but rather as my father. While I appreciated it, I couldn't let them waste time searching for a place I could bring them straight to.

"I can help." The three words came out strangled, and I had to clear my throat before I spoke again. "I can show you where to go."

"We shouldn't bring someone so inexperienced on this mission," Eldin said. "She would only put herself and the rest of us in danger."

"Shaya has proven herself to be plenty capable," Adann countered.

"She's had her keeper for less than a week. She hasn't even declared her guild!"

"Enough," Adann said in the same voice my father used when addressing the villagers. Firm. Authoritative. "If Shaya saw them, she can lead the way and save us time." The two stared at each other in a silent argument. Eldin stood above Adann in experience and respect from others, ten years his senior. Under normal circumstances, Adann would have been expected to defer to him. However, this was a special case. Adann had been chosen by the chief. It was ultimately his decision and no other's.

So Eldin had no choice but to back down. He dipped his head to the younger man, dropping his eyes to the ground in concession. Adann smirked, something wicked in his eyes that made me wonder if maybe he had enjoyed it a little too much.

"There's one more thing," Papa said, drawing everyone's attention back to him. "These strangers have drakons with them. We don't know how many."

That caused another stir among the crowd, uneasy whispers and more than a few glances in my direction.

Adann never faltered, though. "If they have drakons, all the more reason to have Navi with us."

I blinked. I didn't know why him saying my keeper's name caught me so off guard. Maybe because only he and Makai had said it, aside from my father using my full name at my ceremony.

Adann waved me toward the rest of the group. I had to drag one foot in front of the other until I reached his side. I had volunteered for this. Eldin was right to point out my lack of experience, but Adann met my eyes, his gaze steady. He had never once doubted me. I swallowed my fears and gave him a small nod.

"You will prepare to leave immediately," Papa said. "Good luck. May you find the answers we seek."

The rest of the group moved off to gather packs and say their goodbyes. When I turned to my father, I saw the worry in his eyes for the first time.

"Are you sure about this?" he asked softly.

Despite the apprehension gnawing at my insides, I nodded.

Mama rested a hand on my arm, then changed her mind and pulled me into a hug. "Be careful," she whispered against my hair.

"I will," I promised. The hug, true to every hug she had ever given me, lasted longer than necessary, but I waited patiently for her to decide it was enough. For once, I didn't mind. I felt safe in her arms. The chosen hunters were about to venture toward the unknown, with no idea what awaited us when we reached the camp. Perhaps the strangers came in peace.

Or perhaps they would try to kill us.

I squeezed my eyes shut and tried not to cry. When Mama stepped away, I missed the warmth of her embrace.

"Before you go, there's something we want to give you," Papa said. Mama nodded and disappeared inside the hut. By the time I followed and my eyes adjusted, she was over by the chest she shared with Papa, searching its contents.

When she straightened and turned to face me, she kept her hand behind her back. She waited until we came closer before she revealed the knife. "We got this for you. A present, to honor your Crossing, once you chose your guild. We meant to give it to you earlier but…"

But I had returned from my first hunt with news of the strangers. I hadn't declared a guild yet. Even Nell's death had been pushed to the side in light of this potential threat. There hadn't been time for gift-giving.

The fact that they were stealing a moment for it now unnerved me. It took me a moment to put my finger on why:

this might be their last chance to do it. There was always the possibility a hunter wouldn't come back from a hunt—Nell's fate had proved that—but this was different.

I had a feeling a candle would be burning in our hut until my safe return.

I buried the rush of unease and turned the knife over in my hands, admiring the gleam of smooth metal. It was a beautiful blade, straight and double-edged, crafted of iron. They must have gotten it when the traders visited. Had that only been a few days ago? It felt like months.

Someone had carved my name onto the leather wound around the hilt. *Shaya Navi.* Probably my mother's work. I brushed my thumb over the smooth leather, feeling the indentation of each letter. Our people didn't have much use for written words, but Grandpa Enzi had taught me enough that I recognized my own name. My heart swelled to see it written with such care, rather than spoken with fear or derision.

"Thank you." The present represented more than the original intent. An item meant to commemorate the moment I took my place among the Konota had become a symbol of my parents' acceptance. They were still proud of me, still believed in me, and that was the greatest gift I could have asked for.

This time, both of my parents wrapped me in a hug, and I let myself soak up their love, which I'd foolishly thought I had lost. *I love you. I love you so much.* Though the words felt ready to burst out of me, they never made it past my lips.

I could have stood there in their embrace forever, but Papa pulled away, followed a moment later by Mama. She cupped my face and kissed my forehead. "I'm sorry if we ever made you feel like you don't belong. Please come home to us, Shaya."

I nodded once and swiped away my tears before they could fall.

I gathered my pack and stepped outside to find Adann and Ayla finishing their goodbye. My sister and I shared an awkward glance before she murmured, "Please come home. Both of you." She looked like she wanted to hug me but thought better of it, so instead she hurried past me into the hut. Adann gave me a strained smile before gesturing for me to follow.

The others were waiting for us at the base of the hill that led toward Mount Tyir. Eldin and Adann were armed with iron-tipped spears, while Rena and I both carried a bow and quiver. Eldin's keeper sat at his side. Like Illari, the cougar was a mighty weapon all on its own. Rena's keeper, a gray fox, flicked its rust-colored ears restlessly. Rena looked just as impatient.

Adann led with Eldin behind him, while Rena brought up the rear. That left me in the middle, alone except my keeper. At one point I glanced back to find Rena's eyes on me, not hostile but calculating, and for the rest of the hike I could feel that gaze tickling the back of my neck.

I couldn't stop thinking about what awaited us. We could be walking toward our deaths. What if our diplomatic efforts only prompted them to attack? Maybe they would only leave us alone as long as they went unnoticed.

About an hour in, Adann dropped back and Eldin followed suit. "Shaya," Adann said as he fell into step beside me. "You lead the way from here."

I nodded, still nervous but glad to have something to do. Leading forced me to pay attention to my surroundings rather than drowning in my thoughts. Adann walked with me in the front, while Eldin joined Rena at the rear. I picked up quiet conversation between them but couldn't make out any words. Call it self-importance, but I thought they were talking about me.

"I'm sorry about Eldin," Adann said, quietly enough that the two hunters behind us wouldn't hear. "You might be inexperienced, but you were very brave, volunteering to come with us."

I didn't feel brave. Not being a coward didn't automatically make you courageous. "Thank you," I said anyway. I understood how much he put on the line for me. How much he had always done for me. "For giving me this chance. For believing in me."

"You deserve for everyone to believe in you, Shaya. Just because they can't see it yet doesn't mean it's not true." He smiled at me, his warm eyes crinkling at the corners. I understood why Ayla loved him. He would be a great addition to the family, someone—I hoped—I could continue to rely on.

I glanced at Navi, whose eyes occasionally darted back to look at the hunters and their keepers behind us. Illari slunk along at Adann's other side, her lithe but powerful body majestic with every stride she took.

"Do you really think they'll ever accept me?" I asked. "Honestly."

"Honestly?" he said. I held my breath as I awaited his answer. "I think you have something special to offer, and eventually they'll realize it. Then they'll have no choice but to accept you."

I smiled, unable to voice my gratitude, but I think the smile was enough. He returned it before falling back to join the others. They still kept their voices too low for me to hear. Instead of trying to catch snippets of their conversation, I focused on my surroundings as I led the way through the forest. The last thing I needed was to get us lost. It would only give Eldin another reason to loathe me.

When the sun started to descend behind the ridge, Adann ordered us to stop for the night. "There's a stream near here. It's a good place to gather food and water and get some rest." He turned to Eldin. "Take Rena and find us dinner. Shaya can come with me and refill our water."

While Rena and Eldin headed off together, Adann and I gathered all the waterskins we'd brought and walked side-by-side through the forest. This area was only vaguely familiar to me, but Adann knew exactly where he was going as he led the way.

We knelt beside the stream and both dipped a waterskin in. Adann lifted his eyes while he let the liquid run into his. "So... Makai," he said.

I flushed and stared intently at the waterskin in my hand. Water flowed through the narrow mouth, making a soft gurgling that cut off when the waterskin was full. "What about him?" I asked quietly.

"You two seem friendly lately."

The teasing note to his voice made my face grow even hotter. He *knew*. Everyone probably knew about my crush, even though no one had said anything about it before. "So?"

"Hey." Droplets splattered my nose and cheeks as Adann flicked water at me, finally prompting me to raise my eyes. "I'm happy for you, little mouse. It's about time that idiot saw what was right in front of him."

I pulled the waterskin out of the stream and pushed the stopper in before grabbing another to fill. "Thanks." I didn't know what else to say. It seemed like a safe answer.

"Do I need to do the big brother 'if you hurt her...' thing? Because I can." He grinned as he closed his last waterskin. "Put some fear into the boy."

I reached over to swat his arm lightly. "Don't you dare. You might scare him off."

"Fine, fine. But I'm watching him." He pointed two fingers at his eyes and then turned them on me. "Let's get going. It'll be dark soon."

By the time Eldin and Rena returned, Adann and I had the hammocks secured in the trees and dusk had settled over the forest.

"Too bad we don't have time for a proper hunt," Rena said as they joined us on the ground beneath the hammocks. She handed Adann and me pouches full of berries and seeds they had gathered. "We spotted signs that the herd headed this way."

"The four of us wouldn't be able to eat a whole elk, anyway," Adann said. "We'd waste too much of it. Tyir wouldn't approve."

Rena only grumbled in response. After our meal, we settled in for the night, surrounded by the sounds of the dark forest. It was different sleeping with the others and Navi nearby, instead of alone in the night. I slept better than I had during my Crossing, despite the worry that still gnawed at me.

Adann roused us at dawn, driving our party to pack up faster than I thought possible. When everyone was ready, Adann looked us over and gave a small nod. "Alright. Eldin, Rena. Send your keepers out ahead with Illari."

I frowned. *What about Navi?*

Adann caught my expression and guessed my question. "Navi will stay with us, for protection. We don't know what we'll find out here. Be prepared for anything."

Two cougars and the gray fox bounded into the forest. If any danger lay ahead, they would warn us. As we walked, the forest somehow felt more and more unfamiliar. Even hunting parties rarely came this far. More evergreens than oaks and aspens grew around us, the ground littered with dead needles. We had diverged from my Crossing route a long time ago, veering west to reach the section of forest where Caldin and I had first seen the camp.

The search party stopped in unison when Adann lifted his hand. We held our breath as we waited on his next move, but Adann remained motionless. "There's something ahead," he whispered. "People. Illari can smell them."

"Denu sees them too," Rena said.

Adann met my eyes, his expression troubled. "Tell your keepers to stay out of sight. We proceed with extra caution from here."

Soon, the terrain sloped up sharply, and our group ascended the same hill I had crawled up only a few days ago to get my first glimpse of the strangers. Apprehension twisted my stomach as we neared the top. I could feel the tension that emanated from the others as well. Their keepers slunk out of the forest to join us a moment before we reached the top.

It will be okay, Navi told me.

I really wished I believed him.

CHAPTER 13

THE CAMP LOOKED THE same: uniform tents of pale animal hide erected in a neat grid and utilizing every inch of the large clearing. As we watched, two guards and their drakons rounded the edge of the camp, patrolling the border. Different guards than before, a young woman little older than myself with a red-feathered drakon at her side and a middle-aged man. His drakon's scales and feathers were the dark brown of rich soil. Both humans wore their pale hair in long braids.

The sharp intakes of breath around me told me exactly when the others noticed the drakons.

"They have those monsters," Rena whispered.

"We already knew they would," Adann said, unshaken. "Come on."

He stepped over the crest of the hill to reveal himself. The guards and their drakons stalked forward but paused when the rest of us came into view.

"We come in peace," Adann said, though I noticed the tension in his shoulders and the way his hand clutched his spear. "We wish to talk to your leader."

The guards exchanged a look and the man said something in a foreign language. I started to wonder if they even understood Adann, but then the guard let out a laugh and said, "Rajik would love to meet you, valley boy." The man spoke with a stilted accent that made him sound like he was trying too hard to pronounce his consonants. He gestured for us to come forward, but his wicked grin made me think we were making a grave mistake.

Navi strongly agreed. He remained crouched behind the hill until I ordered him to come, though not without plenty of reluctance myself. The guard's eyes widened when they fell on the drakon, and he elbowed his companion in the side. The feathers along the backs of the other drakons rose, followed by quiet growls from deep in their chests. Navi crouched low to the ground with his ears pinned against his head.

The second guard let out a low whistle and the drakons flattened their hackles, though the beasts still watched us with hostile eyes as we passed.

"Your weapons," the young woman said. My hand tightened around my bow, my arm hovering protectively over the quiver at my hip. None of the other Konota seemed inclined to hand over their weapons either. The guard's expression turned to annoyance. "You will not be allowed into the camp with weapons. Surrender them or we can kill you here. Packs too. Could be hiding something in there."

Our group exchanged uncertain glances. When Adann gave a small nod, we reluctantly relinquished our only form of defense, aside from our keepers. I didn't think the fox and cougars would be much good in a fight against the drakons. Navi's ears quivered at the thought.

The female guard led the way, while the man followed behind us. *To keep anyone from escaping,* I thought with growing dread.

We collected a trail of followers as we made our way through the camp. Curious stares and inquiring murmurs surrounded us, but the voices fell silent when we came to a stop in a central area free of any tents. A man sat on a stump, running a dark stone along the edge of a long blade. It resembled a knife, though much broader and probably the length of my arm.

He looked up when we approached. Eyes the color of lichen ran over our party, intrigued. Different colored beads were strung into the long braids of his hair and beard, both so pale they were almost white. Several black feathers were woven into the braid that fell halfway down his back. He was broad-shouldered like my father, but perhaps a hand shorter, though it was hard to tell with him seated. Curved drakon claws and other talismans hung from a string around his neck. Movement to my left drew my eyes to a pure black drakon. Black scales, black feathers darker than the night. It watched us closely from its position beside the stump.

When the man's eyes fell on me, a chill rushed through me. "A valley girl with a drakon." His deep voice carried the same harsh accent. "What is your name?"

I stared back at him and didn't answer, not in defiance but because I was too frozen with fear to speak.

He let out a laugh as cold as his eyes. "Very well. What brings you to our camp, valley folk?"

"We come only to talk," Adann answered. "What brings you to our valley?"

The man studied him with the intensity of someone dissecting every inch of what he saw. I tried to imagine Adann through this stranger's eyes. Young, but tall and strong of body, his gaze steady and unafraid. "We look for new home," he said. "I think we like this one."

Clothing rustled as the other Konota shifted nervously. The words weren't a threat on their own, but his tone carried a dangerous undercurrent.

Adann remained unfazed. "Prey will become more and more scarce as we move into winter. The valley cannot support—"

"No," the man cut him off.

"No?"

"We will not leave. That is what you were going to ask, is it not?"

"Please, there are other places—"

"This is our home now," the man said. "I grow tired of this conversation." He waved a hand at the guard who had led us through the camp and said something in their own language. She looked past us at the other guard, and he laughed at whatever she said to him.

"Let's go, valley welps," the girl said.

"What did he say?" Eldin demanded.

I already had a guess, but the male guard was happy to confirm it. He smirked and replied, "Take them away and kill them."

A shocked silence followed, until Adann broke the spell. "Run." When the word didn't spur us into action, Adann drove his elbow back into the face of the guard behind him and grabbed my arm. He shoved his way past the girl, who didn't have time to draw her weapon.

Rena and Eldin ran behind us as we fled, chased by angry shouts. We reached the edge of the camp and plunged into the forest, our footsteps never slowing despite the tripping threat of roots and undergrowth.

"We should take the ravine down," Eldin said. "It's the fastest way back to the village."

Adann nodded, but a protest tugged at my tongue. The strangers had drakons. If we took the open ravine, they would surely catch up. The safest escape would be through the thickest part of the forest. It would be slower, but they wouldn't be able to fly.

"Wait..." I said, but no one seemed to hear me. They had already turned toward the ravine. I was forced to follow, unease hounding my steps.

Rocks and soil flowed down the hill as the Konota scrambled into the ravine. It had been carved by the river long ago, before Tyir had redirected the water to flow toward the village as a blessing to the Konota. We were able to move quickly down the easy terrain without worrying about tripping on a tree root or uneven ground. For a moment, I thought Eldin might have been right, but the whoosh of wings overhead proved my instincts correct.

It was a time I really wished I'd been wrong.

Two drakons shot over our heads and banked in unison. They landed farther down the ravine, cutting us off, and I recognized the drakons and their riders as the two guards. I locked eyes with the girl before Adann yanked me into motion again.

"Up. Up!" Adann shouted. We turned, scrambling back up the side of the ravine, which was steeper here than where we'd come down. I jumped on Navi's back and he clawed his way to the top, but the others didn't fair as well. Rena and her fox hauled themselves out of the ravine while Eldin lagged below with Adann at his side. Like a good leader, Adann wouldn't leave a man behind. Despite Eldin's arrogance, Adann was younger, stronger, and more capable. He could have scaled the wall of the ravine easily but had to keep pausing to let Eldin catch up.

Behind them, the drakons paced forward languidly. They were toying with us. If they really wanted to catch us, they could have by now.

Hunting, Navi said. Nausea pressed against my throat. He was right. They were playing with us like a cub chasing a doomed rabbit. They thought we had no chance of escape. I was inclined to agree.

I jumped from Navi's back and knelt at the edge of the ravine, reaching down to offer Eldin my hand. He scowled and swatted it aside, only to have a rock give way under his foot a moment later. He cried out in surprise as his whole body lurched downward, his hands scrabbling futilely at the hill until he slid all the way to the bottom.

By then, the drakons and their riders had almost reached him. He wouldn't make it up in time. One of the riders gave a grin as wicked as a soulstealer straight out of a nightmare.

Navi! At my call, Navi launched himself over the edge and landed between Eldin and our pursuers. At first, seeing a drakon standing between them and their prey gave them pause, but it didn't last long. Navi snarled as they took another step, a warning that didn't seem to faze them in the least. The girl laughed, while the man continued to grin like a demon. The brown drakon let loose a roar that made Navi's threatening growls sound like a feisty wolf pup. It swept through me and made bumps ripple up my arms.

Despite the fear that threatened to pin my feet to the ground, I followed Navi into the ravine and probably to our deaths.

Defender, guardian, strength. The traits of a drakon, none of which I had ever seen describing myself, but now I was the defender. I was the only one who stood between my friends and my enemies. Right then, even Eldin was a friend, a member of the Konota, *family.* I wouldn't let them touch my family.

My momentum carried me forward and I sprang onto Navi's back from behind. We faced down the larger drakons while Eldin crawled up the side of the ravine.

I expected them to attack, but they didn't advance again. The two drakons stared at Navi while a low growl continued to vibrate through my keeper's chest. They didn't know what to do with me. Navi didn't frighten them, but his presence was enough to make them hesitate.

"He's up, let's go!" Adann called from above. Navi snarled at the drakons one last time before whipping around and scrambling out of the ravine.

Maybe they didn't want to fight me, but the drakons and their riders weren't done with their pursuit. As we ran into the cover of the trees, I heard the beat of wings and a roar that made the hair on my arms stand on end.

"I'm going to lead one of them away! Keep going," Adann shouted. Before anyone could argue, he split away from the group.

Adann, no! I wanted to scream after him. He needed to stay with us. Perhaps I was wrong, but I thought as long as I could defend the group, the drakons wouldn't do more than follow. I couldn't be in two places at once, so I stayed with the others. Adann was on his own.

He made an obscene amount of sound as he ran in the other direction, more than any self-respecting hunter would ever make and clearly intentional. It worked. When I looked up through the foliage, I saw the girl's red and gray drakon bank to follow him. The other flew over us but didn't attempt to descend through the leaves and branches. The canopy provided a protective net above us, preventing the drakon from reaching us easily. The forest would be our haven.

The hunters were sure-footed and swift, familiar with the forest and the dangers of its terrain. Moving this fast, they might still catch their toe on a stray root, but it was a risk we had to take.

"We're going to lead him straight to the village!" Rena called.

It didn't matter, though, did it? If these people had been here as long as I thought, they already knew exactly where we were. They hadn't attacked us for their own reasons, not because the village was a secret. Besides, we couldn't run the whole way home. We'd be exhausted and captured long before we made it back.

Still, with Adann gone, leadership fell to the most experienced hunter, which was Eldin. At his prompting, one by one they stopped running and found a hiding place. Blending into the forest was usually a skill used to prevent prey from spotting you. Now it proved effective for losing an enemy as well.

But Navi couldn't hide the way a fox or hawk or even a cougar could. Not with his large body and bright feathers. Eldin climbed a tree with thick foliage while his keeper hid in the brush beneath it. Rena ducked into a thicket of scrub oak with her fox. I frantically scanned the forest for a place Navi could hide, but I found nothing. We kept running.

Though I still wasn't worried about leading them to the village, we changed our course away from home and turned toward the river. I craned my neck to look up through the thick foliage but saw no sign of the drakon. Maybe he had lost us beneath the cover of the trees. *Do you hear him?* I asked, glad that I could do so silently.

He's there, Navi said. I tried to listen past Navi's footsteps and my own labored breathing and thought I heard something that could have been wingbeats.

When we reached the river, I slid from Navi's back and splashed my way into the water, not worried about the noise or being out in the open. I bent down to scoop a handful of mud out of the riverbed and returned to Navi. We paused for a few precious seconds so I could rub the mud over his colorful feathers. Navi's eyes scanned the sky, his body stiffening the moment he caught sight of our pursuer.

Hurry, he urged.

I *was* hurrying, but Navi had a lot of feathers to camouflage. When he was more brown than purple and gold, we ran beneath the cover of trees again. I clung to Navi's neck as we raced through the forest and sent a prayer to Tyir for our safe escape.

He's still coming, Navi said, the thought accompanied by a dismayed trill in his throat.

How is he tracking us? I had covered up Navi's feathers. We should blend in with the forest.

But then I realized how foolish I had been. If Navi could hear the other drakon's wings, it could surely hear him tromping around in the forest. With his size, he was anything but stealthy. How were we supposed to get away when the drakon could hear our every move? We could stop and hope they gave up searching for us, but I didn't like our odds.

Then I remembered Eldin mentioning signs of the herd nearby.

Did you smell the herd in the forest? I asked. At his affirmative, some hope started to trickle through my distress. *Find them.*

We turned around and headed back in the other direction. If Navi could pick up the scent trail, maybe we had a chance after all.

Please, Tyir. Please bring us to them.

Excitement ran through Navi when he caught the elk scent. He followed the trail, bringing us north toward Mount Tyir.

It didn't take us long to catch them, and from there it was a simple matter of Navi charging straight into their midst to start a stampede.

The elk barked in alarm and fled through the forest. We stayed with them only for twenty or so paces before we split from the herd and headed south. I hoped the stampede would cause enough noise to cover up Navi's footsteps and confuse the other drakon long enough for us to disappear.

When the thuds of hooves started to fade into the distance, I signaled for Navi to stop and we hunkered down in a thicket. I tried to steady my breathing and joined Navi in listening for sounds of the other drakon. Once the elk were out of range, I heard nothing but wind and bird calls.

I let out a breath of relief. All I could do was pray the others were safe and that Adann had managed to slip away from the other guard. Adann was swifter than Rena, smarter than Eldin, and more experienced than me. Still, I couldn't help but worry that all of Adann's skill wouldn't be enough to escape the drakon rider.

Chapter 14

WE TRAVELED TOWARD THE village until the sun set and we had to stop for the night. I was alone in the woods again, like my Crossing, but this time it wasn't my watcher I imagined in every rustle of the leaves.

Without my hammock, I had to curl up on the hard ground, Navi's warm body curled around me. I was already awake at sunrise, staring at the inside of my eyelids. Rousing myself was surprisingly easy. We paused only once, at the river to drink and wash the mud from Navi's feathers, despite my body begging me to find something to eat. Food could wait. I needed to get home.

People milled around the field at the edge of the village when I arrived. As I descended the hill, I spotted Rena and Eldin in the center of the crowd. Everyone but Adann. The clamor of voices, hundreds of villagers peppering the returned hunters with questions, fell silent at my approach.

I slid from Navi's back underneath the wide-eyed, questioning stares of the Konota. The tension in the air surpassed my return from my Crossing. The hostility only certain people had shown me was now written on dozens of other faces, those that had only been wary before.

"You're okay!" Makai crashed into me and hugged me so tight I thought he might break me in half. "When you didn't come back with the others, I thought... I thought I'd lost you."

I tried to squirm my way out of his arms. "I'm fine. But you might still lose me if you crush me to death."

Makai's grip immediately loosened and he stepped away. He looked down sheepishly. "Sorry. I'm sorry. I'm just relieved."

Something warm unfolded inside me at the knowledge that Makai had been so worried about me.

"She would have been perfectly fine if that beast of hers could hide properly," Eldin sneered. He crossed his arms and turned his disdain on Navi. "It doesn't belong here."

He, I thought. Eldin might be right about Navi not belonging, but his refusal to call Navi anything but "it" was maddening. Like Navi was a *thing* rather than my keeper. I turned toward Makai to silently plead for him to defend me, like he always did, but Makai had vanished.

Eldin raised his voice so others nearby could hear clearly. "Those people have monsters like her own! What if they gave her that drakon and now they're using her to infiltrate the village? How did she escape unless they let her go?"

"No one gives you a keeper." I tried to sound firm. Instead, my voice sounded meek and afraid. "Only Tyir guides our fates."

"Well, maybe you're *fated* to be a traitor," Eldin snapped. He radiated malice and anger. It seemed the only thing saving Eldin's life had accomplished was to make him hate me even more. Did he actually believe that I would betray our people or was he only lashing out in fear?

Pashir joined us and the dread churning my stomach grew. "We should toss her into the pit until the threat has passed. She's a danger to us all!"

To my dismay, murmurs of hesitant agreement answered him. I lowered my eyes, staring at the grass in front of my feet. What could I say to change their minds? I stood alone before them without Makai or Adann to back me up. They could have been the voice of reason, but I didn't know where Makai had gone and Adann was out there in the forest somewhere, maybe still in danger. Maybe dead or captured.

"Enough!" My father's voice cut off any further accusations. "Shaya is Konota, and she will be treated as such until there is actual evidence."

What evidence? I knew he didn't, but the words made it sound like he thought there might be evidence in the future. I *knew* he didn't. He trusted me.

"Guildmasters," he said. "Join me in my hut to discuss what the party has found. Eldin, too. I have more questions for you."

Pashir looked me over with disdain before following my father. Eldin, however, needed the last word. "Your days here are numbered, traitor," he spat.

I forced myself to take a deep breath after he turned away, but I still felt the push of other eyes. Soft voices took up conversations again. About the strangers in the forest. About me.

"Shaya!" I cringed at my sister's voice and pressed back against Navi. "Where is Adann? He wasn't with the others."

She hadn't come to verify my safety, but to ask about Adann. Of course she had. In her frantic eyes, I saw how much she loved him. How much it would destroy her if she lost him.

"I don't know," I said. "He led one of the drakon riders away. I don't know what happened to him."

"Of course he did." Behind her worry, I heard a hint of pride. Always the brave one, always willing to sacrifice himself for others. *That* was why everyone respected him so much, despite his age.

"I'm sure he's fine. It's Adann." I wished I could do more, but all I had were empty reassurances.

"I know... I know." She looked me over, and her concern about Adann shifted to something more tentative. "Are you okay? I'm sorry. I didn't mean to make you feel like I don't care."

"I know," I said, even though I hadn't. Hearing it almost made me cry. After the tension the last few weeks, I feared she had turned her back on me forever. But I could hear the sincerity in her voice and see it in her eyes. Ayla couldn't lie to save her life.

And she could see through anyone else's too. "No, you didn't," she replied. "But it's okay. I know I haven't... been the most supportive since you got back. I'm so sorry." Just like that, I had my big sister back. The anger I had been carrying around at the back of my mind since she suggested I didn't belong melted away. Maybe I was a little quick to forgive, but this was Ayla. She was family.

I threw my arms around her. When she hugged me back, I realized how much I had missed this. Missed her. Ayla had always been a part of my life, and without her I had been teetering off-balance like a hut missing one side of its frame.

"Shaya." My name again, spoken this time without any emotion. No hostility, no relief. Nothing at all.

I pulled away from my sister and eyed Caldin warily. One more person come to yell at me? But she didn't look angry, and Makai stood next to her. His suppressed smile said he was very pleased with himself.

"Makai told me what happened. You saving Eldin." Caldin paused for a long moment before saying, "Thank you for saving my brother's life. I doubt he thanked you himself."

He hadn't, but I didn't confirm it. I hadn't done it for him, or for her. I'd done it because he was Konota, and that meant he was worth protecting. Even if he would have let those drakons eat me were our positions reversed.

Caldin waited to see if I would respond. When I didn't, one corner of her mouth quirked up slightly. "I am in your debt, Shaya Navi."

Those words, coming from a Guildmaster, should have amazed me. I should have acknowledged the weight they held. My mind was elsewhere, though, so I only nodded.

When Caldin left to join the other Guildmasters and her brother, I frowned at Makai. "How did you know?"

"Rena has been telling anyone who will listen about what you did." He laughed at the confused look on my face. "You're not the only one who doesn't get along with him, Shay."

That sounded suspiciously close to someone else actually being on my side. I had thought the strangers with the drakons would destroy any chance at acceptance, but maybe there was hope after all.

I turned my gaze back toward the forest. I told myself that any second Adann would appear at the top of the hill, a grin on his face, alive and uninjured and *safe*.

He didn't.

"He'll be okay," Makai said. He had asked me before what was going on inside my head, but he seemed better at guessing the answer than anyone else.

"I should have done something," I murmured.

"There was nothing you could do. This isn't your fault, any more than Nahdi was mine." He took my hand and squeezed it lightly. "Come on, you can sit with us until he returns. And he *will* return."

He slipped away through the crowd, but Ayla grabbed my wrist before I could follow.

"I know I don't really deserve to do the big sister thing right now." She bit her lip, the way I did sometimes when I was struggling to find the right words. "Be careful with Makai and his friends, okay? They're not always... the nicest group. I don't want to see you get hurt."

While I appreciated her concern, I already knew that Makai's friends, Iliya especially, could be a little prickly. "I know what I'm doing." I gently pulled my wrist out of her grasp and turned away.

I found Makai and his friends sitting in a circle on the ground outside Makai's hut. They looked up as I approached, my steps wary. I feared this new development would turn them against me too, but when I sat down, completing the circle, I didn't see any unfriendly faces. They didn't shut me out or cast fearful looks in Navi's direction, though I still doubted any of them would want to ride him, even if he would let them.

Which he wouldn't.

"There you are," Makai said. "For a second there I thought you weren't coming."

"What do you think they want?" Deira asked. She sounded scared, and I didn't blame her.

"Maybe they just want a new place to call home," Trev said. "You know, to coexist peacefully with us." His tone didn't match the optimistic words.

"Don't be ridiculous." An undercurrent of fear diminished even Iliya's usual haughtiness. "They chased our people through the forest. They're stealing our prey. Maybe Nahdi even got too close and they... took her."

"You mean killed her," Trev muttered. When Iliya and Deira shot him identical glares, his face reddened. "Makai, I didn't—"

"It's okay," Makai said. It wasn't, though. Makai's voice was quiet, his gaze trained on the ground in the middle of the circle.

I hadn't seen that haunted look since our talk by the lake. Everyone might have thought he had accepted her disappearance and moved past it, but he never had. He had just buried the pain.

Now we were dragging it out again.

"She could still be alive," Iliya said. Her voice was gentler than I'd ever heard it, and the way she rested a hand on his knee made me realize she actually *cared*. I had thought she was callous and self-absorbed, but I was coming to see something more substantial hiding underneath. She cared deeply about Makai. About all of them. "Whoever these people are, they wouldn't kill a *child*. Or even a new adult on their way home from their Crossing."

"She's right," I said. "People might have different names for it, but the transition from child to adult is a sacred one wherever you go. The Pajairi call it the Sun Voyage. For the people of the North, it's the Trial by Nature." No matter what they called it, or the differences in how it happened, finding one's keeper was regarded with reverence. There were dozens of stories that mentioned it, ones Grandpa Enzi had told me and ones shared by traders.

The others stared at me for long enough that it made my face flush. Then Deira smiled faintly and said, "You sound like Enzi with all his stories."

"Do the stories tell you anything else about these people?" Trev asked. "Do you know where they might be from?"

I didn't like the attention I had called to myself. Even Iliya leaned forward eagerly. They wanted reassurance, even if that reassurance came in the form of knowledge. Understanding something was the first step to not fearing it.

I thought back to the camp and the drakon riders. Their pale coloring, their camp made of temporary tents like those used by the nomadic people of the North. And, of course, the drakons they brought with them. "The North, probably," I said finally. "In the story of Tavlin Lamere, that's where the drakons live. Where Navi must have come from."

I didn't share what else I knew about the North. I had pestered my grandfather for other stories, trying to learn more about Navi, but he didn't have more legends that spoke of drakons. He did tell me some about the northern people, though. All of them had one thing in common—the people of the Far North were not peaceful. I doubted they had come here to "coexist."

Maybe I should have told them. Maybe I should have warned them about what danger might rain down on us, but I couldn't. They wanted something to make them *less* scared, not more scared.

"It's like Shaya said," Iliya said after a brief silence. "No one would kill someone on their Crossing. Nahdi might still be alive. Maybe once we talk to these people, they'll let her go."

Would they, though? They were more likely to use her as a hostage. The probably false hope in Makai's eyes stirred guilt that would weigh on me until we knew for sure.

A chorus of shouts cut off our conversation. "It's Adann!"

"He's back!"

"Thank Tyir."

I jumped to my feet and darted around the hut. When I reached the north side of the village, I saw Adann descending the hill with Illari prowling next to him. Ayla met him and threw her arms around his neck, clinging to him until he firmly pushed her away.

Hands clapped him on the back as the villagers welcomed him home, but Adann's eyes honed in on me when he searched the crowd. He slipped away from Ayla and made his way over. "See, little mouse? No drakon can catch me."

I ducked away from him as he ruffled my hair—which he *knew* I hated—but I smiled at him, too happy to be annoyed. "What happened?" I asked.

"She was no match for my incredible wits and unrivaled stealth," he replied. "Led her toward the river and then gave her the slip when I was sure we were far enough away. I see you escaped alright too."

"We lost him in the trees." I made it sound simpler than the reality, but I didn't feel like recounting the whole story.

"Well done, little mouse."

"Eldin is still with the Guildmasters. You should join them." I wouldn't mind having someone there to defend me. I had no doubt that Eldin would try to cast me in a bad light somehow.

Adann nodded. He clamped a hand on my shoulder before rejoining Ayla. She would have to wait outside while he joined the meeting, but I understood why she'd be reluctant to leave his side.

We had escaped the drakons this time. I wanted to believe that they wouldn't attack unprovoked, but I knew it wasn't true. My people had lived peacefully in the Konota Valley for generations.

Now we were no longer safe.

CHAPTER 15

THE VILLAGE SEEMED TO hold its breath the next few days, waiting for drakons to appear in the sky over the village. Most people avoided me as much as possible, while others—like Eldin and Guildmaster Pashir—shot me hostile glares any chance they got. They no longer openly advocated for my imprisonment or banishment, but they would happily throw me out the first chance they got.

At least I still had Makai and his friends. *They* hadn't started treating me differently. If anything, the three had acted more friendly, asking me to tell them stories about the North. I selected my tales carefully, avoiding any that might cause fear, which proved difficult. The people of the North were fierce fighters, their clans often warring with each other.

They still had their stories of valiant heroes, though, so I stuck with telling those.

Despite the empty skies, the village readied itself for any impending attack. Anyone not performing essential duties for their guild had to help with the preparations, which mostly meant assisting the crafters in making new spears, bows, and arrows. Some of the older children who had been taught to carve weapons helped as well.

We tended to work by the lake to stay out of the way of any other activity, aside from fishing boats out on the water. At the moment, only our group and one other person—a boy named Keer—sat on chairs we'd carried over from the commons. As I had the past two days, I told stories from the North while we worked.

"Tell us more about Tavlin Lamere," Trev begged. He was one of their favorite heroes, though I'd left out the morbid ending to his story. There were plenty of other daring deeds to recount.

I thought through the stories I knew, sifting out those I had already shared with the others. "During the God Wars, Tavlin faced down many divine enemies," I started. "None more terrifying than Lieth, a powerful and cruel goddess who always hated humans. She unleashed a great darkness upon the land to punish humanity."

"What darkness? What does that mean?" Deira asked.

"Well... the legends don't say exactly." I had pondered the question at length myself. Grandpa Enzi had mentioned multiple versions of this story, all of which only vaguely hinted at what this darkness might be. "In some it seems that it was a literal darkness, casting the world into an eternal night. Others imply that it was some kind of monster created by Lieth to hunt down the humans.

"The gods who sided with humanity during the war searched for an answer, but it was Tavlin who defeated her. He found a way to conquer the darkness, and imprisoned Lieth in her own mountain."

"That's... heroic and all, but *how* did he conquer the darkness?" Iliya said. "We don't know how he defeated it or even what it is. What kind of story is that?"

I couldn't argue with Iliya's complaints. I harbored my own frustration at the lack of details, but I also understood how these things got lost over the centuries. "The war was hundreds of years ago. These stories were passed down by tongue for generations. Eventually pieces... get lost to time."

"I wonder what it was like back then." Makai leaned back in his chair, a half-formed arrow shaft across his lap. "When evil gods roamed free. It must have been terrifying."

Before I could reply, Iliya leaned over and nudged Makai with her elbow. "Look at that poor kid. Someone needs to give him another crafting lesson." Apparently, she was done listening to stories.

Makai craned his neck to look toward the boy who sat several paces away. Admittedly, Iliya was right, but I didn't like the smug look on her face.

Makai let out a laugh and rested his knife on his knee. "It's probably the first time he's tried to do one alone."

"Come on, let's go help him out, eh?" Iliya set aside the spear she had been working on and rose to her feet with fluid grace. Trev and Deira exchanged grins and jumped up to follow her.

"Makai—" I started, but he was already in motion.

I remained in my seat, worry nagging at me, though I couldn't say why. Maybe they did intend to help him, but there had been that *look* in Iliya's eye.

I set down my carving knife and followed cautiously, my footsteps nearly silent on the pebbled beach. Navi stayed at my heel, shared apprehension rebounding between us. No one seemed to notice—or care—that we had followed.

By the time I reached them, Iliya had already taken the half-finished bow from the boy. Keer was a year younger than us and lacking a keeper. His mother was close friends with mine, the two of them often working together in the Crafters Guild.

Keer's wide face and high cheekbones betrayed his southern heritage on his father's side. The man had been a trader who had spent a few days in the village and left unaware that he would have a son in nine months.

"This is the best you can do?" Iliya jeered, turning the bow over in her hands. The work was shoddy, one end shaved too narrow and the mid-section awkwardly lumpy. "I'm not even sure this is salvageable. What do you think Makai?"

She tossed it in Makai's direction. Keer tried to grab it as it passed, but Makai snatched it before he could.

"Hmm... well, we could even it out, but it might snap under the pressure of the bowstring," Makai replied. He twirled it in his hands to inspect the other end. "Isn't your mother a crafter?"

"You'd think she would have taught him better," Trev said. Beside him, Deira laughed.

"Come on, Makai. Give it back," Keer begged as he reached for the bow again. A note of desperation made his voice crack at the end.

"We're only trying to help!" Makai said as he pulled the bow out of Keer's reach. From his voice, you'd think he meant it. Maybe he really did. Somehow that twisted the knots in my stomach tighter.

"Hey!" I said, finally drawing their attention to me. I resisted the urge to cringe beneath their gazes, or to run in the other direction. "What in Tyir's name are you doing?" I snapped, even though I already had an answer. One I didn't want.

Iliya glared at me like I'd stolen her dessert at dinner. "We're just having some fun."

"He doesn't look like he's having fun," I said. Iliya, and everyone else, looked shocked at my tone. *I* was shocked. I had never heard my own voice sound so cold—as frozen as the snow that often dusted the peak of Mount Tyir.

Keer stared at me like a legendary hero come to rescue him, which of course made me self-conscious again. Next time I spoke, my voice was quieter and more timid, the voice that had earned me the nickname *little mouse*. "Leave him alone." Iliya and Trev sneered at me, but Makai looked... troubled. So he did know this was wrong. I fixed him with an accusatory stare, all uncertainty falling away again. "Give it back, Makai."

He held my gaze, and for five heartbeats—I counted—I thought he would refuse. *This* was the boy I'd spent all these years pining for? And I had never noticed this side of him, the version of Makai that taunted younger boys while his friends laughed. *Be careful with Makai and his friends,* Ayla had said.

She had been right.

Makai's eyes dropped from mine. Dizziness washed over me, as if I had used up all my energy staring him down. When he held out the bow, Keer eyed it like an offering of poisonous berries. The boy's eyes darted around the group before he snatched it away from Makai and scurried off, not unlike a mouse himself.

"Makai's sapped," Trev muttered, drawing a giggle from Iliya. Makai winced like the sound had smacked him across the cheek. I willed him to meet my eyes, to *apologize*, even if with only a look. He didn't. His eyes—the brown eyes I had fantasized about, dreamed about—remained fixed on the dirt.

"I'm going home," I said, because no matter how badly I wanted to make some biting comment, nothing came to mind. I was spent from standing up for Keer and from watching the boy I stupidly loved act like someone else. No... not someone else. He'd always been like this, teasing the other kids, but it had always seemed good-natured. Had I been wrong? Blinded by his warm eyes and enchanting smile. Had I missed this all along?

Makai didn't speak. No one did. And when I turned my back to head home, he still hadn't looked up. I wanted to glance over my shoulder, to see if he had lifted his eyes to watch me leave. If he felt guilty or ashamed or *sorry*.

But I didn't. I was too afraid of what I might see. I grabbed the bow I had been working on and my knife, then started up the hill away from the lake. I kept my eyes trained forward until I turned past a hut and broke into a run.

I sat on my bed with my back against the wall of the hut, my arms wrapped around my legs and my head resting on my knees—my typical position when I was hurt or upset or scared, as if making myself as small as possible could make it better. Navi was curled up on the ground beside the bed, his chin on my foot. In a mere week, he had grown too big to crawl onto the bed with me, but he still wanted to be as close to me as possible.

I squeezed my eyes shut and took a deep breath. It did nothing to help the sob that threatened to escape. I'd always seen Makai as perfect. Kind, talented, humble, loyal, handsome. The kind of person to be idolized and adored. Which was ridiculous, of course. No one was *perfect*, but I had been too lovestruck to see it until this had opened my eyes.

Someone kind didn't tease a child. Someone *humble* didn't refuse to apologize for it. Someone loyal didn't betray my trust like this. What else had he done that I had blindly ignored?

I was nothing but a foolish girl. I should have seen the truth all along.

Stop. Navi's order was accompanied by a gentle chirp. I couldn't, though. I couldn't keep my mind from spiraling.

"Shaya?"

My arms tightened around my legs and I didn't lift my head. I didn't want Adann to see me five seconds away from crying.

"I was looking for Ayla, but..." I heard the rustle of the door flap falling shut behind him. "This might sound like a stupid question but... are you okay?"

I glanced up but dropped my eyes without answering. Lying would be pointless. My face betrayed the truth, but I think admitting it aloud would have snapped the last thread that kept me from crying.

Adann came to sit beside me on the bed. I didn't miss the wary glance he cast Navi, but he seemed to accept my keeper's proximity after only that brief hesitation. "Do you want to talk about it?"

No. Another obvious answer, but Adann had never seemed to understand that. Then I realized a part of me *did* want to talk about it before the pressure of keeping it inside exploded. "What do you do when someone you cared about, someone you trusted, turns out to be... not the person you thought?"

Adann didn't answer right away, one of the longest stretches of silence I'd heard from him. When he spoke, his voice was gentle. "You accept you were wrong and try to make peace with that fact."

That answer was obvious too, but it was one that I needed to hear. The rhythm of the words forced me to finally acknowledge the truth. I let out a slow breath and ran my fingers along Navi's forehead. "Thank you."

"Anytime, little mouse." He cleared his throat and reached into his pocket. "I found this yesterday." When he extended his hand and opened his fingers, a bluish-green stone sat in his palm. A river stone the size of a walnut, its surface worn smooth by years of rushing water.

"It's beautiful."

"I saw it and thought of you." He took my hand and pressed the stone into my palm. "How even the tiny things are strong, able to survive the fiercest waters. They might get a little worn down, but in the end they're even more beautiful for it." I looked up at him, my eyes wide, and Adann cracked a crooked smile. "Plus, I thought it was pretty."

I closed my fingers around the stone and smiled back at him. At least when everything else seemed hopeless, I could count on him.

I scooted off the bed so I could kneel beside it and reached underneath to grab my box hidden there. Adann watched curiously as I slid the pieces to unlock it. "My grandfather was a crafter," I explained. "Not Enzi, obviously. My father's father. He made this for me when I was a baby. It's where I keep pieces of things—and people—that are important to me."

"Like... fingers?" I looked up disapprovingly, unwilling to laugh at the morbid joke. He grinned sheepishly. "Sorry. But really, what kinds of things?"

When each of the sliding bars were pushed to the correct side—four bars at each end of the box—I lifted the top off. I didn't quite understand how it worked, but I knew the bars locked on pegs and only released when they were slid into the correct position. My father had taught me the combination once I was old enough to remember it.

I pulled out each of the objects I had collected, all of them small in order to fit inside the box. It was barely long enough to contain the knife my parents had given me, and slightly shorter in width and depth. Along with the knife, which I had decided was too precious to actually use, I had an object from everyone in my family.

A delicate wood carving of a fox's face from my mother, given to me on my eighth birthday. When I was ten, our family's hut was wrecked in a terrible storm that struck the valley. Afterward, my father had handed me a piece of broken wood from the former structure and told me even the strongest things can fall, but they can also be rebuilt with enough patience and resolve.

From Ayla, I had a flower I had pressed between two pieces of leather. Shortly after her Crossing, once she officially became a healer, she had taught me about some of her favorite medicinal plants. The flower was often brewed into tea and used for mild pain relief and to aid restless nights. Just looking at the flower often calmed me, like the other tokens in the box. Finally, there was the smooth piece of antler from Grandpa Enzi. He had said it was from his mother's keeper, a deer like his own.

I tucked the stone between the leather knife handle and the corner of the box.

"See? Now it's safe." I replaced the top and slid the bars back to the middle position, then returned the box to its hiding spot. Adann smiled at me as I sat beside him. "What?"

"I'm something important to you?"

I blinked at him. "Of course. You're like... the big brother I never had. You've always been there for me."

He took my hand, but there was something strained in his smile now. "And I always will be, little mouse."

I startled when shouting rose like a wave outside. First one voice, followed by another and another, multiplying until dozens of voices were raised in the same cry: Attack!

Chapter 16

ADANN AND I SCRAMBLED off my bed. I grabbed the knife I kept under my pillow, the same one I'd taken on my Crossing. After slipping it through a loop in my belt, I hurried outside with Adann right behind me.

Our village had never been attacked before. Theoretically, we all knew enough to defend ourselves, especially the hunters with their experience handling spears and bows. That experience was all *hunting*, though, not fighting. Even as I went to defend my home, I knew we didn't stand a chance against whatever threat had crashed down on the village.

I looked up as a shadow swooped over me, blocking out the sun for a moment before the bright light blinded me again. After my eyes adjusted, I was able to make out the form of a drakon in the sky, banking back toward the village. I watched in horror as the drakon dove and plucked one of the villagers off the ground. It soared upward, only to drop the man from high in the air. He plummeted, his form disappearing behind a hut. Even though I couldn't see him land, I still heard the thud. I jerked to a stop as if I had run into an invisible wall, causing Adann to walk into my back. A fall from that height was survivable, but at what cost?

It seemed the clan was done waiting. Now that we knew they were there, the peace had shattered.

When Adann put his hands on my arms to steady me, I wanted to shrink back against him. I was terrified to face what came next—more importantly, the aftermath. "Shaya." Adann's voice centered me. "Get on Navi. You'll be safer fighting from his back."

Would I? Navi's ears were erect, the feathers along his spine hackled. His fear only magnified my own. My skills were dismal to begin with, and I had no practice fighting from his back. Adann was right, though. Navi had his own natural weapons, and a spear would give me the reach I needed to fight while mounted. If only he could *fly*. More drakons attacked from the skies, only to fly away before our people could strike back.

I swallowed my terror and scrambled onto Navi. Before Adann could run off, I leaned over and grabbed his shoulder. "Promise me you'll be okay."

His only response was a rueful smile, and honestly I was glad he didn't bother lying to me.

My fingers slipped from his shoulder as he turned. When he disappeared around the corner of a hut, a horrible thought hit me: it might be the last time I saw him alive.

At my prompting, Navi raced through the village, toward the building where we kept extra hunting weapons. People swarmed the paths, either running for shelter or to retrieve weapons and fight back. One woman called desperately for her son, who must have gotten lost in the crowd.

When I reached the weapons hut, I found it blanketed by flames.

I stopped to watch as Emry hurried out of the burning building with a bundle of spears in her arms. She started to rush back in after handing them off to Keeton, but the other hunter grabbed her arm. "It's no use!" he called over the crackle of the fire and the shouts of the Konota. The *whoosh* of a dark gray drakon passing overhead drowned Emry's reply.

The roof of the building collapsed, which made retrieving more weapons impossible. Resigned, Emry picked up one of the spears she had rescued, and together the two ran to find people to pass the weapons to.

Neither looked at me once, even though Navi stood no more than five paces away.

I clenched my fist around my knife, the only weapon I carried and one probably useless against the spears and long blades the drakon riders wielded. At least Navi still had his teeth and claws, as well as those spikes at the end of his tail.

I turned my gaze to the sky, counting at least ten drakons. Their skin ranged from black to different shades of gray to brown, their feathers in a multitude of colors. I saw one with purple feathers lighter than Navi's and another with dark blue and yellow. I also recognized the two drakons that had chased us down the ravine. All the riders had light hair worn in long braids that streamed behind them as they shot through the air.

A shadow fell over my vision and a huge black beast—at least three hands taller than Navi—landed with a thud in front of me. Navi backed away, fear snaking through our bond like a bolt of lightning.

The chief stared down at me from the back of the black drakon. He held a metal-tipped spear in his hand, a tassel of black feathers tied around the shaft.

"The valley girl with a drakon," he said, his words as sharp as the spear he carried. His drakon took a step forward, and Navi countered it with a step back. He turned to the side and swung his tail at the black drakon, forcing the creature to retreat from the bone spikes.

The man snorted, maybe in amusement, but it was difficult to tell. I didn't have time to react as his long spear swept out and struck my shoulder with enough force to knock me from Navi's back. My keeper let out a squawk of outrage. I landed in the dirt like the pathetic child I was compared to the man, my hand still curled around my useless knife.

"You are not a warrior. You do not belong on his back," Rajik sneered. He raised his spear again, the tip aimed at my chest. I scrambled backward. Navi growled and tried to lunge at the man, but the other drakon's tail swept into his path.

The man grunted as an arrow struck his shoulder. He didn't drop the spear, but he did lower his arm so he could yank the arrow out like it was a pesky splinter. He didn't seem to notice the blood running down his muscular arm. He turned, looking for the source of the arrow, and I spotted Caldin standing half behind a hut, in the process of nocking another arrow.

The black drakon took off to avoid the second shot. It dove toward Caldin, who disappeared around the edge of the hut. Rajik and his keeper vanished from my sight a moment later.

"Shaya!" Someone grabbed my arm and pulled me up. Pain lanced through my shoulder, and I clenched my teeth to keep from crying out. Makai met my eyes, his worry giving way to relief when he realized I wasn't hurt beyond the ache in my shoulder and my wounded pride. If I'd had any pride to begin with. "What happened?"

"Nothing." I wiped my eyes, hoping he hadn't noticed the few tears that had slipped out. "Are you armed?" Seeing his face again after what happened earlier made my heart ache worse than my shoulder, but I couldn't think about that. Not right now.

He held up his spear in answer, determination set on his face. Makai was too stubborn to be afraid, something I would have admired yesterday but only annoyed me now. He should be afraid. He should be *terrified.*

"There you are!" My mother rushed over to us and pulled me into a hug. "I went to the hut first, but you weren't there."

"I'm okay, Mama." I squirmed out of her embrace and took a step back. "Ayla?"

"In the Healers Hut with Enzi and—" The long, deep note from a horn cut her off. I looked up, searching for the source of the sound, and saw the chief blowing the curved instrument. It sounded again, calling the other drakons to form around him. When they turned away, I realized it was a retreat signal. Triumphant shouts rose from the village, but I knew they weren't leaving because they were defeated. They hadn't attacked intending to win today. They were playing a game, testing us.

A straggling rider glided over our heads, lower than the other drakons as they flew away. Makai's spear struck the man's shoulder, which knocked him off his drakon. He hit the ground with a pained shout but immediately got up and ran toward the forest. Makai sprinted after him.

"Makai, no!" Mama shouted. "Foolish child," she muttered when he didn't listen. She followed, though I didn't know what she intended to do. Hopefully stop Makai before he got himself killed.

My instincts screamed at me to stay put. I still had nothing but my knife, but I couldn't stay in the village and *wait.* I ran after the others. Navi chirped to get my attention, and I managed to loop an arm around his neck so I could heave myself up without him stopping.

With me on his back, we closed the gap between us and the others, but I lost sight of them when they reached the trees. Navi could still hear their footsteps, so we followed the sounds until they came into view again. The man was on the ground just outside a clearing, holding his wounded shoulder. He must have tripped over a root or something else when he reentered the trees. Makai closed in on him, but the man didn't look frightened as he watched the young hunter approach. He looked... almost smug. Then I realized he wasn't looking at Makai but past his shoulder.

I followed his gaze and spotted the archer crouching high in the branches of a tree, her hair a flash of white among the dark green and brown. She had her arrow trained on Makai.

"Up! Look up!" I shouted as loud as I could. My voice broke from the effort, the sound raw and desperate.

It was enough to draw my mother's attention toward the archer, but not Makai's. "Makai Farin, *stop*!" she called, forceful enough that Makai finally ceased his chase and turned. The archer drew the bowstring, her face cold and her arms steady.

A flash of brown caught my eye as Farin shot down from the sky. The falcon flared his wings at the last second and swung his claws forward to grab the archer's arm, but she loosed the arrow a moment before he could throw off her aim. By then, my mother had reached Makai. She gave him a push that sent him sprawling on the ground. The arrow that would have pierced his heart grazed Mama's arm instead.

The archer was still wrestling with Farin, who clutched her arm in his talons while she tried to shake him off. She grabbed another arrow with her free hand and moved to stab at the falcon, but I stopped a few paces from the tree and hurled my knife at her with all my strength. She sat too high for the knife to penetrate when it struck her leg, its momentum lost as gravity pulled it down. It bounced off her thigh and dropped to the base of the tree, but it pulled her attention away from Farin long enough for him to release her arm and glide safely out of reach.

The archer narrowed her eyes at me as she slid the arrow back into her quiver. She swung her legs over the branch and dropped to another below it, landing on a black drakon with dark blue feathers that I hadn't noticed until it launched itself into the sky. Instead of coming after me, the archer and drakon retreated. By then, the other Northerner had disappeared as well.

I didn't bother retrieving my knife. Instead, I ran to my mother's side. She had her hand clamped over her bleeding arm, crimson leaking between her fingers, and Makai was helping her to her feet.

"I'm okay," Mama said when she saw me. "Nothing but a graze. We were both lucky." She shot a sharp look at Makai, who lowered his eyes in warranted shame. "Exactly what were you thinking, young man?"

"I'm sorry, Guildmaster Ora. I thought maybe we could capture one... maybe question him."

"You thought you could be a hero," she corrected him. "You can't—" She broke off as she swayed, her eyes fluttering shut. It was the only warning before she collapsed onto Makai.

With Makai unprepared, her weight almost knocked him to the ground again, but he managed to keep his balance and catch her. He lowered her gently and then looked up at me with wide eyes. Tala made a distressed sound and crept forward to lick Mama's face.

My lips parted. Before I could say anything, Papa and Misni reached us. When my father saw his partner limp on the ground, he looked at Makai so intensely that the boy's posture *shrank*.

"What happened?" Papa demanded.

"She... she was shot. But it was only a graze. I don't know why she fainted." Makai turned a desperate look on me, and I knew what was going through his head. I could blame it on him, tell them she'd only gotten shot because she was trying to save his life. I kept it to myself. Not for him, but because it wasn't important right now.

"Misni, go tell Enzi what happened. I'll bring her to the Healers Hut," Papa said.

Misni gave the chief a sharp nod before pulling herself gracefully onto her keeper's back. The horse galloped toward the village to prepare the healers.

"Makai," Papa said. It was all he needed to get Makai to back away so my father could lift Mama into his arms. Cradling her to his chest like a precious child, he turned and jogged back toward the village, Honovi and Tala on his heels.

Makai got to his feet and brushed leaves and clumps of grass from his knees. "Shaya..."

Before he could finish, I turned my back to search for the arrow. It had lodged itself into a tree, and it took a couple tugs to yank it free from the bark. The arrowhead was unlike any I'd ever seen, several sharp points on both sides angled away from the tip. My stomach churned at the thought of trying to pull that arrow out of someone's flesh.

There was something else on the arrowhead too, a dusting of white on the burnished metal. Poison, maybe? It would explain her passing out. I had to get back and tell the healers.

"Shaya, wait. Can we talk?" Makai said as I jumped onto Navi. I didn't even spare him a glance before my keeper and I raced through the forest back to the village.

By the time we got to the Healers Hut, they had my mother situated on one of the beds, Tala curled up against her side. The fox had her head resting on Mama's stomach, worried eyes staring up at the unconscious human. Grandpa Enzi examined her while Papa and Ayla hovered nearby. Another healer, Lora, sat in the corner with a mortar and pestle and kept darting glances at Mama's bed.

My father and sister looked at me when I entered, but not Grandpa, so I said his name quietly to get his attention. His expression turned curious as I held out the arrow, a flicker of dismay showing after a moment of studying it.

"It's poisoned," he said, the same conclusion I had come to. "Her heartbeat is slow, her breathing labored. We will try giving her our typical antidotes, but I'm not optimistic they will help. I'm sorry." There was something in Enzi's voice, something that said he *knew* they wouldn't help. Maybe he knew more than he would admit to us, something he had learned in his travels.

The way he talked, it was easy to forget that she was more than his patient. He sounded like a healer talking about just another sick person, not his own daughter. I didn't know how he could hold himself together and remain professional. Or perhaps remaining professional *was* how he held himself together.

"How long does she have?" Papa asked softly. I could hear the strain in his voice, the effort it took to get the words out.

"I don't know. A few weeks, maybe."

Papa didn't respond right away. I didn't wait to find out if he ever did. I fled the hut, only to find Makai waiting outside. He straightened when he saw me.

I strode up to him and slammed my hands against his chest before he could speak, hard enough to force him back a step. "What is wrong with you?" I demanded.

He looked as shocked at the violent outburst as I felt. "I didn't mean for it to happen. I was—"

"They were *retreating*!" I was yelling at him now, for the first time in my life. "You should have let them go. If you hadn't tried to run off and be a stupid hero, my mother wouldn't be lying unconscious with poison slowly killing her!"

I turned away, intending to run back home and wallow in my misery, but Makai grabbed my arm. "Shaya, please, let me explain," he said desperately.

"I liked you for years, did you know that? I had this ridiculous crush on you." I jerked my arm away. "Now I'm thinking I had this idealized version of you in my head and I never really knew you at all."

"But you know me now," he said.

"Yeah. And I'm not sure I like that person."

He looked like I'd slapped him. For a moment, I almost felt guilty. Almost. "Shaya—" he started.

"*Stop!* Stop saying my name." I didn't think I had heard it so many times in one day. It was starting to sound like someone else's name, a meaningless combination of sounds. If he said it one more time, I might push him again.

I had finally stunned Makai to silence, and he simply stared at me in dismay until I turned my back and sprinted to my hut.

Instead of flinging myself on my bed, I sat on the floor so Navi could curl up beside me. I leaned against him and let loose the sob I had been holding back since Grandpa Enzi told us Mama was dying.

Navi alerted me when Ayla entered the hut. She hesitated by the door before coming to sit on my other side.

"This can't be happening," I whispered. "I can't—"

"I know." Ayla wrapped her arm around me, and I shifted away from Navi so I could cling to my sister. "I wish... I wish there was something I could do. What's the point of being a healer if—" She broke off into frustrated silence.

"It's not fair. Why *her*? Makai is the one who charged into danger. It should be him laying there dying!"

Ayla rested her chin on top of my head. "You don't mean that," she said quietly.

No, I didn't. No matter how angry I was at him, I wouldn't make him take her place. That wasn't fair. "What are we going to do?"

"I don't know, sis." She let out a shaky breath, and I realized she was crying too. "I don't know."

CHAPTER 17

AYLA SLEPT IN ADANN'S hut that night. She needed the comfort, and it was time to make their union official anyway. That left Papa and me alone, our home now short two people. Neither of us wanted to talk about what had happened, so we went to sleep without a single word.

Early the next morning, I headed to the Healers Hut. Since I hadn't officially declared my guild, I didn't feel beholden to the hunters, and I didn't think either Guildmaster would mind. Caldin and Grandpa Enzi would understand my desire to be closer to my mother.

Adann pulled me aside before I could reach the hut, though. "Come on, some of the hunters are helping the builders clean up. It'll be a nice distraction."

I nodded in silent agreement. Cleaning up was important, and I could visit Mama later. Together, we tracked down Guildmaster Pashir to offer our help. He sneered when he saw me, but Adann at my side kept him from any outright aggression. He directed us to carry rubble out of the village, to an open area near the lake where it would sit until we could decide whether pieces could be salvaged. Several buildings had fallen during the fight, either knocked over by drakons or burned down like the weapons hut.

"This shouldn't have happened," Adann seethed as he hurled a hunk of charred wood into the cart Navi was tied to. Tension radiated off him. I had never seen Adann *angry* before, and it frightened me. "They shouldn't have attacked this soon."

I frowned as I struggled to lift a mostly intact pole. "What do you mean?"

He grabbed the other end of the pole and helped me haul it into the cart. "Nothing. Never mind," he said, shaking his head. "I just thought they'd take more time to consider our offer of peace before attacking."

I pursed my lips and bent down to grab a splintered piece of what used to be someone's storage chest. "They shouldn't have attacked at all," I murmured. The Konota Valley was a haven, a land of plenty guarded by the great god Tyir. How could he have allowed this to happen?

Adann sighed and forced out a smile that looked more like a grimace. "Let's get this load to the lake."

Navi pulled several full carts out of the village that morning. The sun neared its peak by the time Trev interrupted us. "There you are!" He hurried toward us, stopping a pace away only to stare at the ground.

"Speak, boy," Adann said, exasperated.

Trev looked like a rabbit awaiting the perfect moment to bolt from a predator. "It's Makai. I didn't know who else to talk to. He... he told us not to tell anyone, but I'm worried he's going to get himself killed."

I stared at him, but Adann didn't waste a moment on surprise. "What did he do? Where is he?"

"Lora told Iliya those people might have an antidote. He went to their camp to try and get it." Trev's eyes darted to me, scared and apologetic enough that I almost forgave him for teasing Keer. "I tried to stop him, but he wouldn't listen. Iliya went with."

Adann cursed, not even bothering to do it under his breath. "Come on," he said, the words clearly directed at me and not Trev. I trailed behind him as he hurried to where the crafters had been working all morning making new weapons to replace those lost in the fire. He paused to grab two freshly made spears, one of which he handed to me.

I didn't need to ask why. We were going after Makai and Iliya, without Trev or anyone else, because alone we would have a better chance of catching up with them before they reached the camp.

We packed two bags with waterskins and rations and left the village. We made good time through the forest, retracing the path we had taken the time our search party had encountered the clan. I rode on Navi's back, while Adann was a little slower on his own two feet. Illari ran at Adann's side. Navi had to check our pace more than once, but not by much. I'd never seen a man run so fast and so tirelessly. I offered to slow down once, but Adann responded with a sharp "no" that ended any further discussion.

Even Adann couldn't run forever, though. We had to pause now and then, more and more frequently as his strength waned. We needed to stop a few times to fill our waterskins as well.

Makai and Iliya must have left when the sun rose, which meant we were hours behind. Adann wanted to catch up before we got too far away from the village, but they had enough of a head start that we had to break for food. Adann and I could eat on the move, but our keepers needed time to hunt down a few rabbits in the forest. As soon as they had eaten enough to keep their strength up, we moved on.

I knew Adann and Illari were tracking Makai and Iliya, the man by keen attention to the physical trail and the cougar by scent. Though my tracking skill wasn't at the same level as his, I could imagine the forest the way he saw it. Moving this fast, they would mostly be relying on Illari's sense of smell, but Adann would notice footprints, broken twigs, and other telltale signs that the two had passed through.

When night fell, Adann insisted we press on. The forest was dangerous at night, but the moon was close to full, the sky clear, as if Tyir wanted us to catch Makai and Iliya before they did something incredibly stupid.

We grew close to the camp when first light broke. Adann had to be exhausted—*I* was exhausted, even though Navi had carried me the whole way—but he never showed a moment of weakness beyond his heavy breaths. Though Navi had tired as well, his stubbornness rivaled Adann's. He wouldn't stop until Makai was safe.

Adann stopped suddenly, I assumed to rest again, but then he turned to me and said, "You keep following the trail. I need to check something."

"But I don't…"

"You're a good tracker, and it's not a hard trail, since you already know where they're headed. You can do this, okay?"

I wasn't entirely convinced, and I didn't like the idea of him leaving me alone, but I nodded anyway. He patted Navi's shoulder. "Take care of her, alright, friend?" So many of the others wouldn't have touched Navi so casually. He probably would have growled at most for trying, but Navi chirped and flicked his ears forward in response.

Adann gave me a smile that bordered on a smirk. It made me feel better to see him so unbothered and confident. The tip of Illari tail was the last thing I saw before they were both gone.

I dismounted so I could see the ground better. Adann had been right: the trail was almost as clear as fresh footprints in the snow. As a hunter, Makai alone would have been harder to follow, but Iliya was a crafter. She wasn't used to moving through the forest with stealth, and any lessons from before her Crossing had probably been forgotten.

We moved slower now that I couldn't ride Navi, but it wasn't long before he heard quiet voices. He angled his ears in that direction, right along where the trail led. They were close. Soon, I heard it as well. Arguing.

"We can't just *walk in*," Iliya said. I could tell she was trying to keep her voice hushed, but frustration raised it.

"Do you have a better idea?" Makai replied.

"I don't know, cause a distraction or something!"

"Or you could go home." They both jumped at the sound of my voice. I stopped behind them and crossed my arms, staring levelly at Makai. His face flushed.

"Shaya... we were just—"

"Trev told me what you're doing."

"I'm trying to make up for my mistake!"

"You're trying to get yourself captured. Or killed," I snapped, somehow managing to do it quietly. He couldn't make up for his mistake by repeating it. "We're going home."

"Not until I get that antidote," Makai said fiercely.

"No, now." Both Makai and Iliya recoiled as Adann joined us. They might not listen to me, but Adann was older and someone with a certain *presence.* The type of person people instinctively listened to.

They nodded in unison, neither brave enough to meet his eye. We retreated quickly, hopefully before scouts noticed us. The farther we got from the camp with no sign of an alarm raised, the more confident I felt that we had gotten away clear.

After almost an hour of traveling in silence, I couldn't hold it in anymore. I turned sharply and stepped in front of Makai, blocking his path. He barely managed to keep himself from running into me and possibly knocking me over.

I had to crane my neck to look up at him, but I didn't back away. "What in Tyir's name were you thinking?"

"I was trying to help your mother!" He cast a desperate look at Iliya, but *she* couldn't help him. "I can't let her die. Not when it's my fault she's hurt. I don't want you to lose her."

"I don't want to lose you either!" I wasn't full-on yelling yet, but I wasn't quiet either.

"Shaya," Adann said sharply, reminding me to keep my voice down. We should have been far enough away from the camp, but it was best not to risk it.

I checked my anger before I spoke again. "I don't want you to die trying to help her. It's stupid to trade your life for hers."

"But you care about her—"

"I care about you too!" The words slipped out before I could stop them. No matter how hard I tried to bury those feelings, they had been there too long. They still lingered at the back of my heart—my soul—and influenced my every decision where he was concerned. I couldn't shake that godsforsaken *feeling*. "You're part of my village. I'm not going to let you run into danger without so much as a plan."

It was a lame attempt at trying to write off my feelings as less meaningful. From Makai's face, it hadn't worked. He didn't smile, but his lips twitched as he fought to hold one back.

"Shaya, we need to keep moving." Adann spoke too late. I heard the wingbeats before he even finished the last word. "Run!"

He didn't need to tell us. We were in motion before he spoke, fleeing the sound of the approaching drakon. I scrambled onto

Navi's back and he raced after the others. He caught them easily. "I'll try and lead them away!" I called, specifically to Adann. It was my turn to risk my life. I was faster than them, and from the sound of the wingbeats there was only one chasing us this time. I couldn't hear it anymore, but I knew we weren't out of danger yet. "Make sure they get home safely!"

"Shaya, stop!" It sounded more like an order than a request, but I ignored him and urged Navi toward the small clearing I knew we were close to. As we briefly left the cover of the trees, a shadow passed over us. I looked up to see the slate gray drakon following—one of the same drakons that had chased us down the ravine.

"Alright, Navi," I murmured. "Time to lose them."

I directed Navi toward an area where the evergreens grew thicker. The trees there were old—tall and large enough that their branches wove together and blocked out the sunlight, smothering the growth of other plants beneath them. I would be invisible from the air. The perfect place to lose the drakon.

When we reached the thick grove, Navi had to slow down, dodging the massive trunks and jumping over fallen branches. About halfway through the grove, I had Navi stop and crouch down. We went silent, listening for the sound of wings through the wall of needles above us. I heard nothing but distant bird-song and a soft breeze rustling the pine needles.

I think we lost them, I told Navi. We waited a little longer before turning south toward the village. We emerged near the river, so I decided to follow it home.

I had reached the bank when someone called my name. "Shaya!" Adann's shout was urgent, a warning, but I saw nothing except him sprinting toward me from the pine grove. A moment before he reached me, claws wrapped around my arm and yanked me off Navi's back. Adann lunged for my hand, but he only managed to brush my fingertips as the drakon carried me higher.

Navi's distressed cry followed me into the sky. He spread his wings and flapped them desperately, but he was the downed drakon, the one who couldn't fly because he was too afraid to learn. I could feel him wishing then that he had tried harder to conquer that fear.

Though I had thought only the one drakon pursued us, another swooped down and crashed into Adann, knocking him into the river. Illari snarled at the drakon, then raced along the bank after him. The rapids carried him away, no matter how hard he tried to swim toward the bank. Even he wouldn't be able to fight the current until it slowed, which wasn't for at least three hundred paces downstream.

I pried at the talons wrapped around my arm, but I had no hope of breaking the drakon's grip. Even if I did, we were fifty paces in the air, too far to fall.

The girl on the drakon's back leaned down, something small and sharp in her hand. A dart of some kind. Before she could stab my forearm with it, I desperately swatted at her hand, knocking the dart from her grasp. She reached for another, but I managed to wrap my fingers around the edge of the drakon's crimson-feathered wing. The drakon let out a squawk of surprise when I yanked downward.

We tilted, falling into a spiral while the drakon tried to fly with only one wing. I clung to the wing, praying that when we crashed the drakon would release me... if it didn't crush me to death.

The ground rushed closer. Branches snapped all around us as we crashed through the canopy. I braced myself for impact, but when we hit the earth, it gave way beneath us. We kept falling.

CHAPTER 18

I BIT BACK A scream as we both plummeted through the ground. Two girls and a drakon landed in a heap on cold stone. While I was still stunned, gasping to restore air to my lungs, the other girl rolled away and drew a knife from her boot.

Her shout echoed through the underground as she threw herself at me. The sound snapped me back to my senses. I brought up my hands in time to catch her wrists and stop her from plunging the knife into my eye, but she was stronger than me and had both gravity and leverage on her side.

I couldn't stop her, so I let the knife fall, twisting my head to the side to avoid the blade. "*Zera,*" she spat as the knife glanced harmlessly off the rock beside my head. She lifted it to strike again.

"If you want to get out of here, you'll keep me alive!" I said hurriedly. The words gave her pause. She studied me, still trapped beneath her, the knife poised over my head.

She leaned forward and pressed the blade against my throat, not hard enough to draw blood, but I could feel the sharp edge digging into my skin. "And why is that?" she said in the staccato Northern accent.

"Because I can find the way back to the surface." I looked up at the jagged hole at least twenty paces above us. Light shone through it, lighting up the girl's golden hair and sharp edges of her face.

She followed my gaze and narrowed her eyes. I knew the same realization passed through her head: The hole was too high to reach, the sheer walls around us too smooth to climb. Her drakon wouldn't be of any use, either, as the cave was too narrow for it to spread its wings.

She removed her knife from my throat and rose. Without her weight on top of me, I could finally take a deep breath. I pushed myself up so I was sitting and watched her warily.

"You know your way out?" she asked skeptically.

"This is my home. I know every crevice of this valley." I held her gaze and prayed to Tyir she wouldn't see through that lie.

A shower of earth raining down on her head distracted her. We both looked up to see Navi peering through the hole, his gold eyes large and worried.

Are you hurt? he asked.

Fine, I replied. *You should stay—*

I didn't get to finish my warning. Navi had crept forward too far, his long neck stretched down through the hole, and the earth around the edges gave way beneath him. He let out a surprised squawk as he tumbled down to join us. Navi landed on top of the other drakon, who hissed and swung a spiked tail at his head in retaliation. He barely managed to duck in time and scrambled away. A growl rumbled in the drakon's throat as it stepped toward him, the red feathers along its spine raised, even though Navi had his head lowered in submission and his ears pinned back against his head.

"Ryn, *nat!*" The girl's command stopped the drakon, though it kept its narrowed eyes on Navi. "*Ayuh,*" the girl breathed out. "Is your drakon as incompetent as you?"

"He's not incompetent!" I said, feeling the need to defend him rather than myself. Yet, at the same time, I found myself suppressing my own irritation at him. If he hadn't fallen in, he could have helped me locate a way out from the other side or gone to find Adann. Now we were all in the same dark hole in the earth with no sense of direction and my life depending on me finding a way out of it.

I got to my feet and brushed dirt off my pants, then glanced from side to side. The cave seemed to continue in both directions, though it quickly disappeared into daunting darkness.

The girl still watched me with an intensity that made my skin prickle. Her blue eyes were the same color as the sky that taunted us through the hole above, freedom so close but so far away. Like the others of her clan, her skin was pale, and her cheeks looked a bit pink from too much time in the sun. She had red and blue beads in her golden braid, along with scarlet feathers from her drakon.

We simply stared at each other until I broke the silence. "If we're going to work together, we should at least know each other's names. I'm Shaya Navi."

She narrowed her eyes. The pause that followed made me think she would decline to answer, but then she said, "Kota Ryn."

Navi crept toward the other drakon, his nostrils twitching, incorrectly thinking a name meant it was safe to approach. Ryn's growl stopped him in his tracks.

"Carefully, little drakon," Kota said, giving my keeper a wicked grin. "She will bite your nose off." She waved a hand toward where sunlight faded into black. "The way out now, valley girl."

I sighed and peered into the darkness again. "That way," I said, picking a direction at random. I wished I had a torch, any way at all to provide light. Even if I could fashion one out of some cloth and sticks that had fallen through the hole, I had no way to light it.

Kota, however, stepped over to her drakon and rummaged through a bag attached to the keeper's saddle until she found a glass bottle full of some viscous, amber liquid. Tree sap, maybe. She kicked aside a few branches that had fallen through the hole with us, finally selecting one of the bigger ones. After kneeling and placing the bottle by her knee, she unlaced the front of the thick leather vest she wore, revealing the shirt made of thinner hide beneath. Kota used her knife to cut a strip off the bottom and wrapped it around the branch. She drizzled the liquid from the bottle over the makeshift torch, but as far as I could tell, she still couldn't light it. Maybe she had flint in that bag of hers.

But instead of going to her bag, Kota crawled over the ground until she crouched next to Ryn's tail. She held the hide-wrapped branch near the wall and stared at it intently, like she expected it to spontaneously burst into flames.

I took an instinctive step away when the drakon raised her spiked tail. Instead of swinging it at me or Navi, she brought it down against the wall, just above the makeshift torch. I stared in amazement as sparks flew from the impact. She had to strike twice more for a spark to catch, but one spark was all it took. The flammable sap coating the strip of hide lit up like dry leaves.

"*Furj*," Kota said as she turned to me with the burning torch in her hand, a self-satisfied smirk on her lips. Navi's awe mixed with my own. He stared at the torch, the fire glinting off his wide golden eyes. Kota snorted at our gawking. "A drakon is wasted on you. Ignorant child."

The feathers along Navi's neck rose as we both bristled at her calling me a *child*. She couldn't be more than sixteen or seventeen, though there was a hardness in her face that made her seem older.

Kota ignored my silent outrage and stepped past me, her torch lighting the way. I followed, letting her lead even though I supposedly was the one who knew the way out.

"This is dreary," Kota muttered after several minutes without a change of scenery. With every step, the torch illuminated more smooth stone walls, probably carved centuries ago by an underground river that no longer flowed this way.

I didn't respond. I was listening to the quiet, searching for any sign of something new. The sound of flowing water, the whisper of wind through the caverns that might show us the way out. I heard nothing but breathing, our own footsteps, and the scrape of claws from the drakons at our backs.

"You really don't talk much, do you?" Kota said.

I didn't take my eyes off the spot where the darkness swallowed the torchlight. I squinted into the void, wishing for some indication we were growing closer to the surface. "I don't like speaking when I have nothing to say."

Kota glanced back and raised an eyebrow. "Maybe you should work on having more to say." I only shrugged in response. She huffed but let us lapse back into silence.

"How much farther, valley girl?" she asked sometime later.

"A few hours at least." I *hoped* we would be out in a few hours. If we happened to make it to the surface faster, all the better.

Kota muttered under her breath, too quiet to hear, but I suspected I wouldn't be able to understand anyway. The syllables I did catch sounded like her own rough language, full of sharp letters and a jagged rhythm. I still found it surprising how easily the Konota words rolled off her tongue.

"You speak Konota well," I said, a question within a statement.

"I speak many languages. My father said understanding your enemies helps you defeat them, and speaking their language helps you understand them." She stepped over a chunk of rock that had fallen from the ceiling.

"How many do you know?"

She shot me an annoyed look. "*Sio batii nagai, diso mah.*"

"Which language is that?"

"The words of the Pajair *turahi.* It means 'stop asking questions, valley girl.'"

"You were the one who wanted me to talk."

"I have changed my mind."

I looked down at my feet to hide the faint smile on my lips. I was still wary of her and our shaky alliance, but something about her irritation was almost charming. Even a porcupine was still cute.

When we came to a split in the cave, I glanced to either side, as if I were trying to determine which was the correct path. Both led into identical darkness, ominous yet beckoning me forward, into the unknown. Even if I knew a spot above ground where the cave system let out, I wouldn't be able to navigate my way there. I had no way to orient myself, no idea which direction pointed toward Mount Tyir and which to the valley.

I gave a small nod, pretending to make up my mind, and strode down the left tunnel with fake confidence. Kota followed, but I swore I could feel her eyes on my back, studying and judging.

The walls around us gradually narrowed, the roof sloping downward, until I had to duck to avoid hitting my head. Navi and Ryn walked with their necks held low, the feathers along their backs a finger's breadth away from brushing the top of the tunnel.

I started to worry the cave might dead end or narrow so much we wouldn't fit through. Even if Kota and I could, the drakons would be trapped. Maybe we should have turned back, but doing so would have been admitting that I had chosen the wrong direction. It meant revealing that I had no map of the caves in my mind, and therefore no reason for Kota to keep me alive.

I pressed forward, following my own shadow that was cast by the torchlight behind me. I had no choice but to pray to Tyir for a miracle.

Chapter 19

IT WASN'T LONG BEFORE hunger started to gnaw at my stomach. I hadn't eaten since my quick meal in the forest with Adann, and I wondered if my unwilling companion had any food stashed away in her saddle bag. If she did, she didn't bring it out for herself. I was stuck warring between the desire to fill my disgruntled belly and the aversion to asking.

In the end, I didn't have to make a decision. The narrowing tunnel finally opened into a vast cavern with jagged spikes jutting from the ground and ceiling like massive teeth. The stalactites above us looked precarious, deadly stone icicles poised to fall on our heads. I kept my eye on them as we passed beneath until I spotted something growing beside a small pool of water in Kota's flickering torchlight.

I eagerly knelt down beside the patch of pine mushrooms. The multi-tiered, fanned out caps and brown color made them look like pine cones, and I had seen them growing in denser parts of the forest. Their tough texture placed them low on the list for foraging, but they were still edible and would fill my aching stomach.

"What is that?" Kota asked. She kept her distance, looking down at the fungus with her nose wrinkled.

"Food." I pressed my hands into the patch of soil and dug out several mushrooms. Rainwater must have dripped down from above, creating the pool and bringing with it bits of soil. I bit into one of the mushrooms, trying not to make a face at the texture, then offered one to Kota.

"I'm not eating that," she said flatly.

I tossed a few mushrooms to Navi, who eyed them with about as much enthusiasm as Kota before he snatched them up. I ate the other half of my own and straightened from my crouch. "Unless you have food in that magic bag of yours, you might want to," I said. "Who knows how long we'll be down here?"

"I thought you did." She narrowed her eyes at me, her irises darker in the torchlight. "You said you knew the way out. Are we close or not?"

I had trouble swallowing the next bite of mushroom. "Right. Of course." My mind raced for some explanation for my slip. "I know where to go, but I don't know how far exactly. It's not like we played down in these caves."

Kota moved so fast I couldn't react before I found myself shoved up against a thick stalagmite. She had dropped the torch carelessly close to the pool that would have extinguished our only source of light. Navi's cry echoed through the cavern, but Ryn's larger form blocked his path to me.

"You don't actually know how to get out of here, do you?" She had the front of my shirt clenched in her fists, her face a mere three fingers-width from mine. I could only see half her face in the light from the torch, but one eye was all I needed to see the murderous intent.

"Of course I do," I said, but the lie was weaker now. I was stumbling around blind, and Kota had finally caught on.

"*Furj vund kuvar,*" she hissed in her harsh tongue. "I should never have trusted a weak, mewling valley girl. You've probably led us to our deaths."

I wanted to snap back, to tell her she couldn't have done any better, but the retort died on my tongue. What if I *had* led us to our deaths? We might never get out of here. I would never see my family again. I would never prove my worth to my people, or see Adann and Ayla's wedding. And Makai... I shouldn't be thinking of him, but what I wouldn't give to see his smile.

Her grip loosened when she reached for her knife, so I seized the opportunity to twist out of her grasp. I staggered away, trampling over the precious mushrooms and barely managing to avoid splashing through the pool.

"You don't have to do this," I said. "We can still find out way out. Together."

Kota replied with a long string of words that sounded a lot like an insult, but then everything in their language sounded like an insult to me. When she lunged, I dodged to the side, dancing around behind another stalagmite. I might not have been a skilled fighter, but I was faster than her, a little mouse darting from one safe spot to another. Somewhere nearby, I could hear claws scraping against stone, growls and hisses from the drakons as they fought their own duel.

Eventually, our dance brought us out of range of the torch-light. Unable to see my surroundings, I had to move blindly through the cavern, my hands feeling for obstacles, but I couldn't feel what was too low to the ground. My heel caught on something as I took a step back, and I found myself falling through darkness. My shoulder blades struck the hard ground first, causing pain to shoot through my arms. At least I'd avoided cracking my head against stone, a small blessing. Before I could thank Tyir for that, a weight on my stomach forced the air out of my body.

I waited for the knife to fall. Would she slit my throat or stab me through the heart? Or perhaps the darkness would prevent a clean kill, and she would have to strike randomly a few times to get the job done. Either way, I would bleed out on the ground.

Before Kota could end my life, the earth beneath us began to shake. Loose pebbles rattled, and somewhere in the darkness stone crashed against stone. If I had to guess, I would say the roof had one less stalactite.

Thankfully, Kota decided finding somewhere relatively safe was more important than killing the "mewling valley girl." She scrambled off me and her silhouette sprinted toward the vulnerable torch. I rolled to my feet, only to fall back to my knees when the ground shuddered again.

I had never seen Tyir so upset that his anger would rattle the earth.

Before Kota reached the torch, another spike of rock dropped from the ceiling and shattered in front of her. The torch disappeared behind pieces of stone, but the faint glow was still visible. It flickered dangerously, threatening to go out.

Navi, do you see a way out? I asked. I could feel him nearby, even though I couldn't see him. A tunnel might not be any safer than the cavern, but at least we wouldn't have stalactites raining on our heads.

This way. He projected the general direction into my mind, so I felt my way carefully through the cavern while the earth continued to tremble.

Please, Tyir. Stop this, I begged silently. Was it our fighting that had angered him or something else? Maybe it was vain to think the quake had anything to do with me, but I felt it in my soul. I could feel the mountain god's attention as clearly as I felt Navi's presence.

Kota's scream echoed through the cavern. Not the enraged shout from when she attacked me but something else, something full of dismay and anguish.

Against my better judgment, I glanced back. In the light of the torch that still clung perilously to life, I saw Kota on her knees beside her drakon. Two halves of a stalactite lay on the ground beside Ryn's head, and the drakon wasn't moving. Kota tugged at her keeper's ear, screaming something in the Northern language. The drakon didn't stir.

Navi. I didn't have to say more than that. We made our way back toward them, picking our way over fallen rock and between stalagmites.

Kota looked up when we reached them and raised her knife to defend herself, but she hesitated when Navi wrapped his tail around Ryn's neck. He started to drag the unconscious drakon across the ground while Kota pushed from behind. Meanwhile, I went to rescue the torch that somehow remained burning.

Before I could bend down to retrieve it, a chunk of rock—not a stalactite but something much wider—fell from the ceiling and landed on top of the torch. We were plunged into darkness.

I stared in dismay at the spot where I knew the extinguished torch lay beneath stone. *Come on!* Navi said. The torch was lost. I had to get out, lest I suffer the same fate as Ryn. I didn't even know if the drakon was still alive, but I prayed she had survived.

The keeper bond led me back to Navi. I did my best to help drag Ryn toward the exit he had found, though I didn't know how much I contributed, especially since I kept losing my balance each time the ground shook. Most of the stalactites must have fallen by then, because the sound of them shattering had ceased. Instead, I heard something else, something potentially worse than spikes raining down on us.

It sounded like the ceiling itself was splitting in two. The cavern was going to cave in.

"Faster!" I urged, aloud this time so Kota could hear. Navi redoubled his efforts, his muscles straining as we pulled Ryn around an obstacle. We finally reached the opening out of the cavern, just big enough for the drakons to fit through. Navi went first, still dragging Ryn with his tail, while Kota and I helped by pushing.

Kota followed them through ahead of me. I made the mistake of pausing when another quake rippled through the earth. Rock cracked overhead, and though I couldn't see anything but darkness when I looked up, I imagined a jagged line streaking through the ceiling like lightning.

Something grabbed my arm and yanked me into the tunnel a moment before the roof of the cavern collapsed. A shower of rock hit the ground like a series of thunderclaps, so close that I could feel the air move.

The earth gave one last violent shudder and went still.

Only our frightened panting filled the new quiet. I reached out a hand to feel along the pile of rock that now blocked our path back to the cavern, rock that would have crushed me if Kota hadn't pulled me out of the way. I glanced toward where I knew she sat, her heavy breaths revealing her location, even though a shroud of black covered my vision.

"Thank you," I said.

For a long time, her only answer was her breathing, but then she murmured, "You saved my keeper. I am still in your debt, valley girl."

Instead of answering, I got to my feet and discovered the ceiling of the tunnel was high enough that I could stand without hitting my head. I squeezed past Ryn's body, feeling the movement of her chest as I did, and rested my hand on my own keeper's shoulder. Fear still thrummed inside him, mixed with his determination to be brave.

You did good, Navi, I said silently.

We're not safe yet, he replied.

"We need Ryn to wake up," I said to Kota. "Navi can't drag her much farther."

"I know." The heat in her voice had gone, replaced by a weariness that I felt in my soul. I preferred the anger. I heard her move, shifting closer to the drakon. "Ryn," she murmured. "*Deliy, vis.*" She repeated the unfamiliar words, louder this time. I think she shook Ryn's shoulder as well, because I felt the subtle movement of the drakon's body.

Ryn didn't respond.

Kota made a strangled sound. I slid down Navi's side until I hit the cold ground. What would we do if Ryn didn't wake? Losing your keeper was the unthinkable, the worst possible fate. I felt untethered just thinking about it, so I chose to believe the drakon would be fine. She was still breathing. That was a good sign.

"We should get some rest while we wait." I thought I could close my eyes and pass out for a full day, despite the uncomfortable stone beneath me.

Kota's breathing slowed into steady, measured inhales and exhales as she tried to calm herself. I had closed my eyes and was halfway to unconsciousness when she spoke. "You still have some of those mushrooms?"

I slid my pack off and dug out the handful of mushrooms I had stashed there. I reached across Ryn until my hand brushed Kota, and I felt her fingers curl around the mushrooms in my palm.

"Thanks," she muttered.

"You're welcome," I said back, my voice as soft as a summer breeze.

I don't know how long I slept, but waking up was an unpleasant experience. My body was numb from the cold ground, despite Navi's warmth beside me, and I felt disoriented waking to pure darkness. Navi lifted his head when I groaned softly, his concern flooding my mind.

I'm fine, I told him, even though my body strongly disagreed. "Kota?" I said aloud.

"I'm awake," came her quiet response.

"Ryn?"

"Still out."

I tried to work the stiffness out of my muscles while we waited and found myself wishing I had eaten more than a couple mushrooms. Hunger gnawed at Navi's stomach as well. My waterskins were almost empty. If we didn't find our way out of this soon, we would die from thirst or hunger.

Finally, the drakon stirred. Her head lifted, and she let out a tired, bird-like trill. My shoulders sagged with relief.

"We have to go," I said once Ryn proved she could remain steady on her feet.

"Why?" Kota asked in a despondent tone that sounded so wrong coming from her. "You don't really know the way out. We don't have light anymore. We are trapped."

"I'm not giving up until I'm dead," I said. "Follow or don't, it's your choice. Come on, Navi."

I started walking, one hand on Navi's shoulder and the other sliding against the wall of the cave. After a few steps, I heard the unmistakable sound of Kota and Ryn following. I tried to hold onto hope, but Kota's despair dragged at me too. I could feel the darkness pressing against my eyes like something solid, a tangible substance rather than the absence of light.

With every step I grew wearier, until Navi's excitement cut through my exhaustion. *Shaya,* he said eagerly. My human nose couldn't pick up what he smelled, but I knew he had scented something other than dank cave walls. Fresh air.

Ahead, I saw the first pinprick of something new, a lonely star in a black night sky. An opening in the tunnel far ahead of us.

Daylight.

Chapter 20

IT WAS DAWN WHEN we emerged from the caves.

The tunnel opened out a few paces from a rocky cliff, not unlike the one I had almost fallen to my death from during my Crossing. It looked out over the valley, and to the east... the rising sun. A faint glow crept up the valley in an arced line as the sun peeked out. The light glinted off the river that snaked through the valley until it reached the waterfall, where it plunged into the gorge below. I could see the village next to the lake and the patchwork crop fields beyond it.

It was beautiful, and it called up a familiar longing in my heart, that same feeling I'd gotten when I looked out at the northern mountains from the peak of Mount Tyir. I knew there was a whole world out there. Right now I could only see my tiny slice of it. The valley was home, but the more time that passed since my Crossing, the less I felt like I belonged there.

Kota stepped past me and walked toward the cliff. Her keeper trailed behind, but Navi and I stayed by the mouth of the cave. While Kota settled on the ground, her legs dangling over the edge of the cliff, Ryn lifted her head toward the sky and let out a low-pitched call. A sound of celebration, I thought, that we had survived long enough to return to the surface.

Kota glanced over her shoulder. "Come here."

I didn't move. "Are you going to push me off the cliff?"

She snorted with laughter. "Don't be ridiculous. If I wanted you dead, there are easier ways."

I thought about pointing out that she had tried to kill me twice. It was only by my own quick thinking and the blessing of Tyir that I had escaped. Though the earthquake had nearly killed us, in a way it had also saved me. Something had changed in her since then, though. She didn't watch me like a predator waiting for her moment to strike anymore.

Warily, I continued to the edge and sat down, keeping a full pace between us.

She watched me with a faintly amused look, then rolled her eyes and leaned back, her palms braced against the ground behind her. "You don't have to be afraid, you know. You could be one of us, if you wanted. A drakon warrior."

"A what?"

"That's right. Your clan does not have warriors. Fighters. You have hunters and builders and farmers. We have warriors."

I mouthed the strange word. The Konota had no need for a guild of fighters, but it seemed like that was the purpose of Kota's people. "But how do you get food?" I asked. "Who builds your homes?"

"Our *sevan*—lessers—can hunt and gather," she said. "We have no need for your stationary huts. The people of the North are nomads. We don't stay in one place long, and when we have need for something, we move on. And we take it."

We take it. Was that what they intended to do here? Take from us what was ours.

"Drakon-souled are born to be warriors," Kota went on. "Your keeper marks your birthright. You could join us."

I shook my head. "I don't want to be one of you. I am Konota." I wished the words had more force behind them. I wished I truly believed them. *I am Konota.* But I hadn't felt like it for a long time.

Kota raised an eyebrow. "You want to belong to a people who mock and fear you?"

"How do you know they fear me?"

She shifted closer to me, her strange eyes intent. They were pretty, in their unique way, darker toward the edges with lighter streaks closer to the pupil. Bluer than a clear sky. The oddity of her irises captivated me until her voice broke the spell.

"I guessed." She shrugged and leaned away, seemingly unaware of my temporary fascination with her eyes. "People are afraid of the unknown. Things that are different, that they don't understand. It's human nature."

It hurt how on target her words struck. The moment I returned to the village with Navi, people had looked at us with fear and mistrust. Maybe some were coming around, or at least pretending too, but Kota was right. She had very neatly pointed out my worst fear. What if they never accepted me?

Her self-satisfied smirk chased away any possibility I might openly agree with her. I scowled at the colors painted across the sky, unable to admire the beauty because I couldn't stop the conflicting thoughts and feelings rushing through my head.

Navi pressed his shoulder against my back. Comforting me, grounding me. The torrent of confusion dissipated. I stared at my hands, my fingers laced together in my lap, but a peal of warning from Navi made me look up at Kota again. The warrior had scooted closer, inside the space I reserved for the people

I loved. I eyed her, uncertain if scrambling away was a sign of weakness. Uncertain if I even cared.

"Warriors fight for what they want, valley girl," she said. "You can't wait for them to *give* it to you. You take it. Respect isn't given, it is earned."

Was that what I was doing, waiting around for the Konota to respect and accept me? Maybe, but Kota was wrong. I couldn't force them to want me.

She still watched me intently when the rising sun hit her hair. The morning light turned it into sunshine itself, a glowing streak woven with red and blue. It made her look even fiercer, a warrior of the sun.

I lowered my eyes, as if her light were too much to bear. "I know where I belong." I sounded so feeble and defeated. Even looking down, I could feel her staring at me like she could see right into my thoughts. It didn't take much to see past my flimsy denial.

We lapsed into silence as the sun climbed higher, the bands of color fading into blue, until I worked up the courage to ask the question that prickled at me. "If you take what you want, why hasn't the clan attacked yet?"

Kota's lip curled, a flash of disdain I didn't think she meant to show. "Rajik is cautious. He would rather intimidate his enemies into surrender than risk warrior lives in an attack. My father would have called him a coward. Eilzar—our chief before him—would have burned your village to the ground by now."

I doubted any warrior would lose their life fighting the villagers. Perhaps I should have had more faith in my people, but that first mock attack had proved as much.

She looked back at the last traces of the sunrise, a wistful expression crossing her face. "My father always knew the best places to watch the sunrise," she murmured. I wondered if she even intended me to hear. Were the words for herself, secret thoughts that accidentally slipped past her lips? The opposite of my problem.

"Knew?"

She let out a slow breath, and I expected her to deflect the question. She didn't seem like the type to open up. Her guard was down, though, the same way mine had fallen, letting my doubt seep in. I had the sudden urge to place a reassuring hand on her arm but restrained myself. We weren't friends. She was still my enemy, one of the people who planned to conquer my valley.

"My father was a warrior." She glanced over at me before her eyes darted away. Uncertainty radiated from her. "He died in combat two years before my *Jurian*. My Trial—what you call the Crossing. He was a great warrior, respected by the clan. Maybe even our leader someday, if he hadn't died."

"I'm sorry," I murmured. I had been trying to ignore it, but the crushing knowledge that my mother was going to die lingered at the back of my mind. How much longer did she have to live? If her current existence even counted as living. What would I do when I lost her for good? If I lost Papa or Ayla. My family meant everything to me.

Kota shrugged and tilted her face toward the sun. "It happens," she said. "The life of a warrior. I always wanted to be like him, to become a warrior too. When he died, I knew I *had* to. Either I would complete my Trial with a drakon at my side, or I wouldn't return at all. I would wield his sword as my own and carry his legacy."

In that moment, I realized we *weren't* enemies. We were two girls, barely of age, drowning in the pressure and self-doubt the world forced on us. She only wanted acceptance from her clan the same way I longed for the Konota to accept me. The reason for her arrogance and defensiveness became so clear that a piece of my heart broke for her. "That's a lot of pressure to put on yourself."

"Haven't you ever had anything you wanted so much, you'd do anything to get it?"

I ran my thumb along the line of my other palm, my nail sliding across my skin. It was a far too personal question, and she knew that.

Before I could decide whether or not to answer, rustling behind us made Navi's feathers stand on end. I pulled my legs up and spun around to find three warriors and their drakons emerge from the forest.

I glanced at Kota, my eyes wide. She rose calmly and turned to face them.

"You called them," I said softly, thinking back to Ryn's call. I thought it had been a sound of joy, but now I realized it was a signal to summon the others. "I thought..." What had I thought? That she would let me go? She had said she was in my debt, but clearly that didn't mean much.

I recognized the chief at the front, with his multi-colored beads and his massive black drakon at his side. Kota bowed her head to him and said, "I have captured the girl with the drakon."

He said something in their language. Surprise flickered across Kota's face, and there was a certain urgency in her reply. His expression grew irritated, but it faded into something pensive as he considered Kota, then me.

"My name is Rajik Brax, chief of the Drak Clan," he said to me. "I had decided you were too much of a threat to live, but Kota tells me you have potential as a warrior." He looked back at Kota and his pale eyes narrowed. "You have two days to prove you can turn her to our side, to prove she can be useful. I hope for your sake that this valley girl is not a waste of your time."

Kota's jaw clenched at what sounded to me like a threat, but she didn't respond. After that, a warrior bound my hands with a rough rope and used a second, longer piece to tie Navi to Ryn. I struggled against Kota when she tried to help me onto Navi's back, but she grabbed my arms, her fingers digging in hard enough to hurt.

"Stop it," she hissed in my ear. "I am saving your life. You will thank me later."

I think she believed it, but I wasn't so sure. I stopped fighting her, at least, realizing the futility of my situation.

"You can take off now," Kota said, once she had settled into Ryn's saddle.

I hunched closer to Navi's neck and braced myself for the coming ridicule. "Navi doesn't know how to fly."

My words were met with snickers from the other warriors, but Kota only breathed out an exasperated "*Ayuh!*" and urged Ryn into a walk. Navi followed, his ears drooping and his tail dragging, the spikes drawing lines in the dirt behind us.

I had survived the underground, only to end up a prisoner. I didn't know much, but I knew for certain that I would never betray my people. Sooner or later, Rajik would realize this and decide my existence brought only trouble.

CHAPTER 21

A LOUD CRASH JARRED me from my sleep, followed by an enraged snarl from Navi. I opened my eyes, disoriented until my reality settled back over me. I was in the enemy's camp, a prisoner. When we had arrived, they had forced me into a wooden cage, Navi into a larger one beside it. They had left me with nothing but the hard ground to sleep on, not even blankets to keep me warm.

Kota looked down at me from the other side of the wooden bars, her golden hair shining in the sunlight. She held one of those long blades in her hand, and I realized the sound that woke me must have been the weapon slamming into the bars.

"It's time to begin your training, valley girl," she said.

I sat up, while Navi turned in a restless circle inside his cage.

"He can come out when I can trust you not to do something stupid," Kota said. "Incentive to gain my trust, eh?" She unlatched the door of the cage and swung it open. When I didn't move, her expression grew impatient. "*Kuvar'i Zera.* I don't have all day! Get up!" I still didn't move, not until she slapped the bars again with the big knife, which sent me scurrying out.

I looked around as I straightened, automatically searching for an escape, but I knew it was hopeless. They knew it was hopeless. Several drakons and their humans moved about the camp. Even if I could sneak past all of them, I would never leave without Navi.

A sharp whistle drew my attention back to Kota. I jumped out of the way when she threw something in my direction, and a second big knife landed in the dirt where I'd been standing.

"Pick it up," Kota said.

It wasn't a request, so I crouched and wrapped my fingers around the handle. Now that I held it, I realized just how big it was—as long as my arm, the blade three fingers wide except where it tapered to a point. It was lighter than it looked, but the weight of the weapon still pulled my arm around when I moved it experimentally. It felt like it controlled me more than the other way around.

"That's a sword," Kota said in a patronizing tone.

Sword. Like the other unfamiliar words she had shared, I mouthed it silently. I was still staring at the weapon when something flashed in the corner of my vision. I cried out and stumbled backward, narrowly avoiding the sword Kota swung at me. It cut the air barely a finger-width away from my nose. I collided with Navi's cage, the only thing that kept me from falling to the dirt, and my shoulder hit one of the poles hard enough that it sent a twinge through my arm.

I stared at Kota in disbelief. She returned a wicked grin. This wasn't the girl I had sat beside in the light of the rising sun. It wasn't the girl who had thanked me for saving her keeper's life. This was the warrior who had attacked me and then taken me prisoner.

"Got to stay on your toes, valley girl. Don't take your eyes away from the enemy."

I pushed away from the cage, an unfamiliar sensation blooming in my chest. My face felt hot, and my heart pounded with something more than surprise-induced adrenaline. "You could have cut me!"

"Eh, it would've healed," she said, shrugging. "Besides, every warrior could use a nice scar." She flicked the tip of her sword upward and gave mine a pointed look.

Gritting my teeth, I took the hilt in both hands and raised the huge blade. When she swung again, I brought the sword up to block the blow, but I wasn't prepared for the force of it. Pain vibrated down my arms. The impact threw me off-balance, as well as almost knocking my own weapon right into my face. I stumbled again, and this time I cracked my head against the edge of the cage.

Stunned, I dropped the sword and slumped to the ground, one hand pressed against the back of my head. Navi let out a high-pitched trill of distress.

A shadow fell over my face as Kota stepped up to me. The sun behind her outlined her form like some kind of dark spirit, a soulstealer come to devour my soul. She leveled the tip of her sword at my throat. "You'll have to do better than that if you want to stay alive," she said, her lip curled in disgust. "You're as bumbling as a stupid, fat bee who can't fly straight."

I lowered my head, letting my hair fall into my face, but the curtain couldn't hide my shame. I didn't even want to learn to fight and kill like they did, but I hated the derision on her face. It was the same look Eldin and Pashir gave me. Like I was worthless. Like I was nothing.

"On your feet, valley girl." Kota nudged my leg with her foot. *Kicked* might be more accurate.

I lifted my chin and reached for my dropped sword. I grabbed the hilt and stood, immediately off-balance as I lifted the weapon.

"Again," Kota said.

It went on like that as the sun climbed toward midday, until my arms ached, though not as much as my pride. After a quick meal break, we resumed what I could only describe as torture. I didn't think I would be able to sleep that night, but by the end of our training sessions, I was so exhausted I passed out despite the hard ground beneath me.

The next day we did it all over again.

As Kota repeatedly disarmed me with sword and insults, I kept wondering if someone would come rescue me, but I knew it was a fool's hope. They probably assumed I was dead. Even if they did decide to rescue me, they would be woefully out-matched. I was on my own.

The only thing my wistful thoughts accomplished was dis-tracting me. Kota knocked me to the ground—again, this time by darting behind me and buckling my knees with a solid kick.

"*Ayuh*," she huffed. "I'm starting to wonder if Rajik was wrong about you posing a threat to us. And now I'm the one who is going to pay for trying to save you."

She circled me and kicked my fallen sword back to me. "On your feet, bumblebee."

I might have preferred "valley girl."

Again and again I tried and failed to defend myself. She gave me tips on my stance to keep my balance and how to wield the unfamiliar weapon, but it made no difference. I narrowly avoided several scars she seemed to think would somehow turn me into a better warrior. I had at least gotten to the point where the weight of the sword didn't drag me around, but I was still hopeless blocking any of her attacks.

I knew I had only been escaping the tip of her blade because she *let* me, but it seemed Kota had gotten bored with playing nice. When the point of the sword burned across my cheek, I dropped my own weapon and pressed my hand over the stinging wound.

"You get cut and your instinct is to drop your sword?" Incredulous was an understatement. "Gods, bumblebee. You wouldn't last a day in the North."

I grimaced at the blood on my hand, then looked up at her. "Do you miss the North?"

Kota's body tensed, her shoulders hunching forward. I hadn't seen her so vulnerable and guarded since the caves. Instead of snapping at me to mind my own business, she nodded. "It's colder there. But the sun... it's warmer. I miss sitting in the chilly mornings with the sun on my face. The sky is somehow *bluer* there. At least... it was."

There was something ominous in her voice and the way she averted her eyes. She looked guilty, like she had revealed something meant to be kept a secret. "Kota... why did the clan leave the North?"

She hesitated. The words tumbled out after another moment, like she couldn't contain them. "A new chief came to power in another clan. He wanted to rule not only his own clan but the entire North. As the most powerful clan in the North, we were one of his main targets. He wanted Rajik to submit to his will—or die. So we left."

I bent down to retrieve my sword but kept the tip resting on the ground. "If you were so powerful, why did you run?" I didn't mean the question as an insult, but Kota's face darkened.

"Because Rajik is a coward," she spat. "But Rajik wasn't the only one afraid. This other chief was rumored to have the gods' will on his side. Ridiculous, of course, but they did have weapons we had never seen before. When they attacked us, we lost more than a few warriors." Something haunted entered her eyes as she stared into the distance. Remembering.

The look vanished when she returned her gaze to me. "If that weren't bad enough, one survivor came to us with stories of *kuvar* killing his whole clan, a mountain exploding and fire raining from the sky."

"You've used that word... *kuvar.*" Before, it had sounded like a curse.

"It means 'fury.' Specifically, the fury of the gods, but my people use it to refer to disasters. *Natural* disasters. Not the gods destroying whole clans so some power-hungry chief can conquer the North."

I turned my head to look toward Mount Tyir. "Maybe it was the gods." When Kota scoffed, I asked, "What, you don't believe the gods could rain fire from the sky if they were angry? You saw how Tyir shook the earth."

"The gods are stories to scare children," she replied. "Either that or the gods are *always* angry in the North. Blizzards, avalanches, flooding. Why would the gods send so many disasters? It's just how the world is."

"If it's so bad, why live there?"

Kota paused to ponder that. "Because it's home," she answered simply. "Because we were raised there. Because facing the fury of nature makes us stronger. You valley folk... you're weak." She raised her sword again and brought it down on my own in a brutal stroke that knocked my weapon out of my hand. "You would be dead your first raid, if the weather didn't get you first."

When we finished our useless training session, Kota finally allowed me to visit a clan healer to get my cheek tended to.

The healer told me it would probably leave a scar, which drew a smirk from Kota and a dismayed look from me.

"See, bee, at least you'll look like a warrior, even if you can't fight like one," Kota said as we left the healer's tent.

"What if I don't want to fight *or* look like a warrior?" I said, frustrated.

"You had better start, if you want to live."

"You and I both know I'm already dead," I replied flatly. "I won't turn against my people."

I thought I saw a flicker of doubt in her eyes, and underneath that, distress. She wanted me to survive this. Merely because I had saved Ryn or for some other reason?

It didn't matter. Soon, I would be nothing more than wasted time.

After that, Kota showed me around camp. She decided to let Navi out of his cage as long as he was tied to Ryn, which gave him an opportunity to stretch his legs—and his wings—instead of being cooped up in a small space.

His pent-up energy showed. He kept trying to get Ryn to play with him, but the other drakon only batted him away with a swipe of her foot or smacked him with her tail. It didn't deter Navi. He would give it a rest for all of thirty seconds before trying again.

As we walked between the tents and regular workers—Kota called them "lessers," those who had some creature other than a drakon as their keeper—I couldn't help thinking about my dwindling time. Rajik had given Kota two days to prove I could be useful to the clan. With the sun sinking toward the horizon, I knew I would die tomorrow, unless I figured a way out of this. Maybe I could pretend to betray the Konota, like I had pretended to know my way out of the caves. Kota would probably see through the lie, but maybe she wouldn't expose me.

Even if I convinced Rajik, though, I still was useless at fighting.

On our way back to my cage, we passed a warrior with turquoise and yellow beads in his hair. I glanced at Kota's own braid, strung with red and blue. "You all have different colored beads in your hair. What do they mean?" I couldn't explain how I knew they were more than pretty decorations. Maybe it was the fact that Rajik's braid was a multitude of color, while younger warriors like Kota only had one or two, if they had any at all.

She raised an eyebrow at me. I couldn't tell if she was surprised I had asked, or if she was judging me for taking this long to do it. "They're tokens," she said. "Warriors have to earn them by displaying certain traits. Red for courage, black for strength, yellow for intelligence, turquoise for leadership, purple for determination, and blue for loyalty."

I had seen all of the colors in Rajik's hair, along with the black feathers of his drakon. "So... you've proven yourself courageous and loyal," I said.

Kota nodded, the hint of a smirk returning to her face. "And I've only been a warrior for a year. It's rare for someone so young to have two tokens."

And there was the Kota I had first met. She seemed to swing from pensive and insightful to confident and smug. It was like talking to two different people, depending on the day. Or the hour. I didn't know what to make of her, nor did I know how far she would go to repay her debt to me.

I desperately wanted to trust her to help me, but I knew I couldn't rely on her. As I crawled back into the cage where I would spend the night, I intentionally bumped against her leg.

"Clumsy bumblebee," she muttered as she locked the door. She hadn't noticed me slide her knife out of its hiding place in her boot.

CHAPTER 22

O N MY LAST DAY to live, Kota woke me before dawn.

She was acting different, more distant, as she let Navi out of his cage and bound him to Ryn. She opened my cage and set off without a word, leaving me to scramble after them.

As soon as we reached the edge of camp, she climbed onto Ryn's back, so I followed suit and pulled myself onto Navi. She tossed me a pouch of berries, keeping a second for herself, and we set off into the forest. I didn't have to ask where we were going. The sun had yet to rise and we were headed in the right direction, so I rode beside her in silence, eating my breakfast.

Kota had uncanny timing. Only a few moments after we sat on the edge of the cliff, the first spot of light appeared on the horizon. I knew she was thinking about her father as she stared at the colors that slowly filled the sky, and my heart ached for her loss.

We watched the sunrise quietly, not speaking or even looking at each other. Sitting there with Kota was the first true tranquility I had known in a while. Even sitting by the lake with Makai had been rife with grief, but something about the sunrise melted my worries away.

At least if this was my last day to live, I could die having found some peace first.

Navi rested his head on my knee and gave a soft chirp. I felt his apology but adamantly dismissed it. None of this was his fault, even if it had started with him. The clan still would have come to the valley even if I had a different keeper, and being different had started long before I had bonded with him.

He hadn't changed anything except to make me whole.

"Do you believe the stories?" I asked suddenly. "About… people being fated to find their one true keeper."

Kota glanced at me, her face skeptical. "Why?"

"It's just… odd, isn't it?" I asked. "That a valley girl would find a drakon?"

"And you think that *proves* fate? If anything, it shows the bonding is a coincidence. You were together at the right place and the right time." Kota rolled her eyes. "If I had followed the rules of my Trial, I would never have been near Ryn. I only bonded with a drakon because I specifically went to their nesting cliffs. There's no such thing as fate, bee. It's all circumstance."

"But what if it was fate that led you down that path?"

She snorted. "If that's your logic, you can explain anything by fate."

And that was the point, I supposed. Anything could be used as evidence for or against fate, which meant all you had left was what you believed. Looking at Navi, I believed, even if Kota didn't. I couldn't imagine having a different keeper. I had always been meant for this path, even if it wasn't one I wanted. I wouldn't trade Navi, not even to change everything that had happened since my Crossing. Not even to save myself.

Kota gave her head a shake before shifting and reaching into her pocket. "Take this." She pulled out a long, curved claw with a hole drilled through the top so a thin cord could be threaded through it. "It's one of Zeel's claws... my father's drakon. Sometimes we'll keep talismans like this, to remind us of our loved ones."

"Or as trophies from your victories." I knew the various talismans hanging from Rajik's neck weren't to keep his loved ones close. The way Kota glanced away confirmed my suspicion. It also made me think I was getting to her, making her see that not all of her people's ways were *right.* Yes, the North was a harsh place to live, but did that mean they had to be so cruel? "Why are you giving this to me? I thought... well, I thought you would want to keep it." And if Rajik made good on his threat, I would have no use for it after today.

"To remind you of who you are," she said. "And where you belong."

Kota's blue gaze was steady. I broke eye contact first, my heart sinking painfully in my chest. "I really appreciate it, but I can't accept this. I don't belong here."

"Because you belong with *them?*" Kota demanded. "What do you have to return to?"

"A lot. My family, friends..." I faltered, because I didn't really have any friends, and the lie was too obvious. Perhaps Makai's friends could have been mine, if I hadn't realized they weren't the type of people I wanted to be friends with.

"A boy?" Kota asked, smirking.

Heat flooded my face, and Kota's eyes widened as her smirk turned to surprise. She hadn't expected to be right. "It's not like that," I said quickly. "He's not who I thought he was."

"Oh, *vis'ik.* Your face looks like the sunrise." Kota bumped her shoulder against mine and nodded toward the sky. "How bad could he be?"

"It's not just that..." I trailed off, unsure how to explain myself. The more I learned about Makai, the more I doubted my feelings, but it wasn't only my feelings about *him* that left me floundering in my own uncertainty. "I'm not who I thought I was. How can I love someone else if I don't even know who *I* am?"

She laughed, but her mirth faded when my expression remained meek. "If you have something special, isn't it worth it to try? I've never... I've never felt that way about anyone. And no one has ever felt that way about me."

"I find that hard to believe."

She gave me an odd look that I couldn't decipher. "Why's that?"

"Well... you're beautiful. Talented. Smart." Maybe a bit arrogant, but that seemed like a positive trait in their culture.

Kota snorted. "There is one warrior who would love to win my attention, but he's a power-hungry brute. I'm not interested in him. Besides, he doesn't love me. He only wants a trophy. Men like that don't know how to love."

I turned my gaze forward, but the sun had become too bright and I had to drop my eyes. I couldn't speak for Makai's intentions. Though his feelings seemed earnest, I couldn't trust myself to see past his smile. I couldn't think straight when it came to him.

"I'm not sure I know what love is," I murmured.

"Love is sacrifice," Kota replied without hesitation. "Love is giving up everything for another person."

"Love sounds scary, then."

"It is." Kota sighed. "Just keep the claw, okay?"

I let out a slow breath and nodded, unwilling to argue any longer. I knew exactly what I would do with it, if I ever returned home, though I didn't see that happening.

"I have a box at home," I told Kota. "With talismans like this, I suppose. Pieces of the people I care about. Not *literal* pieces," I added quickly, thinking back to Adann's joke and the shriveled ear I had seen on Rajik's necklace. "Symbolic ones. A knife my parents gave me with my name on it, a flower from my sister, a carving my mother made. They're locked away where no one can touch them, in a puzzle box my grandfather made for me."

"You keep them close," Kota said, watching me with her brow furrowed. I didn't know why I was telling her this, either.

I nodded in confirmation. "Under my bed, so they're there whenever I feel alone." And I felt alone a lot, I realized, even with my family sleeping under the same roof. "They're all I have," I said, my voice dropping almost to a whisper.

Her boots scuffed against the ground as she got to her feet. "We should go. Rajik said he wanted to see you this morning."

I pressed my thumb against the sharp point of the claw, hard enough to feel the painful prick. If Kota was giving me this, that meant she thought I still had a chance, right? I rose as well and placed my hand on Navi's side, preparing to remount for the return to the clan's camp.

"When the time comes, just promise me you'll put up more of a fight than that other girl, okay?" Kota said.

I froze halfway into pulling myself onto Navi's back. "What other girl?"

Kota's eyes widened like a child caught stealing sweets. "Never mind that. Let's go."

She gripped Ryn's saddle to haul herself up, but I stalked over and grabbed the collar of her vest. I yanked her backward, eliciting an outraged growl from Ryn. "Kota, *what girl?*"

For the first time ever, Kota looked intimidated. "The valley girl who came too close to the camp. We couldn't let her expose us."

She didn't say it, but I knew. Horror washed over me, bringing with it nausea and disbelief. They couldn't let the girl expose them. So they killed her.

Nahdi.

I felt sick, both at the confirmation that Makai's sister was dead, and the fact that Kota talked about it like... like it didn't *matter.*

I stepped back, my head reeling. Kota watched me, stone-faced, but I thought I saw a trace of something behind the calm exterior. "Can't you see how *wrong* that is? That was someone's daughter, someone's sister! She... she was on her *Crossing.* Doesn't that mean anything to you people?"

"It was for the good of the clan." Her flat tone made it sound like she repeated someone else's words, not something she believed. "It is killed or be killed in the North. You couldn't possibly understand."

No, I couldn't understand. I would *never* understand how someone could murder children, and during their Crossing no less. Was nothing sacred to these people?

"Shaya, please—"

I snatched the stolen knife from where I had stashed it in my boot and threw myself at Kota. With or without swords, I was no match for her, but I had the element of surprise. Before she could defend herself, I slammed the handle of the knife against her skull. *I'm sorry,* I thought as Kota collapsed.

The attack didn't remove Ryn as an obstacle, but it did leave her dazed. I also didn't think she would come after us until Kota recovered. Navi bounded to my side so I could swing myself onto his back, and I slashed the rope around his neck with the knife. Without looking to see if I'd succeeded in knocking out the warrior, we darted into the forest.

The trees were nothing but a blur as Navi raced between them. I closed my eyes, dizzy from the adrenaline and guilt coursing through me. Why should I feel guilty, though? Kota had been holding me prisoner. I didn't owe her anything.

I wished then more than ever that Navi knew how to fly. His desperate sprint was faster than any human could move, but Ryn could take to the sky. If I hadn't knocked Kota unconscious, she could catch us easily. *Faster,* I urged Navi, even though I knew he was already running as fast as he could.

The farther we ran, the more I let myself believe we had done it. Maybe we could escape. We could go home. Then I heard the beat of wings overhead and that fragile hope shattered.

Ryn half-crashed in front of us, landing with a thud that made the earth tremble. Navi skidded to a halt, digging his claws into the ground to avoid a collision, but we stopped far too close to them. Kota hurled herself over Ryn's head and tackled me off Navi's back. The impact left me seeing stars, but I lashed out at her blindly.

"Get off!" The desperate scream came out hoarse and broken. "Let go! I'm going home."

She knocked aside one of my feeble attempts at stabbing her and grabbed my wrist. "*Kuvar'i Zera*, stop yelling! You'll wake all the gods."

Maybe I wanted to wake the gods. Maybe if Tyir heard me, he would send another earthquake.

Kota twisted my wrist in a way that forced me to drop the knife. I couldn't roll over and accept defeat, so I kept flailing my arms in hopes of landing a blow, until Kota pinned my wrists to the ground above my head.

"Gods, bumblebee." Kota's voice was breathless from chasing me down and our recent struggle. I was sure her head still hurt as well. She looked down at me, her blue eyes bright and... was that a smile? "You have guts, I'll give you that. Taking my knife was an interesting choice. A little rash, perhaps. Did you really think I wouldn't notice?"

I glared up at her. "If you knew, why didn't you take it back?"

"Because I was curious what you planned to do with it."

I tried to rip one hand out of her grasp, but Kota didn't budge. Catching her off guard wouldn't happen twice. "You know he's going to kill me," I said. "Why not get it over with?"

"He's not going to kill you."

I didn't understand the certainty in her voice. "You heard him! You know this is all pointless. You'll never turn me into a warrior, and I will *never* join you."

Kota stared at me, her smile gone. I stared back. When the pressure released on my wrists, I didn't move right away, too surprised to do anything but watch as Kota got to her feet. She retrieved the stolen knife and slid it into her boot where it belonged. "Get up, bee. Don't make me tie you up and bring you back at knife point."

The words themselves sounded like an order, but I could have sworn there was an unspoken *please* at the end. That imagined please made me quietly climb onto Navi's back. That please kept me from resisting as Kota reattached my keeper to hers and led us back to the camp, where I was sure certain death awaited me.

CHAPTER 23

THE WARRIORS HAD ASSEMBLED in the center of camp by the time we returned. An agitation rustled through the air—in response to Rajik's anger, if I had to guess. A warrior said something as we approached, and Rajik's head snapped around to glare at us.

"I told you the plan for today," he growled, as if he were a drakon himself, the words rumbling up from his chest. "Why would you take her away from camp?"

The other warriors looked on nervously, but Kota stared back at him without fear. "I had one more lesson to teach."

He held her gaze for another heartbeat before scoffing and turning away. "I'll deal with you later, girl." He faced the gathered warriors and lifted his arms in a grand display. "Today, we decide whether this valley girl has what it takes to be one of us!"

The others booed and sneered in my direction. I gathered only Kota was interested in me joining them. The rest would probably cheer over my lifeless body.

Rajik stepped to his drakon's side and fixed his icy stare on me. "Time to show us what you've managed to learn."

Kota retrieved the sword I had been practicing with, then drew her own from the sheath on Ryn's saddle. I watched her warily, my mind racing. She was going to disarm me in less than a minute, the way she had during our training sessions, and Rajik would know how useless I was. Maybe if I had been given a little more time, but two days of training? I was doomed from the start.

Kota handed the sword to me. I gripped it with both hands, even though it was designed to be wielded with one. The weight still felt unfamiliar, the sword a clumsy extension of my arm. I took a step away from her, mentally preparing myself for the fight and what would follow. How did one prepare themselves for death?

But before the dual could begin, a warrior stepped up to Kota's shoulder. His blond hair had purple and black feathers from his keeper mingling with red and black beads. The beads—I now knew—represented bravery and strength, respectively.

He said something to Kota that I couldn't understand, but I didn't need the meaning of the words to know the gist of them. His tone and the charming smile on his face told me everything. He was probably asking her for a moonlight flight or to watch the sunrise with him. Whatever warriors found romantic. On second thought, maybe he had offered to spar with her. That could very well be their version of wooing.

From her scowl, she didn't share his feelings. This had to be the warrior she had mentioned earlier. She didn't even look at him when she said, "I would sooner eat my sword."

His smile quickly transformed into a sneer. "You would rather spend time with the *valley girl?*" Kota and Rajik always made those two words sound like an insult, but this warrior took it one step further. It sounded like I was dung stuck to the bottom of his boot. "She's just some worthless—"

He reached for me, but Kota moved faster than a striking cobra and grabbed his wrist. He cried out in surprise and pain as she twisted it, spinning him around with his arm bent behind his back.

"If you try to touch her again, Tam, I will break it," she said calmly. I knew she had said his name for my benefit. Or maybe she wanted to spit it out like *he* was dung under *her* boot. She released his wrist and shoved him away hard enough to make him stumble.

He managed to keep his feet under him and twisted around to glower at both of us. "We both know she will be dead within the hour. Valley folk are weak."

"We'll see," Kota murmured. She turned her back on him and nodded for me to take my fighting stance. I did so, falling into a position that at least felt natural, even if the sword didn't.

We stared at each other for a long time. I waited for her to strike, like she had every time we practiced, but Kota was a statue beyond her measured breathing. I tried to get a handle on the fear that coursed through me. I had gotten better in the short time she had trained me. Maybe that was all I needed—to hold my own long enough to show I had potential. My fingers tightened around the sword.

"Get on with it!" one of the warriors hollered.

Kota still didn't move, so I did. I stepped forward, going on the offensive this time instead of desperately defending myself against her attacks. She easily turned her sword to block my swipe, then brought her weapon around in a fluid arc, aiming to slash at my right side.

I found the attack odd. I might still be awkward and slow fighting with the sword, but I had picked up *some* of what she told me. She should have attacked my unguarded left side, where it would have taken more effort on my part to block or dodge. Instead, all I had to do was raise my sword to deflect the blow. I braced for the impact, gripping the hilt tightly so it didn't go flying from my hands, but the attack lacked much power behind it. I knew full well she was stronger than that.

Kota was going easy on me.

She moved a hair slower than normal—not enough to be obvious, but after fending off her much faster attacks, I was able to block her with relative ease. She narrowly avoided my own strikes or barely managed to block them. She cut me once, nothing more than a shallow, tiny nick on my arm. It stung, but not enough to slow me down.

In the end, she disarmed me. Anything else would have been too obvious. A valley girl with so little experience would never beat a fully trained warrior. We faced each other, panting, me empty-handed and Kota's sword leveled at my throat. After a few seconds, she lowered it and turned to Rajik.

Neither of us spoke while Rajik regarded me thoughtfully. We had put on a good show, but would it be enough to fool him and the other warriors? The longer he went without speaking, the more I wanted to scream at him to announce his verdict. If they were going to kill me, I wanted it over with.

When I felt about ready to burst, he said, "I'll admit, you did better than expected. Perhaps Kota is right. Your drakon keeper is a sign from the gods that you belong with the clan."

I highly doubted that Kota had called Navi a "sign from the gods," but she had called being a warrior my birthright.

He stepped closer so he towered over me. I had to tilt my chin up to look him in the face, the broad-shouldered monolith with pale, calculating eyes. "But are you prepared to betray your clan?"

No. I wanted to scream the word back at him in defiance, but I knew it would only result in my death. I tried to keep my voice steady when I said, "I want to be a drakon warrior."

Rajik only grunted in response. He drew a knife as he approached Navi, and a pulse of fear ran through me. Had he seen through my lie? Was he going to kill Navi? My keeper tried to retreat, his ears flattened against his head, but Ryn's tail blocked his path.

"Please, wait—" I stepped forward, but Kota grabbed my arm to hold me back.

"It's okay," she murmured.

Instead of attacking like I feared, Rajik cut the rope that bound Navi and Ryn together. "Here is my offer, valley girl. To-day, you will return to your people. Convince them to surrender. Do this, and you may join us. You will be trained as a proper warrior. I'll even give you the antidote to save your mother's life. If you fail, we will crush your pathetic village. You have five days. I doubt she will live much longer than that."

My stomach fluttered. They did have an antidote.

He knew *exactly* how to manipulate me. I didn't even know if my mother was still alive, but Rajik seemed to think so, if he was offering her life in exchange for my loyalty. I could save her... but the price would be unthinkable. How could I betray the Konota? Surrendering to the clan would mean the Konota would become *sevan*, if they were even allowed to carry the title of "lessers." Perhaps they would be lower than even that.

Or perhaps it was all a trick and Rajik would kill everyone the moment they surrendered.

Kota nudged my arm. She didn't meet my eyes as she handed me my pack, and when I checked the contents I found a water-skin and dried meat, enough for the journey home.

"Five days, valley girl," Rajik said. He turned away and the other warriors dispersed, murmuring amongst themselves. Only Kota remained.

My fingers curled around the straps of the pack. I met Kota's gaze, but only briefly before she looked down at her feet.

"Why did you do that?" I asked.

"What?"

"You know what. You made it seem like I have any promise as a warrior."

Her eyes darted in the direction her chief had gone, then back to me. "There's more to being a warrior than wielding a sword, bee. My father taught me that." She pulled her long braid over her shoulder and brushed her thumb against the blue bead. Loyalty. "Good luck, Shaya Navi. You'll need all of Atu's strength behind you."

I doubted her god would lend me strength, but perhaps mine would. Aside from the earthquake, Tyir had been silent, watching the threat to his beloved valley. Would he intervene when the gathering storm broke?

"It doesn't have to be like this," I said. "You know this is wrong. You can help me stop it."

She averted her eyes and didn't respond. Our fleeting friendship was over.

I let out a resigned sigh before turning my back on her. It wasn't my ears but Navi's that caught Kota's whispered answer: *"But how?"*

CHAPTER 24

W E WASTED NO TIME on the return trip, aside from a few breaks for Navi to eat, drink, and rest. On foot with the other Konota, the journey had taken a full day, but we reached the village before sunset.

I didn't know what they assumed had happened to me. Did they think I was dead? Held prisoner? Or that I had turned against them? The last one hung over me as I made my way through the village. No one ran to greet me. No one cheered my return. Instead, suspicious stares followed me all the way to my family's hut.

I rapped my knuckles against the wood frame. Walking in felt like intruding, even though it was my own home. Or it had been. I wasn't sure that was true anymore. "Papa?" I called. "I need to talk to you."

The long silence that answered me made me fear he was elsewhere, but then an arm batted aside the door flap. Papa swept me into his arms, lifting me off the ground. The scent of lavender clung to his shirt, as if he'd been drenched in it. "You're alive," he murmured. "I thought I had lost you too."

"Papa," I protested weakly. I could hardly breathe in his embrace. Realizing this, he set me down and cupped my face in his hands, wiping the tears off my cheeks. Seeing him almost made me forget everything I wanted to say. Why had I been afraid to enter the hut? I *was* home.

"My beautiful girl," he said. "What happened?"

The villagers that had trailed behind me were now gathered near the hut, keeping their distance but close enough to hear. Before I could answer, Makai stepped into view from between two others. His eyes widened when he saw me, shock transforming into joy as he accepted what he saw. He broke into a run and crashed into me. It wasn't the welcome I had expected after I yelled at him, and I didn't know how to react. Though I was still furious at him for everything, his arms around me still made my heart beat faster.

When I didn't hug him back, Makai released me and stepped away, watching me uncertainly. Had he really expected a happy reunion? Even if I set my conflicted feelings aside, it was difficult to share his excitement with the truth about Nahdi sitting like a lump in my throat. I would have to tell him eventually.

But not yet. I forced myself to turn away and face the crowd, but it still took me some time to find the courage to speak. My eyes scanned the sea of faces. People I had known my whole life, people who hardly knew me at all, except for a few. I finally spotted the two I sought. Adann and Ayla were side by side as they pushed their way to the front of the crowd. Unlike everyone else, they both looked relieved to see me alive, their faces a small spot of dry land among an ocean of hostility and mistrust.

"The clan took me prisoner," I began timidly. "I learned things..." I trailed off, subconsciously shifting closer to my father. The skepticism that stared back at me wasn't an encouraging sight. They wouldn't like what I planned to say. Would they even listen?

You're weak, valley girl. How many times had I heard that from Kota, from the others? *Run back to your weak clan.* They were right, though. We were weak compared to them. There was no point in denying that.

"Go on, Shaya," Adann said. "What did you learn?"

Ayla left Adann's side and came to take my hand. Makai nudged my elbow. He didn't speak, but it let me know he was there for me too. I still didn't know how I felt about him, but his presence provided reassurance anyway. Kota had been wrong. I *did* have people here who cared about me. People who would listen.

"They're never going to agree to peace. I... I've talked to their chief, their people." My voice grew stronger as I went on, until my words rang out over the village with impossible clarity. "This is what they *do*. They want our land, and they aren't afraid to kill us all if we resist. They're going to attack in five days, and we don't stand a chance against them."

"And why should we trust anything you say?" Eldin demanded. Always my first dissenter. "They let her go! She's probably working for them."

"They *want* me to join them, but I won't." I had known this would happen, and I had nothing but my words to convince them. In my experience, words were rarely enough.

"So they let you come back instead of killing you?" Iliya asked. She and Makai's other friends had reached the front of the crowd as well. "Do you really expect us to believe that?"

"Stop, Il. Shaya wouldn't do that!" Makai said, coming to my defense once again. This time, it wasn't enough.

"Of course you would believe her. You're nothing but a love-sick pup padding after her. Open your eyes, Makai! She's one of *them*."

Makai stared at her. His eyes darted to Deira and then Trev, but both studied the ground intently. "You *know* her," he said, frustrated. "She's your friend."

"Come on, Makai." Trev's eyes darted up. While Iliya's whole demeanor was scathing, Trev shifted uncomfortably. "She was never our friend. I know you like her, but Iliya's right. Stop ignoring the signs."

"What *signs*?" Makai sounded desperate now. I had dragged him into my shadow and now he was experiencing the backlash.

"You have a choice to make," Iliya said. She cast a sneer at me before looking back at her so-called friend. "It's the drakon girl or us."

The world was collapsing in on him. I could see it on his face. An impossible choice, one he couldn't make. I wanted to tell him to choose them, to stop being foolish. I wasn't worth losing his friendships over.

I couldn't do it, though. I needed him by my side more than ever, so I made the selfish choice and kept silent. He would have to choose on his own, them or me... and I couldn't stop myself from praying to Tyir it would be me.

Makai shook his head, which apparently was answer enough for Iliya. "Fine. I hope she's worth it."

In a last-ditch effort, he turned to his final friend. Her reluctance was written in the hunch of her shoulders and the way she refused to look at him. "Deira, please."

She took a deep breath and let it out slowly. "I'm sorry. They're right."

He stared after his friends in dismay as Iliya looped her arm through Deira's and the three retreated into the crowd. I knew they would stay close, listening to what would follow, but they had walked away from him. Because of me.

I understood how he felt, but I was done trying to convince the villagers. I turned my back on those who would believe I had betrayed them and fixed my gaze on my father. "They will not make peace, and we can't fight them." I paused, and everyone seemed to pause with me. Waiting. For once, *listening.* "We have to leave."

An uproar of voices followed, shouting in disbelief and anger, but Guildmaster Pashir's rose above the rest. "We can't *leave.* This is our home! Are we really going to entertain the ideas of a near child whose keeper is one of *them*?"

"Leaving is the only way! Please, listen to me. If we fight, they'll kill us all." The clan had faced the same choice in the North. *Submit or die.* Kota had called Rajik a coward for choosing to run, but I understood why he'd done it. Against hopeless odds, you did what you had to in order to survive. Would she call me a coward too, if she knew I was asking my people to do the same?

"Shaya's right." Adann's voice was enough to silence the others, at least temporarily. "Their first attack was a test. They retreated before any of their own even got hurt. We came out of it with several wounded and one still slowly dying."

Beside him, Ayla winced at the unsubtle mention of our mother. It sounded like she was still alive, at least. Not that it mattered, since Rajik wouldn't give me the antidote unless I joined them. I couldn't tell them that part. I had to choose between my mother and the Konota, and no matter how much I loved her, I wouldn't betray my people.

"I don't trust her," Eldin said. "She's not Konota. She's not even part of a guild. She missed her choosing."

The reminder clawed at my insides. With everything that had happened, I had forgotten about that. Inside, I had chosen the hunters, but only because Adann told me to. I had never announced it to the rest of the villagers. Because there hadn't been time or because I didn't really want to?

Adann snorted, though. "It's an arbitrary tradition. It's not like the gods are going to smite her for missing the deadline. She can still pick a guild."

"We can't leave." Guildmaster Belvir put us back on track with an echo of Pashir's protest. "The Konota have been here for generations. Where would we go?"

Anywhere but here, I thought, but it was Adann who answered. "And what else would you have us do? Die in a foolish attempt to defend it? Or perhaps you would ask us to surrender to them."

"Maybe we should surrender," Belvir snapped back.

"I'd rather die than surrender!" Pashir argued. "There's no telling what they'd do to us if we showed our bellies to their spears. They might kill us anyway."

"Enough." My father didn't shout, but his deep voice carried anyway, the single word enough to cease the argument. His eyes were as unfathomable as the face of Tyir. Dread pooled in my stomach. "We will not abandon our home. We will keep trying to settle this peacefully until there is no other choice," he said. "And if it comes to it, we will fight for our valley."

I loved him, but my father was too proud to see the truth. "There *is* no other—"

"Enough!" His voice was like a clap of thunder this time, sharp enough to make me flinch. "There will be no more arguing about this. Remember your place, Shaya Navi. My decision is final."

I could count the number of times I'd heard my father raise his voice on the fingers of one hand. To count the times he'd raised it at *me*, I didn't need any. *Remember your place.* Those cold words made ice creep through my chest. My heart ached, struggling to beat. Remember your place.

I clamped my jaw and didn't speak again.

Chapter 25

I WENT STRAIGHT TO bed, even though the sun hadn't set yet, pausing only to retrieve my box from its hiding place. My throat tightened at the thought of Kota as I pulled the drakon claw from my pocket. I should have gotten rid of it—we *weren't* friends—but I couldn't bring myself to discard it like it meant nothing. Instead, I tucked it inside the box with the other treasures I held close to my heart.

Navi had to squirm his way through the door and lost a few feathers in the process. He climbed up on the bed, practically on top of me, and once again I feared the frame might break. I didn't make him sleep on the floor, though. His presence was a comfort I needed.

"Shaya." My father's voice followed the rustle of the door flap. I could hear the apology inside my name, but I wasn't ready to accept it. I kept my back to him. Navi had his eyes open, his head resting on my hip. I could picture the way his golden eyes glowed in the darkness as he stared down my father.

Eventually, Papa sighed and left the hut, rather than going to his own bed. He still hadn't returned by the time I fell asleep, nor was he home when I woke the next morning.

I had finished getting dressed when the screams started. Too many voices and too far away to make out words, but they were coming from the direction of the lake. After shoving on my boots, I ran out of the hut with Navi on my heels.

When I came down the narrow path, a group of people had already gathered around something on the shore, blocking my view. More and more made their way down from the village to see what the fuss was about. Soon, the entire Konota people would be there—children, adults, and keepers all crammed together on the shore. Makai stood at the edge of the group, trying to peer over someone's shoulder to get a look, but his continued attempts told me he hadn't succeeded yet. Farin was nowhere in sight—off hunting, perhaps.

"Do you know what happened?" I asked as I jogged up to him.

He shook his head. "Someone's dead but I don't know who. I can't see."

My mind immediately jumped to the worst conclusions. What if it was Adann on the other side of this wall of gawkers? What if it was my father? As far as I knew, Papa had never come home last night.

My throat too tight to swallow, I pushed my way forward. Navi squawked in frustration, unable to squeeze through the crowd, the Konota for once too distracted to part around him. But I was small and determined enough to squirm through.

I almost wished I hadn't.

My world stopped as I fell to my knees beside my father. Papa was sprawled out on the shore, face down, his wet hair and clothes clinging to his body. They must have pulled him out of the lake. Dried blood crusted the edges of a tear in the back of his shirt.

They had laid out Honovi's body beside him as well. The wolf looked too skinny, his black fur soaked, seemingly uninjured but unmoving. Papa's lifeforce had been keeping Honovi alive well past the wolf's natural years. With his human gone, he had nothing to sustain him.

"Papa, *no!*" Ayla dropped to the ground beside me, her face distraught and streaked with tears. Her fox sniffed at Papa's wounds, then pressed his nose against a lifeless arm. Ayla bent over the body, her head resting on his shoulder as she cried.

I stared down blankly, my own face dry. This couldn't be happening. *Not him too.* He had been stabbed in the back, killed by someone without a drop of honor in their blood.

"It has to be one of *them,*" someone murmured.

I looked up to find Caldin looking down at me, her eyes empty. Her grief was buried in there somewhere, but Caldin was always the one to hide away those feelings. She never flinched, never gave ground. And she was exactly what we needed right then.

Eldin stood beside her, the one who had spoken a moment before. "We can't wait any longer. We have to strike back."

"We don't know anything for sure," she replied softly. Her eyes never left mine.

"Look at his arms!" Eldin's words drew my attention to my father's arm, to the long gashes that ran across his skin. Too large for a cougar, too neat for a wolf. "He was clearly attacked by a drakon." His eyes fell to me, accusatory and furious. Where Caldin buried her grief, Eldin let his out as rage. "Unless *she* did it."

The accusation was too absurd for me to process right away. I stared back at him, my eyes widening when I realized what he had said. "How could you even—" My voice broke, cutting off my reply.

"Shaya would *never* kill our father," Ayla snapped. She had lifted her head, and while her eyes were red from crying, they were also fierce and filled with outrage. "How *dare* you? Accusing my sister when the real killer is out there in the forest somewhere!"

Eldin blinked, taken aback by her sudden anger. Ayla was the gentle healer, not this. Even Caldin looked surprised. Eldin held up his hands and said, "I was only—"

Ayla stood faster than I thought possible and shoved Eldin hard enough to knock him back a step. "You were only *nothing*. You've hated Shaya since she returned from her Crossing. You should leave unless you have something useful to say."

Eldin continued to gape at her. Before he could either obey or make his next retort, Adann appeared and rested a hand on Caldin's shoulder. "I found something," he murmured to her. His eyes darted to me before he pulled Caldin away. Adann's back was to me as they talked, but I thought he was showing her something. Her glance in my direction made apprehension settle over me, thick enough to smother.

When she stepped past Adann, I saw she carried a knife in her hand, her fingers curled tightly around the handle. Dried blood crusted the double-edged blade. "Attention, everyone!" she shouted.

I hadn't realized how many voices had clamored in the background until they all fell silent. The sound of *nothing* crept under my skin and made me shudder. Caldin still stared at me, her expression as blank as ever.

What? I wanted to scream.

"Adann found the knife that was used to murder our chief." She switched the blade to her other hand, resting it on her palm so she could hold it out for those close enough to see.

I'd thought I had hit the bottom when I saw my father's body, but I'd been wrong, because I was falling again. No one spoke as the realization sunk in, until someone from the back of the crowd shouted, "What? What is it?"

Eldin snatched the knife away from Caldin and held it up so the carving on the leather faced the crowd. I doubted most of them could see it, but Eldin shouted it for all to hear. "The knife belongs to Shaya Navi."

I stared at my name on the leather, carefully carved by my mother. Confusion and disbelief coursed through me. My knife had been used to kill my father. But how? It had been safely tucked away in my box the night before.

Hands seized me from behind. I didn't know who and I didn't bother to look. I shook my head slowly, my eyes pleading with Adann, but his face was a muddied mess of emotions.

"You don't know that." Makai had made it to the front of the crowd finally. Farin perched on his shoulder now, his feathers ruffled. "Someone could have carved her name to make her look guilty!"

"No," Ayla said quietly. Confused and reluctant, but not un-certain. A pang ran through me. So soon after defending me, she was going to make it worse. "Our parents gave it to her after her Crossing. It's hers."

Ayla, why? I had so many things I wanted to say, but all of them stuck in my throat. How could I defend myself? How could I say anything that would make them listen? My knife, drakon claw marks on his arms. I couldn't blame her for telling the truth. It was the way she looked at me that squeezed the air out of my chest.

"I knew it," Eldin said. He sounded far too pleased for the circumstances. "She's working for them! They let her return so she could kill our chief."

A ripple of voices came after, each word a knife to my own back. *Traitor. Murderer. Monster.*

"Enough," Caldin said sharply. Everyone fell silent to listen to the Guildmaster. "This situation will be investigated and judgment will be passed once we have enough evidence. In the meantime, we must choose a new chief."

Her eyes fell on me again. I searched for something in them, something to give me hope that she believed me, but Caldin gave nothing away. I looked at the ground, and my next exhale stuttered and stumbled. How could they believe I would do *this*?

"What evidence?" Eldin snapped. "We don't need more evidence than what we already have!" Shouts of agreement echoed his words, and suddenly the fear and grief and dismay snapped together in one unfamiliar emotion—rage.

"He was my *father*, you soulless pile of rat droppings!" I shouted. Something finally broke inside me and I tore away from whoever held me. I took a step toward Eldin, but someone caught my arm and pulled me to the side. Though Adann's hand gripped my arm tightly, the pressure of his fingers wasn't what hurt. It was the way that he stared at the ground, unable to meet my eye. Did *he* believe it too?

All of the fight went out of me. My shoulders slumped, and I think Adann's hand on my arm was the only thing that kept me standing.

"Take her to the pit," Caldin said. "We will deal with her soon."

"I'm sorry," Adann whispered as he pulled me away. I could hear how deeply he meant it. The grief, the regret. I didn't struggle. I couldn't. I had nothing to say and nothing I could do, so I let him lead me away and left my heart behind on the lake shore.

CHAPTER 26

MANY DECADES AGO, THE Konota dug a deep pit in the earth to hold prisoners—traitors, enemies, anyone who posed a danger to the village. It hadn't been used in my lifetime, probably not even in Enzi's. I was the first to set foot on the ground at the bottom in generations when Adann lowered me in.

They had Navi sedated somewhere nearby, probably tied up in case it wore off. Whatever poison they'd used cut me off from his mind. I could still feel him there, in the back of my head, but it felt like he was all the way at the peak of Mount Tyir.

The pit was too deep and the walls too steep to attempt climbing. Even if I could, they had placed a web of strong wooden poles weighed down by stones over the opening. Completely and utterly helpless, I curled up against the wall with my arms hugging my knees. I bowed my head and cried until I was too exhausted to continue.

The villagers mistrusted me already. They would banish me, and they might not even wait for a new chief to make the decision. With no chief to pass official judgment, the Guildmasters could hold a vote. More than half needed to favor my banishment. I hoped that Grandpa Enzi would be on my side, but the rest of them? Mama was still dying in the Healers Hut, unable to speak on my behalf. Belvir and Pashir would vote against me for sure. Caldin... I never knew with Caldin. She had said she owed me a debt, but traitors didn't get to collect. If she believed me to be guilty, it wouldn't matter.

There was nothing I could do, but that didn't stop my mind from desperately searching for an answer. How had someone used my knife to kill my father? Eldin had been right the first time—it had to be someone from the clan. It left only one logical conclusion, and that was Kota. I had told her about the box beneath my bed and the knife inside. Maybe getting me exiled was a last-ditch effort to convince me to join them.

Knowing Kota had betrayed my trust added another shot of hurt on top of everything else. I should never have trusted her in the first place, but I'd thought I had seen something in her. Something different from the others.

But I was wrong. Kota was my enemy, the same as any of them. When she drove that blade into my father's back, she had stabbed my back as well. I didn't know for sure she had wielded the knife, but any involvement was enough.

Telling the Konota this wouldn't change anything, though. They would ask why I had confided in one of the drakon riders, giving enough information to frame me. They already had the killer in their minds. Nothing I said would make a difference.

My father, too, had been wrong. When he gave me that piece of wood, he had said the strongest things could be rebuilt even if they fell. The bond between my family was the strongest thing I'd ever known, but nothing could rebuild what I had lost.

He had been the strongest person I knew, but nothing would bring *him* back.

The morning led to midday, and midday faded into evening and then twilight. Darkness fell over the pit. I had always preferred being alone in the silence, or I thought I had. It wasn't until this moment that I realized I'd never *truly* existed in silence. There was always the sound of distant voices, the wind in the trees or over the grass, the gentle breathing of my family as they slept. I had never known the sound of silence, the complete *nothingness,* but this far in the ground and away from the village, the emptiness pressed against my ears. I found myself holding my breath so even that sound was absent, my eyes closed, fading into the nothing. Maybe it could take me away from here.

I opened my eyes and looked up as a shadow fell over the pit, blocking out what little moonlight filtered through the slats of wood. I couldn't see his face clearly, but I knew his silhouette. Knew the way his hair fell around his face as he crouched at the edge of the pit.

"What are you doing here?" I asked, my voice dead. Had they uncovered anything that pointed to the actual killer? Were they even looking? I prayed he came with good news, but I had sunken too far into my pit of despair to believe it.

"I'm going to help you escape," Makai said, too loudly for those traitorous words. Great Tyir, what if someone heard him?

"Don't be an idiot," I said, making sure to keep my own voice quiet. Just loud enough for him to hear from the edge of the pit.

"I won't let them banish you!" he said. The fierceness in his voice chased away some of the dread. Makai cared. Despite everything, a part of me was still drawn to him. And I hated it.

I shifted, but it did nothing to help. My backside had gone numb hours ago. "Escaping would only assure them I'm guilty."

"But you're *not*! They can't do this."

I blinked up at him. "What makes you so sure? All the proof says otherwise."

"I refuse to believe you would do this."

"Everyone else seems to believe it. Why put blind faith in my words?"

He paused. Though I couldn't see his face clearly, I knew he looked at me with genuine confusion, like he couldn't understand why I would ask that. I could *feel* it. "Because I love you. I'd stand by you through anything. And I know you. I know you wouldn't do this."

For a second, I forgot to breathe. I forgot to think about anything except Makai's words echoing in my mind. *Because I love you.* He'd said it so casually, like that previously unspoken sentiment wasn't a big deal. Part of me wished I could see his face better because I wanted to know how he looked at me in that moment. I wanted to know his eyes when he said he *loved* me.

Again, I reminded myself that I shouldn't care. I didn't love him. My crush was silly and pointless. And Makai didn't love me either, even if he thought he did.

"You don't know me," I said. "Not really."

His confidence never wavered. "But I do. You're not unknowable, Shaya. It only takes someone willing to see past the walls."

And he had managed to do that in a few weeks? *Stupid boy,* I thought. Stupid boy with no sense and a heart that loved blindly.

Then there was me, a stupid girl with a heart that didn't know what it wanted but somehow still wanted him.

"I'm not escaping," I said when I thought something foolish wouldn't slip out. "They'll find the real killer."

"They have your knife, Shaya. They have drakon claw marks on the body." I winced at the words *the body*, like it was nothing more than a corpse. Not my father. "They're not even looking for anyone else."

That ceased my flimsy protests. I didn't know why I bothered arguing against the very words I'd told myself earlier.

I stared across the tiny pit at the crumbling dirt wall. Were they really that afraid of Navi and me? No one seemed to even second guess the "evidence," no one but Makai. Even Ayla... even *Adann* hadn't spoken in my defense. *I'll always be here for you,* he'd said. It seemed in the end, promises meant nothing. Empty words.

"There's no way out anyway," I said. "Do you even have a plan? Where would I go?"

"I can't just..." he started, but I tucked my head into my arms and he trailed off. He was coming to realize the pointlessness. Escaping wouldn't do me any good. Either way, I'd lose my home and my family—what was left of it. I may as well let them banish me.

I felt helpless again. Trapped in a cage with no way out. My soul, which so craved freedom, was destined to remain trapped. By the clan, the Konota, or my own fear. "Go home, Makai," I said. "Before you get caught and they throw you in here too."

Thankfully, he didn't argue this time. His face disappeared, leaving only the night sky. Through one gap, I could see the front half of Etris, the cougar constellation, which brought back distressed thoughts of Adann. I hoped it was the knowledge that there was nothing he could do that kept him away, not that he believed I was guilty. I tried to hold onto that hope, but as the night dragged on, it slipped away piece by piece.

When they came for me the next morning, I didn't bother asking what they had decided, and they didn't bother telling.

The verdict became evident when they handed me a pack. It looked like the one I had taken on my Crossing, only without the hammock attached to the bottom. I didn't have to look inside to know what I would find. A waterskin, flint, and a knife, the blade tucked away where I couldn't reach it until after my banishment. Theoretically, the things I needed to survive after they threw me out of the valley.

No food, no bow, no spear. Just a knife, water, and a way to make fire.

They brought Navi to me as well, his wings bound firmly to his sides with thick ropes. Adann led him by a halter fashioned from more ropes, which held his jaws shut as well. They couldn't completely disable him—there was still his tail and those wicked claws—but Adann didn't look concerned. I was beaten, and therefore so was Navi.

I slid the pack on over my shoulders before they tied my wrists together in front of me. Rena tied the final knot a moment before Makai broke through the group of people chosen to escort me to the Falls.

I tried to turn away before he did anything else stupid, but he threw his arms around me. "Please let me do something," he whispered fiercely. "I can't let this happen without *doing* anything."

I twisted and squirmed until he let me go. The others were watching us, most of them blank-faced, but Eldin wore his typical sneer. "No," I said quietly. "This is happening. And you're going to let it." I gave him a weak smile. "It's okay. None of this is your fault. You'll be fine without me."

"It's *not* okay," he said. "Tahck is dead, you're getting banished, the real killer is still out there, and there's an evil clan threatening us all. Nothing is okay!"

I let out a slow breath. He was right, of course, but there was nothing I could do to comfort Makai or help myself. I was useless. I always had been.

Makai mentioning the clan reminded me of something else, something I needed to tell him before I never saw him again. It didn't change anything, but he still deserved the truth.

"Makai... there's something you need to know."

He eyed me warily. "What?"

"While I was with the clan... someone told me about a girl that got too close to the camp. They couldn't have her expose them." I watched him deflate, his earlier determination to help me escape whisked away like smoke on the wind.

"They killed her, didn't they?"

I gave a small nod. "I'm so sorry."

"That's enough talking," Eldin interrupted.

"Goodbye, Makai," I murmured.

"But I need you." I heard Makai's whispered words as Eldin grabbed my arm and pulled me away, but I didn't acknowledge them.

We set out before the sun was fully above the horizon. It would be a long hike to the Falls, and the party would take their time to conserve energy for the trip back home. There would be no trip back for me.

With my hands tied, navigating the terrain was difficult, but Rena and Eldin flanked me and caught my arm whenever I stumbled. They had Navi surrounded by hunters and their keepers, wolves and cougars that could take down the drakon if he tried to escape. He wouldn't, though. Where was there to escape to? Our fate was sealed. We were Konota no longer.

Adann brought up the rear, but whenever I twisted to catch his eye, Eldin would swat the back of my head. "Eyes forward," he demanded.

We stopped for breaks five times during the trip. My escort broke out food and water for themselves, and while I was gifted a few swallows of water, no one offered me any dried meat or crackers.

The agonizing journey ended when the sun peaked. I could hear the thunder of the waterfall before it came into view. We continued past the Falls, following the gorge for another twenty paces before stopping at the place where my banishment would become official. The location had been carefully selected ages ago as a survivable drop, though as far as I knew, only a handful of people had walked this path. Now I was one of the unfortunate few, joining them in infamy. Would the Konota tell stories of my betrayal for generations to come?

"Shaya Navi." Caldin's strong voice sounded behind me, but I didn't look at her. I stared past the gorge, toward the forest that existed southeast of our once sheltered valley. Beyond the familiar pines and oaks, a stark line cut the land where the forest ended and the Pajair Desert began. I had heard of the people who lived there, as tough and merciless as the land they called home. The Pajairi, formidable fighters—warriors—who worshipped the sun that baked the sands. Directly in front of me, the land stretched out to the southern forests of Payan, also known as Nagnar, where according to the legends the people drank the blood of their enemies. When I turned my head to the west, I could see the plains and beyond that the kingdom of Emirdom.

I would have to make my home somewhere out there. Alone.

"You have been accused of the highest treason, taking the life of our great chief, Tahck Honovi," Caldin said. "The sentence for such a crime is exile, banishment from the Seagar Falls."

Seagar Falls. I had rarely heard it called by the full name. Seagar, the first man to face banishment from the valley. He had done the very thing I stood accused of—killing the chief, in his case in an attempt to seize power for himself. The Falls became a warning to those who would dare betray our people.

No one asked how I pleaded or if I had any words to defend myself. My fate had already been decided. Fervent pleas and desperate explanations would fall on deaf ears. I wouldn't give them the satisfaction of ignoring me.

Eldin cut my hands free, then he and Rena pushed me forward. A few feet away, keepers herded Navi to the edge of the cliff. Chips of rock and clumps of dirt crumbled away from his claws and plummeted into the gorge, soon to be followed by a girl and her keeper.

"Guildmaster... may I speak with her for a moment?"

The sound of his voice was almost enough to bring tears to my eyes, but Adann's face gave nothing away as he approached me. For a second, I dared to hope that he would tell me he believed I was innocent, that somehow he would help me. Instead, he reached into his satchel and pressed a wooden box into my hands.

"I thought you should have something left you care about," he murmured, too quiet for anyone else to hear, not even the keepers.

I looked at the box, at the whorls of the wood and the sliding pieces I knew so well. It looked the same as last time I'd seen it. Unbroken. And lighter.

My eyes flickered up to Adann's face. At first, I thought his expression was sad, but then something hard and callous crept in. Without another word, without warning, he shoved me backward into oblivion.

As I fell, I realized why our ancestors had pitched traitors into this gorge. I had fallen from my place among our people, lost whatever respect and trust I'd once held. Now I was falling from my home, never to return.

Part III: Outcast

Kast'am

Parote

Tōl-gasit

CHAPTER 27

THE TERROR AT THE first few seconds of free-fall faded into a detached weightlessness a moment before I crashed into the river. It felt like breaking through a wall of ice, the solid surface meeting my back before the water gave way and swallowed me whole.

The impact forced the air out of my lungs, so there was no breath to hold as the current swirled me around. I kicked my legs in an attempt to right myself, but I didn't know which way was up or how to fight against the swift water. Even though my arms might have helped, I clutched my box desperately to my chest. I could feel Navi nearby, struggling as well, as both of us were swept away from the Falls.

By mere chance, my face broke the surface. I gasped instinctively, only to be pulled back under so nothing but water flooded my throat. If I didn't get a breath soon, I would drown in this river. Survivable didn't mean *easily* survivable, it seemed. I kicked my legs again, trying to get back to the promise of air, but the current overpowered any attempts to swim.

My back bumped into something steady, not stationary like a rock in the water, but not twisting wildly in the rapids either.

Navi. His strong legs pushed at the water, cutting across the current toward the shore. I couldn't hold onto him with my cold hands still clutching the box, but the force of the river pressed me against his side.

The bank at this section rose a full two heads above the water. I hurled the box up onto land and reached for the edge of the cliff as Navi's claws dug in, holding us from being swept back into the river. My wet fingers slipped on grass and loose earth at first, before I managed to get purchase.

I hauled myself out of the water, gasping and sputtering, but it wasn't my waterlogged body that dragged me down. I lay on the shore with my cheek against the spiky grass, wishing the earth would open up and take me to my early death. What was the point anymore? My father was dead and I couldn't even mourn with the village.

I could picture the events that would transpire after my escort returned home. The proceedings would be even more extravagant than Nahdi's funeral. Silence would reign in the village until sunset, when everyone would feast in his honor. After night fell, they would light the funeral pyre. The Konota would dance and sing and the children would play games in the light of the fire that burned away my father's body so his spirit could freely travel to the next life. All hearts would be filled with a mix of joy and sorrow as everyone celebrated the life of their beloved chief.

Everyone but me.

My eyes burned. Warm tears mixed with the droplets of river water that still clung to my cheeks. Instead of grieving beside my sister, I lay on this bank alone, too angry and betrayed to mourn properly. But I could still hold the silence that paid respect to the father I had lost, whose death I had been blamed for.

Wet feathers brushed my hand. *No, not alone,* I realized. I had Navi with me. No matter what, I would always have Navi with me. He was the other half of my soul, bound to me forever.

I don't know how long I lay there, paralyzed by grief and regret and hopelessness. It could have been hours or a mere handful of minutes.

The sun had dipped behind the western mountain range when I pushed myself onto my hands and knees. It felt like I had a boulder on my back, forcing me down as my whole body trembled with the effort to rise from the ground.

I crawled over to where the box had landed when I threw it. My fingers shook as I brushed them over the damp wood. I was afraid to open it to see the damage. Ayla's flower probably hadn't survived. Adann's river stone was still inside, or so I assumed.

The truth danced at the edge of my mind, but I refused to let it in. Whenever it got too close, I would squeeze my eyes shut and chase it away. I didn't want to think it. I didn't want to *believe.*

But I couldn't hold it off forever.

I felt like I was plummeting again, only this time Navi wouldn't save me and there was no river at the bottom. This time I would shatter against ragged stones. The truth threatened to suffocate me. I'd thought I had felt betrayed when Adann said nothing in my defense. I'd thought it had hurt when I believed Kota had killed my father. That was nothing compared to this.

Only three people had known how to open the box. Me, my father... and Adann.

He must have memorized the combination when he watched me open it. Someone had gotten into it without breaking it. *Why, Adann?* I wanted to scream it at the uncaring cliff, but no one would hear and the river would swallow the echoes. The answer wouldn't make it better anyway.

Navi let out a low, melancholy whine as he rested his head on my knee. He felt my pain as his own, the bitter sting of grief streaked with anger. I leaned against him, longing for whatever comfort I could find, even though nothing was strong enough to hold back the cold creeping through me like frostbite.

What now? Navi asked.

I looked up at the top of the cliff far above us, an impossible barrier blocking our return to the valley. Impossible... except for the girl with a drakon keeper. *We need to go back.*

Despite the ache in my heart and the lingering hopelessness, I felt no hesitation. I couldn't walk away and let Adann go unpunished. Worse, I had no idea why he had killed my father or what he planned to do next. There had to be a reason.

I had no choice. I had to go back to the place that was no longer my home, carrying with me the fragile hope that someone would believe me.

Makai. I glanced at Navi when he said Makai's name, but the drakon wasn't looking at me. I followed his golden gaze upward to see a falcon soaring above us, a spot of motion in the darkening sky. *Farin?* The thought was simultaneous between us.

A splashing drew my attention to the river, and I scrambled to my feet when an arm broke the surface. "Makai!" I shouted when his head came into view from beneath the river surface.

Without me having to ask, Navi plunged into the water. He swam through the current to reach Makai and guided him back to the bank. I fell to my knees at the waterside, grabbing Makai's arm to help pull him up, then sat back on my heels to stare at him as water streamed down his face and from his hair.

"What are you doing here? Are you insane?"

Even after his attempt to break me out, even after his confession of love, I never expected him to do *this*. Following me into exile was easily the dumbest thing he'd done, and Makai was an expert at making dumb decisions.

Once he caught his breath, he lifted his head and gave me a crooked smile. "Maybe."

I almost pushed him back in the river. "Makai, you—"

"I couldn't let you be alone. What if you didn't survive?"

"So you left the village and jumped off a cliff? That's... that's..." The only word I could think of was insane, but I had said that already. "The valley is your home. You shouldn't have followed me."

He shrugged and slid the pack he carried off his back. It was soaked, of course, the same as mine, but it was also fuller. "There's nothing left for me there. Not without you."

"What about your parents? Your friends?"

"I don't have friends anymore," he said bitterly. "And my parents..." He winced and averted his eyes. "They haven't been the same, not since Nahdi." He lifted his gaze again, determined once more. "It doesn't matter. What's done is done."

He was right about that. When the villagers realized what he had done, they would never allow him back. He would be killed if they found him in the valley, the same as me. There was no point in dwelling on it.

He started unpacking the contents of his bag to lay them out in the sun to dry. A few changes of clothes, one for him and one that looked smaller for me. Another waterskin and two waterproofed leather bags. He pulled one of them open and handed me a strip of jerky. "Thought you might be hungry."

I tore into the food eagerly, accepting a few thick crackers when he offered those too. It was a far cry from a feast but better than nothing. Makai didn't eat, instead opening the second pouch to check the arrow fletchings and bowstring inside.

Maybe he had made a terrible decision, but at least he had left the village prepared. We could carve our own bow and arrow shafts, craft some arrowheads from stone, but a bowstring and feathers for the fletching would be harder. He had brought a decent amount of food to keep our strength up until we could hunt, along with some kindling in a third leather pouch.

He must have spent all night planning this, after I sent him away, gathering what he needed so he could follow me into banishment.

When I finished eating, I scooted back and combed my fingers through my still-wet hair. Makai's continued to drip onto his shoulders. "Who became chief?" I asked.

"I don't know. They hadn't announced it yet when I left. I snuck out while the Guildmasters were still in their meeting."

"Who the new chief is could affect whether he gets what he wants," I murmured. "Whatever that is." Belvir wanted to surrender. Pashir wanted to fight. I didn't know where Caldin or Enzi stood. They were the only two Guildmasters who hadn't spoken during the argument about what to do.

Makai gave me a puzzled look. "Who will get what he wants?"

I let out a heavy breath. If I told him, it made it real. If I explained it all, it would confirm what I already knew in my head but hadn't fully accepted. There was a part of me that still hoped I was wrong, that it wasn't true. Makai waited while I looked past him at the river, the rapids the only sound that filled the pause.

"Adann," I said finally. "I don't know why, but Adann killed my father... and framed me for it." Navi made a pained sound. I think Makai was staring at me, but the world tumbled too fast for me to focus on his face. I wanted to throw *myself* back in the river rather than see his reaction. Would he even believe me?

I could hardly breathe as I waited for him to respond, which took far too long. I would have thought time had slowed down if

I hadn't been staring at the river, the water moving along at the same swift pace.

"How do you know?" he asked, his voice almost inaudible.

"The claw marks. At first, I thought someone from the clan had stolen my knife." I didn't say that it was someone I had almost come to trust, whose supposed betrayal had hurt almost as much as Adann's. "But when I was at the clan's camp, a girl gave me a drakon claw. Adann must have found it when he stole the knife and used it to fabricate more evidence against me. But mostly this." I held out the puzzle box I had been clutching so hard that my fingers ached when I relaxed my grip. I showed him the sliding bars that locked the box. "The knife and claw were inside. Adann knew how to open it, the only person other than my father."

The look on Makai's face said he believed me, which was somehow worse than him trying to deny it. I set the box aside and buried my face in my hands, all the hurt flooding back in a new wave.

"Adann killed him and no one will believe me." Now that it had been spoken, it hung in the air and mocked me, the foolish girl who thought there was anything she could do. Exiled, mistrusted, and helpless.

I dropped my hands and resummoned my resolve. "But I have to go back."

"You... what?" Makai looked at me with the same disbelief I had shown when he followed me and probably just as warranted.

"I have to do something. Expose him. We'll tell everyone the truth. If he killed my father, there's no telling what else he'll do."

"We have no proof! It'll be your word against his," Makai protested. "You said it yourself: they'll never believe you. If they even let you get two words out before they kill you for breaking banishment law."

"Well maybe I'll just kill *him* then!"

Those words rang through an stunned pause as Makai stared at me. "You don't mean that," he said softly.

My shoulders slumped as the rage left me, expelled in that one shout. I felt like I'd gotten the breath knocked out of me again. "No. I don't."

He went silent while I was wrapped up in my own thoughts, my own distress. Then he said, "What do you want to do? Wherever you lead, I'll follow."

"I want to try."

Makai met my eyes for a heartbeat and nodded. I had called him insane for following me into exile, and now I was planning something equally foolish. Returning to the valley immediately after they banished me? Perhaps stupider than anything Makai had done so far.

But it had to be done.

We had four days before Rajik led the clan to attack. I prayed the Guildmasters wouldn't vote on a course of action before that. It didn't give us much time to get home, but luckily we had a drakon.

I turned toward my keeper, who stared back at me with trepidation in his gold eyes, because he already knew what I was going to say. "Navi. It's time for you to learn to fly."

The last traces of dusk had disappeared by the time we found an area clear of trees where Navi could get a running start. We had to work by moonlight, but I didn't want to waste time waiting until morning.

My drakon was reluctant to participate in the flying practice, to say the least. His attempts to get off the ground mostly resulted in gliding until he ran out of room and had to land to avoid crashing into a tree.

"You have to flap your wings to go higher!" Makai called helpfully. He held out his arms and flapped them twice to demonstrate.

Navi chirped irritably and glared up at the falcon circling above his head. If I had to guess, I'd say the bird was mocking my flightless drakon.

"Makai," I said wearily.

He laughed but called Farin back to his side. The falcon landed on Makai's shoulder and ruffled his feathers before starting to clean them.

I sighed and turned back to Navi. "Try again. And Makai's right. You have to flap if you actually want to go up."

I couldn't differentiate my own frustration from his as he turned and bounded along the bank. He spread his wings once he got some speed and jumped. As soon as his wings caught the air, he gave them one powerful flap, lifting himself higher. Before he could beat them again, a gust of wind knocked him off-balance and he fell from the air. He crashed into the ground, falling from no more than my own height, but remained limp on the grass like he had plummeted from three times that.

I strode over to stand in front of him and crossed my arms. "Navi! If we're going to get back in time to stop something terrible happening, you have to learn to fly!"

Navi's ears flattened against his skull and he ducked his head. His apology rang through my mind, and my burst of anger melted away. I slumped against the tree behind me.

"This is hopeless," I muttered. How were we supposed to help if we couldn't even get back to the valley?

A thud startled me. I looked at Makai, who had dropped our two packs on the ground nearby, fully packed and ready to go. "So we find another way back," he said.

"Do you *know* another way back?" I asked.

"No," he admitted. "But you do." When I continued to stare at him, he rolled his eyes. "Come on, Shay. I know you spent hours looking at that map of Enzi's. Just think."

I tried to remember the layout of the map I had pored over. I had been fascinated with the world and its extensiveness, but my brain was so frazzled that any memory of the image escaped me. "I... I can't. I don't know—"

Hands clamped down on my shoulders. Makai's face was a breath away from mine, his eyes intent, almost forceful. It was an expression I'd never seen from him. "You can. Everything is riding on you. You can do this."

I stared into his eyes, my doubt still threatening to overwhelm me, but something about the way he looked at me made me believe. *You can do this*. I closed my eyes and conjured an image in my mind. The small table in my family's hut, the smell of old parchment, the feel of the brittle page beneath my fingertips. I traced the line of the valley from Mount Tyir to the Falls, continuing along the river after it dropped into the gorge. It turned west and flowed through the plains until it reached the ocean. The gorge carved by the river, with its high, unclimbable cliffs, went on for miles. The only way was to follow the river until forest turned to plains and we could travel north again.

"I know how to get home." I stepped out of Makai's grasp and picked up my pack. "It'll take a few days, but if Adann's goal is to get the Konota to attack the clan, it won't be immediate. We can still get back in time." We had discussed other scenarios earlier, but it was the one that made the most sense. Adann had agreed with me that we couldn't fight the clan, but it must have been a lie.

Makai nodded. His smile creased crow's feet at the corners of his eyes. "That's my girl," he murmured.

I turned away so I didn't have to respond. Makai jogged to catch up with me, and I heard a rush of wings as Farin took flight. We had a long way to go, a difficult journey through unfamiliar territory. Still, it was shorter than the Crossing, and we didn't have to climb a mountain. We had both survived that. We could do this too.

Together.

Chapter 28

THE JOURNEY TO THE plains was a lot farther than it looked on the map in my mind. When I went from tracing the path in my head to actually walking it, every step chipped away at my determination. We traveled through the night and into morning, taking as few breaks as possible.

As I watched the trees pass—pines and the occasional oak with leaves fading from green to bright orange or yellow—my worries came back to me. What if we didn't make it back in time or I was wrong about Adann's plan? What if it was already too late? What if I was wrong about the route back to the valley and we couldn't even make it at all? *What if, what if, what if.*

"Shaya."

I continued to stare at the line of the cliff where the land met the sky.

"Shaya, look at me."

With a sigh, I obeyed. Makai looked as weary as I felt, his tawny skin gleaming with sweat. It was barely noon and the day was already one of the hottest of the season. "What?" I asked.

"Stop thinking. Unless you're thinking about how to stop Adann, it doesn't do any good to fret."

In truth, I didn't even have a plan. My only goal at the moment was getting back to the valley. "I don't suppose you have any ideas."

"Tell the villagers he's a traitor. That he stole your knife and killed Tahck..."

I shook my head. "Really? Who do you think they'll believe, the exiled drakon girl or their golden boy?" He was trying to help, but simply *talking* was pointless.

I felt a twinge of guilt at Makai's wounded look. "I'm sorry," I said quietly. Makai's sagging shoulders and bowed head reminded me of everything he had given up to follow me off the edge of our world. He had left behind his family and home with the knowledge he would never return. For me.

"We trick him, then," he said, undeterred. "Somehow get him to confess where others can hear him."

"Maybe. I need someone else on my side to make it work." If I could get one person to listen, to believe, others might follow. "And I think I know who to talk to. Caldin." She was a highly respected Guildmaster, maybe even the chief by now. Enzi, too, would be willing to listen. I just had to get to them alone without anyone else seeing me. "Maybe we can do this."

"We *can*," he said, words he had spoken twenty times over. I was only now starting to truly believe them.

When the sun started to set, we had to stop for the night. Not only did we need the rest, but clouds had rolled in. They would block the moon and steal what little light we'd had the night before. Makai had only been able to carry one hammock with his pack of other supplies, and he set it up between two sturdy branches while I waited on the ground, chewing at my lip.

His feet hit the bed of pine needles at the base of the trunk. "You take the hammock. I'll sleep down here."

I swallowed. "Don't be ridiculous. It's dangerous and you'll be freezing. There's plenty of room for both of us."

He blinked at me in the fading light. "Are you sure?"

I wasn't, but I nodded and began my climb before I could change my mind. Navi scrambled up the other side of the trunk and found a thick branch to cling to for the night. He settled down where the branch met the trunk and wrapped his tail around it to keep him steady. Farin landed nearby and fluffed up his feathers.

I waited for Makai to reach me so he could get in first. Once he was situated, I carefully slid into the hammock after him. It was a tight fit, my body pressed against his side and one leg resting over his. He put an arm around me and rested his cheek against my hair. Instead of tensing, I nuzzled my face against his neck.

I'd never felt more secure.

Makai was warm and solid in my world that had suddenly turned cold and uncertain. His gentle breath stirred my hair, and I could feel the steady rhythm of his heart in his chest. I had doubted everything I'd once believed about him, and yes, maybe Makai wasn't the person I had thought. He wasn't a *bad* person, though. He was loyal and thoughtful, maybe a little bit reckless. A lot reckless. But he stood by me when he had every reason not to.

A few tears escaped my eyes, but Makai didn't notice until I sniffled quietly. "Hey... what's wrong?" He gently wiped the droplets from my cheeks.

"Thank you," I whispered.

His arm tightened around me. "For what?"

"For coming after me. I don't think I could do this alone."

He was silent for a few seconds, the space between our voices filled with rustling leaves and a distant hooting. "Yes, you could. But luckily you don't have to."

I love you, I thought. But I couldn't make my lips form the words.

"Tell me a story?" Makai murmured.

"What?"

"A story. Like the ones you told us before. About a hero who triumphs despite impossible odds and formidable enemies. Something... something to give us hope."

His tone was light, but a desperation hid underneath it. He knew what we were up against. He knew we would probably fail. The hero always won in the stories, though. It never mattered how hopeless it seemed, how outnumbered they were, the hero always pulled through in the end.

Of the stories Enzi had told me, NokaMia's was my favorite, so it was that tale I began as the sunset faded into twilight and then to darkness.

Once, a kind and just queen ruled over the magnificent city of Darajin. The city rose from the desert sand like an oasis, a paradise for its citizens. Outside the mighty walls, warlike roaming clans and thieving bands ruled the dunes, but inside Darajin the people were safe.

Then a stranger from a far-off land arrived at the city with words of magic and enchantments. He promised the queen he could grant her great power, for a small price. Dazzled by the visitor's promises, the queen agreed, but it was a trick. Instead of gifting the great ruler with magical abilities, the man poisoned her and fled in the night with as many gems as he could carry.

The healers had never before seen the poison the traitorous stranger had used. They said the poison was slowly immobilizing her body, and that their beloved ruler would die in less than a month. All hope seemed lost. Only one refused to believe this.

Her name was NokaMia, a young woman in the Queen's Guard. The Guard was devoted to protecting the queen, whatever the cost, and so NokaMia would fight until her last breath to save her. She had heard of a mythical flower that grew deep underground, beneath the western plains. Others had scoffed at the stories, but Noka believed the Eleir flower was real.

Everyone else believed she was wasting her time, so Noka left the city alone, with only her owl keeper for company. With her wits to aid her, she evaded the desert clans and thieves and journeyed across the sand dunes to reach the western plains.

Noka had heard the flower would be surrounded by dangers, but none of the stories described exactly what dangers. All she knew was it could be found deep in a cave that ran beneath the wind-blown plains.

For three days Noka searched, to no avail. She began to lose hope, starting to doubt her earlier certainty that the flower existed. She had almost given in to despair when she encountered a group in the plains. The Salla, they called themselves. When asked, the Salla confirmed the flower was real, but they refused to help her retrieve it. All but one, a young hunter named Running Wind. He was a rash young man with a thirst for adventure, and so Wind led the way across the plains to the hidden entrance to the cave.

Their two keepers refused to go inside, pleading with their humans not to enter. Noka had come this far, though, and would not turn back. Together, Noka and Wind entered the cave and journeyed into its dark depths.

It soon became clear that it wouldn't be as simple as walking down the tunnel and finding the flower. Running Wind had brought torches to illuminate their way, but even deep inside the cave there was a fierce draft that extinguished any attempts to light them. Eventually, the two gave up and continued in complete darkness, with only their sense of touch and sharp instincts to guide them.

For a while, only the sound of their breathing filled the emptiness inside the cave. Then the *noises* started. The sound of claws scraping against stone. A quiet hissing that Noka and Wind both thought they had imagined, so neither brought it up. Noka thought she saw monsters, glowing eyes watching her from the darkness. Hallucinations, surely, brought on by the pure darkness and her imagination.

When they came to what appeared to be a dead end, a place where their path dropped off into a deep pit, even Wind implored her to return to the surface. Again, Noka refused.

She dropped one of their useless torches over the cliff, counting ten seconds before the wood clattered on the cave floor. Too far to jump, the cliff too slick to climb down. Undeterred, she threw another torch farther out, rewarded with the sound of it hitting a surface on the other side. A horizontal surface, not a wall, as the torch skidded across the rock rather than striking once and falling.

Ignoring Wind's questions about her plan, she started throwing pieces of rock she chipped away from the cave wall with her knife. Different distances, different heights, to determine how far and how high the other side of the gap was. When she felt confident in her ability to make it, Noka took a running start and hurled herself into nothing.

Despite her efforts, she hit the ground earlier than expected. The impact buckled her legs, bringing her jarringly to her hands and knees. The rock scraped her palms and tore through her pants. She stumbled when she rose, pain in her hip making it difficult to walk. But Noka pressed on, leaving Wind behind on the other side.

Deeper she went, the tunnel sloping downward still, until she came to a cavern.

A faint light filled the open space, at least twenty paces to the other side. Mighty stalagmites reached toward the ceiling, while their twins hung ominously from above.

The light itself came from an impossible garden of glowing purple flowers.

Noka stood at the entrance of the cavern, awed by the sight before her. The large flowers grew sporadically, here and there a lone flower pushing up from cracks in the rock. She counted only five of them.

She picked one flower and tucked it carefully inside her satchel. Though she knew that taking too many would be selfish, she had her reasons for reaching for a second.

The moment her fingers touched the second flower, a soft hissing filled the cavern, followed by the sound of claws scraping rock. A creature crawled down the side of the wall, its slitted green eyes reflecting the light from the flowers. It looked like a huge lizard, almost as long as Noka was tall. Another rasping hiss and a second one joined it, then a third.

She recognized the sounds—the hissing and the click of long claws on stone—and the glowing eyes from earlier. They had been watching her and Wind all along, but had only chosen now to reveal themselves. To attack. From the way they stalked forward, she knew they didn't intend to let her leave alive.

"Please," she said. To Noka's surprise, the word made them pause. She swallowed and met the eyes of the creature at the front. An intelligence lurked in those eyes, staring expectantly back. "One is for my dying queen and the other for the man who helped me. I wouldn't have gotten this far without him."

All three of them hissed again, but then the one in the front turned away. The others followed, and together they climbed the wall and disappeared into a tunnel Noka hadn't noticed before.

She let out an unsteady breath and started back the way she had come.

When she reached the gap, she almost didn't make the jump back across. She hit the edge of the cliff, barely managing to hang on long enough for Wind to pull her to safety.

"Did you find it?" Wind asked, his voice echoing off the walls of the cave.

Invisible to Wind, Noka grinned in the darkness. "I did," she replied.

When the two emerged from the complete black of the cave, the bright sunlight burned their eyes and left them blinded at first, but Noka continued to smile through the pain. She had succeeded in finding the flower her people said did not exist. She could only pray that her queen still lived.

She parted ways with Wind, giving him one flower to take back to his people in thanks for helping her. The return trip took another week, and by the time she reached Darajin, three weeks had passed. Noka ran through the streets to reach the palace, delivering the miraculous cure only minutes before the queen would have drawn her last breath.

Such is the story of NokaMia, the hero of Darajin, who risked death and ridicule in order to save her queen.

I finished the story and tilted my head to look at Makai. His eyes were closed, his breathing steady. Asleep. I sighed and shifted to get more comfortable. How much of the story had he heard? At least it had helped him fall asleep, which had been the point.

Even wrapped in Makai's arms, I didn't sink into sleep with the same ease. Everything swirled through my head in a windstorm that only spun faster the harder I tried to calm it. The future terrified me, the past broke my heart, and the truth of the present haunted me.

I wasn't NokaMia. I wasn't Tavlin Lamere the Godslayer or any other hero. How was I supposed to stop what lurked ahead? Hardly able to breathe, I snuggled closer to Makai and tried to block it all out. At least I had him with me. At least I wasn't alone. Right then, that was all I could ask for.

I woke up cradled in Makai's arms, our bodies pressed snugly together by the sides of the hammock. I had daydreamed about this very moment countless times, but I never thought it would happen like this. Far from home after being banished from the valley, on our way back to expose a traitor and stop a war.

When I tilted my chin up, I found Makai looking at me with a tender smile on his lips. He moved as if he intended to kiss my forehead before he thought better of it and rested his head against the hammock again. "Sleep well?" he asked.

No, I hadn't, but Navi saved me from replying. It was his insistent chittering that had woken us both in the first place. His impatient chirps sounded again from a nearby branch, followed by the sharp crack of his tail spikes hitting the bark. *Wake up! Lovey cuddles later.*

I flushed at those words and pressed one hand against Makai's chest to push myself up. It was an awkward clamber out of the hammock, but I managed to avoid falling out of the tree or stepping on Makai. I carefully made my way down to where Navi already waited while Makai untied the hammock and let it drift down to me. I had it rolled up by the time Makai's feet hit the ground.

"Ready?" he said as he slid his pack over his shoulders. I secured the rolled hammock to the bottom, picked up my own pack, and nodded.

We followed the river until we reached a section where its path dipped south. It took us a little time to find a safe place to cross without needing to wade through a treacherous current, but once on the other bank we continued northwest.

I focused my thoughts on tracing and retracing our path in my head. I was so absorbed in the map I created in my mind that Makai almost knocked me over when he stumbled into me. I caught him with one arm, the other flinging out to steady myself on a tree trunk.

He pulled away and stared at the ground, embarrassed. "Sorry. I tripped."

I frowned. He *tripped?* My feet could navigate the forest terrain while my mind was preoccupied. Makai had more awareness than that. "Are you okay?"

"Fine. Just tired."

I eyed him. We were both hungry, having only eaten the food he'd brought since we had no time to hunt, but this journey was shorter than his Crossing. His body was used to long hunting trips. I was tired as well but not on the verge of falling over. "Let me carry your pack then. Mine is lighter."

"No, I'm fine. Let's keep going."

"Makai." My tone left no room for further argument. Reluctantly, he slid the pack off and handed it over, accepting mine in exchange.

We pressed on, but I kept my eye on Makai as we followed the afternoon sun. He definitely wasn't "fine." His face looked pale, his uneven steps far from the confident tread of a hunter. Even an inexperienced hunter shouldn't stumble over roots or accidentally kick rocks through the brush.

I stopped and put a hand on his shoulder. "You need to rest." He looked like he might fall over again.

"We don't have time for that," he protested. "I'll manage."

"I think you're sick."

"I can still walk."

"*Makai.*" This time he only stared back at me obstinately. Strong-headed, stubborn, *stupid* boy. Arguing about it was only wasting time, and the look in his eyes said I wasn't winning this one anytime soon. "Fine. But if you fall again, we're stopping."

"Fine," he agreed.

We continued at a slower pace, with Makai stepping carefully to avoid any tripping hazards. At least it would prevent him from hurting himself, unless he outright fainted from whatever illness was invading his body.

Unfortunately, he was right. If we stopped, we would be wasting precious time we didn't have, maybe only waiting for the sickness to get worse. What would I do if it got bad enough that he couldn't go on? I had to get back to the valley, but I couldn't leave him behind.

Excuse me. I looked over at Navi, who watched me with mild amusement as he walked. *I could carry him, you know.*

Of course. Maybe I had a sickness of my own addling my brain, because I should have come to that conclusion a long time ago. Carrying the extra weight would eventually tire him out, but I had ridden Navi the whole return trip of my Crossing.

"Wait," I said.

"What now?" Makai asked, the annoyance in his voice muted by exhaustion.

"You can ride Navi."

He glanced between me and my keeper, a long pause preceding his weak laugh. "Okay." Even he wasn't too stubborn to concede to the obvious solution.

I had to help him onto Navi's back, which was further proof that he shouldn't be walking. Makai slumped forward against the drakon's neck, looking woozy. *Don't let him vomit on my back please,* Navi said, horrified.

I fought back a smile and replied, *I'll do my best.*

Makai seemed to get used to the rhythm of Navi's gait and closed his eyes to rest. No vomit to worry about. At one point, I thought I heard him murmur, "Shut up, Farin," but when I glanced back he still appeared asleep.

By the time the trees ended and I stepped into the tall grass of the plains, I was wishing I had another drakon to ride. I stopped and leaned against Navi, taking a moment to rest. His concern floated through my mind, but I assured him I was fine. I hoped that was the truth, rather than Makai's blatant lie earlier.

Makai had dozed off, but now he lifted his head to look down at me groggily. "Are you okay?"

I nodded and smiled up at him. His face had returned to its normal color, and aside from the lingering sleepiness, he didn't look ready to topple over anymore. "How are you feeling?"

"Better. Maybe I just needed a little rest after all."

Navi crouched down so Makai could slide from his back without having to jump. When Makai stepped forward, he seemed steady on his feet again. My relief at seeing him back to full health was short-lived as his widening eyes drew my attention behind me.

CHAPTER 29

THE PEOPLE SEEMED TO grow right out of the plains. They wore swaths of grass on their shoulders and heads, camouflaging them in the tall grass, and soil painted their cheeks. They leveled their spears at us and traded quiet words in an unfamiliar language.

"We don't want any trouble," Makai said. He stared them down, unintimidated, and I was torn between exasperation and affection.

"Valley folk," the man at the front said. A pale-furred coyote with long legs stood beside him. "What are you doing here? You do not come to trade." The Konota words came out stilted and awkward.

"We're just passing through," I said.

He took a step forward, his eyes narrowed, and a growl rumbled from Navi's hiding spot in the grass. *Navi, no!* But the drakon had already stalked forward, teeth bared, revealing himself to the hunters.

"Drakon!" After the first shout, murmurs rustled, repeating the one word. *Drakon, drakon, drakon.*

It felt like my return from my Crossing all over again, confronted with the awestruck and fearful faces. I put a hand on Navi's shoulder and he stopped snarling, but he remained crouched, ready to spring. "Please, don't be afraid! He won't hurt you."

I realized then that these faces weren't fearful. They stared at Navi and me with reverence. One by one, they started to kneel. Spears flat on the ground, their heads bent, a whole hunting party *knelt* before me.

"Great drakon soul. You bless us with your presence," their leader said. He raised his face, and to my shock there were tears in his eyes. "You look weary. Please, come and we will give you food and water." When he stood, the rest of the group followed suit.

Makai and I exchanged a glance, but when the leader gestured us forward again, I followed. Makai hurried after me, sticking close to my side and looking like he was ready to fight all of the hunters single-handed if it came to that. *Fool.*

"My name is Tripping Root," the leader said. "You may call me Root. It is not far to the *daram*."

"What's a... *daram?*" Makai asked.

Root considered the question. "It is similar to a family, but beyond blood alone. It is what we call our people. You can rest there and fill your bellies."

"Thank you, but we have to—" I started.

Root held up a hand to cut me off, though there was nothing spiteful in the gesture. "You must rest. I am sure you have very important things to do, but you cannot do them run ragged."

As if to prove his point, Makai staggered a little and grabbed my arm to steady himself. "I'm fine," he said in response to my concerned look. Maybe he wasn't entirely over his sickness.

"Come," Root said. He started walking again, the rest of his people following. I glanced at Makai, who shrugged and started after them. It couldn't hurt, I decided. We needed food, and maybe they had a healer who could help Makai.

We walked at the head of the hunting party, a pace behind Root, my arm wrapped around Makai in case he stumbled again. I offered to help him onto Navi's back, but he refused. I think he was worried about looking weak in front of the plains hunters.

He spent a lot of time studying Root, who led the party with his lanky coyote beside him. Makai stared so intently that the man stopped and looked back at us with his eyebrows raised. "Yes?" he asked.

Makai's eyes widened. "I, um... why is your name *Tripping Root*. It's just... it's a little weird."

I knew how the plains people chose their names, but I wasn't sure whether Makai did. Their names held special meaning, which was why Root had shared his in our language instead of his own. A verb and a noun, the verb belonging to the keeper. Root's coyote was named Trip. It *was* an odd name, even for one of his people, but I still elbowed Makai in the ribs for being so rude.

Fortunately, Root looked amused rather than annoyed. "Trip is not the most graceful of canines," he replied. Trip whined softly and laid his ears back, but Root didn't look the least bit embarrassed.

"You shouldn't ask questions like that," I whispered to Makai once we started walking again. "It's impolite."

Makai waved a hand. "It's fine. He didn't mind."

"That doesn't mean it's not rude."

Makai shrugged in response. Root hadn't been offended, so no harm had been done, but still. Makai should learn to filter his thoughts.

It took us perhaps thirty minutes to reach the *daram's* camp. Tents similar to the ones I'd seen in the clan's camp, except conical and made from thinner animal hide, were set up in a non-uniform cluster. A cheer announced the hunting party's return. Heads poked out from the tents as we walked through the temporary village, and awed words passed between the onlookers. I couldn't understand them, but I guessed at the general reaction. The hunting party had returned empty-handed, aside from two strangers, one with a drakon keeper. I caught that word several times.

The other hunters split away, leaving us alone with Root. He stopped in front of a tent and held the flap open for us. "I am sorry, but your keepers must wait outside."

We nodded in unison. I gave Navi a reassuring pat before ducking into the shelter, followed by Makai and then Root. Inside, a woman sat on a rug laid out on the packed earth. She watched us with curiosity as she spoke in the language of the plains.

"They come from the Konota Valley. The girl has a drakon," Root responded. The woman's eyes widened.

"Valley folk with a drakon?" she said, switching to Konota, though the way her words ran together still made them difficult to understand. "Fascinating."

"You are a long way from home, valley folk," Root said. "Come, sit. We will talk." He laid out two more rugs for us and then took a seat on the one already waiting beside the woman. I studied the pattern on mine before I sat down—it looked like Konota work.

"My name is Storming Sky," the woman said. "What brings you so far from home?"

I wondered if I looked as much like a deer in the torchlight as Makai did. I didn't want to lie to these people who seemed so welcoming, but I couldn't tell them the truth either. They might not react so kindly to someone who had been banished by her own people.

"If you don't mind," I said slowly, "I would prefer not to say."

"She has her own secrets," Sky said, amused. She and Root shared a meaningful glance that made me uneasy.

"It is her," Root said. "Tammae has returned."

I looked from one to the other, completely baffled by the knowing smile they shared. "I'm sorry but... what are you talking about? Who is Tammae?"

Root waved a hand as if brushing away my question. "Later. First, you must eat."

The meal our hosts prepared was simple—small amounts of meat with a mixture of seeds and edible roots. We sat in Sky's tent while we ate, cross-legged on the rugs.

Root had spread out a fifth rug, which remained unoccupied until another woman joined us. "Valley folk, this is Singing River, our shaman," Sky said as she waved the woman in. "River, this is Makai Farin and the drakon-souled, Shaya Navi."

River sat on the open rug between me and Root. I recoiled when a rattlesnake slithered across the ground toward us, but I realized the animal was the woman's keeper when it settled in her lap. It flicked its tongue at me before going still. "It is a pleasure to meet you both," River said.

We dipped out heads to her. "I'm sorry, but... shaman?" I asked. I had never heard the word before.

"Our healer," Root answered. "And spiritual woman. She leads our people through what Sky cannot."

Makai looked at him quizzically. "Like what? Why wouldn't your chief be able to lead?"

"I lead our *daram* in body and mind, but River leads us in spirit," Sky answered. When we continued to stare blankly, she sighed and gave River an exasperated look. "You valley folk do not know much, do you?"

River laughed. "There is more to life than gathering food and roaming the plains. I prepare our children for their *Prot Kyn*—First Hunt—and direct the *daram* in our tributes to the gods."

"I heard the valley folk do not pay tribute to their god," Root said, still sounding amused. I wasn't sure there was anything that *didn't* amuse him. "They live in his valley, farm his earth, and drink his water, but they do not pay thanks."

The words weren't accusatory, but I still flushed. I had never thought about it, but he had a point. We took what Tyir gave us for granted, never officially honoring the mountain god.

"We don't need to pay tribute," Makai said. "Tyir gave us those lands in thanks to our people, generations ago!"

"You overlook your god's generosity. He continues to give and you continue to take," Sky said. "It is a wonder he does not send a storm or earthquake to swallow your village whole. Your people must have done something incredible to earn his gratitude for this long."

I frowned, trying to remember any stories that told of what specifically the Konota had done. They mentioned his thanks, but not what the people had done to earn it. Had we already forgotten?

"We're not here to talk about Konota history," I said. "I'm sorry, I don't mean to be rude. But you said you would tell us about this... Tammae you mentioned."

"Of course." Root set his empty bowl on the ground in front of him. "Many generations ago, a drakon warrior saved our *daram*. Her name was Tammae Lakki. She came from the North, cast out by her own people for refusing to fight. In her land, people with drakons were fighters. Killers. Tammae was not like them. She was a wanderer, a free spirit with a taste for the sky." As he spoke, he lifted his hand and traced his fingers through the air. "Tammae was weak and weary, so the *daram* offered her food and shelter. She traveled with them for many days as they headed south. They asked her where she was going, but she always gave the same answer: 'Wherever the wind carries me.'

"On her seventh day with the them, they were attacked by invaders from the southern forests. They were unprepared and unequipped, but Tammae came to their rescue. She did what she had fled the north to avoid doing—fighting and killing. Our leader then asked how he could ever thank her, but she told him there was no need. When they woke up the next morning, Tammae Lakki was gone. Their wise shaman said someday she would return to us, finally giving us the chance to repay her kindness."

I glanced at Makai to see his reaction to the story. He stared at Root with the same expression he had while listening to Roubin's story about Avarttha.

"Three generations later, our people came across a young man with a drakon keeper. He had been born in the plains but exiled from his own *daram*, so we eagerly welcomed him into ours. The shaman at the time named him Tammae Lakki's next life. He did much for our *daram*, and after his death we eagerly awaited the next reincarnation of Tammae. Hundreds of years passed with no sign of a drakon-souled... until now."

I stared into my empty bowl, caught up in his story and the rhythm of his voice. Several seconds passed before I realized he had stopped talking. When I looked up, he was staring at me. "I... I'm sorry, but I'm not some legendary savior from hundreds of years ago."

"But you are," the healer broke in. She reached over and placed two fingers on my forehead. I forced myself to sit still instead of pulling away. "You share her soul, her spirit. You share her courage."

Root smiled at my owl-eyed expression. "Are you not a wanderer exiled by your people because you do not belong?"

It wasn't the whole story, but... yes. I was exactly what he said, when you broke it down to the most basic truth.

But was I really a reincarnation of their beloved savior?

"In your past lives, your soul came to us and saved us," Sky said. "Now, we seek to repay that kindness. If there is anything we can do to assist you, you need only ask."

"Thank you, but I'm afraid there's nothing you can do to help us." I thought about the valley, the clan, Adann. But these people weren't warriors. I wouldn't drag them into my fight simply because they thought I had helped their people several generations ago. "Besides, you've done enough by giving us food and a place to rest."

Sky dipped her head. "For now, it will be enough."

"Thank you, but—" I broke off when Makai's bowl hit the ground. He followed a moment later, his back and then head hitting the hard earth. "Makai!" I scrambled over and put a hand on his shoulder. He didn't move, his eyes closed and his face pale again.

I turned to River, my eyes wide. "Please. I think he's caught some kind of sickness."

River was already in motion before I finished speaking. She stood and gestured to Root. "Bring him to my tent. I will do anything I can."

I stayed at Root's shoulder the whole way there, then hovered beside Makai once the man laid him down on a pile of animal skins. I only backed away when River calmly asked me to give her room. I forced myself not to fidget while she examined him, my arms wrapped around my body and my fingers digging into my ribs.

Finally, River sat back on her heels and lifted her head. "I have seen this sickness before."

"Will he recover soon?"

Her silence was answer enough, and dismay snaked around my heart. He couldn't die. Not with all that I had lost already. I couldn't lose him too. "Please, there must be something you can do."

River looked to Sky. A long pause filled the tent as the healer and chief stared at each other. I wished I knew what passed between them, what Sky's pensive look meant when she turned her eyes to me. I couldn't breathe, the panic at the thought of losing Makai crushing my chest. I thought I might collapse inward if they told me they couldn't save him.

Finally, Sky dipped her head, not to me but at River. The healer gave a sharp nod in response and hurried out of the tent.

"What? What is it?" I asked.

"We have a medicine, but it is not common. For you, we will use it."

For me, their fabled returning savior. I didn't care why they thought I was this Tammae Lakki, or if it was true, as long as it saved Makai's life. "Thank you," I breathed.

"I know what it is like to lose someone you love," Sky said gently. "I would not wish it on anyone."

"I don't—"

"Come, Shaya Navi. Let us walk while the shaman helps your friend."

I had no choice but to follow Sky outside, leaving Makai behind with Farin perched worriedly on his chest. Navi and Sky's keeper—a dusty-furred plains wolf—trailed us through the temporary village until we reached the edge. If Sky planned to say something, she didn't for a long while. Tall grass brushed my hands and legs as she led the way around the outskirts of the camp, her expression serene.

"Thank you for everything," I said when I couldn't stand the silence any longer. "I don't know how I'll ever repay you."

"There is no need." Sky walked with her arms folded, her back straight, and her head held high. She looked more like a queen described in the stories than the chief of a small *daram*. No jewels or lavish robes, but with an air of dignity even my father had never possessed. "We already told you, we are repaying *you*."

I grimaced at the ground. "I'm not who you think I am. I'm not a hero. I'm not a mighty warrior. I've never helped anyone in my life."

"Tell me, child, where are you in such a hurry to get to?"

"To save my—" I broke off when I realized she had proved her point rather effectively. "To save my village," I finished.

"The one that cast you out."

"I never said—"

"You did not have to. Listen, wanderer." Sky stopped and rested a hand on my arm. "You are only beginning. You are young. Believe me, you will be a hero yet."

I didn't have the energy to argue. I still didn't believe it, despite the conviction in her voice. I knew in my soul that I would probably fail to save the Konota Valley from the threat of the clan, but I had to try anyway.

Maybe that's what a hero is. Navi flicked one ear and tilted his head. *Someone who does the right thing, even when it's hopeless.*

Even when it's hopeless. I knew he was trying to be encouraging, but instead I felt like I had crashed into that river again. Every new hurdle was like an unexpected change in the current, dragging me away from the surface until I didn't know which way I was swimming.

"Can we turn back? I would really like to check on Makai."

Sky dipped her head. "Yes, of course."

Makai was awake when we returned. He looked better but still weak, struggling to keep his eyes open as he focused on me. He gave a crooked smile. "If it isn't the great Tammae Lakki returned."

I sat cross-legged on the ground beside him. "Please don't," I whispered.

His smile faltered. "Sorry."

"It's okay." I hadn't meant to make him feel guilty, but I didn't want to hear that name again for at least a month. "How are you feeling?"

"I don't feel like I'm dying anymore, so that's something." He tried to keep his tone light, but there was a shakiness in his voice that destroyed the illusion. "Shaya... River says I'll still need some time to recover. The night, at least."

My heart sank when I realized what he was saying. It would be a longer delay preventing us from reaching the valley.

"You need to go on alone."

I stared at him, his words running through my mind several times before they fully registered. "I'm sorry, what?"

"You can't wait. You have to get back and try to stop Adann. You have to save the valley from the clan."

"Shut up. I'm not leaving you, idiot."

"The village is more important. My parents are there. Your mother and sister. You have to go. For me. For Tahck." My throat tightened at my father's name. He was right: I had to end it before anyone else suffered the same loss.

"We will care for him," River said gently. "He will recover soon."

"I'll catch up when I'm better," Makai promised. "But you have to leave *now*."

I bent my head and rested it on his shoulder. "I need your help, though. To talk to the villagers."

"You don't need me. You have the words. You just have to find the right ones." He took my hand and gave it a squeeze, although a feeble one. "I believe in you. Hero or not, you're more than you think you are."

I let out a slow breath. "Okay. Okay, I'll go."

Makai smiled, relieved when I finally agreed. "I'll be right behind you. I promise." He pulled his hand out of mine and reached up to brush his fingers against my cheek. "You've got this, Shay."

After a brief hesitation, I leaned forward and pressed a kiss to his forehead. His skin burned my lips, another reminder that—despite the promises that he would live—Makai was not well. "If you die, I'll never forgive you," I whispered. Then I scurried out of the tent before I could change my mind.

Outside, Root approached with my pack and held it out to me. "I refilled your water and added some food. You will have plenty to make it home." He stood by while I slid it on.

"He should be better by morning," he assured me. "I do not know what troubles plague you, wanderer, but I wish you luck. I hope we meet again." He rested a hand on my shoulder before disappearing inside.

Leaving Makai in the plains felt like leaving a piece of myself. I knew it was only for a day, maybe less, but as I left the tents behind I felt like I was facing my Crossing all over again. It was me and Navi, my faithful watcher, crossing unfamiliar territory to expose my father's murderer, stop an evil chief, and save the people who would likely kill me on sight.

It made climbing a mountain sound easy.

CHAPTER 30

I RODE THE REST of the way on Navi's back. As we entered the valley through the narrow pass, I sent a silent prayer to Tyir that nothing had changed in the past two days. That a battle hadn't started and no one else had died. That Adann hadn't done anything else to betray the Konota.

Being back in the familiar forest hurt. Something vital had been torn away when Adann pushed me off that cliff. A part of me that had been washed down the river and would never return—the part that called this valley home.

The village? Navi asked.

Yes. I didn't have a plan yet. I had tried to solidify one between the plains and the valley, but nothing I had come up with seemed right or even feasible. I couldn't walk into the village and demand they listen. Still, I needed to find out what had happened since Makai and I left. Most importantly, who had been selected as the new chief.

It was risky but my only option. We were both on high alert as we passed through the forest. Night had fallen, so we shouldn't encounter a hunting party, but I didn't want to assume we were safe. If I got caught before I even reached the village, I wasn't a very good mouse.

I felt exposed as Navi and I crossed the wooden bridge north of the lake, but we made it to the other side without anyone spotting us. Though I didn't want to, I left Navi behind by the river, since it would be easier for me to stay hidden alone. As I had hoped, the night meant the village was quiet. Most people were in their huts, although a few sat around the firepit at the center of the village.

I slunk through the shadows cast by the huts and made my way to Adann and Ayla's. I crouched behind it, hidden from the moonlight as I listened. Nothing. Either they weren't home or they were asleep. I moved on to the Healers Hut, to Caldin's, to Eldin's. Silence everywhere. The longer I spent in the village, the more my frustration and apprehension grew. When all else failed, I went to the fire pit to see who had gathered there.

I found a deep shadow to shroud myself in and peered carefully around the edge of a hut. Enzi sat among the group, telling a story I had heard before—the very one I had told to Makai, about the Eleir flower and NokaMia.

I knew I increased my chances of being caught by sticking around to listen, but I couldn't help myself. My storytelling would never compare to that of our Healer Guildmaster. The way his voice wove the words together made the story come to life. I could picture every scene in my mind without even trying. It was impossible not to get drawn in, clinging to every word as if dangling from the edge of a cliff by my fingertips. I had entered the story somewhere in the middle, after Noka leaves her city and reaches the plains in search of the mythical flower.

When the story finished, the small group sat in silence, taking time to process. The first time I heard the story, I had spent more time than most pondering the events and implications, the finer details about the world it described and *what it all meant*. More importantly, I had wondered how much of it was true.

I shook myself free of my trance. As much as I wanted to, I couldn't sit around listening to stories. I started to move away from the fire, but then Iliya broke the silence.

"Too bad we don't have some brave hero to save us," she said bitterly. "We're doomed."

"Don't say that," Lora said, her voice soft enough that it was almost swallowed by the crackle of the fire. "Everything might work out okay." The young healer didn't sound convinced by her own words. She always struck me as an optimistic person, but even she was losing hope. She reached for Iliya's hand, but the other girl pulled it away.

"How?" Iliya demanded. "The clan has won. Chief Tahck is dead and Caldin is going to surrender tomorrow, like a coward! I can't believe she agreed to that. Tahck *never* would have given up. And Makai is missing too! What if they took him?"

"Don't be ridiculous," Misni said. "He probably followed that traitor over the Falls."

"That's not true," Iliya spat. I could hear in her voice that she still cared. She was worried about Makai, even after turning her back on him.

She had given me something important, at least: Caldin had been chosen as chief. Learning that someone who might actually hear me out now led the Konota was a relief, but the rest of the conversation I found concerning. They planned to surrender to the clan.

"To be honest, I'm surprised Adann suggested we surrender," Emry said. She sat opposite Iliya, her troubled eyes trained on the fire. "He doesn't seem like the type to give in."

"He's right, though, isn't he?" Misni said. "Adann might be brave, but he isn't stupid. We're beat. Fighting would only result in more people dying."

Emry sighed. "I suppose so. There's a reason he was chosen to replace Caldin."

Bumps rose on my arms. Adann was a Guildmaster. Perhaps the youngest in history, further proof that the villagers trusted him. This was going to be even harder than I thought.

At least I knew why he had killed my father. Adann wanted the Konota to surrender, and Papa never would have allowed it. Chief Tahck had advocated for peace, but he would have gone down fighting if it came to that. An alpha wolf didn't roll over and surrender. I was still missing a piece of my answer, though. *Why* did he want them to surrender? Emry was right about Adann, on both counts. He wasn't a coward, and he wasn't stupid. He had to know surrendering wouldn't end well.

If I understood his motives, maybe I would have a better chance of convincing the villagers, but that would require talking to Adann. Facing my former friend and father's killer was the last thing I wanted to do. I knew it would happen eventually—it loomed over my head like a storm cloud threatening to break, but I wasn't going to run brazenly into the rain.

Maybe it was the rational decision or maybe I was scared. Maybe both.

Either way, I knew I had to—

"Shaya?"

My body stiffened at my sister's voice. She sounded confused, shocked to find an apparition before her. A traitor would never return to the valley after being banished. Surely she was seeing things.

I turned slowly, my heart pounding so hard you'd think I was facing a drakon attack. I had to focus on taking deep breaths to keep from passing out. "Ayla, please..."

She shook her head slowly. For a few racing heartbeats, I thought she might let me go, but then she raised her voice and shouted, "She's here! Shaya has returned!"

It took my broken heart and stomped all over the pieces.

I broke into a run and dashed past her. My sister tried to grab my arm, but I slipped from her fingers before she could get a good grip. More shouts rose throughout the village, repeating Ayla's alarm. *The traitor has returned. Shaya Navi.*

I wove between the huts, darting down a different direction whenever I saw someone emerge. Every time someone laid eyes on me, I thought I was done for, but I was small. I was fast. The little mouse evaded capture.

Navi waited for me at the river with his ears perked, his body tense and ready to run. I hurled myself ungracefully onto his back and he raced toward Mount Tyir. By then, I could hear pounding hoofbeats—keepers and their riders chasing me. Navi was fast, but I didn't think he could outrun a horse.

I tugged on one of his feathers, drawing an outraged sound from my drakon, but he turned toward the lake like I wanted. I ordered him onward, guarding my other thoughts so he didn't understand my plan until it was too late.

His startled question crashed into my mind the moment he realized our destination.

You're going to jump, I said.

I can't!

You have to fly if we're going to get away. He slowed his steps, but I dug my heels into his sides, my will power pushing against his. I didn't like it, ordering him against his own wishes, but it had to be done. We dashed up the slope to the overhang where we had jumped into the lake with Makai and his friends.

"Navi, *jump.*"

It wasn't a long drop, but I hoped it would be enough. His wings caught the air, his claws grazing the surface of the water as we glided over the lake. He flapped, and this time we remained steady. We climbed into the sky and left the yelling voices behind us.

I left my worries on the ground. Everything that had been weighing me down for the last several days got swept away by the wind as Navi's wings carried us higher. The rush of cold air stung my eyes, making them water, but I didn't care. I couldn't hold in my shout of pure exhilaration, spreading my arms out like a second pair of wings.

He still wasn't the steadiest flyer, and when he wobbled I had to throw my arms around his neck to keep from toppling off his back.

I gave a nervous laugh and waited until I was sure he had his balance again before I straightened and twisted to look back at the village. A group stood on the lake shore, illuminated by the moonlight, staring up at us as we fled. Adann stood among them. Was he worried about my return? Or did he think there was nothing the little mouse could do? *I'm coming, Adann,* I thought. *You can't hide for much longer.*

Except I was the one hiding. I had wanted to keep my return secret for as long as possible, but now the village knew I was here. They would be looking for me as soon as the sun rose. I wouldn't be able to sneak back in to talk to Caldin or Enzi.

I needed Makai. He didn't hold the answers, but at least he offered support. At least I wouldn't be alone in this.

Without me having to tell him, Navi carried us to the cliff where Kota and I had watched the sunrise. It was far enough away from both the village and the clan's camp that it would be a safe place to rest and think. Though I was wary about entering the cave again, it provided shelter from the wind, as well as a hiding place if anyone did come along.

Thinking led absolutely nowhere, though. I kicked a stone in frustration, sending it skidding into the darkness. I had messed everything up so quickly.

Navi made a quiet sound of disappointment and nudged my arm with his nose. *In the morning,* he said.

I sighed and slumped against him, curling up beside his warm belly when he settled down. He was right. I had until tomorrow afternoon before they surrendered. They still had to make the journey to the clan, and they might even put it off longer to try to find me. By then, Makai would be at my side.

But I still couldn't clear my mind long enough to fall asleep. I spent the entire night with every horrible thing that had happened running on a loop.

CHAPTER 31

THE MORNING YIELDED NO better results. No matter how hard I wracked my brain, there was no solution. I wouldn't get remotely close to the village. Even if Caldin or Enzi did enter the forest alone for some unforeseen reason, I would never find them in the expansive valley.

By midday, I had basically given up.

I stopped half a pace from the cliff and stared out over the forest, my shoulders slumped in defeat. The cliff faced southeast, so I couldn't see the pass that led into the valley, but I kept glancing in that direction as if I might see a falcon roaming the sky.

Makai should have caught up by now, but how would he find me way up here? If he even made it into the valley. Maybe River had been wrong and whatever medicine she had given him hadn't worked. He could still be sick or even dead.

Navi's ears quivered when he heard someone moving through the forest. It didn't matter if they were Konota or Drak Clan. Everyone in this valley was my enemy. *Coming this way,* he said.

The easy option was to soar to safety and go find Makai. Except I didn't know where to find him. The Konota might surrender before I returned.

You need to find him. Make sure he's okay, I told Navi.

Come with, he pleaded, but I couldn't. I wouldn't run away. I had to stay here and do what I could. Stall, keep them from surrendering. Maybe if Navi found Makai, he could make them listen, if I survived long enough for Navi to carry him back.

"Navi, *go.*" I shoved his shoulder, but my true force came from the willpower I threw into the command. "You have to find Makai." Navi made a distressed sound, but he spread his wings and dove off the cliff. I watched him soar upward, his figure growing smaller as he flew away... away...

I stood alone and waited to face my enemies.

Footsteps crunched the grass behind me. "I knew you'd come back." Adann's deep voice sent ice through my veins. I wanted to scream at him. I wanted to cry. I wanted to ask him the question that had resonated in my head since he pushed me off that cliff. *Why, why, why.*

Instead, I turned and met his treacherous eyes without a word.

"Kota told me about your little spot. You should have joined the clan, little mouse," he said. I almost flinched at the nickname. "This could've all gone so differently for you. For both of us. Maybe your father would still be alive."

"Don't you dare try to place this on me," I said. "*You* killed him. *You* drove that knife into his heart. And for what?"

"To end this," he replied simply. "Tahck was never going to agree to surrender. His death removed him as an obstacle."

"Why do you want us to surrender? I would have thought you would fight."

"And let the clan slaughter us? No. I didn't get away that day, when they chased us. They caught me, and they offered me a deal. They wanted us to surrender. When they attacked us, I saw their strength and knew we didn't stand a chance."

More pieces settled into place. Before Kota captured me, he had followed me. Led them right to me. He had framed me so I couldn't convince the Konota to leave, also probably hoping I would go to the clan if I decided to return. Then there was Rajik's offer to provide the antidote. I hadn't realized it at the time, but he had no reason to know my mother had been poisoned. Adann must have told him.

He took a small step toward me. "If I get them to surrender, there are no casualties. The Konota get to live with the clan."

"You mean they get to live as slaves."

His voice was steady. Certain. "It's better than dying."

"Is it?"

Adann narrowed his eyes. "Everything I did was for the Konota."

"Oh? I suppose you personally don't get anything out of this. Are you some esteemed member of their clan now? Was it worth killing your chief and betraying your people? Was it worth betraying *me*?"

I was still that silly innocent girl, somewhere deep inside. Somewhere I still loved him, and I thought he had cared about me too. My mentor, my guardian, my big brother. Adann had been so much to me, but apparently I had been nothing to him.

I saw the flash of hesitation in his eyes, but in the end he only shrugged. "Rajik trusts me. I'm going to be a warrior, one of the few without a drakon." He stalked forward, moving with the same predatory grace as the cougar at his side. "You're not Konota anymore. Join the clan. Join *me*."

"*No.*" I would keep giving that answer until they stopped asking. "I'm not like you. I'm not a traitor."

"Why do you *care?* You're not one of them. You never were. Didn't you see how easily they turned against you? How readily they believed you would murder your own father? In the clan, you won't be an outsider. You'll be respected, revered even. You'll be a warrior. Powerful. Unstoppable."

I shook my head. "I'm not a warrior. I'm not a killer."

"Why do you have to be so *stubborn?*" The frustration in his voice said something I didn't want to accept. Maybe he *did* care, enough to want me to join the clan with him, even if it meant killing my father and getting me banished. It made everything hurt that much more. "We could have everything, Shaya. If only you would see sense. If you would just *join* me."

He held out his hand. I took a step back... right off the edge of the cliff I had forgotten loomed behind me. I started to topple backward, but only for a moment before Adann caught my wrist and pulled me back to safety.

"It wasn't supposed to be this way." He sounded so genuinely sad that it fueled my hatred. If I was someone he cared about, how could he justify everything he'd done?

He raised his hand, his fingers curled into a fist. Faint rustling sounded behind him, and I looked past him to see two warriors slither out of the forest. I was outnumbered, trapped between them and the cliff. My only escape option was hurling myself over the edge, and Navi wasn't around to catch me. I could feel him growing farther and farther away.

Adann's touch was surprisingly gentle as he wrapped a rope around my wrists to bind my hands behind my back. "I'm sorry," he murmured as he took me prisoner. *I'm sorry,* he had said when he led me to the pit. Had he been apologizing for that or for killing my father?

They could take me, but I wouldn't come quietly like a good little mouse. Not this time.

I let all of my anger and grief out in a furious yell and twisted, driving my elbow into Adann's stomach. He gave a very satisfying grunt of pain, and I felt his grip loosen. I turned and threw my weight forward, knocking the still off-balance Adann toward the cliff. His toe landed on the edge, stabilizing him. Then the rock beneath him crumbled. Adann cried out as he started to fall, only to catch the cliff with his fingertips.

I held my breath as hands seized me from behind and forced me to my knees. I waited for the earth to give way again, to send Adann plummeting to his death... but then one of the warriors stepped forward and pulled him up.

Adann's face was a mosaic of disbelief, betrayal, and anger—the same emotions I had felt when I learned the truth about him. "I thought you weren't a killer," he said.

The demon I'd once called a friend stared down at me, looking so hurt. I spat at his feet. "Maybe I was wrong."

I wasn't prepared for the sudden pain that left me dazed as Adann backhanded me across the cheek, splitting open my half-healed cut. A glorious and terrifying sound reverberated through the forest. *Navi.* I had never heard him roar before, but I knew the sound like I knew my own breathing. I could feel his anguish, his rage and fear, though distance had dulled our connection. My keeper, my other half, separated from me. He wanted to come back. *Stay away. Stay away,* I pleaded. *Find Makai.*

I blinked through the pain and lifted my gaze to Adann, ignoring the feeling of warm blood dripping down my cheek and along my jaw. Everything inside me wanted to curl up, play dead, admit defeat. Everything except one spark of defiance that I think resided in Navi. He was the fire inside me, burning despite the distance.

I thought Adann might hit me again out of frustration, except one of the drakons chirped. "Someone is coming," a warrior said. "Konota."

Adann waved his hand. "Go. Hide." As suddenly and silently as they had emerged from the forest, the warriors vanished again. Not five seconds later, they were replaced by a somewhat odd group of seven: Caldin, Eldin, Rena, Pashir, Belvir, Canton, and Ayla. The chief, two Guildmasters, two hunters, a crafter, and a healer. The reactions to seeing me ranged from dismayed shock from Ayla to disgust from Eldin and Pashir.

Caldin's face gave nothing away as her eyes settled on me, on my knees in front of Adann the Great. "The keepers heard voices. What's going on?"

"Look what I caught wandering the woods," Adann said. "I guess she couldn't stay away."

"We'll deal with the traitor later. There are other tasks to handle first," Caldin said.

Other tasks. Like surrendering to the clan like Adann wanted. Was that why one of each guild was present, including the Guildmasters? Ayla instead of Enzi, since he was too old to safely make the trip, and Canton in place of the indisposed Ora. Adann must have been planning to meet them at the camp but came to find me first. The extra hunters were... what? Protection? As if they could actually do anything against the clan's warriors.

"Rena, Eldin, take her back to camp for—"

I spun, still on my knees. The ground scraped through my pants, but I didn't wince. "Caldin, please. I didn't kill my father." Her face tightened in anger at my interruption, but I pressed on. If only I could make her *listen.* "It was Adann. He's working with the clan."

Adann let out a sharp laugh that was echoed by confused chuckles from the others. "Why would I be working with the clan? The ridiculous accusations of a desperate child."

I took a deep breath, frantically searching for some evidence against him. If it was my word against his—the treasured hunter of the Konota and new Guildmaster versus the banished drakon girl—I may as well stop talking before I wasted anymore breath. I stared at the ground in front of me, and shockingly the earth yielded my answer.

"Look at the ground," I said. "Claw marks in the dirt, left by the warriors' drakons. They were here, not ten seconds before you arrived."

Heads turned down to study the dirt, where the two drakons had left faint imprints and claw marks. Eldin spoke first, looking at me with a sneer. "That means nothing. These tracks could be from your beast."

"Navi's tracks are there." I jerked my head toward the place my own drakon had left marks in the earth. "He's young, so they're smaller. Those tracks are different." Not all of them would see the difference, but the hunters would.

"That's still not proof," Eldin continued to argue. "The drakon warriors could have been with you."

Ridiculous accusations of a desperate child. I was desperate, more than I'd ever been in my life. Everything came down to this moment. I *had* to make them believe me. "If they were with me, why am I the one tied up and on my knees? Why wouldn't they have overpowered Adann?"

Canton and Belvir exchanged a look. I might be getting through to them, though Eldin and Pashir still watched me with unimpressed scowls.

I didn't care what any of them thought. There was only one person I needed to convince, but her face may as well have been the barren peak of Mount Tyir. "I can explain everything. The claw marks on my father's arms, the knife. Caldin, *please.*" The new Konota chief had been studying the ground, but she looked up when I said her name. "You know I wouldn't have done it. You *know* I wouldn't kill my own father."

Eldin snorted. "I've heard enough. Just push her over the cliff and be done with it." He took a step toward me, but Caldin held up a hand.

He gave her an astonished look. Caldin didn't acknowledge it, her focus on me—the girl who had been banished for a terrible crime, the evidence all too damning, but who had saved Caldin's brother at risk to her own life. She had once told me I was in her debt. Now I was counting on her upholding that, despite my fall from grace.

"Speak, then," she said. "Explain."

I let out a shaky breath. "There's a puzzle box. My grandfather made it. Ayla can verify that." Heads turned toward her, and my sister gave an uncertain nod. "I kept my knife in there, along with a drakon claw talisman I was given by a girl in the clan. Adann is the only other person who knew how to open it, because... because I trusted him."

I almost choked on the word "trusted." My voice quivered as my vision started to swim from unshed tears. The initial hurt of learning the truth came rushing back, but I didn't let it break me. "He stole the claw and my knife and used it to kill my father, framing me because... I guess it was all too convenient to pin it on the girl everyone already mistrusted."

"Ridiculous," Adann repeated, shaking his head. "That's quite a tale you've spun, little mouse. Perhaps you should make up stories like the ones Enzi tells."

When Ayla stepped forward, his smirk vanished. "Is it true?" she demanded. She stared him down, searching for any lies his eyes might reveal.

"Of course not." For the first time, I saw something falter in him. In the slightest shift in his posture, the way his shoulders hunched forward and the way he leaned away from her, I saw the truth.

And Ayla did too. "Is it *true?* Did you kill my father?"

"No. She's making it up. Ayla—"

"You're lying," she whispered. The look on her face was a reflection my own pain and shock, the realization that someone you loved and trusted completely had betrayed you. It cut deeper into the soul than any knife could. Seeing it destroy my sister opened a new wound for me, right next to the one Adann had so callously carved.

She took a step away from him. "He's *lying*. He did it."

I could almost hear the snap when Adann's expression changed. His features twisted in rage as he turned on me. "You ruined *everything,* you stupid girl."

"Rena, Eldin. Seize the traitor," Caldin ordered. The two hunters stepped forward. Rena's face was unreadable, but Eldin's was still riddled with disbelief. Everyone behind them looked like their world had fallen through. How could *Adann* betray the Konota? Unbelievable, unthinkable, impossible.

Adann glared at the approaching hunters. "This isn't over," he said. He let out a high-pitched whistle, then ran and launched himself over the edge of the cliff.

Ayla's impulsive *"No!"* rang out, hanging in the air for a moment before the whoosh of wings cut through it. A drakon soared upward with Adann on its back. Out of the corner of my eye, I saw Illari whirl and bound into the forest. As the drakon flew toward the clan's camp, Adann twisted around. Our gazes locked, and there was a promise in his cold, dark eyes. He would repay me for destroying his plans.

Even after he had turned away, my eyes remained on the drakon as it shrank into the distance. I couldn't stop staring, like it had carried away something I desperately wanted back.

That was silly, though, because the Adann I thought I knew wasn't on the back of that drakon. He had never existed.

I flinched when someone rested a hand on my arm. "Are you hurt?" Ayla asked. "Your cheek..."

Yes, everything hurts. "I'm fine," I answered. Aside from the reopened cut on my cheek I had almost forgotten about, Ayla's medicine couldn't touch my wounds.

"That's why he wanted us to surrender," Caldin murmured. She still gazed after the drakon, her eyes more distant than the retreating keeper and its riders. "He was working with them all along." I could guess what ran through her mind: she should have seen it. He had been under her command, her most talented hunter. She should have realized he had been lying for weeks.

Like I should have realized he had been lying to me. I wanted to tell her it wasn't her fault, but like so many times before, I knew my words would be pointless. So I kept them to myself.

At least everything made sense now, even if it had come together in a way twisted by Adann's warped mind. I did believe that *he* believed he had done this for his people, trying to protect their lives by getting them to surrender, even if it meant taking one life to save many.

"We have to get back to the village," I said. "Now that Adann is exposed, the clan knows you won't surrender. They're going to attack."

Caldin tore her eyes away from the drakon that was nothing more than a dark spot in the sky and nodded sharply. She helped me to my feet before cutting the ropes that bound my hands.

When she waved her hand in a circle, the party turned and fell into a swift jog back toward the village.

I stayed near my sister as we ran. She didn't look at me, her eyes focused on the terrain ahead. She didn't have the same practice navigating the undergrowth and tree roots as the hunters, but the furrow of her forehead told me she was concentrating harder than she needed to.

"I'm glad you were there," I said. Adann might have convinced them to let Eldin push me over the cliff if she hadn't been.

Ayla answered with a small nod. I listened to her somewhat ragged breathing and counted our synchronized steps. Ten paces before Ayla's hesitant, "Shaya—"

"Not now," I cut her off before she could apologize. I loved my sister as much as I loved my parents, which was why it hurt so much when even she didn't speak up for me. That Ayla could think I would drive a knife into our father's back hurt almost as much as Adann's betrayal. I knew she was genuinely sorry, and I was sure she had plenty of words prepared, but I wasn't ready to hear them. Not with Adann still out there, the clan's impending attack, and Navi still growing farther away by the second.

CHAPTER 32

THE VILLAGE WAS LOCATED almost due south from the cliff, closer to us than to the clan's camp. The trip still took far too many hours. I feared the warriors would have beaten us there on the backs of their drakons, but the village was undisturbed. The sky had darkened by then, the sun obscured by gathering clouds. A warning from Tyir—the clan was coming.

My return with the rest of the Konota was met with more confusion than hostility. I knew I should be thankful for that, but the uncertain murmurs dragged up memories of my return from my Crossing. In a way, my banishment had started the moment I crested that hill with a drakon at my side.

The crowd of nearly four-hundred parted to allow Grandpa Enzi through. "Caldin, what is happening? We weren't expecting you back so soon." He didn't look at me. I hadn't seen him since my father's death, so I had no idea what he believed about the accusations.

"There was no surrender," Caldin answered, but there was too much to explain and too little time.

I had no way to do it delicately, so I interrupted the chief... for the second time that day. "I didn't kill my father, Adann is a traitor, and the clan is attacking. We have to get ready."

Astonished gazes turned toward Caldin, who nodded. The words were passed through the crowd for those at the back who couldn't hear. I could see the moment each villager understood and accepted the truth.

"And how are we supposed to win against trained fighters?" Lora asked, her voice thin with fear. "There might be more of us, but we don't stand a chance." At her side, Iliya avoided meeting my eyes, keeping her focus trained on the ground while she clutched the other girl's hand like it kept her tethered. The two of them—a healer and a crafter—would be less equipped to fight than a hunter or even a builder.

Healers were important in battle too, though. Even as she voiced her doubt, I started to form a plan. "The leader," I said. In all the stories of great battles and victory under hopeless odds, they had always gone after the leader. "We have to find Rajik. If he falls, we win." At least, I hoped so.

"Gather the weapons," Caldin ordered. "They attacked us once unprepared. That won't happen again."

"And Enzi, prepare the Healers Hut," I said. My grandfather finally looked at me when I addressed him directly. For a moment, I forgot what I intended to say to him. I expected something cold or blank on his face, but nothing about it had changed. He was more serious now, but the same attentiveness he had always shown me lived in his eyes. It almost made me weep with relief, even if a small bit of anger that he hadn't tried to help me lingered. I would sort that out later.

I took a deep breath and continued. "Emry and Misni can guard the door. Your healers can be ready to help the wounded, maybe even patch them up enough to return to the fight." Hopefully, a hunter and a builder would be enough to keep warriors out of the hut if they decided to attack it. I would have liked to believe they wouldn't do such a thing, but I knew enough that I doubted they had any honor at all.

He dipped his head and turned. The healers peeled away from the gathered Konota, along with Emry and Misni.

They were listening to me. The people who had regarded me with fear and mistrust for weeks, who had been so quick to cast me out, were obeying my orders. It was startling enough that it took my breath away for a moment.

"Trev and Deira," Caldin said. My eyes fell on Makai's former friends, who avoided looking at me as they stepped forward. "Escort the children out of the village. You can take shelter in the Acorn Grove."

The two nodded obediently and hurried off to round up the Konota who had yet to complete their Crossing. One such member pushed his way to the front of the crowd, though.

"I want to fight," Keer announced. He stood straight, his chin up as he dared to address his chief in such a way.

"You're to go with the other children," Caldin said firmly. "You'll be safe with them."

"My Crossing is less than a year away!" Keer argued. "I'm old enough to help."

Caldin let out a slow breath. She didn't have time to waste arguing with him. "Very well. You can help by assisting the healers."

Keer bobbed his head, satisfied by the compromise. The villagers started to disperse, gathering weapons and taking up positions around the village. My eyes scanned the sky, waiting for the first drakons to appear.

I didn't realize Keer hadn't left until he said my name. "Yes?" I replied uncertainly.

"Thank you." He somehow seemed more intimidated now than when talking to Caldin. "I know it was you who got Makai to apologize."

My gaze had started to wander back to the gray sky, but I blinked at that. "Makai apologized? When?"

Keer frowned. "After the first attack... I assumed it was you who told him to do it."

I shook my head slowly. My mind reeled from this revelation, but I didn't have time to dwell on it. "Go to the Healers Hut. They'll be here soon." He scurried to obey, his figure disappearing between two huts.

Caldin appeared a moment later, carrying two spears, one of which she handed to me. The new chief rested a hand on my shoulder and gave it a squeeze. "I hope to see you on the other side, sister."

Not everyone would make it out of this battle alive. Perhaps none of us would. The knowledge that these might be the last words I would speak to her made my throat tighten. I had to stretch my arm up to reach the taller woman's shoulder and return the gesture. "You too, Chief Caldin," I managed to get out. *Tyir, watch over her.* The Konota needed a leader like Caldin.

She moved away to call orders and encouragement to the waiting villagers. Crafters, farmers, and builders stood in line with the hunters, grim-faced and prepared to defend their home with their lives.

We had only a few more minutes before the clan appeared in the sky. Drakons soared over the forest in a v-formation, not bothering to hide their presence. This wasn't a sneak attack. This time they wanted us to see their numbers, to fear what we were up against.

Armed with the spear and standing amidst a line of hunters, I craned my neck to watch as they flew over our heads. My eyes sought Rajik's Brax, but the black drakon wasn't in the formation.

My heart sank when I spotted another familiar keeper. The drakon's gray scales faded into the storm-warning sky, but the red feathers stood out like a splash of blood. *Ryn.* What would I do if I had to face Kota? I didn't think I could fight her, and I wasn't sure she would share the sentiment. Her loyalties rested with the clan.

All I could do was hope I wouldn't have to find out.

"Fight in pairs," I called to the others. "There are more of us, so stick together if you can." A few nods acknowledged my words, but for the most part they watched the drakons with trepidation as the formation swept around.

Swords met spears as the drakons swooped down at the village. The Konota fought in pairs as I had suggested, one villager warding off warrior weapons while the other attempted to stab at the enemy. Keepers did their best to assist, but they couldn't do much against the drakons. Out of the corner of my eye, I saw an eagle dive at a drakon rider's face, talons outstretched.

Another warrior coming straight at me stole my attention. I lifted my spear, prepared to parry a sword stroke, but none came. Instead, the drakon grabbed my arm and hauled me into the sky.

I shouted in surprise and terror as we rose higher, the battle shrinking away below us. But I recovered quickly. Even in the claws of the drakon, I wasn't helpless. I stabbed upward with my spear, trying to hit the warrior, only to realize the drakon had another rider. His hand grabbed my spear and wrenched it out of my hand all too easily.

The drakon glided downward and dropped me while we were still several paces off the ground. Another scream rose in my throat as I plummeted, but I hit the earth hard enough to cut it short.

I tumbled several paces before my back crashed into the side of a hut. My cheek stung from my open cut, new blood running over dried streaks on my face, and my body ached in several other places. My shoulder hurt the worst. It had taken the first impact. I bit my lip to distract myself from the pain as I pushed myself to my hands and knees.

I squinted through the cloud of dust the drakon kicked up as it landed. It was only on the ground long enough to drop off Adann before it took back to the sky.

"Hello, little mouse," he said, then slammed the butt of my own spear into my already injured shoulder.

I cried out as I was knocked backward, unable to keep the tears out of my eyes anymore. The pain, both physical and emotional, overwhelmed me. It almost blinded me. I wanted to curl up in the dirt and pretend none of this was happening. Where was the girl who had tried to shove him over a cliff to his death? Wherever that fire had come from, it was gone now, extinguished like the last embers of a campfire.

He stood over me, his face deceptively regretful. "It could have been so different." He cast the spear aside and drew his knife, then hauled me to my feet by the collar of my shirt. Another jolt of pain shot through my shoulder as he pulled my back against his chest. The point of his knife pressed into my side.

"Do it." I tried to sound defiant, but the words came out weak and defeated. I *was* weak and defeated. Illari stalked toward us, while Navi was still far away. I was without my keeper and therefore hopelessly outmatched. The time training with Kota had accomplished nothing in the end. I wasn't a warrior. I was still nothing more than a pathetic child playing hero in a game of pretend.

He laughed, the sound cold and sharp and too close to my ear. "Oh, no. I'm not going to kill you. That would be too easy. We're going for a little walk."

When he pushed me around the side of the hut, I realized which one the drakon had thrown me against. Adann's home, the one he would have shared with Ayla, if things had been different. He shouldered his way past the door flap, dragging me with him, then kicked the back of my legs. My knees buckled. I dropped to the ground at his feet, unable to resist.

Adann tied my hands behind my back. Again. Another rope bound my ankles together, a third secured me to the bedpost, before Adann stepped around to stand in front of me.

I craned my neck to look up at him. Adann had always been tall, but on my knees before him, he felt like a giant. "Do you even care that you hurt Ayla?" I demanded. "Did you ever love her?"

"Of course I did." His face remained cold, at odds with his words.

"But you were willing to betray her. To kill her father."

"It was necessary." He crouched down, bringing himself to eye level. "I don't expect you to understand. You were blinded by your love for him, but Tahck was going to ruin us. Something had to be done."

I shook my head. "You should have loved him too. He loved you like his own son."

Adann narrowed his eyes. "When I first sought out Ayla's affections, I wanted to get close to the chief. I was a nobody before my Crossing, and I remained a nobody after it. Just another hunter. My own parents were dead, so I thought maybe having Tahck as a father figure could benefit me. I would stand out as the beloved of the chief's daughter. I always wanted to be a Guildmaster, and Ayla was going to help me get there."

I tried to remember Adann before he had started courting Ayla. Once, I had thought Adann had always been adored by everyone, but I hadn't known much about him until Ayla introduced us. Was it possible the entire village had ignored him until Ayla pulled him into the light?

"It became more than that," he went on. "I love Ayla. I know you won't believe that, but I do. I loved Tahck, too."

"You don't kill people you love," I snarled.

"That's what you don't understand. I do what I need to. I always have. That's what you learn when you're orphaned young and you're raised by everyone and no one at the same time."

Adann straightened and sheathed his knife, then went to retrieve his spear from the corner. Ayla had carved the designs on the shaft herself. He was going to use my sister's gift to fight his own people. The cold-hearted, soulless monster.

He ran his fingers over the carvings. When he glanced back at me, his gaze was scrutinizing. "You really do love him, don't you?"

I stared at him. My tears had stopped, but my eyes still hurt, just like the rest of me. "Love who?"

He rolled his eyes. "Don't give me that." We watched each other until he broke into laughter. "Oh, Tyir, you really are that deep in denial!"

"What are you talking about?"

"Makai. I know you sent Navi to find him, wherever that idiot is instead of by your side like the lovestruck pup he is." He knelt in front of me, too close, but I had no space to back away. "You were willing to let yourself get captured—possibly even die—to protect him. If that's not love, I don't know what is."

"Love is sacrifice," I murmured. Like Makai's sacrifice when he followed me into exile.

He gave me a wry smile. "It's a shame. You could have had someone far more worthy of you, if you weren't so foolish. You're something special, Shaya Navi. At least, I thought you were." He straightened, his spear held loosely in one hand. "You wait here for me, alright little mouse? You should sit down. You'll be more comfortable." He patted my cheek before stepping past me to leave the hut.

I rocked backward off my sore knees... and onto my sore butt. No part of me remained unscathed, every bit bruised and scraped, inside and out. I was a patchwork of pain and my arms twisted behind my back wasn't helping.

This was not how this would go down. I wasn't going to sit there and wait for him to return. I needed to fight in the battle. If I found Rajik, I could end this. But what chance did I really stand against the clan's chief? I couldn't even fight Adann. A little mouse challenging a drakon.

I let out a frustrated scream and hit my forehead against my knees. I still didn't know who I was or what I was meant for, but it wasn't battle. Not a hunter, not a warrior. I was nothing. Guildless. Purposeless. My breathing turned shallow, only to be squeezed off as tears leaked from my eyes again. I had thought eventually they would run dry, but I always seemed to have more.

Calm down. Navi's voice in my head evoked another sob, but for a different reason. He had to be near, if he could speak to me. I reached out for him and felt him growing steadily closer.

I don't know what to do, I said.

Fight back.

Somehow, that was enough. Strength, protection, *guardian*—the traits of those with drakon keepers. Maybe I wasn't a warrior like Kota or Rajik, but I wasn't worthless either. That fire hadn't come from Navi. It had been inside me all along, waiting for him to unlock it.

This wasn't over. I closed my eyes and took several deep breaths. When the urge to cry had passed, I looked around Adann's hut. He wasn't stupid, so he wouldn't have left anything sharp out in the open. That didn't mean he hadn't left something hidden.

Searching his things was anything but easy. The rope that tethered me to the bedpost only allowed me to roam so far. With my hands and ankles bound, every movement was a reminder of my tumble from the air. It was a slow process.

I checked under his bed first, my own favorite hiding spot, but Adann wasn't me. The small gap beneath his bed was empty. *Where, where, where.* Where would Adann keep an extra knife or something else I could cut the ropes with?

The wooden chest at the foot of his bed might contain something useful, but it was tied shut with complex knots. After a brief struggle with the knots, I realized I had no idea how to undo them, especially behind my back where I couldn't see.

The longer I searched, the more my hope diminished. I checked between the cracks in the walls I could reach, between pieces of straw for anything small he might have hidden. Nothing. Finally accepting defeat, I sat down on top of the chest. *I'm sorry, Navi.*

I bowed my head and took a deep breath. Adann had been gone for ten minutes at the least. I could hear the shouts of humans and various cries of keepers, muffled through the hut walls. How long would the battle last? How long could the villagers hold their own against the warriors?

How many Konota had died already?

I stared at the dirt floor, trying to ward off the flood of helplessness. I might have been right when I said we needed to leave. We didn't stand a chance against the clan. Still, I knew willingly enslaving ourselves to them would have been worse. Some of us might still end up there, but at least we had tried. At least we had fought for our freedom.

Maybe Navi would arrive before Adann returned. His claws could cut through the rope. He drew closer still, already in the valley, flying as fast as he could. I could picture the forest rushing by below. Makai was on Navi's back—I could feel it. Surely that meant he was okay. They could help me, if only they got here fast enough.

Something in the dirt drew my attention away from Navi. A faint line in the earth, almost trampled to nonexistence, but enough of a trace left to form an arc, as if someone had dragged one corner of the chest out. I stood, hope returning like a flower thought to be dead, only to bloom in vibrant colors with the help of a little water.

Unfortunately, moving the chest was no simple matter. I sat on the ground with my back against the bed frame, my knee wedged behind the chest. I screamed as I *pushed*, the strain tearing at my muscles. The wood chest pressed against the bruise on my knee. My back arched, the bed frame dug into my shoulder, but then I felt the chest move. Barely three fingers, but it was enough to expose a sliver of the hole someone had dug in the ground. I paused to recover and let the pain fade, then went again, moving it another three fingers.

Stashed inside the hole beneath the corner of Adann's chest was a drakon claw.

It was the one he had taken from my puzzle box, the cord still strung through the hole. The claw he must have used to carve marks on my father's arms. He had kept it. My stomach twisted at the image conjured to my mind: Adann kneeling beside the body and meticulously dragging the claw across my father's skin to frame his victim's daughter.

I didn't know why he had kept it. As a reminder of what he had done? Perhaps a tiny part of him felt guilty.

I scooted around so I could lean back and run my fingers over the dirt floor until I found the claw. After carefully manipulating it so the sharp underside pressed against the rope, I started to saw.

It wasn't fast work. A knife would have cut the bindings in one or two slashes, but the claw was meant to pierce skin and tear through flesh, not rope. I also couldn't apply much pressure. I counted each stroke as the claw worked through the rope strand by strand.

Finally, I felt the bonds loosen enough that I could twist my hands the rest of the way out. Triumph flooded through me. I sawed through the bindings around my ankles and scrambled to my feet, but I regretted it when a wave of dizziness almost sent me to the ground again. I grabbed the edge of Adann's bed to steady myself until it passed and my vision cleared.

I took a step toward the exit but froze when a shadow ghosted the doorway. I feared Adann had returned and my escape was foiled already, but then a different face appeared as an arm pulled the doorflap aside. The pale light from outside illuminated Kota's blue eyes.

CHAPTER 33

K OTA STEPPED INSIDE AND let the flap swing closed behind her. She wore her leather armor, the thick material shielding her torso and legs. Bracers covered her forearms, and she had purple lines painted on her cheeks. She looked fierce, beautiful, and dangerous. She looked like my enemy.

Neither of us moved, neither spoke, two girls who had been on the path to shaky friendship staring at each other across the dim hut. I didn't want to attack her. Whatever her allegiances, I knew too much about her head and her heart to wish her any harm.

"I saw Adann go after you and thought..." Her voice was quiet, strangled. Whatever she planned to do, she hated it. "I'll help you find Rajik. If he dies, the others will lay down their weapons."

I let out the breath that had been holding me motionless, feeling dizzy again with the realization that Kota was *on my side.*

"Come *on*, bumblebee," she said when I didn't move. I laughed at her scowl and hurried to her side. She handed me a knife that I took with trepidation. "I almost brought a sword, but I was afraid you'd hurt yourself with it."

I threw my arms around her, and after a moment of hesitation she returned the hug. "I'm so happy you're here." I squeezed her tighter, which elicited a grunt of protest.

She gave my back an awkward pat. "Okay, okay. I'm happy too. We need to go." She disengaged herself from my arms, her face bright scarlet as she stepped away.

"Well, isn't that sweet." My muscles locked at the sound of Adann's voice.

Kota didn't hesitate. She drew her sword as she spun, but Adann jumped back through the doorway and Kota's sword cut only animal hide. *"Met-sulit,"* she snarled as she ran after him.

I lingered inside, clutching the knife like it could somehow solve all my problems. I could do this. Adann had to pay for all he had done, to me and to everyone I cared about. Thunder cut the air as I threw back the door flap and stepped outside. Kota and Adann dueled a few paces away, while Ryn faced off against Illari.

Navi. I called out to my keeper with my heart and mind. I could feel him there, distant but never gone.

I'm coming. Still too far away, though. I didn't have time to wait for him.

Kota slashed at Adann with her sword, but he knocked it aside with a swipe of his spear. Ryn and Illari lashed out at each other with extended claws. I was the extra in this fight, and despite Navi's absence, that gave us the advantage. Instead of joining Kota against Adann, I slipped around his hut and circled the building so he didn't see me come up behind him.

Maybe I should have felt worse about literally trying to stab him in the back.

I might have succeeded if Ryn and Illari's tussle hadn't turned so the cougar faced me. She let out a snarl and sprang away from the drakon. It left her side unguarded so Ryn could rake her claws down the cat's flank, but it didn't slow Illari down. She charged me as I tried to attack Adann from behind.

I lifted my knife to defend myself before a hundred pounds of angry cougar crashed into me. The blade sank into flesh when I hit the ground, and Illari's momentum drove it deeper as she landed on top of me. Right into her heart.

As much as I hated him and every dark corner of his soul, I wouldn't wish the agony that saturated Adann's scream on anyone.

My muscles strained as I shoved the limp cougar off me. Adann had fallen to his knees, his horror fading into emptiness as he stared at his dead keeper. Kota stood over him with her sword still raised. "I'm sorry," I said. My voice cracked. "I'm so sorry. I didn't mean to—"

Kota grabbed my arm—thankfully my uninjured left arm—and hauled me roughly to my feet. "We have to find Rajik."

I stumbled as she pulled me away from my victim and the weeping man who had lost half of himself. Because of me. I had wanted to stop him, but not *this*.

"Bee, move your butt, we need to go!" Kota shoved me forward.

When we reached Ryn, I climbed up behind Kota and wrapped my arms around her torso, but Ryn didn't move.

"Kota?"

She didn't speak right away. I bit my tongue to keep from saying we were wasting time and forced myself to wait. "I betrayed my clan," she said at last. "I turned against them. My father always told me a warrior should be three things above all else: honorable, loyal, and brave. But he never told me what to do when honor and loyalty conflict. What if I did the wrong thing?"

I rested my chin on her shoulder and tightened my arms around her. "I think when your father told you to be loyal, he didn't mean to a man like Rajik. What you did was very honorable and brave, and I think he'd be proud of you."

Kota twisted around to face me, her blue eyes like a clear sky. Then she nodded, a new determination settling on her face. I barely managed to hang on when Ryn suddenly spread her wings and took off.

"Rajik will be watching from somewhere close," Kota called, the words almost buried beneath the rush of wind. "He loves the glory of victory but not so much the danger of battle."

He really was a coward without honor. The clan had quite the chief.

My eyes scanned the ridge above the village. "There," I said, reaching past Kota to point. One massive oak stood above the rest of the trees, even its high branches thick enough to hold a man, even a drakon. Children would sometimes dare each other to climb as high as they could and mark the bark. I had watched Makai surpass every mark except one: Adann's, which sat high above the rest.

I held on tighter to Kota as Ryn turned toward the tree. When we got closer, I could make out the form of a large, dark shadow crouching on one of the branches, near the trunk. *Brax.* Rajik had to be nearby, hidden among the foliage. "He's there."

"I see him," Kota said.

Ryn flapped her wings and brought us higher, then folded them close to her body and dove at the tree.

I didn't realize Kota's plan until it was too late to protest. Instead of landing on a nearby branch, Ryn shot directly toward the dark form of Brax. The other drakon shrieked in surprise as Ryn plowed into him, knocking him from the tree. Ryn's claws ripped bark free as they grazed the branch. As soon as we cleared the oak's trunk, her wings snapped out and slowed our dive enough that she could land on the forest floor rather than crash. The impact was still jarring. My head snapped forward, my jaw colliding with Kota's shoulder.

Ryn spun to face the fallen drakon a moment before Rajik jumped from a branch as high as he was tall. He landed in a crouch beside his keeper.

"This is disappointing," he said as he rose. "It seems you're as gutless as your father, Kota Ryn."

"My father was a great man," she said, her words punctuated with a snarl from Ryn.

"Your father was *weak*," Rajik said. "If he had lived, he would have been the chief who led us to ruin with his foolish honor."

Something felt off—as if he were bragging about the death of a man rather than stating a fact. Kota picked up on it too, and her body stiffened. "What do you mean?"

"I think you know what I mean." He stepped forward, Brax at his side, his thick spear held at the ready. "When Eilzar died, that worthless son of his gone for *this* place, he was going to name me or your father and everyone knew it." He smiled. Brax's low growl filled the pause. "It had to be me."

Kota drew her sword and threw herself from Ryn's back, a reckless move fueled by rage. Ryn's eyes were on Brax, but the black drakon didn't move as Rajik stepped forward to meet Kota. Her sword clashed with his spear, but the sound was almost covered up by Kota's yell.

My breathing went shallow. I wanted to help but knew I would only get myself hurt if I tried to step in. This was Kota's fight—one it quickly became apparent she was going to lose. Kota might be talented for her age, but Rajik's experience outmatched her. He was toying with her, and I wasn't sure she realized it.

I swung my leg over Ryn's back in preparation to jump down—maybe me getting in the way would be enough to end this before Kota died—but then Rajik lifted one leg and kicked the young warrior in the chest. Kota shouted as she fell, until her back slammed into the earth and the cry broke off. Rajik lifted his spear to deal the final blow, but I hurled the knife Kota had given me at his chest.

It bounced off the leather armor that covered his shoulder, but it was enough to distract him and, as Ryn prowled forward, to make him flee like the coward he was. After kicking the fallen knife into the brush, he swung himself into Brax's saddle and took off.

"Kota!" I called. Ryn bounded forward as Kota scrambled to her feet. I expected to see rage, but her face was blank, nothing but determination in her eyes. I grabbed her arm and hauled her onto Ryn's back. The drakon snapped out her red wings and launched us into the air.

CHAPTER 34

A FEW MIGHTY BEATS of Ryn's wings brought us past the treetops and into the open sky. I searched the darkening clouds, looking for Brax. The black drakon had the advantage in this storm, but a flash of lightning lit the sky and revealed the black shadow streaking across the clouds.

"There!" I called, pointing, but Kota had already seen him. Ryn shot after him, flapping her wings to gain speed. We flew toward Mount Tyir, the great mountain ever watching, ever silent. What did the god think about the battle happening in the valley below? Maybe he had sent the storm as a sign of disapproval, not a warning, but of course the clan didn't care about our god's approval. No storm would stop this war.

The flash had only exposed Brax for a moment. Barely five heartbeats later I lost him, his dark form disappearing as if into smoke. My eyes darted across the sky fruitlessly. "Where did he go?" I shouted, squinting at the storm clouds. I prayed for another streak of lightning, but none came.

"I don't—"

Kota's reply was lost as something crashed into us from the side, knocking me off the drakon. I twisted as I fell to see Ryn evading Brax's snapping jaws. The two drakons and their riders went out of view as I kept spinning, and I braced myself for the impact. It came sooner than I expected. The air rushed out of my chest as I hit a tree, but I managed to cling to a thick branch.

I really needed to stop falling out of the sky or my body would never forgive me.

When I had recovered enough, I lifted my head. I found Ryn's red feathers immediately, but Brax and Rajik were gone.

"He's getting away!" Kota called from where she and Ryn hovered.

"Go! I'll catch up!"

Kota gave me one last reluctant glance before Ryn turned and chased after the clan leader.

I climbed down to the ground, my progress slow as every motion tugged at some injury or another. My chest hurt from colliding with the branch, making it difficult to get enough air.

Keep going, Navi said. *I'm coming.*

He was close, so close. I could feel him coming toward me from the direction of the village. He must have dropped off Makai and then come to find me, because he no longer had a passenger.

My feet landed on the ground at the edge of a clearing. By now, I knew this forest well, the layout springing to my mind like one of Grandpa Enzi's maps. I knew what I needed to do. Navi's desperation crackled through our bond as he raced toward me.

Instead of waiting, I ran away from him.

I raced across the clearing until it ended and I plunged back into the trees. I pumped my legs as hard as I could, squeezing out every last drop of speed from my battered body. Eventually, I forgot about the pain in my chest and my shoulder and everywhere else, the only thing in my mind the next step that would carry me closer.

Navi. I called to him with my heart and soul rather than my voice. *I need you.* He was closing in, moving with even more speed as he soared over the forest, despite his exhaustion. I knew he would find me. He knew what I wanted him to do. We were one mind. One soul.

I left the edge of the trees three steps before I launched myself over the edge of the cliff.

For a few seconds, I was suspended in free-fall. I plummeted, gathering speed, but I didn't look at the ground rushing up at me. My eyes remained trained on the horizon, at the end of the valley where the river dropped off into the Falls. I kept my arms and legs out, trying to control my fall as best I could and keep my stomach toward the ground.

My body hit something solid. I was no longer falling but swooping upward on the back of my keeper. The sudden change in direction made my head spin, but I clung to his neck while I tried to orient myself and brushed Navi's worry aside. *Find them.*

Navi banked, turning us toward the two shapes in the distance. A flash of red feathers streaked across the sky—Ryn racing after the jet black beast that was nothing more than a shadow. Brax was bigger, but Ryn was faster. She was closing the gap between them. When Ryn was only a few drakon-lengths behind him, he turned sharply, circling around to fly straight at them. The two dipped so Brax shot over their heads.

Faster, Navi. Faster.

He was already tired from flying all the way from the plains and his dash to catch me after I hurled myself off a cliff. I sensed his irritation at that too, along with his exhaustion. I wasn't doing much better myself. My body ached and all I wanted to do was pass out on his back, but I couldn't. Not until this was over.

Then the storm broke. We flew from open air one moment to a downpour the next. Rain beat at my skin and Navi's wings, running down my forehead and into my eyes. The wind picked up, throwing Navi off course.

You couldn't wait a little longer? I thought, which came dangerously close to reprimanding a god. At least the rain would hinder Rajik as well. I blinked water out of my eyes, clearing my vision in time to see Brax rake his claws over one of Ryn's wings. The red drakon swerved, the wind making it that much harder to regain control.

"Kota!" I shouted as Ryn spiraled out of the sky. Human and drakon crashed in a spray of mud and rainwater. Rajik twisted in his saddle to grin at me before Brax plunged after them.

When Navi folded his wings against his sides, I pressed myself to his back as tightly as I could. We dropped like a diving falcon. I expected Rajik to go after Kota and finish her off, but the black drakon flared his wings to slow his descent and twisted in the air.

We didn't have time to slow down. Navi crashed into Brax and pain enveloped my body as the other drakon's claws plunged into Navi's underside. Brax rolled again, reversing our positions so Navi was under him. I clung to my keeper desperately, my back facing the approaching ground. Another flash of lightning blinded me, so all I saw was a shadow across my vision as Brax spread his wings and let go.

Navi managed to extend one wing and flip us around so he hit the ground first instead of crushing me beneath him, but it didn't make the fall painless. I tumbled off his back and into the mud, gasping for breath, only to have rain flood my mouth and nose. I rolled over, coughing and sputtering.

I only took three shallow breaths before lifting my head to squint in search of Kota. I spotted red feathers first, then the mud-coated human figure nearby. I dragged myself over to Kota, praying she was still alive, even though she lay unmoving in the mud. Her eyes shifted beneath her eyelids when I grabbed her hand, but she didn't open them.

"Kota?"

Her hand gave mine a light squeeze, and that was all I needed. I bent my head over her, resting my forehead on her chest as if I were crying over the loss of my friend. A wet thud sounded behind me as Brax landed.

I rolled away from Kota to face the approaching Rajik. Rain dripped down his face and turned his light hair and beard a muddy brown. He drove the butt of his spear into the ground with each slow step, his expression a mixture of triumph and rage. I dragged myself backward with my elbows, my feet sliding uselessly in the mud. I tried to get up, but I felt Navi's pain as if it were my own, the life bleeding out of him.

Rain and the throbbing of Navi's wounds blurred my vision as Rajik bent over me. "You actually thought you could beat me? Two pathetic girls who are barely adults?" I wanted to glare up at him, but the rain kept getting in my eyes. I had to keep my face tilted down, my gaze trained on his knees. It was better anyway. Appear defeated. Make him let down his guard. "You are weak. You are *nothing*," he snarled.

Behind him, something moved in the rain, nearly blending in with the mud. I forced myself to looked up, keeping my eyes open despite the stinging rain. Weaponless and barely able to move, I stared at him without fear. "We're stronger together."

Rajik pressed his spear against my chest and pushed me down into the mud. I had to close my eyes against the rain, unable to look at him even as the weight of the spear lifted. I didn't have to see to know he was flipping it around, preparing to stab. "Your ancestry means nothing, valley girl. You were never going to be a warrior."

No, I wasn't. But Kota was already a warrior.

I drew my knees up to my chest and kicked blindly upward. My boots slammed into Rajik's abdomen with enough force to knock him back a step. His foot stuck in the mud and he toppled backward, right into Kota's waiting sword.

I squinted through the rain to see Kota shove the much larger man off her. The sword protruded from Rajik's chest, the blade driven all the way to the hilt. He remained on his side in the mud, trembling.

Kota got to her knees behind him and grabbed the hilt of the sword. In a powerful jerk, she twisted the blade, drawing an agonized scream from the dying warrior. "That's for my father, you soulless monster," she spat.

I let my head fall back against the ground. More mud seeped through my hair and clung to my scalp, but I didn't care. Rajik's ragged breathing had gone silent. Kota staggered over and practically collapsed beside me, favoring one leg as she attempted to lower herself to the ground.

"It's over," she murmured, echoing my own thoughts, her voice almost lost beneath the torrent of rain.

"It's over," I agreed.

"He killed my father."

My chest tightened, my throat closed up, and all I could think about was Adann and my own father. "I'm so sorry." I winced as I sat up, barely able to make my muscles respond. A gust of wind angled the rain at my face, the drops of water like jagged ice against my skin. My body shuddered from cold and exhaustion.

A low keening filled the air, audible despite the pounding of the rain. I had never heard the sound of a grieving drakon before, but I recognized the same anguish from Adann's scream.

I tensed when I realized Brax stood not three paces away, his head bent over his dead human's body. Even Kota's eyes were sad as she watched him.

"To live without one's other half is a fate no one deserves," she murmured. "It's not Brax's fault he bonded with such a vile human."

"Why doesn't he die?" I asked. "Without Rajik's life to sustain him..."

"Drakons live a long time," Kota answered. "Longer than humans. For us, it's the other way around. Our chief before Rajik was nearly a hundred when he passed."

"What will happen to him?"

"He'll either live out his days in misery or find a way to join Rajik on the other side so they can enter the next life."

The drakon lifted his head, a growl rumbling in his chest. I thought he might attack, but instead he whirled and took off into the rain.

I touched Kota's shoulder lightly, and when she leaned against me, I put my arm around her. We huddled there, soaked in rain and mud and sweat and grief—two girls without fathers, two outcasts.

When she pulled away, the way she wiped her eyes despite the rainwater pouring down her face told me she'd been crying. Her father's death was an old wound, but learning the truth about it had reopened the scar. It would take time to heal again.

Kota struggled to her feet. "We have to go back. Stop the fighting." Hard-faced, she yanked the sword from Rajik's body and used it to cut off the dead chief's braid.

I couldn't feel my body as I staggered to my feet. It had gone numb from cold, but at least I couldn't feel the pain anymore. "Can Ryn fly?"

Kota nodded as the drakon limped through the mud to reach us. "Her wing is hurt but we'll manage."

Navi?

I'm okay. He rose from the ground, his legs so unsteady I thought he might topple over again. I knew more than rain soaked the earth around him, but the bleeding had stopped. He struggled toward me, and I rested my head against his neck. *I'm here now.*

I could feel his guilt, as if it were somehow his fault he hadn't been around to protect me before, but I was the one who had sent him away. If anything, I should feel guilty for causing him grief. I had done it for a reason, though, and I didn't regret it. *Makai?*

He's okay. Or had been when Navi left him in the village. What had happened next we had no way of knowing.

"Let's go," Kota said. She was already in Ryn's saddle with Rajik's braid draped around her neck.

The moment I settled on Navi's back, the rain turned into nothing more than a drizzle, as if Tyir knew the battle was over. Navi's wings trembled as he spread them, and his first attempt to follow Ryn into the air failed. I feared we might have to walk back to the village, but he got a running start and managed to lift himself out of the mud.

Halfway there, the rain stopped completely. The clouds dissipated, allowing a sliver of sunlight to shine through.

The first sight of the village made me nauseous. Unmoving bodies littered the ground, and several huts had been dismantled or burned. It would take time to recover from this disaster, but nothing could completely diminish my hope as Kota flew in a circle above the village.

Ryn roared, drawing every eye upward to see Kota holding out the severed braid. The black feathers and colorful beads woven into the light strands unmistakably marked it as Rajik's. The rest of the warriors lowered their weapons upon realizing their chief had been defeated.

I searched the crowd for Caldin, praying she hadn't fallen in the battle. Though I couldn't find the chief, I spotted her eagle flying over the village instead and let out a slow breath. She was alive, at least.

I turned to the closest Konota. "Makai. Have you seen Makai?" I asked, grabbing Emry's arm when she didn't look at me right away. She had been gawking at Kota and jumped when I touched her. The hunter mutely pointed toward the Healers Hut before looking back at the sky.

I stepped past her and raced toward the hut. Did that mean Makai had been injured in the fight? Who else had died? Why had it taken him so long to get back? I passed bodies as I ran through the village, my mind noting the fallen even as I tried not to look. Some dead, some with their lives still hanging in the balance. Iliya sat on the ground next to Lora, holding her hand while another healer stitched a wound in Iliya's side. I saw Rena's unmoving form, her blank eyes. Pashir, too, had an arrow through his chest. I had no love for the Guildmaster, but my heart ached for the death and destruction around me.

A cold thought made me shiver again. Had Adann been right about surrendering being better?

When I reached the hut, I pushed the flap back and ducked inside. My eyes took a moment to adjust to the dim light. Once they had, I took in the scene. Woven blankets and animal furs had been laid out on the floor, each makeshift bed housing the wounded dragged from the battlefield. My mother was still unconscious in one of the few actual beds, with Ayla sitting on the edge of it. Makai and Grandpa Enzi stood nearby.

A huge grin split Makai's face when he saw me. "Hey, Shaya. I hear your banishment has been lifted."

I stepped around one of the makeshift beds and hurried across the room to throw my arms around him. "I thought you'd be back before midday. When you didn't come I thought... maybe something went wrong and you weren't better."

"Yeah... sorry about that. I had something to take care of first." He squeezed me in return before pulling away so he could smile at me. The tenderness in his eyes was everything I wanted when I was younger, for him to look at me that way. It warmed my face and body despite my still soaked clothes.

Adann had been right about one thing, at least. Navi had gone to help Makai, leaving me in danger. He wouldn't have done that for anyone. Makai had made a lot of mistakes, but he had come through when I needed him.

"Makai brought us a miracle," Ayla said. Her voice drew me away from the warmth of Makai's smile, and I realized she held our mother's hand. She had tears in her eyes—not the hopeless tears we had both cried when Grandpa told us the poison was killing our mother, but tears of happiness and *relief.*

"This young man showed up with a rather rare flower," Grandpa Enzi said. "I hear it only grows in the western plains and is very treacherous to retrieve."

I looked back at Makai, whose smile had turned a touch smug, like he was proud of himself but trying to keep it off his face. "You found it? It exists? How?"

"I remembered that story you told and realized what they had given me."

"You... you were listening to my story? And believed it?"

"I listen to everything you say." He took my hand and gave it a squeeze. "And yeah, I believed it. I could tell from the way you told the story that it wasn't just a myth to you. So I asked River what she gave me. She said it was a rare plant that grew nearby but was difficult to harvest. They had been saving the one flower they'd kept for many generations. But it was worth it to help the friend of Tammae Lakki."

Hearing the name of my supposed past life was both surreal and thrilling. A familiarity brushed against my soul. Maybe they weren't wrong about Tammae. About me. Maybe I had been a wanderer once, traveling the world and helping people.

"Thank you." I could hardly get the words out. They weren't enough, and we both knew it. He had saved my mother, the way he intended to when he left the village to steal the antidote from the clan. He had risked his life in a stunningly reckless way in an attempt to make up for his mistake. Twice. I realized now that it was a part of who Makai Farin was. Taking bold risks to help people ran in his blood, and I couldn't change that. "But you're still an idiot. Going after the flower alone? You could have died."

He laughed, as if him dying were something to treat lightly. "I would have if it weren't for that story. The whole thing was like... a guide to surviving the cave. The gap and how to get across it safely. Taking only one flower so the creatures don't attack. I'm glad Navi showed up, though. Enzi says I probably wouldn't have made it back in time without the ride."

I shook my head slowly. *Fool.* But I'd never been so grateful for Makai's stupid bravery. I gave him another hug before going to sit across from Ayla at my mother's bedside. Mama was going to be okay. The battle was over, Rajik defeated. My banishment had been lifted. I had lost my father along the way, and in a way I had lost Adann too, but it was *over*.

CHAPTER 35

I STAYED BY MY mother's bedside through the night. Ayla and Grandpa Enzi sat with me, all of us waiting for her to wake. Makai had curled up on the ground in the corner of the Healer Hut, since any cots or makeshift beds were occupied by the wounded. He could have gone home, but I didn't blame him for staying. His parents had tried to come talk to him once, but Grandpa had sent them away, saying there were too many people in the hut and they could talk to their son later.

I dozed off for short periods, only to be disappointed to find Mama still unconscious when I woke. Grandpa Enzi never seemed to close his eyes, sitting nearby reading something by candlelight. Ayla spent most of the night bent over the cot, her head resting against our mother's leg as she slept.

I forced my way out of uncomfortable sleep for the fifth time that night. Grandpa's candle had either been extinguished or burnt out, because the hut was completely dark. I could hear his gentle breathing and thanked Tyir he was finally getting some rest. Mama remained motionless, but Ayla shifted in the darkness.

"Can we talk?" my sister asked softly.

If I hadn't already lifted my head, I might have pretended to still be asleep. I wasn't ready to talk to her, not when all my feelings were a boiled over pot of stew. It had to happen eventually, though, so I stood up and left the hut without a word.

Ayla followed me into the moonlight. The village was quiet, everyone asleep in their huts—the ones that still stood. Many families had opened their homes to fellow villagers this night. My eyes ran up Mount Tyir, toward where I knew the clan's camp was nestled in the forest. Kota hadn't even said goodbye before leading the clan away from the village. I didn't know what she planned or if I would ever see her again.

"I don't expect you to forgive me." Ayla spoke quietly, but something about the village demanded to remain undisturbed. It looked abandoned, with the destroyed huts, the smell of smoke lingering in the air. The funeral for the dead would happen tomorrow. Until then, the village itself was dead, waiting for the moment it could come back to life.

I remained with my back to her, still staring at Mount Tyir. I had avoided thinking about it, but now I had to decide where I stood.

The first time Ayla had hurt my feelings badly enough that I had never wanted to talk to her again, my father had sat me down and told me forgiveness wasn't a sign of weakness. "Forgiveness is strength," he had said. "To accept the hurt into our hearts and make the choice to move forward. People make mistakes, but they can make up for them too. Do you think your sister deserves a chance to move beyond this?"

I had forgiven Ayla for a lot of things over the years—and she had forgiven me for plenty as well. That was what siblings did. But could I forgive her for turning her back on me when I needed her most?

"I just wanted you to know that I'm sorry," Ayla pressed on when I didn't give any reaction. "I'm so, so sorry. Everything... everything happened so fast and I didn't know what to think. I didn't know what to do."

"Did you think I killed him?" I asked, my voice little more than a whisper.

"What? No! Of course not. But what was I supposed to do? The evidence—"

"Was fake," I cut her off. I turned to face her and immediately regretted it. Her desperate, imploring eyes proved the sincerity of her words, but I still didn't know if it was enough. "Because he wanted everyone to think I did it, and he knew it would be all too easy."

Ayla winced, even though I didn't mention him by name. She raised her eyes to the sky and blinked several times, her lips turned down in a grimace. "I would never have thought he could do it, any more than you. What do you think will happen to him?"

"You know what will happen." The same thing that had happened to me when the Konota thought I had killed Papa.

"I know what he did was terrible. I know he doesn't deserve our sympathy but..." Ayla's words left her like a heavy exhale, too fast and too breathy. "Without Illari, he'll never survive. And what about his soul?"

No, he didn't deserve our forgiveness. After everything he'd done, I should be happy to see a demon devour his soul. Except I wouldn't wish that fate on anyone. After the way he screamed when Illari died, I never wanted to be responsible for doing such a thing ever again.

To live without one's other half is a fate no one deserves, Kota had said. It would be a mercy to send him to the next life. How long did he have before the soulstealers found him, unprotected and vulnerable?

I didn't want to talk about Adann. It hurt too much. This conversation was painful enough without bringing him into it. "I won't say what you did doesn't still hurt," I told her. "I'm not going to say it won't haunt me for months. I don't know if I'll ever trust you the way I used to." Ayla lifted a hand to delicately brush tears out of her eyes. Her shoulders hunched, as if preparing to handle the blow of my final words. "But... you're my sister, and I love you. I *forgive* you, but that doesn't mean I've forgotten."

I stepped back but was too slow to avoid her as my sister threw her arms around me. "Oh, thank you! *Thank* you. I promise I'll make it up to you." I had enough experience with Ayla's hugs to know trying to escape was futile. I had to stand there until she decided she'd had enough.

Thankfully, Grandpa Enzi cut it short. "Girls?" Ayla released me and we turned to him in unison. I didn't have to look at Ayla to know she wore the same mix of hope and apprehension that I felt. "She's awake."

Inside the hut, Mama sat propped up by pillows and blankets piled behind her. She smiled when she saw us and held out her hands. "There are my perfect girls."

"Mama!" Ayla squealed as she dashed forward to take one of Mama's offered hands. I followed more slowly, clasping my mother's other hand between both of mine.

"Where is your father? Is he too busy to come see his miraculously recovered partner?" The amusement in her voice made what we had to tell her hurt that much more. Tears welled in my eyes, and I looked to Grandpa for help, only to realize he hadn't followed us inside.

When I turned back to my mother, I found Ayla looking to *me*, her face streaked with tears. "Mama..." I started hesitantly. "There's a lot we need to tell you."

The amusement vanished from her face like something had ripped it away. I told her everything that had followed her poisoning: Makai trying to get the antidote, me getting captured, Papa's death, my banishment. Her tears started at the lake, at the body of her dead partner, and doubled when I told her who was responsible. The young man we all loved. Ayla turned her face away, but I told the entire story with the same detachment with which I had told Makai the story of NokaMia. As if it weren't *my* story, but something that had happened to someone else.

When I finished, the three of us simply sat together, Ayla and Mama crying, me sinking deeper and deeper into the pit I had buried my emotions in so I could tell the story without breaking down, until I couldn't feel anything at all.

CHAPTER 36

WHEN I COULDN'T SIT any longer, I glanced toward the corner where Makai had been sleeping. The space was empty. He must have slipped out of the hut while Ayla and I talked to Mama, so I went looking for him.

I didn't have to look hard. I found him at the lake, at our spot by the tree. Farin perched on a branch, restlessly ruffling his feathers while Makai sat as still as stone. He had his knees pulled up to his chest, his arms wrapped around them. As I had done many weeks ago, I sat beside him and simply looked out over the lake. As before, I waited for him to speak first.

He was still staring at the line where the water lapped at the shore when he broke the silence. "When you left me in the plains, I realized it was the first time I had been on my own, other than my Crossing," he said. "Even then, I knew Nahdi was out there somewhere, facing the same trials. I knew the village was waiting for me back home, waiting to celebrate my return. It kept me going."

Makai looked almost as troubled as he had when he learned Nahdi had died. His face, the face I had memorized long before I should have even been thinking about love, showed his distress as clearly as the lake reflected the glow of the nearly full moon.

"Then, suddenly, I was alone," he went on. "With the plains *daram*, but more alone than I'd ever been in my life. I didn't know what I would find when I reached the valley, if you would be even alive. And I felt... empty." He lowered his chin to rest it on his knees. "I've always tried to *be* something for someone else. The perfect son, the best hunter, the funniest friend... or everything you wanted me to be. I needed everyone to like me, so I needed to become what they wanted."

I remembered back to when I had thought of Makai as a color-changing lizard. He was coming to realize something I had put together a long time ago.

"I don't know who I am without other people, Shaya." He finally looked at me, and for a heartbeat the pain in his eyes pressed against my chest like a boulder. He looked so *lost*, like I had felt when the Konota turned against me. "I don't want to only live for others anymore. I want to be my own person. But I don't know who that is."

I scooted closer so my shoulder touched his. "Let me ask you something..."

He cast me a wary look but didn't interrupt.

"Why didn't you tell me apologized to Keer?"

He blinked, taken aback by the question. "Because I didn't do it for you."

A smile tugged at my lips. It was the answer I'd been hoping for. "I know who you are, Makai. You're someone who cares about other people, enough that you're willing to risk your life for them. You care a little too much what people think, which is why you sometimes do the wrong thing trying to impress them. You're a good, loyal person who needs to learn which people are worth your devotion."

"You are," he said softly. "I've never been more sure of any-thing in my life. Whoever I am, I want to be someone worthy of your love. I like who I am around you. I want that to be the real me."

"You can be whoever you want to be, Makai. And whoever that is... I love you. I love you and I'm sorry it took me this long to figure it out." When I brushed my lips against his, everything stopped moving. We were trapped, frozen in that heartbeat. Then I leaned into him, my fingers curling into the cloth of his shirt, and the world sprang into motion with a jolt that left me dizzy.

"Sorry?" He sounded breathless. He smiled and lifted his hand to brush a strand of hair behind my ear. "That's part of who *you* are. Taking your time, over-thinking, worrying... I'm the idiot who was too stupid to see how amazing you are for far too long."

I started to reply but he cut me off with another kiss.

When the kiss ended, he pressed his forehead against mine. One hand rested against the side of my neck, his thumb gently brushing my jaw. "I love you, Shaya Navi," he whispered. "And I'd follow you over those Falls all over again. To the ends of the earth."

I smiled, my eyes still closed. "And I will call you an idiot the entire way, but I'll be glad to have you by my side."

He laughed and kissed me again, making a quiet, disappoint-ed sound when I pulled away. I looked up the path that led to the village, toward the hut where they were holding Adann. They hadn't bothered putting him in the pit. Even the man who had betrayed them all and killed their chief wasn't considered much of a threat now that his keeper was dead. I hadn't seen him since he'd been crouched over Illari's body, weeping. I was terrified to see what he had become. Did he even still have his soul or had the demons found him already?

Makai glanced over his shoulder to follow my gaze. "Are you okay?"

"There's something I need to do."

Somehow, he knew exactly what I meant without me having to say it. "Do you want me to come with?"

"No... This is something I have to do alone."

I stood up, but Makai caught my wrist before I could leave. His fingers were gentle but firm. "Be careful. I know they think he's not dangerous, but..."

"I know." Whatever the villagers thought, Adann would never be harmless. Not beaten and broken, not keeperless, not even dead. Especially to me. Seeing his face would be enough to hurt me. Thinking his name sent a pang through my soul, bringing with it a longing for everything to be different. If I could change one thing in this world, I would turn Adann into the man I'd thought he was. Papa wouldn't be dead, and so many broken hearts would have been spared.

"I don't care what he's done or how self-serving he is," I said. "No one deserves to go through this." I already knew what needed to be done, but I didn't want to say it aloud.

"Do you want me to?" Makai asked, his voice barely above a whisper.

"No." I took a deep breath. "I killed Illari. This is my fault. It's my duty to fix it." I was sure my smile was riddled with sorrow and guilt. "Thank you, though." I leaned down to kiss Makai's cheek before stepping away. His fingers uncurled reluctantly, letting me go like it was our final farewell.

I stopped by my own hut on the way. Its emptiness felt eerie at night, the beds waiting for inhabitants that wouldn't come. The family-sized hut shouldn't be so lonely. I only stayed long enough to grab a candle and match to light it before moving on to my real destination.

Adann's hut wasn't even guarded, which I found foolish, but it meant I didn't have to explain to anyone why I was here. Still, I knew the stories about what people became once their soul had been ripped away. Adann the man might be beaten, but who knew what damage a soulless could do? I braced myself for what I might find before I pushed my way inside.

When I entered, Adann didn't move beyond lifting his eyes. The candlelight flickered over his face, the play of the light making him look gaunt. He didn't blink. He hardly seemed to breathe. He sat on his bed with his back to the wall, one hand tied to the wooden bed frame. That haggard, defeated look in his eyes made my heart clench. I couldn't begin to imagine what pain had tunneled deep into his soul and left behind this husk of a man.

"Hello, little mouse." It hardly sounded like his voice.

"Hello, Adann."

"Have you come to gloat?" Adann stared at me from across the room, his eyes empty. Once, those eyes had been full of life and humor. His smile had been infectious, and his words brought people to listen. Not anymore. His voice was as fragile as a newborn bird. It was still him, though—still Adann, his soul intact.

"Do you not know me at all?" I asked.

"No." He gave a barren laugh that rose bumps over my skin. "I guess I don't. I thought you would be easy to beat. I was a fool." Adann tilted his head, studying me in the dim light. "You don't let people see who you are. And when I underestimated you... Well, here we are. So what are you going to do now?"

I stepped forward and set the candle on the side table, then knelt on the edge of the bed. I wasn't worried about him attacking me. When he saw the knife in my hand, a flash of fear rose from the dead nothingness that had taken him over, but the terror quickly turned to relief.

"I can't live like this," he whispered.

I didn't know if it was a plea or permission, but it didn't matter. I had already made up my mind. "I know," I murmured back. Adann didn't move as I placed a hand on his shoulder and drove the knife between his ribs, into his heart. His body shuddered.

"Thank you," he breathed. Then he slumped against me, eyes closed.

I pulled the knife out and let it drop to the hard-packed dirt. Burying my face against his neck, I released my pain and grief. Adann had betrayed me, betrayed all of us, but once upon a time he'd a brother to me. I had done the worst thing anyone could do to another person and killed half of his soul, leaving the other half alive and in agony. The least I could do was put him out of his misery.

I wept, Adann in my arms, until the last ounce of life drained away and his breathing went still. When gentle hands tried to pull me away, I only held on tighter. "Shaya," Makai said. "Shaya, you have to let go."

My fingers dug into Adann's arm, clinging desperately to his body like I could bring back the Adann I thought I knew from this lifeless corpse. "It's all my fault."

"He made his choices." Makai finally succeeded in prying me away from Adann. "None of this is your fault, Shay." His arms wrapped around me and he stroked my hair, murmuring meaningless reassurances in my ear until my tears ran dry.

Chapter 37

T HE PERSON I REALLY longed to talk to I hadn't seen since she glided through the sky, triumphantly holding the long braid of a fallen murderer. After a failed attempt to get more sleep, I told my family where I was going and left the village just after dawn.

I feared Kota had led the clan away without saying goodbye. As Navi's wings carried us up Mount Tyir, I prayed to the great mountain god that I would find the camp and not an empty clearing.

I was amazed to find that the journey, which took nearly a full day on the ground, required less than two hours in flight. I exhaled in relief when I saw the tents. People, drakons, and other keepers roamed between them. They were packing, though, some in the process of taking down tents.

I spotted a familiar drakon and his human and landed beside them. Tam turned to me, his eyes narrowing suspiciously. "Where is Kota?" I asked.

"You tell me," he grumbled. "No one has seen her since last night. She's not in her tent."

Without responding, I turned Navi around and returned to the air. "Hey!" he shouted after us. "If you find her, tell her we'll be ready within the hour!"

I didn't have to search for her. Navi carried us over the forest to the one place I knew I'd find her.

"Not a very good hiding place, you know," I said as I slid from Navi's back. Kota sat with Ryn curled up behind her. The gray drakon lifted her head when we landed but settled down and closed her eyes again when she realized who had arrived. I joined Kota at the edge of the cliff, letting my legs dangle over the side. How had this one place come to hold so many memories, good and bad?

Kota had her long sunshine hair pulled over her shoulder, her fingers running over the braid and the red feathers woven into it. "I wasn't hiding from *you*."

"Who were you hiding from?"

She gave me a wry smile. "Everyone else." Her fingers slid down and pulled on the leather cord that bound the bottom of her hair. It fell to the ground, where she left it as she started to unwind the braid. When she finished, she braced her palms on the ground and leaned back, letting her hair fall in a curtain of loose waves behind her. Freed from the braid, the golden threads touched the ground when she tilted her head back, closing her eyes against the light.

After letting her sit there for a while, basking in the sun, I asked, "Why?"

Kota shrugged and didn't answer, not right away at least. Eventually, she sighed and reluctantly opened her eyes. "I thought I wanted what my father never got to have, but this morning made me realize something. I want to be a warrior, not a chief. Maybe someday but... I'm sixteen. I'm not ready for this."

I thought about everything that had happened in less than a full month. From bonding with Navi to my father's death to battling a drakon warrior in a stormy sky. "Sometimes life throws things at us that we're not ready for. It's how we handle it that matters." I reached over and took her hand. I worried I had made a mistake when her eyes widened, but she didn't pull away. "You have an amazing opportunity. You can lead the clan down a different path. Make it *better* than he did."

"Down a different path," Kota murmured. She turned her head north, though it was impossible to see past Mount Tyir.

"You want to go home, don't you?"

She nodded. "I'm sorry."

I pulled my hand away and tucked it into my lap. "You were right before. I don't belong here. I don't know if I belong with the clan either, but the valley isn't my home anymore. I know I'm not exactly the hardened warrior but—"

"You helped bring down a clan chief," she cut me off. "You're not weak, bee. You never were."

I didn't know about that, but somewhere along the line I had found the strength to fight instead of hiding in the background. "Whatever awaits us in the North... I think we can handle it."

"Together?"

"Always."

She smiled, her blue eyes bright. That smile chased away her earlier gloominess. It warmed me from the inside out, as brilliant as the sunshine that lit the valley. "Alright. Then let's go to the North."

My stomach rolled at the thought of leaving the valley behind, but it wasn't all dread. No matter how scared I was, this felt right. Being with Kota felt right, though there was one more person I wanted at my side. "There are some things I have to do first."

True to Tam's word, the clan was ready to go when we returned to the camp, the tents disassembled and carts loaded. Kota and I landed together, our arrival drawing the attention of the clan. They gaped at their new chief with her loose hair falling to her waist. She somehow looked more fierce, I thought, with her hair blowing freely in the breeze. I knew she was aware of their stares from the way she pointedly ignored them.

"There you are!" Tam said as he approached. "We're just about ready. Where to, chief?" To my surprise, there was no hint of a sneer in his voice. The clan would follow her despite her age, their rightful chief by their customs. Even if Rajik lacked any honor, the same wasn't true for his warriors.

Kota glanced at me before answering Tam. "We're not leaving yet."

Tam stared at her, as if expecting her to add more or explain the reason for this ridiculous statement. "Excuse me?" he said when she didn't.

"You heard me. We will depart after sunhigh. Perhaps the warriors can take this time to learn some patience." To me, she added, "I need to stay here. Good luck, bee."

I watched her with a faint smile until I noticed Tam scowling at me. I stared back calmly until he averted his eyes. "If you have something to say, you can say it," I said.

"This is all your fault," he spat. "If it weren't for you, we would have taken this valley for our own."

I had never been happy to hear the words "this is all your fault," but yes... yes, it was my fault. And I was *proud* of that.

"Everything is about to change for your clan, Tam. I would forget about what might have been and start thinking about the future."

I left the clan behind and returned to the Konota village. Not *my* village, not anymore. *I am Konota.* The words had felt like a lie when I spoke them weeks ago. Maybe I never had been.

The village was bustling with activity by the time I landed. They had a lot of rebuilding to do. I felt a touch guilty for skimping on my part, but Kota and I had ended the battle by killing Rajik. They could let me have this.

I landed outside the Healers Hut and knocked softly on the doorframe before pushing my way inside. My mother lay on the cot, asleep again, and Grandpa Enzi sat beside her. He watched me warily, like he knew why I had come.

"Did you believe it?" I asked. Might as well not waste time.

"Of course not," he said firmly. "I tried to speak in your defense. So did Caldin, but the other Guildmasters outnumbered us. There was nothing I could do, and for that I am sorry. Perhaps I should have tried harder but... perhaps I knew you would be okay, no matter what happened. You're strong. I knew you would survive."

I couldn't find it in my heart to stay angry with him. "You did what you could." And that was what mattered. He was right, ultimately. He couldn't have stopped my banishment. Only Adann had possessed that power.

Grandpa glanced down at my sleeping mother, his eyes troubled. Father and daughter, with the same brown hair that had been passed down to me. Then there was his skin. I had always thought it had paled from lack of sunlight, but now I questioned if maybe there was another reason.

"You weren't born in the valley, were you?"

He looked up, his eyebrows raised. "What makes you say that?"

"You recognized the poison. You knew it would kill her slowly. You knew the clan would have the antidote. And then there's your name... unusual for Konota, isn't it? You always made it sound like you had left the valley to travel before returning home, but that's not the truth, is it? You came here from the North."

He let out a slow breath. "No one was supposed to know anymore. A secret long forgotten, painted over with half-truths." I watched him silently, waiting for him to continue. "Yes, Shaya, I wasn't born here. I came to the valley when I was a young man. My mother left the village shortly after her Crossing, longing to see the world. She found her way to the North, where she fell in love with my father."

"Eilzar."

Surprise flashed over his face. "Yes. He wasn't clan chief when they met. His father was. By the time I was born, he had inherited the position. I grew up with the expectation that I would become the next chief, but I never wanted it. My mother told me many stories about the valley. Where her soul had longed to leave, mine longed to return. After she fell ill and died... I left. I came home."

"And they let you?"

"The Konota had no reason to fear outsiders. The chief remembered my mother and welcomed me with open arms." He sighed and rubbed his hand across his forehead. "Perhaps you take after my mother, and that is why you want to leave."

"What makes you think I want to leave?"

He looked at me steadily. "Am I wrong?"

I shook my head. After another long pause, I said, "Thank you. For the stories. For... I don't know, giving my life meaning."

He stood and left his place by his daughter's bed to join me near the door. "Promise me one thing, Shaya Navi. Be careful, okay? The North is a dangerous place."

"I know."

He shook his head. "I'm not sure that you do."

"I'm going with Kota and the clan. I'll be fine."

He frowned and tilted his head slightly. "The young chief? You two bonded while you were with them."

I nodded. "She's... special." There was something about her that drew me to her from the beginning. "She'll keep me safe," I promised. I wrapped my arms around him and squeezed him tight. "I hope we see each other again."

Grandpa gently patted my back. "I think we will. In this life or the next." He smiled at me when I stepped away. "Good luck, wanderer."

He said "wanderer" in a way that made it sound like hunter or crafter or healer. The guilds the Konota chose became part of their identity, but I was guildless. *Wanderer.* That was what the plains people had called Tammae.

It felt like I had finally found that small piece of me that had been missing all this time.

I gave him a nod and turned to leave, but I stopped with my hand on the door flap. "One more question... have you heard of Tammae Lakki? I don't remember her mentioned in any of the stories."

Grandpa Enzi's brow furrowed. "Tammae Lakki was Tavlin Lamere's sister. She's not in the stories because she wasn't a hero to the people of the North."

"Why not?"

"Because she betrayed Tavlin." My heart sank. "She killed him and fled the North."

A tingling ran over my skin. The *daram* had called Tammae a hero to their people, a wanderer who had left the North because she refused to kill. But if what Enzi said was true, she had lied to them. She was a villain to the Northern people, slayer of their greatest hero. Which one was she then? Hero or villain?

"Thank you," I said quietly. I slipped out the door before he could respond.

I went looking for Makai after that. I found him with his friends by the lake, at the base of the hill with the tree, the rope still tied to its branches. Tension hung in the air as I approached, and it only grew worse when they noticed me.

Makai's face lit up, though, and warmth flooded my body at the memory of our kiss. "Perfect timing, Shay. They have something to say to you."

The three exchanged a sheepish look. Trev spoke first, offering a murmured, "We're sorry." The others echoed the apology.

"We should have trusted you," Iliya said. I would have thought she'd be the most reluctant to apologize, but I found no bitterness in her voice.

I didn't know how I felt about any of them. Honestly, I didn't care. So I shrugged and said, "I forgive you." I turned to Makai, the person I actually wanted to talk to. "Kota told me another clan drove her people from the North. I want to help them reclaim their home." I took a moment to search his eyes. His expression was open, equal parts curious, hopeful, and worried. "I want you to come with us."

Makai's lips twitched. "Are you testing whether I'll live up to my promise to follow you to the ends of the world?"

I gave him a small smile. "I didn't think I had to test it."

"No, I guess not." He looked back at his friends, who stared with identical shocked expressions.

"You can't be serious," Deira said. "You're leaving?"

Iliya actually smiled a little. "An adventure like this? You know he wouldn't pass it up. Besides..." She glanced at me and said grudgingly, "He wouldn't let Shaya go alone." She reached out and pulled him into a hug. "You better come home, you idiot." She released him and stepped back. "I need to get back to Lora." I got the feeling, as she turned away, that she was doing her best not to cry.

The other two hugged him as well. "Stay safe," Deira murmured. Then she took Trev's hand, and they followed Iliya around the lake to the village.

"So, when do we leave?" Makai asked.

"As soon as we're packed." This wasn't a Crossing, a relatively short journey up Mount Tyir. This was the *North*.

Makai gave a small nod. "I guess we better get started, then."

Makai's parents didn't take it as well as his friends, but he shut down any attempts to order him to stay.

"I'm an adult now," he said adamantly. "I make my own decisions." They didn't have anything more to say to that, except heavy goodbyes.

My farewell to my mother and sister wasn't met with any surprise or protests. They simply hugged me and told me they loved me, like they'd seen this coming all along. Maybe they had.

"Just promise you'll come back to us," Mama said, in a way that made me wonder if they'd burn my favorite candles until they ran out.

When we were packed for the long journey north, Navi flew us back to the camp. I wondered what Makai was thinking as we passed over the familiar forest, the village rapidly growing more distant.

"Are you afraid?" I asked.

"No," he said. It felt like a lie. "Are you?"

"No," I lied back.

The clan was all set when we arrived, awaiting our return. Navi landed near Ryn and Kota, who was leaning against her drakon with her arms crossed. She straightened when we touched down. Farin landed atop Navi's head instead of Makai's shoulder where he usually perched. The drakon flicked his ears irritably, but he didn't shake the falcon off.

Like Navi, Ryn carried supplies in bundles secured to her back, as did the rest of the drakons around us. Kota eyed Makai, who sat behind me with his arms wrapped around my stomach, and I realized this would be the first time they'd spoken. "So, this is him?"

"This is him," I confirmed.

She looked him up and down, clearly unimpressed. "You better be worth it, valley boy."

"Worth what?" he asked.

"Her devotion," she replied, thrusting a finger in my direction. Makai gave me a panicked glance, and I bit my lip to keep from smiling. I remembered how intimidating Kota could be. He'd be fine once he got to know her.

Satisfied that he was properly warned, Kota gave a small nod. "Ready?" she asked. Makai and I both nodded. "Then let's move out."

She mounted Ryn, the other warriors following suit. The drakons remained grounded, since the *sevan*—I needed to talk to Kota about the whole "lesser" thing—had to travel on foot. We made our way up Mount Tyir, leaving behind the valley I had once called home and riding into the unknown.

I had once thought Mount Tyir had been calling me, before my Crossing. Now I understood that hadn't been it at all. Beyond the peak lay a land of great mountains that put Tyir to shame. A land where—as Kota put it—the gods were always angry.

The people of the North had once called the drakon riders godslayers. I was ready to face whatever the gods threw at us.

ACKNOWLEDGEMENTS

The Sound of Nothing isn't the first book I've written, nor the first book I published, but it is my baby. I'm so grateful to everyone who helped make it possible to publish the first book in the Soul Keeper series. As always, thank you to my loyal writing friends: Clayton, Audrey, Cassie. You're always there for me and a huge support on my publishing journey. Special thanks to Cassie McDonald for the amazing maps of the Soul Keepers world.

A giant thank you to my parents and sister. You all went through hell this past year and somehow still found the time and enthusiasm to support my writing. I'll always be grateful for my amazing family and how much effort they've dedicated to making my dreams come true. Lexi, thank you for nitpicking every detail of the cover and for drawing the amazing chapter header and scene break images.

For all the beta readers who saw the Sound of Nothing through it's many drafts (and titles...), you helped bring this book from a mess of a first draft to something I could be excited to share with the world. Your feedback was invaluable. Thank you to Nikki for offering to do some line edits on incredibly short notice.

For everyone who supported the Kickstarter: Thank you so much! Lisa, Stefanie, Nikki, Nancy, Aira, Chris, Hannah, Nastasia, Laurel, David, Rachel, Jamie, Kaitlyn, Leslie, Melissa, Carly,

Kimi, Chelsea, Anisha, Zephyr, Gail, Rea, Josefine, Terri, Seth, Ari, Michael, Caroline, Cassie, Audrey, and Lexi. Every bit of support helped make this book a reality and will provide funding to publish future books. I hope you continue to support this series through the other four books, which will have their own Kickstarter editions.

So grateful for JV Arts and the stunning cover illustration. You took my vision for the cover and made it a reality. Getting the cover done was perhaps the most stressful part of publishing this book, due to a false start and quite a bit of searching before I found JV Arts, but they made it all worth it in the end.

About the Author

Nicole Aisling is equal parts biology nerd, animal lover, and story enthusiast. She studied biology in college, but an incurable thirst for knowledge led her astray to philosophy and psychology classes, which inspired stories like her debut novel, *Chasing Nightmares*. She loves merging magic with science, creating worlds grounded in physics and biology... but still fantastical. When she's not outside enjoying nature, she can be found cuddled up on the couch with her dogs, settled in for either a good book or the latest TV episode.

https://nicoleaisling.com/